# Praise for the novels of I

"In pitch-perfect prose, Heidi McCahan effo _____ to be a modern woman in all its complexities in her heartwarming new page turner. A story of reinvention, second chances, and finding love that truly conquers all, *One Southern Summer* is an absolute must read by a standout voice. Fans of Susan Mallery and Debbie Macomber will devour this captivating novel."

—Kristy Woodson Harvey, *New York Times* bestselling author
of *Under the Southern Sky*

"Second-chance romance steeped in southern sweetness…what's not to love? In this heartwarming story set in the fictional town of Camellia, Alabama, Heidi McCahan's characters prove it's never too late to reclaim your true self and build the happy-ever-after you deserve. The end result? A sentimental escape that leaves readers smiling."

—Julie Cantrell, *New York Times* and *USA TODAY* bestselling author
of *Perennials*

"In *One Southern Summer*, Heidi McCahan pens an engaging story about family ties and starting over when life takes an unexpected turn. Realistic characters, poignant moments, and a romance that celebrates second chances will leave you as satisfied as a glass of sweet tea!"

—Kathryn Springer

"A touching, tender story about hope, second chances and new beginnings. Lose yourself in *One Southern Summer*."

—RaeAnne Thayne, *New York Times* bestselling author

"Heidi McCahan's *One Southern Summer* is true southern women's fiction, complete with sweet tea and gossip and a feisty, meddling grandma. But it's also a contemporary story of family dynamics, social media, and the important issue of human trafficking. The small Alabama town, the summer heat, the foibles of the imperfect characters who nevertheless steal your heart, all are portrayed in rich prose that kept me turning the pages. I loved this story!"

—Lee Tobin McClain, *New York Times* bestselling author

# ONE
## *Southern*
# SUMMER

## HEIDI McCAHAN

## LOVE INSPIRED
*Stories to uplift and inspire*

# LOVE INSPIRED®

*Stories to uplift and inspire*

Recycling programs
for this product may
not exist in your area.

ISBN-13: 978-1-335-66259-0

One Southern Summer

Love Inspired
22 Adelaide St. West, 41st Floor
Toronto, Ontario M5H 4E3, Canada
www.LoveInspired.com

**Printed in U.S.A.**

For Susan May Warren and Rachel Hauck.
Thank you for teaching me how to write a novel.
Your wisdom and encouragement helped me put this story together.
I'm forever grateful.

# ONE
## *Southern*
# SUMMER

# Prologue

*One year earlier*

With the Carolina blue sky cradling the mid–May sunshine, every blade of grass on the manicured lawn standing at attention and the humidity unexpectedly missing in action, she almost believed nothing could go wrong.

Almost.

In the unwritten rules of Southern etiquette, every woman innately understood the expectations regarding a proper social gathering. And more importantly, the ramifications of an unforeseen party planning faux pas. That's why Avery Lansing Crawford had hired Raleigh's premier event planner to oversee the flawless execution of her baby's gender reveal festivities.

She stood on the back steps of her screened porch and surveyed the yard like an offensive coordinator mentally preparing for the first play of the football game. Ice rattled against the galvanized steel buckets as the caterer packed the containers with bottled drinks. A woman wearing black pants and a white blouse strode past her, balancing an oval tray of cupcakes. A rogue wave of emotion washed over Avery and she blinked back tears.

Finally. She'd stayed pregnant. This party was actually happening. Those pastel pink– and pale blue–frosted cupcakes crowned with custom-made pacifier-shaped candies symbolized victory. Avery smoothed her hand over the royal blue fabric of her maternity dress and caressed her rounded abdomen. After last year's miscarriage all she wanted was an unremarkable full-term pregnancy.

Was that too much to ask?

For the past twenty-two weeks she'd held her breath at every cramp and mysterious backache. Her frequent visits to the restroom were fraught with anxiety. She'd been terrified her worst fear would manifest—bleeding. When the twenty-week ultrasound results confirmed a healthy pregnancy, Avery allowed the first inklings of hope to take root. Pax said he'd be happy with a girl or a boy, but she suspected he had a strong preference for a boy. And she longed to give him the gift of a healthy son.

Sure, she had tried to convince herself contentment was possible with only one child. After all, they had a beautiful home, wonderful friends and a thriving business. But ever since that miscarriage, her need to have another baby consumed her. Like a woman tearing through the pantry looking for the good chocolate, Avery couldn't escape her obsession with getting pregnant again.

Was she selfish for wanting to grow their family?

No. She banished that thought as their three-year-old daughter skipped across the backyard. Lots of people had multiple children. Addison needed a sibling.

A breeze kicked up, blowing a lock of the little girl's curly honey-colored hair across her face. She stopped and tossed her head impatiently then tugged the strand free with her hand. Avery smiled. So precious. Addison spun around, her blue eyes finding Avery.

"Mama, can I have a balloon, please?" She stretched the single syllable word and twirled in a clumsy circle. Her yellow polka-dotted dress billowed around her bare legs.

"Not yet, baby. The balloons are for the party, remember?" Avery stopped short of asking how Addison knew they had balloons. The event planner had received explicit instructions to keep them tucked away in the enormous trunk in the middle of the yard until they were ready for the big reveal. Once the guests arrived and had their drinks and appetizers, she and Pax planned to open the trunk together. Whatever color balloons emerged would indicate the gender of their baby. Avery's heart fluttered with anticipation. She could hardly stand the wait.

"I. Want. A. Balloon." Addison stopped twirling and pooched out her lower lip.

"Do we get anything when we ask like that?" Avery admonished. "And where is your father?" she whispered to herself, surveying the yard for Pax or the babysitter she'd hired to keep Addison entertained. The professional photographers had just arrived and she wanted to go over her expectations one more time. The event planner had positioned the photo booth in the wrong place. They needed a better location or all the guests would have to squint into the sun during their pictures.

"If Daddy says yes can I have a balloon?"

Avery smiled. This girl. She was relentless. Addison crossed her arms over her tiny torso. Anticipation gleamed in her eyes.

"Do you know where your daddy went?"

"He's inside." Addison tipped her chin up, well aware that she provided a crucial piece of information. "Talking to Uncle Trey."

Avery's shoulders sagged. Uncle Trey was Pax's best friend and partner in the Crawfords' successful home renovation business—an enterprise launched from Avery's widely read lifestyle blog. Trey had recorded the highest number of closings this spring of any Realtor in Raleigh, Durham or Chapel Hill. The housing market wasn't showing any signs of cooling off, so she couldn't blame them for plotting their next move. But couldn't they take a break? Production had wrapped on the first season of their new TV show. The camera crew had left yesterday. Two magazines had wanted to feature the gender reveal in upcoming issues, but she'd declined. Today was all about gathering with their family and friends, and celebrating this new life growing inside of her. Hadn't they earned a reprieve from eating, sleeping and breathing real estate?

She'd lost more than a little sleep over her decision to keep the event private. The pilot episode of their home renovation show had pulled in an enthusiastic audience. Her popularity on social media had skyrocketed. Along with her almost constant fear that she'd somehow mess it up. When she'd first started out, mingling with strangers on the internet, the conversation had been light. Fun. Encouraging. It wasn't long before their small company's unexpected success had brought out a mean streak in her opinionated followers. Comments could be deleted and the most offensive trolls blocked, but she never quite got over the sting of hurtful words flung at her with casual indifference.

Oddly enough, now she felt guilty for depriving their fans of an exclusive look at their family life. Trey and Pax had roped her into becoming the face of their brand. Despite her initial reluctance, she couldn't deny that the dopamine rush she earned when her pretty posts gained the approval of her capricious demographic motivated her to keep producing more appealing content. Always on a relentless quest to go viral. Again. No one had to know she had nothing to do with staging that home. Or the content of the pictures she posted.

"Mama, when can I have a balloon?"

Addison's question tugged her back to the present. "When the party is over. I'll make sure we save one just for you."

"Oh-kay." Addison heaved a sigh then slinked away, like a defeated athlete who'd unexpectedly lost a competition.

Avery pulled her phone from her pocket to check on the babysitter's status. An incoming text from her sister Harper bubbled up.

**We've been delayed another twenty minutes on the ground in Atlanta. I'm so sorry. I hope we get there before the party is over.**

Avery glared at the update. What a bummer. She really wanted Mama and both her sisters here. She couldn't hold off a hundred guests another two hours, though. Maybe longer, depending on how long it took her family to get their luggage and catch an Uber from the airport. She put her phone away without responding.

Furrowed brows and fierce whispering between the event planner and her assistant demanded Avery's attention. Uh-oh. What had gone wrong?

Panic quickened her steps as she strode toward them, casting another glance around the yard. The caterer had the food situation under control. Two women guarded the cupcakes and Addison chased a butterfly. Other than Pax not yet making an appearance and her family's delayed flight, nothing earth-shattering triggered a warning.

"Hey, Meredith." She infused her voice with calm and stopped beside the event planner. "Are we about ready?"

Meredith and her assistant exchanged nervous glances.

Avery's mouth went dry, and she pressed her palm against Meredith's slender arm. "What is it?"

Color splashed across Meredith's cheekbones. "Avery, two of our white tablecloths have hideous red wine stains on them. I'm so embarrassed and I hate to ask, but do you have two we can borrow?"

The weight of dread lifted from her shoulders. "Now, that I can handle." She rewarded Meredith with a reassuring smile. "Of course you can use mine. I'll be right back."

She turned and strode across the yard with a spring in her step. Stained tablecloths. If that was the only detail they'd overlooked, this party was going to be golden. She hummed softly as she pulled open the door to the screened porch, crossed to the back door then stepped inside. The fragrant aroma of fresh flowers enveloped her as she paused in the quiet kitchen.

A gorgeous floral arrangement from Pax's parents sat on the large island's marble countertop. So thoughtful. They'd booked a speaking engagement in California and couldn't reschedule. Avery had silently rejoiced when she'd received her mother-in-law's regretful text. They managed to get along when they were together, but Pastor and Mrs. Crawford had a way of commandeering the spotlight. Avery wasn't the least bit interested in sharing today.

Her heels clicked on the hardwoods as she passed through the den. She'd stored her round tablecloths in the laundry room's spacious custom cabinets. Michael Bublé streamed from a wireless speaker nearby. The rumble of masculine voices filtered from the laundry room and Avery paused. Then she heard Pax's familiar throaty chuckle. She angled her head as she inched closer. What was he doing in there? And who was he talking to in that tone of voice she thought he reserved only for her?

She tapped her manicured nails on the door then gently pushed it open. "Pax? Are you—"

Her mind refused to comprehend what her eyes saw, and her legs quaked like her nana's Jell-O salad at Christmas dinner.

*This isn't happening.*

She cupped her hand over her mouth to silence the scream fighting to break free from her constricting chest. Pax and Trey were pressed up against the washing machine, locked in an intimate embrace.

Through the window overlooking the backyard she watched as Addison opened the lid on the trunk and dozens of pale blue balloons sailed into the cloudless sky.

# *Chapter One*

Maribelle Hurst Lansing was mad enough to drown puppies. Ever since Olive McPherson waltzed into town and wormed her way into every club and committee, she'd made it her mission to aggravate people.

And tonight was no exception.

Ignoring the group's obvious distaste for her yammering, Olive, The Queen of Book Club, blathered on about this month's selection—the same mindless pablum she'd insisted her previous book club in Memphis enjoyed reading. She was always carrying on about Memphis. Maybe if it was so wonderful, Olive should consider moving back. Just saying was all.

Maribelle shot a pointed stare at Lucille, her across-the-hall neighbor at Westwood Manor and self-appointed chauffeur. Lucille conveniently avoided eye contact and loaded her fork with another bite of pear and pomegranate salad. Lucille's husband had passed six months ago and she hated to go home to her empty apartment. Maribelle didn't exactly love living alone either, but after ten years she'd gotten used to the idea. Besides she'd started binge watching *The Good Place* and if she convinced Lucille to leave now, there'd be enough time to watch a full episode before her eyes gave out and she fell asleep.

When Nell, bless her heart, interjected and managed to shift the conversation toward the upcoming fundraiser for Imari's Place, Maribelle groaned inwardly then drained the last of her sweet tea. She cared about human trafficking as much as they did, but were they really going to put an end to such a travesty during book club? Probably not. Which is why they should call it a night and write that handsome director a check like they did every year.

Heaving a dramatic sigh, Maribelle made a big show of checking her wristwatch. Lucille didn't even bat an eyelash. Instead she carved her fork through another pear slice and nodded vehemently at whatever Nell was saying. Oh, for Pete's sake. *Finish your fancy salad already. It's probably not even that good.*

Not to be outdone by a community service project, Olive made a desperate grab for the spotlight and launched into her diatribe on the merits of authentic character arcs. Maribelle had had about all she could take. She pushed her chair back and stood then reached for her good pocketbook—the one with that Michael fella's logo her granddaughter Avery said all the young people were crazy about.

Evidently, her body didn't get the memo. For one terrifying instant, her brain and limbs battled, and she tottered precariously off-balance.

*Dear Lord, do not let me fall in front of Olive McPherson.*

She'd never let her forget it. Ever since Maribelle suggested they hire a ventriloquist for the family fun night at church and he'd offended half the congregation with his off-color jokes, Olive went to great lengths to remind her of her missteps.

How was she supposed to know his act wasn't appropriate for children? Whether she had one week or a hundred left on this earth, Maribelle vowed Olive would not hold one more iota of mortifying information over her head.

The young lady serving their table and hovering nearby must've questioned Maribelle's judgment because her unsightly fingernails clamped around the sleeve of her cashmere sweater faster than a dog on a jackrabbit.

"Can I help you, Mrs. Lansing?" Her wide green eyes and polite smile did nothing to obscure her pity.

"No thank you, sugar." Maribelle straightened, confident she'd dodged the proverbial bullet, and readjusted her sweater. "By the way, there's a lovely nail salon in that new shopping center on Highland Circle. You should stop by sometime."

The server's smile faded, and she fisted her hand at her side. "I'll keep that in mind."

"They have complimentary coffee, sweet tea or sparkling water. What's not to love?"

Without waiting for a response, Maribelle started toward the ladies' room. They'd been meeting for drinks and dessert—or salad if you were dull and boring like Lucille—after book club at The Flowering Vine for over a decade. By now the management should've figured out that a group of older women didn't need to sit so far from the restroom. Didn't they know how their lives revolved around frequent and unfettered access to the facilities?

And the table placement. So cramped. Now she had to focus on navigating through the narrow gaps, while waving and smiling to folks she'd known for three-quarters of a century. No doubt a few wanted to bend her ear, but she couldn't be bothered given the circumstances. Her incident back at the table left her a little flustered. She needed to focus on her footing. Who knew when some irresponsible patron might bobble into one's path, or an unsightly spill no one had bothered to tend to might cause her to slip?

Then her gaze landed on Cole Whitaker and she quickly forgot her list of the restaurant's offenses. The handsome non-profit director of Imari's Place sat near the windows at a table for two, staring at his phone. Perhaps she'd delay her visit to the ladies' room.

"Hey, Mr. Cole." She gripped the edge of his table and offered a sweet smile. Poor thing. Dining alone.

"Hello, Mrs. Lansing. How are you?"

"I'm well, hope you are." Maribelle gestured to the empty seat across from him. "Mind if I sit down?"

"Well, I'm expecting—"

"This will only take a minute." She sank into the hard spindle-backed chair and folded her hands on the worn wooden table. "I guess you heard my granddaughter Avery is moving back to Camellia."

"Is that right?" Cole set his phone facedown beside his napkin-wrapped silverware. "I hadn't heard. Avery and I don't keep in touch."

"Oh, what a shame. You two were thick as thieves back in the day."

Cole hesitated. "That was a long time ago, Mrs. Lansing."

"Well, it's never too late to rekindle an old friendship." Maribelle studied him, certain that regret had flashed in his eyes when she'd mentioned Avery. She'd leave out the extraneous details. Avery's husband had left her with two little ones, forcing her to sell that gorgeous house in Raleigh and move back home. Cole would hear it all soon enough. News that juicy spread like the plague.

"I'm sure Avery will be busy getting situated."

Huh. That polite, stiff smile wasn't the response she'd hoped for.

"Please tell her I said hello." His phone buzzed on the table, and he reached for it. "It's lovely to see you again, Mrs. Lansing. Excuse me."

Maribelle pushed to her feet. "I'll make sure my daughter-in-law invites you out to the house real soon."

Cole nodded then pressed his phone to his ear.

Maribelle frowned and resumed her journey to the restroom. That hadn't gone as well as she'd envisioned. Maybe he was having a stressful day. She'd regroup and visit him again soon. Ever since her good-for-nothing son abandoned his family all those years ago, she'd gone out of her way to look out for her daughter-in-law, grandchildren and great-grandchildren. Avery's life might be a wreck now, but she'd find a way forward. Maribelle was just giving her a little boost. It's what any thoughtful grandmother would do.

She shouldn't be here.

Avery tapped her brakes and eased her SUV and trailer to a complete stop as the traffic light in Camellia, Alabama, blinked from yellow to red. The muffled sound of live music caught her attention and she lowered her window. Blooming crepe myrtle trees and old-fashioned black lampposts with glowing lights formed a protective canopy over the downtown sidewalks. A crowd of people fanned out from the stage near the roundabout, enjoying the concert. The warm evening breeze filtered into her car and she inhaled deeply, thankful for a respite from the stale aroma leftover from their fast-food lunch and Hayes's recent diaper change.

This might be her hometown, but she had never intended to return. Parts of her childhood had been idyllic. Fishing in the pond, catching fireflies and roaming the neighborhood on their bikes for hours. But after Daddy left, it had meant frequent visits to the food pantry and wearing someone else's jeans she'd bought at the thrift store. When she'd married Pax, she'd finally been set free from the hole her father's absence had carved out of her heart. And the longer she'd lived in Raleigh, the more her accomplishments had granted her a false sense of security.

Together, she and Pax had curated a lifestyle more glorious than she could've imagined as a young girl living in a small Central Alabama town. Sure, she'd visited a few times over the years. But a tiny part of her had always been relieved when she could bid Mama and her sisters goodbye and get back to Raleigh. Camellia represented the lonely, confused teenage girl who ached to escape her abandonment issues. Now here she was, wounded and humiliated, tugging all her possessions along with her kids back home to Mama.

Feeling abandoned all over again.

The light turned green and she hesitated, giving the familiar surroundings another sweeping glance. The same brick buildings flanked Main Street, although the names of the stores had probably changed. Folks in Camellia knew how to weather hardship. After the steel, textile and manufacturing industries all faded away and left families destitute, Camellia had rallied once again. Now this was a family-friendly city known for great schools and stable jobs.

Maybe she'd learn a thing or two about reinvention while she was visiting. Because that's all this was. A visit. At least that's what she kept telling herself and her daughter every time Addison asked how long they'd stay in Alabama.

Avery tapped her thumbs against the steering wheel as the theatre where she'd begun her reign as Miss Camellia flashed by her vehicle. She'd advanced to the state beauty pageant in

Birmingham where she'd won Miss Congeniality. Hard to believe that was fifteen years ago. She could only imagine what the town gossips were saying about her now.

Camellia's residents loved a second chance redemptive story, but they also loved drama. The kind of salacious stories that only grew the longer they circulated. Avery shivered involuntarily and rolled up her window. She didn't want to be the topic of discussion at book clubs, church committee meetings and supper tables. Her ex-husband had cheated on her and dragged their family through the mud, but she desperately hoped all that was behind her now.

A few minutes later, she obeyed her GPS instructions and turned onto a road with a gated entrance. She punched in the PIN her sister Harper had texted her, waited for the black wrought iron gates to swing open then pulled into her mother's circular driveway. Mama had told her that she and her new husband had bought a lake house with enough room for Avery and her kids to stay for a while. She'd failed to mention the gorgeous white craftsman-style home deserved to be on the cover of the South's most popular magazine. Ferns hung symmetrically on either side of the porch and the freshly mowed grass framed a flagstone path. A wreath adorned the candy-red door and potted flowers lined either side of the wide steps.

"Wow," Avery whispered. Quite the upgrade from the cramped two-bedroom rambler in Camellia where Mama had raised Avery and her two sisters alone after Daddy left. The setting sun spilled orange and crimson streaks across the cloudless blue sky. Through the trees in her mother's yard, she glimpsed the lake. Wooden docks jutted out like long fingers, and she recognized the familiar silhouettes of boats bobbing in the water.

Coming home had never felt so miserable.

Oh, she wanted to be happy for Mama. Really, she did. After scraping by for years as a single mother trying to support a family on a public school teaching salary, Mama deserved to marry a man who cherished her and provided a beautiful lakefront home. But Avery struggled to celebrate anyone else's blessings since her life had unexpectedly nosedived. Her marriage had ended when she caught Pax with Trey in a compromising position in their laundry room. Divorce was final last month. She'd lost her husband, both her business partners and a solid chunk of retirement savings. Evidently, Trey not only had a thing for her husband, but he loved to overspend too. Thankfully she'd delivered a healthy baby boy, but grieving her failed marriage, trying to keep track of a precocious four-year-old and caring for a newborn by herself had nearly done her in.

Pax and Trey had wanted to keep filming their popular home renovation show, but she refused to sign on for a second season. How could she film a reality TV show when she couldn't stand to be in the same room with them? But the money she'd walked away from made her stomach hurt.

Okay, so she had issues to work through. Take a number, anger management. Leave a message, grief recovery.

She still had her blog and her social media presence, but she hadn't posted since Hayes was born. The words had dried up. Repackaging her heartache into an appealing, well-filtered post intended for mass consumption was impossible. And the comments. Oh, the comments. Total strangers felt compelled to weigh in on the most intimate details of her life. She couldn't take it.

Hot tears pressed against her eyes and she leaned her forehead on the steering wheel. After ten hours of driving and five stops to soothe a screaming baby and appease a feisty pre-schooler, she should be crying tears of joy. She didn't have to drive alone on the interstate, navigate through thunderstorms or bribe Addison with goldfish-shaped crackers to give her baby brother his pacifier. Her arrival in Camellia was supposed to signal an end to the nightmare of betrayal and divorce.

But it wasn't an end to the pain.

She'd left Raleigh devastated and unemployed. Selling the house had been inevitable because she couldn't afford the mortgage. Well-meaning friends had introduced her to new clients, but the home-staging appointments were awkward. She used her newborn son as an excuse for her scatterbrained presentations. A pathetic excuse really, because the truth was Trey had been the driving force behind all their endeavors.

She'd fooled everyone. Only a handful of people who'd produced the television show knew the truth. Her degree in fashion and textile design wasn't all that useful in the real estate business. At least that's what Trey had made her believe. Slowly but surely, one passive-aggressive comment at a time, Trey had reduced her to nothing more than the public face of their business. A social media influencer who couldn't deco-rate a house and was too humiliated to engage with her audi-ence. He'd been so subtle about it too. Publicly, he'd embrace her suggestions for renovating a kitchen's backsplash or updat-ing a bathroom's fixtures. Then he'd go behind her back and submit a last-minute change order, claiming she must've been distracted with caring for Addison. Trey had undermined her confidence and used her to get what he wanted. Shame seeped in, reminding her yet again that she'd been distracted by her own foolish need for approval.

Coming back to Camellia with what little she still owned and moving in with her mother and stepfather wasn't part of her vision for her future. Almost every square mile of this close-knit community served up another memory. Not that she wasn't proud of where she came from. Her family and her upbringing had shaped her. But her current reality fell far short of her lofty expectations.

"Mama, are we here?" Addison's voice interrupted her reluctant stroll down memory lane.

Avery sniffed and dried her tears with the back of her hand. "Yes, baby. We're here. Let's go inside and say hello to your grandmother and Papa Greer."

"I want to get down," Addison whined. She'd fought sleep all day, finally losing the battle about forty-five minutes ago. Which meant she'd be grouchy and difficult to deal with until Avery could get her settled down in Mama's guest room.

"Hang on." Avery turned off the ignition, unbuckled her seat belt and slid from the car. Although she needed help, she hated asking. Her mother, sisters, grandmother and now her new stepfather, Greer, were probably more than happy to have her and her children in Camellia. She sensed a storm on the horizon, though. Another difficult season. She'd learned resilience growing up without a dad, but her heart broke knowing Pax's choices had forced her children down a similar path.

Resentment burned hot. Part of her wanted him to be happy, but she hated what the divorce had done to their family.

As soon as her flip-flops hit the ground, Avery stretched, wincing at the tightness in her back and shoulders. Between packing, getting up to feed Hayes in the middle of the night and driving all day, she was weary all the way to her bones. The last twelve months had depleted every ounce of her fierce determination.

This wasn't the life she wanted. She'd spent the second half of her childhood looking for a way out of Camellia. After her father abandoned them, she'd never been the same. His departure splashed a painful stain on nearly everything she'd loved about this place. Now here she was, back in town, a single mom of two and desperate for help. Desperate for hope. She didn't want her husband back, but she had no idea how to rebuild when her well-crafted life was all a facade.

Cole Whitaker pushed his bagel aside and slid his laptop closer, pretending to read his email. Except the news of Avery Lansing Crawford's return to Camellia had captured the interest of the locals. And his assistant, Millie Kay, was doing her part to keep everyone informed.

"My mama cleans houses for some folks over on the lake and she was at the Macintoshes' place last night. They're the ones with that new white brick mansion on Wilder Road. Anyway, she saw Avery pull in next door, towing a trailer. She had everything but the kitchen sink jammed in that thing." Millie Kay paused for dramatic effect. "I guess she'll be sticking around. Which is no surprise, seeing as how her husband left her high and dry."

Cole leaned further out of his chair to hear what Millie Kay said next then chastised himself for eavesdropping. Did he really need to know? Half of what she repeated likely wasn't true, anyway. Not that Millie Kay wasn't a wonderful administrative assistant. She just liked to talk. About anything or anyone.

Cole had to prepare for a board meeting, but curiosity about Avery shot to the top of his to-do list. He quickly searched the internet for Pax Crawford's social media accounts. The guy was easy to find. Several pictures filled the screen, commemorating a recent trip to Vegas, a fancy meal at an iconic restaurant and the interior of a stunning home. There weren't any photos of Avery. Instead, the images with people often included Pax posed beside a man Cole didn't recognize.

"Pax Crawford prefers men?" Cole quickly scrolled through several more posts. Still nothing about Avery or any children.

*This is none of your business. Get back to work.*

He ignored the wise counsel looping through his brain and searched for Avery online. Although he wasn't surprised when numerous articles and links filled his computer screen mentioning a television show about home decorating, the photo of her that appeared first captivated him. *Mercy.* Her dazzling smile still made his pulse stutter. And a precious little girl, a carbon copy of her beautiful mother, sat beside her. The same corkscrew curls, pale blue eyes and porcelain skin. Only the hand-smocked dress and the giant pink bow pinning back her curls were different.

Cole's chest tightened. In the last decade, Avery had only become more beautiful. How was that even possible?

*Stop.* He closed his web browser and reached for his Auburn War Eagle mug. Taking a sip of coffee, he forced his attention back to the task at hand. The conference call with the foundation's board of directors was scheduled for one o'clock this afternoon. He didn't have time to worry about local gossip.

But this wasn't just any local gossip. It was Avery.

Pushing back his rolling desk chair, he stood and crossed his cramped office to the wall with the map of the United States. Dozens of pushpins marked the locations where his team had identified potential trafficking victims. This is what mattered. Those precious girls plus the hundreds or even thousands more they hadn't reached yet, all in desperate need of education and marketable skills. Imari's Place was bursting at the seams. He had to secure funding, at least two hundred and fifty thousand, to give the girls scholarships and expand the housing options. His life's work and highest priority. And he wouldn't rest until he'd avenged his little sister's abduction, and the suffering she'd endured at the hands of her captors.

This wasn't the time to get sucked into the drama of some silly middle school crush whose world had unexpectedly unraveled.

Although if he was honest, his relationship with Avery was anything but silly. They'd gone to school together from preschool to twelfth grade. Lingering on the periphery of her life at first, he'd been mesmerized by the glow she emanated, until it came time to study. She was all business then. They were one-two in their graduating class. He'd edged her by a point that last semester. They'd strived to overachieve. Driven by the hurt and grief that had consumed their home lives. Education provided their tickets out of Camellia.

When he'd gone to Auburn, and she'd left for Raleigh to major in fashion and textile design, he'd lost track of her for a while. Lord knows his first career had swallowed him whole. Until he came to his senses. By then Avery's engagement to Preston Yates Crawford, affectionately known as Pax, had claimed the headlines of Camellia's newspaper.

*The only son of prominent pastor marries schoolteacher's daughter.*

That wedding was all anyone talked about for weeks. His mother tried to get him to attend. He'd refused. Admiring Avery Lansing Crawford from afar became a role he no longer cared to play. So what if they'd once scribbled their commitment to one another on a cocktail napkin—a foolish promise to marry if neither one found someone else by the age of thirty-two. An age he'd selected. It seemed so distant at the time.

They'd sat at a table in an upscale Camellia reception hall that night, supposedly celebrating their senior year with the customary milestone Senior Ball. But Avery's date had been in the corner making out with someone else, and he'd come alone. Both were stressed about school, their parents' struggles and fear of what the future might hold.

Now less than ten months stood between him and his thirty-second birthday, slightly more for her.

*Wonder where that napkin went?*

He took another sip of his coffee and quashed the question as quickly as it materialized. Nobody cared. Besides, he wasn't about to swoop in and offer a shoulder to cry on. It wasn't his place.

Someone knocked on his door. He turned to see Millie Kay hovering. "Cole? There's a woman here to see you."

"I really can't see anyone, not with the board meeting—"

"It's Maribelle Lansing."

Oh, boy. "Send her in."

He hurried to set his mug down then straightened the papers stacked near his computer and scooped his messenger bag off the worn leather chair facing his desk.

Maribelle's shoes tap-tap-tapped on the floor, announcing her arrival. "Good morning."

"Good morning, Mrs. Lansing." Cole smiled. "Would you like some coffee or water?"

"No, thank you. Please, call me Maribelle."

He tried not to look relieved. If she'd declined his hospitable offer then maybe she didn't intend to stay long. What could she possibly want?

"To what do I owe the pleasure of your visit?" Cole waited while she perched on the edge of her seat. Then he rounded his desk and sank into his own chair.

"I need to speak with you about my granddaughter Avery."

Maribelle cut her eyes toward his open office door then leaned forward. "It's a rather sensitive topic."

He smothered a sigh then stood. "Right. I'll get the door."

She tipped up her chin, obviously pleased with his compliance.

Cole eased the door closed, but not before earning a disapproving glare from Millie Kay. Honestly, the woman had no shame when it came to eavesdropping.

He sat down again, clasped his hands on the desk and offered his most patient smile. "How can I help you today?"

Her cerulean gaze bore into him. "I want you to offer Avery a job."

"Excuse me?" He shifted in his seat. Not that he wanted to be disrespectful to one of Camellia's most philanthropic residents, especially a true friend of the foundation, but he didn't see how Avery's tragic situation had anything to do with human trafficking.

"Your connection to Avery is no secret." She tapped one well-manicured nail against the handle on her leather handbag. "If anyone can help her find her sparkle—her purpose—again, it's you, Cole."

"I'm afraid I'm not following."

Her brow puckered. "I seem to recall your face at more than one family gathering in my daughter-in-law's home over the years. Wasn't that you in Avery's graduation photo?"

"Yes, of course. We go...way back."

"Aren't you in need of a designer for all those houses you will build?"

"I appreciate your enthusiasm for everything we're trying to accomplish here, but we haven't even secured the funding to expand Imari's Place. It will more than likely be one house."

"But if you had the funding, you'd proceed with your plans?"

"In theory, yes." Cole smoothed some crumbs from his unfinished bagel off his desk.

"What if I guaranteed you the funding you needed in exchange for offering Avery a job?"

Cole's mouth went dry. "I—I mean—I think—that—uh, does Avery know you're here?"

Maribelle ran her fingers through her short, curly white hair. "We haven't discussed next steps."

"So that's a no." He leaned back in his chair and linked his arms across his chest. "I'm guessing with a baby and a little girl to look out for, she'll have more pressing objectives than decorating a house that doesn't even exist yet."

"Or it might thrill her to have something to occupy her mind." Maribelle smiled. "You know Avery. She's at her best when the creative juices are flowing."

"I'm touched that you reached out to me during your family's darkest hours, but I'm afraid I can't accept your generous proposal." The words pained him, and he regretted them the second they left his mouth, but he had to call her bluff. No way she had access to that kind of funding.

Maribelle's right eye twitched, and a tense silence filled the space between them. "Very well. I guess I'll have to rip this up." She extracted a check from her handbag, unfolded it long enough for him to see the six digits then pinched it between her fingers. "What a pity."

Surprise bolted through his veins. He flung up one palm. "Now, hold on a minute."

She paused, the check only a second from being torn in two. "Care to reconsider?"

"Where did you get two hundred and fifty thousand dollars?"

"That's none of your business. Do we have a deal or not?"

Her inscrutable expression made him sweat. "I need to know that Avery is in agreement."

"You let me worry about Avery." Maribelle pushed the check across the desk. "I hope you and your board of directors have a productive meeting this afternoon. I'm certain they'll have no trouble coming up with the additional funds you need."

"Thank you, Maribelle." The words were inadequate, but all he could muster.

"You're welcome, darlin'." She pushed to her feet. "No need to walk me out."

"Yes, ma'am." Cole stood on wobbly legs and waited until she left the office.

*This changes everything.* With more funding, the housing options expanded. With a safe place to live, the women could focus on work and furthering their education. Lord willing, they wouldn't have to return to life on the streets or worse, their pimps.

As he sank into his chair, his breath rushed out in a groan. He should be ecstatic. Instead, guilt blew in like a storm rolling in off the Gulf. He hadn't spoken to Avery in years, but he knew one thing for sure. If she found out her grandmother bribed him, she would be furious. Cole wiped his sweaty palm on his pants then reached for the check. He'd have to make sure Avery never discovered the truth.

## Chapter Two

One simple post. That's all she needed. One photo with a brief caption to announce her resurgence. Her social media resurgence, anyway. If only the rest of her professional life could be revived as easily.

Avery sat on the white linen sofa in Mama and Greer's lake house, clutching her phone in her hand, and scanned the room for inspiration. The soothing color scheme mirrored the outdoors. Green- and blue-patterned pillows dotted the sofas and the armchairs flanking the white brick fireplace. Between the white shiplap on the walls, green plants on the rustic wood mantel and baskets artfully arranged on the floor, the living room looked like Joanna Gaines herself had blessed it with her sensibilities. The whole room was stunning.

She shuddered to think what might happen if Addison had her way with the furniture all slipcovered in white. Hayes wasn't crawling yet, but he'd figure it out soon. She envisioned him gripping the sharp edges of the modern wood coffee table to pull himself up. Maybe Mama and Greer wouldn't mind if she babyproofed a few things. That table spelled trouble. The baskets underneath needed to go too. Hayes would probably empty every single one. Or chew on them.

"Is everything all right?" Harper, Avery's sister, sat on the love seat with Hayes napping in her arms. Harper's curious gaze pinged between Avery's face and her phone. "Did someone send you a nasty DM?"

"I haven't bothered to look." Social media had been easy to ignore. Mostly. If she didn't pay attention, then she didn't have to see what people said. "But now I feel like I should get back out there."

Harper's smooth brows scrunched together. "Give yourself grace. Y'all have been through it."

"Yeah, well, hiding isn't going to change anything." Avery held up her phone and opened the camera. "And I need to earn some money."

She'd start simple. An appealing photo of a vibrant bouquet in a glass vase beside a stack of home decor magazines. Mama's coffee table wasn't kid-friendly, but it made for an attractive background. Surely it would gain some likes and comments. Right?

What if the unwritten rules and norms of social media she'd grown to understand had been replaced with new lingo and trends she'd have to learn all over again? Frowning, she stared at the image she'd just taken. Inspiration for a clever caption had vanished, replaced by another wave of self-doubt. Her relationship with social media hadn't always been this complicated. At first, she'd had a ball connecting with people who had a passion for design and home decor. When the stakes weren't so high, and the comments were nothing but heart-eyed emojis. But the last year had zapped her enthusiasm for living life in plain view of the public. Would she ever feel comfortable putting herself out there again? Did she even want to?

Heaving a sigh, she leaned forward and slid her phone onto the coffee table.

Julene, her youngest sister, sat crossed-legged on the striped throw rug, flipping through a magazine. In her denim shorts, red tank top and her blond hair piled in a messy bun, she resembled a high school student instead of a young woman who'd finished her junior year at Auburn.

Julene tossed the magazine aside then stood and snatched Avery's phone. "I've got an idea."

"Wait," Avery called after her as Julene crossed the room then stepped outside onto the screened porch.

Hayes whimpered in his sleep. Avery winced and silently willed him not to wake up. At least not yet. They'd had a restless night. Poor little guy's routine was all out of whack.

"No need to worry." Harper shifted Hayes to her other arm and gently patted his diapered bottom with her palm. "Julene manages the social media account for a regional magazine."

"I still want to see what she posts." Avery craned her neck and stared out the window. She couldn't see her sister. The lake looked amazing, though. Tree branches waved in the morning breeze and blue-green water lapped against the shoreline.

"What kind of job are you looking for?" Harper asked. "I'm sure if we spread the word, folks would line up to have you style their homes."

"They'll also have plenty of questions. I'm not ready to rehash all the drama." Avery held up a folded copy of the *Iron City Gazette* that Greer had brought her at breakfast. "There are exactly zero Realtors advertising for assistants in the classifieds. If I don't find something soon, I'm going to have to think outside the box."

Camellia had morphed into one of Alabama's most desirable midsize cities. Surely some of those shops she'd driven past when she'd come home were looking to hire.

"Isn't Pax required to pay child support?"

"Only the minimum amount required. It's better than nothing, I suppose." Avery fought to keep the tremor from her voice. Addison stood only a few feet away in the kitchen, working with Mama to finish making chocolate chip pancakes. The gentle soothing lilt of Mama's voice mingled with Addison's determined preschool-sized proclamations—insistent that she stir the batter herself. The last thing Avery wanted was for Addison to overhear a discussion about Pax, Trey and their lack of involvement with the kids.

Harper cast a furtive glance toward the kitchen. "Have you asked Pax or Trey to increase their contribution? Or set up consistent visitation?"

Avery cringed. "Please, not now."

Too late.

"Is my daddy coming here?" Addison skipped to the sofa and leaned on the arm, no doubt smearing pancake batter across the fabric. "Is he, Mama?"

The hope and enthusiasm in Addison's blue eyes undid her. How many times would Avery have to rip the proverbial Band-Aid off the raw wound and tell her little girl yet again that her daddy wasn't coming around?

"No, baby." Hot tears pressed against Avery's eyes as she smoothed Addison's hair back. "I'm sorry."

Her legs itched to run. The logical part of her mind implored her to stay and bravely face another barrage of questions, but she couldn't. She didn't possess the strength. Sidestepping her daughter, Avery rushed past her mother watching wide-eyed from the kitchen, pancake batter dripping from the whisk in her hand. If anyone would know what to say in this situation, it was Mama.

Because she'd lived it.

The hardwood floors felt cool against her bare feet as she slipped into the downstairs powder room and shut the door. Yanking a hand towel from the bronze-plated towel holder mounted on the wall, she slumped onto the commode and buried her face in the fluffy white terry cloth to muffle her sobs.

How was this her actual life?

The dizzying trajectory to success had started as a simple partnership selling real estate then morphed into home decorating and flipping houses. Vendors suddenly offered her free product in exchange for her social media influence. Although she enjoyed scrolling through images of spectacular homes, she didn't want to spend that much time on social media. Especially once Addison had started walking and talking. But Pax and Trey had insisted. Convinced her she had to capitalize on the groundswell of internet popularity. Soon, the production company came calling. She and Pax had cultivated a family, a business and a successful home renovation television show. Every aspect of her life had seemed so incredibly perfect.

She'd never paused to question why Trey edged her out, gradually decorating homes and making major business decisions without her.

Eventually doing *everything* without her.

Maybe she hadn't asked more questions because deep down she secretly feared that she didn't deserve to be successful. It had been easier to bask in the glow of the nation's approval rather than dread the day when a fickle audience might turn on her.

But now, more than a year later, she still wanted an explanation. Something more substantive than they'd offered that gut-wrenching day in the laundry room.

*We fell in love, and we were waiting for the ideal time to tell you.*
How could she have been so naive? And when would she
officially get over their betrayal? She'd chased these questions relentlessly, unable to grasp an answer that offered lasting peace. In her weaker moments, a small part of her still
secretly hoped that Pax would come back.

But that was impossible.

Their marriage had ended. Her last text message to Pax in-
dicating she and the kids had left Raleigh went unanswered.
He and Trey were allegedly on a book tour, promoting Pax's
new memoir.

"Mama?"

Addison's voice on the other side of the door made Avery's stomach twist. She quickly swiped at the moisture on
her cheeks.

"Mama? I need you."

The simple plea tightened Avery's throat again. She refused to give in this time. Pushing to her feet, she put the
towel back then turned on the water and forced herself to
confront her reflection in the oval gold-framed mirror hanging above the pedestal sink. Red-rimmed eyes, splotchy skin
and frazzled curls springing from her head like errant cork-
screws greeted her.

"Ma-ma." Tiny knuckles rapped clumsily on the door.
"Come. Out."

*She needs you.* Squeezing her eyes shut against the poignant
reminder, Avery splashed cool water on her hot skin. Teaching her daughter to be brave and resilient meant opening that
door instead of cowering alone. She turned off the water, dried
her face then pasted on a smile and opened the door.

"Hey, sweetie."

Relief flooded Addison's blue eyes. She flung herself at

Avery. Scooping her into her arms, Avery planted exaggerated kisses on Addison's cheeks until her deep belly laugh echoed off the walls.

Harper and Julene stood in the hallway, their expressions guarded.

"Mommy needed a minute." She kept her smile in place, both for her sisters and for Addison. Now more than ever she carried a desperate longing to be understood. To know that her family believed in her. At least until she had the confidence to believe in herself.

"I love you, Mama." Addison planted slobbery kisses on Avery's cheek. She still smelled of pancake syrup and her favorite strawberries and cream bubble bath. Her precious words soothed Avery's fragile heart.

"I love you too, sweet pea."

"And I also love Daddy. When is he coming?"

And just like that the tender moment vanished.

"Come on, let's go to lunch." Harper gently passed Hayes to Julene. "My treat."

"But I can't leave my kids." Avery winced as Addison twisted her fingers in her hair.

"Why not?" Harper stared at her like she'd sprouted a third eye. "Mama's having a ball with them, and Julene is here to help."

Julene swayed side to side, smiling down at Hayes as she settled him in her arms. "I don't know, holding this sweet fella is a miserable assignment."

Avery hesitated. Her sister did love babies. She'd have to be back to feed Hayes soon, though. He wasn't great at taking a bottle. Add that to her list of obstacles to conquer before she went back to work.

"When was the last time you enjoyed a kid-free outing?" Harper asked.

"I can't recall." The allure of adult conversation and a menu that didn't feature chicken fingers or macaroni and cheese won her over. "All right, but only if we stop by the boutique on Main Street. They're hiring part-time salespeople and I want to apply."

Another pointed glance pinged between Julene and Harper.

"That's not the first place I'd go if I needed a job," Julene murmured.

Avery kissed Addison's head then set her on her feet. She ran back to the kitchen.

"I've worked retail before." Avery propped her hands on her hips. A short stint at the general store in high school wasn't the same as an upscale women's clothing store, but she'd figure it out. Why did her sisters have strong opinions about where she worked?

"It's not about experience." Harper cupped Avery's shoulder and gently guided her toward the guest room down the hall. "Go put on a cute dress."

Avery glanced at her pink cotton T-shirt and denim skirt. "What's wrong with what I'm wearing?"

Harper's bangle bracelets jangled together as she smoothed a strand of hair behind her ear. "If you're applying to work at that boutique you need to look fashionable."

Avery bit her lip to keep from arguing then followed her sister's orders. Twenty minutes later, she emerged from her room wearing a pink floral maxi dress and metallic sandals, with her hair tamed into submission. She'd even put on a little makeup for the first time in ages.

After she collected her phone from Julene and reassured Addison that she'd be back before her nap time, Avery followed

Harper outside. "Want to stop by and say hello to Nana?" she asked, settling into the front seat of Harper's red sedan.

"Not really." Harper turned the key in the ignition. "She's coming to supper tonight."

"One visit with Nana today is enough for you?"

"Have you met our grandmother?"

Avery laughed as they buckled their seat belts. "Nobody tells it like it is quite like Nana."

"Facts." Harper fiddled with the AC then selected a pop station on the radio.

Avery felt untethered riding in the car without Hayes and Addison. She surveyed Harper's center console, noting the lipstick, powder compact and travel-sized hand sanitizer stored in the cubby. There probably weren't any crushed-up goldfish crackers or forgotten sippy cups littering the floor mat behind her seat. Oh, to be twenty-something again. Harper taught middle school math, and she was on summer break until early August.

"Tell me more about why you're interested in working retail." Harper steered her car onto the road leading toward downtown Camellia. "I thought you were a lifestyle blogger. No, wait. What's the word? *Influencer.*"

Avery smiled at her sister's good-natured teasing. "Pax and Trey had the real estate licenses. I maintained the blog and social media, and occasionally helped stage houses." She'd felt more like Trey's administrative assistant most days. Shame burned deep. She didn't want to talk about them today. Or confess to Harper that she'd pretended to be something she wasn't.

"So home decor is your niche then? What happened to fashion and textiles?"

Staring out the window, Avery caught glimpses of the other

homes along the lake. At least the ones not tucked away behind wrought iron fences or meticulously manicured hedges. Before she could formulate a response, Harper's phone rang, saving her from coming up with an answer.

To be honest, she didn't know how to define her niche. Or if she even wanted to. Was there any value in clawing her way back to the top, just to share trite staged photos of summer picnics, beach reads and place settings on Mama's table by the porch? More questions she couldn't seem to answer. That didn't mean she'd stop searching for clarity, though. Time had softened the raw edges of her heartache. She wasn't Trey's puppet anymore. Somehow she'd have to rediscover her true passion. Her authentic self. The version of her life she'd curated and portrayed to the rest of the world didn't exist anymore.

"Sorry." Harper ended the call and gave an apologetic smile. "Mary Catherine and I have been talking about spending a long weekend in Destin. I think we've finally agreed on the dates."

"That sounds fun." Envy sailed in and she promptly batted it away, like she'd swung at the birdie in their childhood badminton game. *Not today, jealousy.* The ugly feeling had crept in far too often in recent months, especially if she ran into friends from her former life as a married woman. Only a few had stuck by her after everything imploded. Sure, they'd promised to keep in touch, but she didn't expect any of them to visit her in Camellia. Or invite her to spend a weekend at the beach.

Harper slowed to claim a parking space on Main Street then eased the car between the white lines and turned off the engine.

"Oh, good. You nabbed a space close to the boutique. Let's

pop in right quick." Avery grabbed her purse then reached for the door handle.

"Avery, wait. You should probably know—"

"Oh. My. Word." Avery punctuated every syllable as she locked eyes with Pax's mother, Whitney, standing on the sidewalk.

"Pax's mother owns the boutique." Harper's words left her mouth in a long, defeated breath.

Cole stepped out of the historic brick building where his foundation rented office space, sandwiched between the pharmacy and an art gallery, and immediately halted his steps. Avery Lansing Crawford—with her trademark platinum curls fluttering in the warm breeze—stood across the street. His breath caught. Even from a distance, she was striking. He let his gaze sweep from her gorgeous hair to the feminine curves of her upper arms and the pink flowery dress that emphasized her petite figure. He had a lunch meeting in five minutes at the deli two blocks down Main Street, yet his feet behaved as though anchored in the concrete.

He couldn't look away.

*Stalker much?*

Avery faced her mother-in-law, Whitney Crawford. Evidently former mother-in-law if what he'd heard around town was accurate. He glanced at Avery's sister Harper standing between the women. Harper recognized him and waved.

Oh, no. To be honest, he'd imagined his reunion with Avery countless times over the years. He'd even scripted the conversation, including clever lines he'd say, and of course Avery would laugh at his witty sense of humor. Except Pax's mother had never been a cast member in his outlandish dream sequence.

Mrs. Crawford and her husband, Dalton, led a prominent megachurch known as The Oasis. Their congregation had rapidly expanded from fifty families to almost eight thousand members in the last ten years.

Cole didn't worship at The Oasis. His family had been First Presbyterian people for as long as the church existed. His great-grandparents' names were engraved in the stained glass panels in the foyer. He'd grown up in the beautiful old church, its spire visible from where he stood now, and he still attended every week. Sat in their family's usual pew third from the front on the left. It just felt right to continue the Whitaker family tradition.

Besides, Pastor and Mrs. Crawford gushed publicly about their commitment to fighting social injustice, but somehow never had time to attend an event benefiting Imari's Place or make a charitable contribution. Last he'd heard, The Oasis had declined all solicitations to become a ministry partner.

Cole had vowed he'd avoid any messy entanglements between the Crawfords and he hated to be late for a meeting, but his loyalty to Avery kept him from turning away. His brain screamed, *Don't do it!*

But his legs argued, *Let's go!*

He tugged at the collar of his gingham-checked button-down. Two young women standing on the corner holding shopping bags jabbed at the silver button to change the traffic light so they could cross the intersection. Cole stood behind them. The hair on the back of his neck prickled. Cars traveling on Main Street cruised to a stop, yielding to the pedestrians. He racked his brain for something intelligent to say as his feet found their way across the asphalt.

Mrs. Crawford's bright yellow dress fluttered in the breeze like a caution flag at Talladega racetrack. Her three-inch heels gave her a distinct height advantage over her former daughter-in-law. Avery stood tall with her shoulders back. Their encounter reminded Cole of the Westerns he used to watch on TV with his dad, featuring the hero and the villain pitted against each other in a showdown at high noon in front of the saloon. Hopefully no one in this situation planned to inflict harm.

At least not physically.

He couldn't hear what they were saying, but he could tell by the anxious expression on Harper's face and the telltale tip of Avery's chin that this wasn't an easy exchange. Harper caught his eye again. Her tight smile silently screamed *help*.

Man, this was a really, really bad idea. Maybe he should wave back then duck into the closest store and pretend he needed to buy a new tie. Then Avery shifted, and her blue-eyed gaze locked on his. Like a compass destined for true north, he couldn't have turned away even if he wanted to.

"Cole? Cole Whitaker?" Her smile was like a ray of sunshine bursting through the clouds after a stormy day. "What are you doing here?"

His mouth suddenly dry, he stopped beside Avery and pretended not to notice Mrs. Crawford's curious gaze. "Hello, Avery." He shoved his hands in his pockets to keep his defiant arms from pulling her into an embrace. "It's good to see you again."

"You too." Her voice sounded as sweet and melodic as he remembered.

"Harper." He grinned. "It's been a minute. How are things?"

"Splendid. I'm a teacher on summer vacation without a care in the world."

"Enjoy your well-deserved break." He turned toward Mrs. Crawford. "Good afternoon, ma'am. Cole Whitaker."

Her near-perfect smile faltered as she regarded his out-stretched hand for a long second then shook it briefly. "It's nice to meet you, Chris."

Ah. The accidentally on purpose mispronounced name. *Well played.* He wouldn't abandon his Southern manners, though. Not even in these circumstances. Especially not in these circumstances. "It's Cole. Not Chris." He offered his most genuine smile. "I'm the director of Imari's Place. By the way, we've invited you and Pastor Crawford to attend numerous fundraising events. It's a shame y'all haven't been able to join us."

"Oh, right. You do look familiar. I'll ask Dalton's assistant to give your people a call." She tried for another smile, but looked like she'd bitten into an onion. Or maybe she needed more Botox.

"Sorry to interrupt." He held up both palms. Neutral as Switzerland. "I wanted to say hello."

"You're not interrupting." Mrs. Crawford's wide smile was back in place. Her gaze slid past him and settled on Avery. "I've got to get to a lunch meeting with the elders' wives, but I couldn't miss the opportunity to welcome Avery back home. Give my best to the children, darlin'. You wouldn't *believe* how busy we are. Tell those sweet grandbabies how much we love them. We'll have y'all over to swim in the pool real soon."

Avery's mouth opened, but no words came out. Disbelief crossed her face. Cole shot Harper an is-she-for-real glance.

Then Mrs. Crawford leaned in and kissed the air somewhere in the vicinity of Avery's cheek. "Enjoy the rest of this gor-geous day." She stepped around them and strolled away, her heels clicking out a staccato rhythm on the sidewalk.

"Oh, Mylanta." Avery tucked an errant curl behind her ear with trembling fingers. "She is really something."

"That went better than I expected." Harper released a shaky laugh.

Avery still looked stricken. "I don't know what to make of her invitation. She can't be serious. I mean, Addison loves to splash in the pool, but I'm not ready to drop her off at her grandparents' house unsupervised. Hayes isn't ready for pool floaties and sunscreen and—"

"One day at a time, all right?" Harper cupped her palm on Avery's shoulder. "Let's assume positive intent. Surely she wants to see her grandchildren and reconnect with you."

Cole withheld a snarky comment. Whitney Crawford and positive intent was a stretch. *Dude, not helpful.*

Harper linked her elbow through Avery's. "Cole, would you like to join us for lunch?"

Disappointment arced through him. He'd like nothing more. "I wish I could, but I've got a meeting as well."

His gaze found Avery's again. He had so many questions. Maribelle's words echoed in his head.

*You two were thick as thieves back in the day.*

"Mama's having some people over to the house tonight for supper." Harper readjusted her purse strap on her shoulder. "Why don't you come by around six?"

He hesitated. "I don't want to intrude."

"You're not intruding. Our stepfather built Mama a beautiful new lake house. She's more than happy to give you the grand tour. I know Julene would love to see you too."

He politely waited, giving them both one last opportunity to retract the invitation. Harper elbowed Avery in her side. "Exchange phone numbers with Cole so you can text him the address and code for the gate."

Over a decade had passed since he'd exchanged texts with Avery. The thought of having her number again made his palms sweat.

Avery retrieved her phone from her purse. The device pinged repeatedly. She stared at the screen, her smooth brow furrowed.

"Everything all right?" Cole asked, discreetly swiping his hands on the legs of his chinos.

"Yeah, it's just…" she trailed off then glanced at Harper. "Julene's post."

Harper grinned. "She showed me the picture. Spectacular shot. So people are responding?"

"The most notifications I've had in quite a while." Avery swiped her fingertip across the screen then scrolled. Nervous laughter bubbled from her lips. "This is wild."

"How about that." Harper turned toward Cole. "Avery's been on a social media hiatus. Julene posted a stunning photo of the lake this morning. Evidently Avery's audience is glad to see she's back."

Cole studied Avery as she passed him her phone. Her expression didn't quite match her sister's enthusiasm.

"Put your number in my contacts, please."

His fingers skimmed hers. That brief encounter sent his mind into a tailspin. Super. Just like old times. Could his heart handle that romp down memory lane? Probably not, but the check from Maribelle he'd already deposited made the decision easy.

"Thanks for the invitation." He entered his number then gave Avery her phone. "I'll see you around six."

# Chapter Three

"I'm guessing after today's encounter with Whitney you probably changed your mind about applying at her boutique." Harper sat across from Avery on Mama's screened porch, her phone in one hand and a plastic tumbler full of sweet tea in the other.

Avery had fed Hayes and now he'd almost fallen asleep in her arms. She rocked in the white rocker, hoping to lull him into a pre-supper nap. "I'm going to have to look elsewhere. I don't feel comfortable asking her for a job."

Harper offered an empathetic look. "For what it's worth, I'm proud of you. That was a tense scene. You handled it with grace and class."

"Thank you. Whitney and I have struggled to communicate well. Even when Pax and I were married."

"Tough to share the spotlight?"

Avery stopped rocking. Harper's question touched a still-tender wound. "Sometimes I wonder if she knew that Pax felt conflicted. Now that I've had time to reflect, I can see how she might've had some insight into her only son's dilemma. Our business had taken off, but he must've been wrestling with honoring his commitment to our family and wanting to pursue a relationship with Trey, but..."

"But she didn't know what to do about it." Harper finished the sentence for her. It was still hard to wrap her mind around all that had happened to their family. A family she would've described to anyone as satisfied and content. Her ignorance about Whitney owning the boutique served as another painful reminder of her failed marriage and the lack of honest communication.

"There's no manual for how to navigate a complex situation like this, right?" Harper shifted in her seat. The ice in her drink clinked against the side of the plastic tumbler. "I'm sorry for all that you've been through. You are so brave and resilient, and we're all thrilled that you're here. Take some time and find your lane."

"I don't feel brave," Avery whispered, lowering her voice to keep her words from traveling through the porch's screens and out into the neighbors' yards. "I'm scared to death. How am I supposed to provide for these kids?"

Harper's eyes widened. "Say what now? I thought Pax and Trey were promoting Pax's new memoir? Don't book tours help sell books?"

"They're on a tour, as far as I know. But we couldn't agree on filming another season of the show, and Pax won't receive a royalty check for several months. Trey spent almost every dollar we had in our savings account on horse races." She swallowed against the familiar sour taste clawing its way up the back of her throat. Being honest and vulnerable and saying the words out loud gave in to the panic, gave her fears all the power, and she hated that.

"I'm so sorry," Harper said. "What are you going to do?"

"That's the problem. I truly have no idea. It about killed me to ask Mama and Greer if we could move back in. Not that I had much choice. Rent for an apartment in Raleigh is unaffordable without a steady income. After the house sold and I paid off the loan, I have enough to cover expenses for about six more months."

"You could create a cookbook." Harper grinned. "That's the next logical step for a lifestyle blogger, right?"

"That's cute," Avery said. "Except I can't cook."

And she was done pretending to be something she wasn't.

"You've always been good at making things pretty." Harper stared out at the lake. "In a perfect world, what would you do for a living? Design clothes?"

Avery hesitated. Making things pretty? Is that really all she was good at? She'd mulled the notion for months, ever since her marriage imploded. She'd tried to find her new lane, binging countless podcast episodes, hoping to find inspiration in the stories of other women making a positive impact in the world.

"I'm not that great at designing clothes," she confessed.

"So not true. You whipped up a few outfits for me when we were younger."

She ignored her sister's protest. "Posting on social media about my non-Instagrammable life won't pay the bills, either. Besides, I want to do something more substantial. I want to help women bounce back from devastating circumstances."

There. More words she'd feared saying out loud, because frankly the idea sounded ridiculous.

Harper's brows sailed upward.

"Before you say anything, let me explain."

"I'm listening."

"Social media is a wonderful tool. I'd be lying if I claimed we could've been successful without it. But at the same time, the content we created wasn't necessarily authentic. It's a slippery slope, creating content for an audience that can turn on you overnight."

"But you're so good at it." Harper set her tea aside and scrolled through her phone. "Did you see there are more than five hundred comments to that picture Julene posted for you this morning?"

"But that's the thing." Avery fought to keep irritation from her voice. "It's just a pretty picture. It doesn't change the world or inspire a woman who feels hopeless to keep going."

"It might. You don't know for sure." Harper kept scrolling. "Most of these comments are super kind."

"Don't tell me about the ones that aren't."

Insights, analytics, likes, comments and shares—all the data that used to make her world go around—she'd been able to ignore since her self-imposed hiatus from social media. Hayes released a deep sigh and she resumed rocking. Julene had paired the lovely photo of the lake with an intriguing caption, something about hitting the reset button and making a fresh start.

So folks had noticed. Big deal. She couldn't buy diapers with a social media post.

Inside, the doorbell rang then footsteps thumped across the hardwood floors. Addison squealed with delight.

Harper and Avery exchanged glances. "Nana," they said in unison. Greer had been kind enough to pick her up and bring her to the house for supper.

Then Avery recognized the familiar rumble of Cole's laughter. Her pulse sped. She didn't want to feel excited about his visit, yet she couldn't stop her thoughts from circling around all the childhood memories filled with Cole. During the storms in her life, he'd reappeared at the exact moment she needed him most. That had always been the way with their friendship.

Until she'd let Pax woo her into a whirlwind courtship.

"Let me see if Mama needs help." Harper stood. "But I want to talk more later about the engagement and the reach of Julene's post."

*I don't.* She'd longed for her sisters' support, and she understood Harper's enthusiasm for revamping an account that had been successful. But she couldn't ignore the thoughts that kept resurfacing. The idea that maybe she was meant for something more substantive than "making things pretty." She had to focus on something more practical—like a traditional job with a steady paycheck and health insurance.

Harper went inside and slid the screen door closed. Cole's voice grew louder. Kind, loyal Cole. Steadfast. She smiled at the bittersweet memory of their vow to marry at thirty-two if they hadn't met anyone else. It had been a rough night. A silly proclamation, really. Besides, she'd been inebriated from whatever her loser date had slipped into her soda. Cole had kept her company, and they'd scrawled their vow on a cocktail napkin embossed with their high school's name and the date. She still had the napkin somewhere—probably in the bottom drawer of her jewelry box. The whole evening might've been an epic disaster, but he'd redeemed it by making her laugh and driving her safely home without an expectation of anything in return.

Right on cue, he stepped onto the porch with a Tervis tumbler full of ice water and a plate of cheese, crackers and fruit.

"Hey," he said. "Julene sent me with sustenance."

"Thanks." She smiled, strangely shy at his presence.

Cole set the water and the plate on the table next to her then sat on the opposite rocker. He'd rolled up the sleeves of his gingham-checked button-down to reveal chiseled forearms. His gray slacks were impeccably pressed, and concern was evident in his expression as he studied her. Harper always said he had the prettiest hazel eyes. Those long dark lashes were to die for too.

"This must be the handsome baby boy I've heard so much about." Cole's warm gaze settled on Hayes. "Your grandmother likes to brag."

Avery laughed. "It's one of her many gifts."

"What's his name?"

"This is Hayes. He's five months old."

"Nice. Congrats."

"Thank you. He's a sweetie."

Cole nodded then sipped his water. A comfortable silence settled between them. Birds chirped in the trees nearby, and the citrusy fragrance of Mama's bee balm flowers wafted on the breeze. Her chair squeaked as she continued rocking. She wanted to ask about him and what was new in his life. Except part of her didn't really want to hear if he had a wife and children.

Surely Nana would've told her *that*.

"How are you, Avery?" His tender concern seeped into his voice.

She looked away. He'd always been able to see right through any facade she tried to construct. No sense pretending all was well.

"I'm all right. It's a big adjustment coming back here."

"Especially with two small children." He leaned forward, elbows on his knees and hands clasped together. "Are you looking for work?"

She nodded.

"Mama? Can I come out there with you?" Addison pressed her palms and her face against the screen, the tiny metal squares squishing against her porcelain skin.

"You stay in and help get ready for supper. Go wash your hands in the bathroom, please."

"You. Come. In." Addison stomped her bare foot on the floor, emphasizing each word.

"No, ma'am." Avery mustered her stern voice, still determined not to wake Hayes. Addison had impeccable timing for testing her patience. "That's not how you speak to me. Go wash your hands, please."

Addison hesitated then scampered away.

"She greeted me at the door." His mouth curved in a knowing smile. "She's feisty. Kind of like someone else I know."

"Hardly." Avery scoffed and reached for the water, her mouth suddenly dry.

"Oh, don't be skeptical. You had all of Camellia and most of Alabama wrapped around your finger."

"Yeah, well, that was a long time ago."

Warmth heated her skin as he stared at her.

"It's never too late to be what you might have been," he said.

"C.S. Lewis?"

"George Eliot."

She gulped half the glass of water then resumed rocking. "Here's the thing. I'm still not sure what I want to be when I grow up."

Amusement flashed in Cole's eyes. "I've seen pictures. My mom told me all about the show too. When it comes to home renovation, you're a natural."

"That's sweet of you to say, but we had a producer and talented camera people. Pax and Trey…" she trailed off, stopping short of confessing how little she had to do with their past success. She was sick and tired of her own narrative. And what that meant for her future. For her children's future.

Cole sipped his water. The birds chirping in the trees near the porch filled the silence. When he met her gaze again, the empathy and the hope she saw there made her breath catch.

"I've known you almost my whole life, Avery. While I admire your humility, I refuse to believe that all you've accomplished is because of someone else's savvy. You have a gift. A creative energy that no one can stifle. Don't let someone else determine your worth."

His words knifed at her. Is that what she'd done? Placed too much focus on Pax's rejection?

"See? You know I'm right."

"My life's been an absolute nightmare this past year, Cole."

"And yet you're still standing."

Staring out over the lake, her baby boy nestled in her arms, she wanted to believe in herself the way Harper and Cole did.

Cole topped a cracker with a slice of cheese. "I know how much you love a good project, especially when you're dealing with your problems. I have something that's right up your alley."

Curiosity outweighed her uncertainty. "Do tell."

"Imari's Place is due for an expansion. I need an interior designer—someone to make all the decisions from paint color to cabinets in the kitchen and choose all the furniture."

Avery stopped rocking. Chill bumps pebbled the skin on her arms. "You're kidding, right?"

"I'm serious. The board approved it. We're scheduled to break ground next week."

Wan laughter escaped her lips. Hayes flinched and cried

out. She leaned down and planted a gentle kiss on his head then patted his backside until he fell asleep. Cole's offer scared her. She was a single mother and an irrelevant lifestyle blogger abandoned by her husband and her temperamental audience. Could she really design and decorate a large-scale project without Pax and Trey? "I appreciate the offer, but I've never worked solo before. I'm not sure I can handle a major assignment right now, given all the upheaval in my life."

Cole dusted cracker crumbs from his fingertips. "You have a bachelor's degree in fashion and textiles, right? Plus, extensive experience. Once I send you the specs, you can make a final decision. Funding's approved to pay you, although it isn't as substantial as you may want."

She sifted through the details, trying to discern what he wasn't telling her. Hadn't he heard what she'd said?

"Yes, I have a degree, but in a mostly unrelated field. There must be more qualified candidates available. My experience is not as extensive as you might think."

Her heart hammered. Telling Cole her most vulnerable thoughts and feelings had never been difficult. But they were adults now. There was so much at stake. "Trey, my ex-husband's partner, did almost all the work and I let people believe that I deserved the credit. A few clever shots of me tossing pillows on a sofa and arranging flowers in a vase had everyone fooled."

She forced herself to look Cole in the eye. She couldn't mislead him. His work with Imari's Place meant so much to him. He battled human trafficking out of his own personal loss. She'd never forget how he'd suffered when his sister disappeared. Or the agony he'd endured as the news of her murder had split his family in two.

"Please, Avery." Cole's voice implored her to reconsider.

"Everything you've experienced personally and professionally adds value to this project. You can mold this building into a beautiful home. I looked through the pictures on your website and watched three episodes of your television show. Your style is unmatched."

Her throat tightened. His gaze was so earnest she had to look away. This was the kind of meaningful work she'd told Harper she wanted. A job that helped women get back on their feet. How could she say no?

He'd enjoyed his reunion with Avery's family far more than he should have.

The laughter, effortless conversation and delicious food pulled him in, slowly weakening his defenses.

While the realization made Cole uneasy, he still couldn't bring himself to say his goodbyes. Then Julene refilled his glass with more sweet tea and Mrs. Lansing—Mrs. Huntington now—served a second helping of that scrumptious pulled pork and he settled back in the upholstered dining room chair. Greer regaled them with his misadventures hiking the Appalachian Trail, woefully unprepared among a bunch of buddies from his financial advising firm.

One glance at Avery sitting across from him, the candlelight from the centerpiece flickering in her eyes, and everything felt good and right in his world. His devastation over her decision to marry Pax was conveniently erased.

*Seriously, it's time to go.*

He'd missed her.

"Cole, can I interest you in some peach cobbler and vanilla ice cream?" Mrs. Huntington asked.

He groaned and pressed his palm against his already full stomach then opened his mouth to politely decline.

"Now, don't you go trying to scoot off, young man." Maribelle shot him a pointed glance from the far end of the table where she'd held court all night.

"Maribelle, you aren't shy about expressing your opinion, are you?" Greer teased, the lines around his eyes crinkling.

*You have no idea.* Cole forced a smile and plated his utensils while Julene and Harper cleared the table.

"And don't pretend you don't play tennis." Maribelle shook her finger at him. "You can afford a few extra calories every now and then."

Avery laughed, her oversized feather-shaped earrings swaying above her shoulders. Heat climbed his neck as Avery's eyes locked on his. He glanced at Julene, hovering at his elbow to collect his plate.

"Thank you," he said. "It was delicious."

"You're quite welcome." Julene smiled. "We'll be back with dessert in a second."

Now was the ideal time to make his exit. Maribelle's presence at the table tonight jolted him back to reality, reminding him this was anything but a casual meal between childhood friends. She had bribed him. Plain and simple. If Avery found out, their friendship would end before he even had a chance to rekindle a spark.

He'd meant what he'd said on the porch earlier. Avery might be struggling now, but she had a natural gift for design. Raw talent that Maribelle and everyone else in her life clearly recognized. She just needed the right opportunity to showcase her strengths. The expansion at Imari's Place was the ideal project for her. Besides, if he returned the money to Maribelle, the foundation wouldn't have sufficient funds to expand and he'd have to turn away young vulnerable women.

Except he couldn't leave without an answer from Avery about his job offer.

Avery's mother stood. "I'll start the coffee maker."

"Coffee? You can't drink coffee before bed." Addison's spunky observation drew another round of laughter. Even Cole smiled. She was a carbon copy of her mother.

Avery reached over and smoothed the little girl's hair from her forehead. "Don't worry, baby. We'll drink decaf. Speaking of bedtime, we need to start your bath soon."

"No way." Addison pushed out her lower lip. "It's too early for bed, Mama."

Avery tipped her head to one side, her smile still in place. "It's not too early for you, sweet girl."

Cole's heart squeezed. Her patience and attentiveness impressed him.

"Can I have a little taste of ice cream? Just a teeny tiny taste?" Addison scrunched up her face then pinched her thumb and first finger together.

How to resist that? Cole was glad he didn't have to be the enforcer. He'd be putty in Addison's hands, just like he couldn't say no to Maribelle.

"You may have a teeny tiny taste of vanilla ice cream." Avery mimicked her daughter's hand gesture and higher pitched voice. Addison grinned then shot a glance around the table as if she secretly knew attention was directed at her.

"How are things at Imari's Place?" Greer asked as he helped clear the serving dishes and platters from the table.

Cole's stomach clenched. He stole a glance at Maribelle.

*Please, please not a word*, he silently pleaded. He'd about died when Maribelle arrived in time for supper. Her appearance almost made him bail on the whole evening. Almost.

He smoothed his fingertips along his jaw, carefully measuring his response. "Things are good. Really good. The board of directors approved an expansion and we plan to break ground next week. Hopefully Avery will consult with us regarding interior design of the home."

Avery slid her hand over the sea green place mat in front of her, brushing away crumbs. Or plotting her own exit strategy.

"You'd be perfect for that job, darling," Maribelle chimed in.

Oh, boy. Cole shifted in his chair. See? That's why he'd sidestepped the topic. Greer had initiated polite conversation, but this was dangerous territory.

Avery reached for her water glass. "I appreciate your vote of confidence, Nana."

Cole resisted the urge to lean forward, eager to hear her response. What if she said yes?

Although he couldn't blame her for saying no. She had a baby and a four-year-old. Moving back to her hometown as a single mom probably wasn't her dream for her future. With her life at a crossroads, she had plenty of reasons to decline. Yet against his better judgment he found himself hoping she'd say yes.

They weren't sixteen anymore. He'd find a way to work with her and keep their interactions professional. They were friends. Two friends who'd made an impulsive promise to bail each other out after they'd exhausted all their other options.

Except he didn't want to be Avery's last resort. He'd wanted to be her first choice and she had chosen Pax.

Greer and Julene carried cups, saucers and a carafe in from the kitchen while her mother delivered peach cobbler topped with generous scoops of vanilla ice cream.

"Here you are." Mrs. Huntington set a plate in front of

Cole. Ice cream ran in creamy rivers off the top of the peach cobbler.

"Thank you." He sliced his fork through the dense dessert then took a bite, enjoying the sugary explosion in his mouth. Despite his thoughts and intentions battling against each other, part of him loved being back with these people who used to feel like his second family.

After his sister was gone and his parents divorced, Cole spent countless hours with Avery at her family's old place on Crabtree Lane. This gorgeous lakefront home was the opposite of the shabby rambler in one of Camellia's working-class neighborhoods. He surveyed the massive trestle table with more than enough room for all of them, fresh flowers and candles in the center and a stunning view of the lake through the broad expanse of windows. What a relief to see Avery's mama so happy and content. Greer had given her a second chance she'd so desperately deserved.

Spoons clinked against china as creamer and sugar were stirred into the coffee. Conversation ebbed and flowed while they ate their dessert. Cole half listened as Julene and Greer talked about the local festival coming up, the minor league baseball team's winning record and Greer's plans to take a client out on his boat the following day.

Cole scraped the remaining pool of ice cream from his plate then glanced at Avery. He didn't have kids or nieces or nephews, but he knew from hanging out with his friends that bedtime was a lengthy production. She wasn't required to give him an answer tonight but if she said no, he'd have to find other candidates quickly.

Maribelle would never stand for that.

How could he catch a few minutes alone with Avery before he left? He was down to his last few sips of coffee when the grandfather clock in the living room chimed eight o'clock.

*Really. It's time to go.* He couldn't stall any longer. Cole drained his coffee then pushed back his chair and stood. "Thank you so much for supper. Everything was fantastic and it's great to see you all again."

He intentionally let his gaze glide around the room, careful not to land on Avery.

"C'mon, Addison, I'll start your bath while your mama says goodnight to Mr. Cole." Harper stood and plucked Addison from her chair before the little girl protested.

Bless Harper. He made a mental note to buy her coffee next time he saw her in town. Avery's thin brows arched but she didn't argue, either. "Sounds good." She stood, skirted the end of the table and followed Cole toward the front door.

"Don't be a stranger now," Greer called after him.

"Wait, wait don't go." Addison's bare feet slapped against the hardwood floor and Cole turned around as she ran toward him. "Bye-bye, Mr. Cole." She squeezed his legs and he didn't even care that she smeared vanilla ice cream on his pants.

Avery pressed her fingertips to her mouth.

"Nice to meet you, sweet girl." Cole patted her head. "Sleep tight."

She turned and skipped away. "I'm comin', Aunt Harper."

Avery wrinkled her nose. "Sorry about your pants."

Cole shrugged. "No worries. She's adorable."

He headed for the door, his thoughts waging war. Did he ask for her decision? Establish a firm deadline?

"So about your job offer."

Cole stilled, his hand resting on the doorknob.

"I have a couple questions."

His pulse quickened and he turned to face her. "Yes?"

Avery tapped one fingertip against her chin and her other arm was draped across her torso. "Flexible hours, I'm assuming?"

"Of course."

"You recognize I've never tackled a project of this magnitude? And that I don't plan to stay in Camellia long-term?"

He waited for her to keep talking, his breath held.

"But I feel like I'm supposed to say yes."

Inside he was all fist bumps and high fives. Outwardly, he downplayed his enthusiasm. "Great. Thanks for letting me know. I'll give you a call when we're ready to schedule our first meeting."

He turned to leave.

"Cole." The sound of his name on her lips still had the power to take him down. He swallowed against the dryness in his mouth. "Yes?"

"It's good to see you again. Thanks for coming by."

If hearts did backflips, his just executed a gold medal–worthy performance. "It's good to see you too, Avery."

He slipped out and pulled the door shut then paused on the porch. Despite his excitement over Avery's decision, guilt gnawed at him. Maybe he should tell Avery that Nana's generous contribution was the driving force behind his offer. Except then Avery would change her mind, and he couldn't stand the thought of wrecking their fragile bond.

Sometimes it was better to beg for forgiveness than ask for permission.

# Chapter Four

*Why* had she said yes?

Only twelve hours had passed since she'd accepted Cole's job offer. Way too soon to panic. Except fear had barged its way in during Hayes's 4:00 a.m. feeding, drove in tent stakes and set up camp. Like it planned to stick around a while.

"Sweetheart, are you okay?" Mama walked beside her on the paved path circling a man-made water feature in the center of Camellia's new community park.

"Mmm-hmm." Avery tightened her grip on the stroller's handle and stared straight ahead, determined to keep an eye on Addison. They'd already had one epic battle of wills this morning. Addison had picked out her own outfit. A red-and-white-striped T-shirt and lime green shorts. Maybe the lack of sleep and rude awakening was to blame, but Avery foolishly took issue with the clothing selection. When she'd suggested Addison change into something that matched, the poor girl had melted. Avery knew better than to criticize a four-year-old's clothing choices.

After she'd apologized for hurting Addison's feelings, she'd encouraged her to leave the scooter behind. At least until she'd had more time to practice. The thought of scooping her baby girl off the pavement and tending to skinned knees or elbows made her feel panicky. Mama had mentioned the brand-new play structure and Avery had promised they'd stop and hang out there.

But Addison would not back down. She'd even tried loading the thing in the back of the car by herself while Avery was busy getting Hayes ready to go. Determined to regain control of the situation, Avery mandated that Addison wear her new helmet. Addison had happily complied—probably because it had purple sparkly paint.

"You're quiet this morning." Mama slanted her a curious look. "Sounds like y'all were up early."

"Too early. I tried to go back to sleep after I finished feeding Hayes around four thirty, but Addison came in at five fifteen."

"Oh, dear."

Addison had tiptoed in and crawled into bed beside her then peppered her with questions, diminishing all hope of anyone going back to sleep.

"Where she gets all that energy is beyond me." Avery leaned over the handle and adjusted the light blanket she'd tucked around Hayes. He'd stayed awake since she'd transferred him from the car. His little brow furrowed as he squinted at her from underneath the stroller shade.

"There's a place where we can stop and see the ducks and look for turtles." Mama unscrewed the cap on her water bottle. "Between the scooter ride, seeing the animals and playing on the new play structure, maybe that will tire her out."

"Please, let it be so."

The lush canopy of trees overhead offered a reprieve from the warm morning sunshine. Squirrels skittered through the underbrush. Birds perched on branches nearby, preening. The peaceful setting did nothing to soothe the thorny knot of emotions inside.

Mama twisted the cap back on the water bottle. "You don't have to talk to me if you don't want to, but I'm here and happy to listen."

Her gentle words crumbled the last of Avery's stubborn resolve. "I shouldn't have accepted that offer from Cole. I really wish I hadn't and now I don't know what to do."

There. She'd blurted it all out.

Mama slowed her steps. "Are you concerned about starting a new job when you have small children?"

*Sort of.* "I'm not really qualified to take on a project like this."

"Oh, I don't know about that. You're very talented. Cole and his staff are fortunate to have you. I wish you'd been able to decorate our new place. But I hated to ask, what with Pax leaving you and all. Besides, you were seven months pregnant by the time we were ready to move in."

"Mama, I haven't decorated a room or designed anything on my own for eons. And even though I'm still so mad at Trey and Pax for leaving, they did a lot of the work and—"

"Hey, watch me!" Addison looked over her shoulder then glided along the path. Her toe caught and she stumbled, but quickly recovered and shot them a proud smile before getting right back on the scooter.

The child was fearless.

"You're doing great," Avery called out. "Remember to watch where you're going, please."

"Julene, Harper and I are available to babysit. Or we can find someone local to help if that's what you'd prefer. What else is giving you second thoughts?"

Avery's flip-flops smacked against the pavement as they

walked faster to keep up with Addison. "I don't want to sound ungrateful. I need a good job and my children are a huge blessing. Hayes especially has been such a gift. After my miscarriage, I wasn't sure I'd ever get pregnant again."

"You don't sound ungrateful. You sound normal," Mama said. "Lots of women are in your position, trying to provide for their families and pay attention to their career."

"How'd you do this, Mama? I'm not just talking about work. You kept it together so well after Daddy left. I never heard you complain."

Mama's expression grew serious. "I tried not to ever complain in front of you girls or let you see me crying. Nana is quite generous now, but when your grandfather was alive, he did not like to part with his money. I had to ask for help and I hated it. Hated that you had to buy somebody else's used clothes, and we never got to take fancy vacations."

"We went to the beach lots of times."

"And stayed in a condo that my students' families let us borrow."

"Julene, Harper and I didn't care. Those trips are some of my best memories."

Mama's chin wobbled.

"Please don't cry." Avery pressed her hand against the small of Mama's back. "You're an amazing mother. We're so grateful for all the sacrifices you made for us, and I'm so happy that you and Greer found each other."

"Thank you." Mama blinked back unshed tears. "I know you are. Now, tell me what's really bothering you."

"I'm afraid I'll fail. Cole's put his trust in me. Not to mention the fundraising, grants and donations to make this all happen, right?" Despite the heat and humidity blanketing the park, a chill raked her spine. "I can't let everyone down."

"You will not fail," Mama said. "Cole chose you as his partner. You'll be a team."

"Add that to the list of things keeping me up at night." Avery's attempt at humor fell flat. "It seems I'm a lousy teammate."

"That is not true, and this is an extraordinary opportunity. Who knows? Sometimes friendships have a way of turning into something more."

"That *cannot* happen."

"Why not?"

"Because he needs somebody who..." she trailed off, unable to finish the sentence.

Someone who isn't living with her parents. Someone whose ex-husband didn't leave her for a man.

"Avery, you are worthy of love. I want you to remember that. Don't allow rejection and disappointment to shape your future."

Avery's knees threatened to buckle. Mama's words landed like a truth bomb in the middle of her ransacked heart. "But this hurts so much."

"I know." Mama gently rubbed Avery's arm. "But new opportunities and support from your family have a way of soothing some of the hurt. Maybe you can't see it today, but someday not too long from now, you won't feel so wounded all the time."

Oh, she wanted to believe that. She really did. But she couldn't shake the nagging feeling that saying yes to Cole had opened her up to a whole new brand of heartache.


"Well, don't that beat all." Lucille examined the flyer Maribelle had plucked from the console table in the atrium downstairs. "You reckon his mama arranged all this?"

Maribelle huffed out a breath and snatched the flyer back.

Words failed her. And that rarely happened. She was as mad as a mule chewing on bumblebees. Through the lenses of her reading glasses, she examined the announcement again. Pax would be in Camellia in a matter of weeks, hawking his wares in his daddy's church. The notion soured her stomach. He had a lot of nerve, coming back to the place that had raised him and demanding that folks buy his book. She leaned closer and examined the professional photo of Avery's ex-husband filling the middle of the page. Maribelle refused to admit it out loud, but he still looked as handsome as all get-out.

But not as handsome as that Cole Whitaker.

"The Oasis has a right nice sanctuary." Lucille reached for her teacup and saucer. "I imagine he'll fill the place up."

"Bite your tongue." Maribelle scowled from her red recliner beside Lucille. "That book is probably a dreadfully mediocre retelling of his uneventful childhood. Nothing good happened to that boy except for Avery."

Lucille took a dainty sip of her tea in silent compliance.

Even though she'd invited Lucille over to discuss this horrid news, Maribelle desperately wanted to be alone now. She needed space and time to process this latest development and she always did her best thinking in the afternoon.

Lucille was good to her, though. And Maribelle didn't have the nerve to ask her to leave, especially when she needed a loyal friend with decent eyesight and the freedom to drive. They'd be traveling hither and yon until this mess was all straightened out.

Sunlight filtered through the windows overlooking the courtyard outside Maribelle's studio apartment at Westwood Manor. Her tea sat untouched on the mahogany Queen Anne coffee table. Lucille's cup rattled against her saucer. Maribelle tried to make sense of what Pax and his partner were up to.

Why a book tour? And why stop here in Camellia where his presence would only cause Avery more pain?

This only reinforced Maribelle's confidence in her decision to intercede. His calculated plans for self-promotion couldn't go unhindered. Not if she had anything to say about it.

"Maribelle, I wonder if—"

"Now, I know what you're thinking." Maribelle folded the flyer and tucked it inside the cover of her Bible on the side table situated between the chairs. "Nell already read me the riot act on the way back from lunch."

Lucille's normally serene expression puckered. "How could you possibly know what I'm thinking? I've barely said a word."

Honestly. So sensitive. "Now, don't go and get your knickers in a knot. Your feelings are as plain as the nose on your face."

Lucille's chin dropped. The pain flashing in her eyes gave Maribelle pause. But only for a second. She had too much on her mind to be concerned about anyone else's feelings. "You think I've meddled. Stuck my nose where it didn't belong and caused all sorts of trouble. Let me tell you a thing or two about what it—"

"Maribelle, I never accused you of meddling." Lucille pressed her lips into a thin line as she leaned forward and slid her cup and saucer onto the table. "Nell and I have every right to be concerned about your behavior."

She ignored that barbed comment and drew a breath. She'd address the gossip circulating behind her back another time. "Despite what you might have *heard*, I didn't make that donation for my own selfish gain. Lord knows I watched my family burn to the ground once before when my son walked out on those beautiful girls and their precious mother. I'm not going to sit around and watch Preston Yates Crawford get all the glory."

"You certainly have strong feelings about your granddaughter's well-being."

"You're darn right. And who better than me to advocate for Avery and her children?"

Lucille's brows arched toward her silver curls. "Well, now I'm not sure if you're the best person for the role."

"But how in the world could I live with myself if Cole wasn't able to move forward with his project because they lacked the necessary funds?"

"Excellent question."

"See? I knew you'd come around to my way of thinking." Relief swept over her and she flashed a satisfied smile. To be honest, she'd gotten all fired up and tried to pretend that she didn't care what her friends thought, but a pang of uncertainty settled under her sternum when Lucille mentioned she and Nell had discussed her family's ugly situation. They had no business judging. It wasn't like they'd shared in the experience. "My son had no excuse for behaving the way he did. I still don't understand it and I won't take up for him. But I have dedicated my life to rectifying a horrible situation."

Feeling winded, she slumped back in her chair. There. A ribbon of satisfaction wound around her heart, nudging that pesky uncertainty out of the way like her grandmother used to sweep the dirt off the front porch. If Lucille was going to overstay her welcome, at least she'd have ample time to consider Maribelle's perspective.

"I have a question." Lucille twisted her charm bracelet in a slow circle around her bony wrist. "If you don't mind my asking, what will Avery and her sisters think about your donation to Imari's Place?"

Maribelle frowned. Now, what kind of a question was that? Just when Lucille had regained Maribelle's confidence, she had to go and plant a whole garden of doubt with her poorly timed inquiry. "It's none of their concern."

Maribelle's late husband had squirreled away more than a million dollars and left his fortune to her when he'd passed. Since her son had abandoned his family, she'd kept those details to herself. But that didn't mean she wasn't acutely aware of how her granddaughters might react to her choices. "You may think I overstepped going to see that adorable Cole Whitaker, but trust me, I know what I'm doing."

Avery was exactly who he needed on his design team. And on his arm. Even if he wasn't ready to admit it yet. Maribelle took great pride in her matchmaking skills and credited herself for bringing numerous couples together over the years.

"I have every confidence in your abilities, Maribelle."

Lucille's smile was a little too thin to be believable. "You do?"

"Absolutely." Lucille reached for her tea again. "I just hope you're prepared for every possible outcome."

Another cryptic comment. Maribelle filed that one away to examine later. As best as she could tell, Pax hadn't demonstrated any remorse for ruining his marriage. The only possible outcome Maribelle could envision was making him regret his choices.

"As long as I live, I'll never get over what Pax has done, leaving my sweet Avery and those precious children. To quote my daddy, may he rest in peace, 'Somebody oughta teach that boy a lesson.' Now, revenge isn't a path I often advocate, mind you. Ask anyone in town who knows me. That's not my forte."

Lucille coughed.

Maribelle cast her an annoyed glance then fisted her arthritic hands in her lap. Since she couldn't go after her son and drag him back to town and force him to support his family, she'd devote all of her time and energy to making sure her granddaughters and her great-grandchildren flourished. As soon as she had this whole mess straightened out, she'd channel her resources into Harper's marriage prospects. Her decision to teach math was noble and all, but she'd be veering into old maid territory shortly if she didn't find herself a man.

Her face flushed, Lucille regained her composure. "Avery's done quite nicely for herself. It's a shame what's happened, but she'll find her way through this."

Maribelle wanted to believe her. She really did. But all the success in the world couldn't ease the pain of a humiliating rejection. That lovely girl had lived it twice. First as a daughter and then as a wife. Avery had to rise from the ashes of her fractured family, more successful and deeply admired than ever before.

Maribelle would make sure of it.

He should've told her already.

Cole swung hard, punctuating the humid afternoon air with a grunt. The neon green tennis ball popped off his racket and went sailing out of bounds on the other side of the net. Love–thirty.

"You are exceptionally awful at this today." Hemby swiped his tanned forearm across his face then pulled another ball from the pocket of his shorts. "What's the problem?"

"I did something ludicrous." Cole spun his racket in his hands and rocked side to side, pretending to focus.

"Wow, that's intriguing. Ludicrous as in you might get arrested or was this more of a slightly questionable activity?"

"I accepted a bribe."

Hemby stopped bouncing the ball and straightened without serving. "Now, there's four words I never thought I'd hear from you."

A rivulet of sweat trickled down Cole's back, making his T-shirt stick to his skin. Why had he confessed? If he needed to bare his soul, there were more empathetic listeners in his life.

"Let's take a water break." Hemby let the ball bounce away and strode toward the blue metal bench on the sideline. "Unless this confession of yours calls for dinner inside?"

Cole shook his head and walked toward his bag slumped on the end of the bench. He didn't have the energy to shower and meet his friend at the country club's restaurant. Or make polite conversation with the board members and benefactors he'd likely run into.

Henry Everett McDougal Broughton, nicknamed Hemby by his little brother more than twenty-five years ago, had been Cole's closest friend for at least that long. They'd both gone to Auburn and roomed together for four years. Hemby had witnessed the destruction Cole's younger sister Kimberly's death had rained down on their family. Even though there was very little his best friend didn't know, Cole had often struggled to find the words to describe his feelings for Avery.

Hemby tackled every obstacle life threw at him with a brutally pragmatic approach. Sometimes his tough love pep talks were exactly what Cole needed. Today was not one of those times. Despite multiple attempts by Hemby and his wife to set Cole up on dates, none of those connections had ever panned out. When Cole broke up with his last girlfriend, Evangeline, and Hemby's wife questioned why, Hemby had remarked that Avery had stolen Cole's heart and never bothered to return it.

The sarcastic comment had stung, mostly because it was true. Avery had captured his heart and he'd never recovered.

"Want one?" Hemby twisted the top off an electrolyte replacement drink.

The offer pulled Cole back to the present. "Please."

Hemby passed him the bottle coated in condensation. Cole took a long sip. The sweet orange liquid coated his parched throat.

They sat side by side on the bench. Tennis balls plunked against rackets and thumped off the hard surface behind them. Hemby swabbed his face with a white towel. "What's on your mind?"

"Avery's grandmother donated a generous sum of money to Imari's Place."

"Maribelle Lansing?"

Cole nodded.

"Excellent." Hemby tapped his bottle against Cole's in a pseudo toast. "How much?"

"A quarter of a million."

"And your problem with this is what exactly?"

"Her donation is contingent upon me hiring Avery to help design the expansion project."

"What's wrong with that?"

Sweat dribbled into Cole's eyes and he wiped it away with the back of his hand. "Avery will be furious when she finds out."

"Who's going to tell her?"

"Forget it." Cole pressed the side of his sports drink to his cheek, desperate for anything to draw the suffocating heat from his flushed skin. "I knew you wouldn't understand."

"Take it easy, sparky." Hemby slung his towel over his shoulder. "Donors make contingencies all the time. Names on buildings, specific bricks on certain courtyards. Mrs. Lansing wants her granddaughter, who happens to be a popular lifestyle guru, to be closely involved. I don't see why that's an issue."

"Why am I not surprised?" Cole dug in his bag for a towel. "You have no skin in this game."

"Not true." Hemby scoffed. "I'm your best friend, and

you're miserable company right now. It's my job to try and improve the current situation."

"Yeah, well, I deserve to be miserable."

"Another false statement." Hemby grinned then lightly punched Cole's shoulder. "C'mon, man. Stop worrying. This might be a serendipitous opportunity."

"Or the perfect way for me to ruin my future."

Hemby paused, his drink halfway to his mouth. "That's cryptic. Say more."

"Avery will be livid when she realizes she's being used, especially given the way her marriage fell apart."

"Is it safe to assume this won't be the regular kind of anger where you apologize, grovel then she forgives you and life goes on?"

If only. Cole shook his head. "Afraid not."

"But what do you gain by telling Avery about your agreement with her grandmother?"

Cole shot him a withering glance. "Peace of mind. Absence of guilt. The ability to sleep at night. I—I just got Avery back in my life. I don't want to lose her."

*Again.*

"Ah." Understanding dawned in Hemby's eyes. "I get it."

"Do you?" Cole stood and shoved a can of tennis balls and his soggy towel into his bag. Shame blanketed him. He shouldn't have confessed his feelings. This was going to come back to bite him in the worst possible way. Besides, Avery deserved to hear the truth directly from him. Especially when she'd been so vulnerable and revealed her doubts and fears.

Man, he was a fool.

Hemby finished off his drink then stood and launched the empty bottle toward the recycling container nearby. The plastic rattled against the rim then fell inside. "Here's what you need to do."

"Oh, great. Can't wait to hear your sage advice."

Unfazed by Cole's sarcasm, Hemby retrieved his racket and shouldered his bag. "Keep the money, finish the project then convince Avery she can't live without you."

Cole blew out a laugh. "Golly, what a brilliant plan. Thanks so much. I'll get right on that."

"Do you have a plan B?"

Nope. "Sorry I was so lousy today. See you around."

"Think about what I said," Hemby called after him.

He waved his hand in the air and kept walking toward the court's exit.

The board of directors had been flabbergasted by Nana's generous donation. In the best possible way. They hadn't asked the most pertinent questions. Not that they needed to know about Mrs. Lansing's stipulation. Or contingency as Hemby called it. Between the board's enthusiasm, their impromptu brainstorming session about raising additional funds, and their collective joy about providing housing and scholarships, there hadn't been time to mention Avery's role. To be honest, Cole couldn't think of one person who'd object.

The only one who seemed to have issue with this unconventional agreement was him.

He pushed open the wrought iron gate, stepped through and let it clang shut behind him. Heat radiated off the asphalt as he worked his way toward his white sedan parked near the center of the lot. The news of the expansion was supposed to be an opportunity to celebrate. The young women at Imari's Place had a shot at a normal life now. Every step of forward momentum for the foundation meant a step away from the unresolved guilt he still carried about his sister's abduction. If he'd been paying closer attention, maybe she'd be alive today. Still, he wasn't comfortable with Maribelle's insistence that he bring Avery on board. Based on their conversation, it was clear Avery had no idea what her nana had done.

*That didn't stop you from offering the job, though, did it?*

He kicked at a pebble in his path. That nagging voice of reason was really getting to be a problem. Why couldn't he be more like Hemby and roll with this?

"Because it's not that simple," he grumbled, tugging his keys from his bag then unlocking the door to his trusty vehicle. Experience had taught him that if he wasn't careful, he'd get swept up in the drama he'd promised himself he'd avoid.

Avery's downfall wasn't his concern. Her battles weren't his to fight. Sure, Maribelle's generous contribution made his biggest dream a reality. It also came at a significant cost. Because following through on their agreement wouldn't be easy for him, either. Running a foundation meant coordinating a lot of moving parts. It wasn't like he'd be at the job site every day. He could leave a project manager in charge—not that he had one of those—and avoid seeing Avery. Except she'd be closely involved in the decision-making process. Maybe even digging in and getting some of the work done herself.

Could he handle being that close to her again after all these years? He'd dated other women since he and Avery had gone to college. Even one woman in particular who he'd thought might be The One. Until he admitted to himself that she wasn't. Evangeline was a beautiful and talented woman and he'd cared deeply for her, but he didn't love her.

Because she wasn't Avery.

Evangeline had wanted an engagement ring, but he'd ended the relationship. Avery had clearly moved on, married Pax and started a family. But he'd never been able to see himself standing at the front of a church reciting vows with anyone other than Avery.

He ached for all that she'd endured when her marriage unraveled. But selfishly, he was terrified to let her back into his world. He couldn't risk his heart again.

*Why* couldn't she escape this punishing self-doubt?

Avery sat at Mama's kitchen table with her laptop open. She'd spent almost an hour scrolling through social media accounts, searching for design inspiration. She blew out a long breath and reached for her coffee. Only a smidge remained. She drained the mug then grimaced when the lukewarm beverage hit her taste buds. Gross. Maybe a second cup would ease the headache forming behind her eyes or somehow ignite a spark of creativity. Nothing she'd seen felt right for Imari's Place.

Worse, the nagging sense of dread that she couldn't succeed without Trey and Pax still clouded her thinking. So frustrating. Pushing back her chair, she stood and crossed to the coffee bar in the corner of the kitchen. She didn't need them.

A quick glance at Hayes rocking in his baby swing nearby, eyes closed and his precious mouth curved into a toothless, dreamy grin, reminded her that she had a limited amount of time before he woke from his morning nap and needed her full attention.

Greer came into the kitchen and sat down at the table. "Mornin'."

"Good morning." She smiled then popped a new capsule in the single-serve coffee machine. He looked dressed for a round of golf in his lavender polo shirt and pressed white trousers. "Have you had time to review the agreement?"

He held up a thin stack of paper then removed his reading

glasses from their perch on top of his head and slid them into place. "I'm going to read it right now."

He'd agreed to review the document Cole's assistant had emailed yesterday. Avery had read through it twice and didn't have any concerns, other than her lack of confidence that she was the right person for the role. Greer wasn't an attorney but she trusted his judgment implicitly. She longed for his quiet reassurance that she wasn't making a huge mistake.

The front door opened. A flurry of whispered conversation preceded her sisters' arrival in the kitchen. Plastic bags filled with groceries rustled as they plunked their provisions on the counter.

"Hey." Avery poured almond milk creamer into her coffee. "Thank you for going to the store."

"Not a problem." Julene slipped past her with frozen berries destined for the freezer. Why had she avoided eye contact?

"They were out of some of the baby food you wanted." Harper held up a two-pack of pureed peaches. "I hope this will work?"

"I'm sure Hayes will love peaches." Avery offered a grateful smile. She'd planned to start introducing solids soon. Harper turned away and quickly emptied the next bag.

"All right, what's going on?" Avery opened a drawer and pulled out a spoon. "You two are unusually skittish, and the whispering is a bit of a concern."

"Nana called me while we were at the store and said to be sure and grab a copy of *Camellia Today*." Julene pulled a glossy magazine from the bottom of a shopping bag. "There's an upcoming event that has her all fired up."

Oh. Avery's scalp prickled. She hesitated, the spoon suspended above her mug then feigned a smile. "Well, that could mean anything, right? Nana might be concerned about a garden club announcement or the latest book club selection. So what is it? What's the issue this time?"

Julene and Harper stood side by side at the counter, their foreheads crinkled. Harper fidgeted with the tassel on the zipper of her straw purse.

"Here." Julene flipped open the magazine. "As your sister and the magazine's social media manager, I want to apologize for not warning you first. I don't always know what articles are being featured. I'm still really new and—"

"Julene." Avery stopped stirring then reached over and squeezed her sister's arm. "It's okay. There's nothing to apologize for. Y'all. C'mon. How bad could one little article be?"

Julene scrunched her nose in disgust.

Harper glared at the publication like it harbored a flesh-eating bacterium.

Avery took a fortifying sip of coffee then let her gaze slide over the article dominating two pages of the magazine's spread. A professional headshot of Pax standing next to a stack of hardback copies of his book sent a pang of surprise arcing through her. Of course, Camellia would be proud of him. He'd just published a book.

"Nana is worried because he's coming for a book signing and he'll be speaking at The Oasis," Harper said.

Oh.

"Good for him." Avery shrugged then turned away. She popped the spoon inside the dishwasher then retrieved her mug. Why the hushed whispers and worried glances? They'd divorced. Who cared if Pax's book tour garnered positive press?

The way her gut coiled in a tight knot hinted that she cared. At least a little. Okay, maybe a lot. And maybe other people cared too. Especially if a popular local magazine featured him.

She peeked at Greer. He was pretending not to listen. But she could tell, since he hadn't flipped to the next page of the contract yet, that he was paying attention.

"W-when's the book signing?" Avery managed to squeak out the question.

"I haven't seen the flyer yet." Julene closed the magazine then tucked it inside her tote bag. "Nana says it's during Father's Day weekend."

How ironic. Avery nodded, drumming her fingertips on the counter. That was three weeks away. She could be mentally and emotionally prepared by then.

Right?

"Thanks for letting me know." She carried her coffee to the table and sat down again across from Greer. "I need to sign that contract today. Unless you have any concerns?"

Greer hesitated, undoubtedly waiting for Harper and Julene to comment. When they kept quiet, he spoke. "My advice would be to honor your word and follow through on this. It might lead to future endeavors."

Future endeavors. The tactfulness of his words did little to ease the sting. She had to think about the future and providing for Addison and Hayes. Through the slider, she caught a glimpse of Mama and Addison down on the dock. Her heart pinched. Pax was coming to Camellia. Would he want to see the kids?

"I'm curious." Harper's voice pierced Avery's thoughts. "Why would you say yes to helping Cole?"

"Because he asked me." It was true. He'd looked at her with those hazel eyes and she saw the earnestness there, his passion for helping young women in a desperate situation and she couldn't say no. Didn't want to say no. This was meaningful work. Her involvement in the process—no matter how small—made a lasting impact. It was the kind of work she'd said she'd been looking for.

Except she couldn't overlook the fact that even when she'd been completely honest with him, he'd brushed off her concerns. She'd tried to politely decline his offer, yet he'd insisted she was the woman for the job. When she'd tried to explain that she wasn't exactly qualified, he'd misconstrued her doubt as humility. Wasn't that the way with Cole? Always placing her on a pedestal? It felt good to be admired and praised by a man again, instead of overlooked and discarded.

But could she really handle this project? There wasn't a producer or an assistant or even a camera operator to dress up her decisions with a clever shot that tricked the eye. This home was more than a cute idea or an opportunity to earn a commission. Imari's Place meant a life-changing opportunity for women who had lived through unimaginable circumstances.

She drew a deep breath then picked up a pen and scrawled her signature across the blank space at the bottom of the contract.

"There." She gave her sisters and Greer a resolute nod. As if the definitive gesture paired with her signature absolved all her doubts and insecurities.

Pax had done a number on her. Healing still seemed like a destination on the other side of a canyon-sized wound.

That's why she had to keep moving forward. Even if she had to drag her latent creativity kicking and screaming into the light. No, this wasn't the opportunity she'd envisioned when she thought about going back to work. But this was not the time to ignore an open door. People would be talking, and she was going to make sure they had something positive to discuss besides her failed marriage.

## Chapter Five

The pungent scent of diesel fuel filled the air. It had to be nearly a hundred degrees already, but Cole couldn't stop a smile. The backhoe punched through the earth and scooped up a bucketload of dirt. As the equipment operator dumped a pile of coppery red clay on the ground then went back for more, Cole's throat tightened. He removed his hard hat and swiped his palm across his face.

Seventeen years had passed since his sister had disappeared. For a few months, he and his family had clung to the hope that she'd be rescued from whatever stronghold had trapped her in its clutches. Trafficking? Had she been murdered and her remains undiscovered? Those questions had cycled through his mind countless times. Until the investigators found her body. It never got any easier thinking about her demise.

There wasn't anything he could do about Kim's murder. But helping others and making a difference in the world eased his pain. A little.

He put his hat back on then reached for his phone to take a picture. Every time the foundation raised more money or another woman was rescued, Cole documented the milestone. Sometimes he sent the pictures to Millie Kay for sharing on social media. Often he stored a folder of the photos on his phone as a reminder that they were making progress.

One bucketload of dirt at a time.

Thankfully Dale, his new project manager, had stopped to get iced coffee, and the women who lived in the house had left for work already, so there wasn't anyone else here to see him getting emotional. At nine in the morning, the early summer humidity pressed in hinting at what was in store for Alabama in the weeks and months ahead. Sunshine warmed his back and spilled across the soon-to-be expanded Imari's Place. The current facility had served its purpose, but it was long overdue for an upgrade. He captured a few more photos, sent them to Millie Kay then turned to the architectural plans he'd spread across the hood of his car.

Adrenaline surged through his veins as he mentally calculated what this expansion offered. It was more than a home for sixteen additional women. The buildings offered a refuge, a second chance at a life these ladies never imagined possible. Thinking about the lives that would be impacted with the sudden influx of cash inspired him to do more, to keep pushing, to keep fighting against the injustices of this world.

Sweat trickled down his spine. The fabric of his polo shirt stuck to his lower back. Dale must've stopped to take a phone call, or else run into a line at the coffee shop. He should've been back by now. Another twenty minutes in this heat and he'd need to find some water. Movement in his peripheral vision caught his attention. Finally. Coffee.

A beige SUV followed by a News Channel Nine van and

Millie Kay in her compact car rolled around the cul-de-sac then parked on the street nearby.

What in the world?

Millie Kay rolled down her window and shot him an apologetic grimace. Cole couldn't hear her over the rumble of the backhoe, but he thought she mouthed "I didn't know."

The back passenger door of the SUV swung open and Adrian Caldwell, Camellia's mayor, emerged.

Seriously?

The van driver cut the engine. A camera operator and a woman who often covered local events and breaking news emerged. Who'd summoned the press and the mayor?

Another vehicle arrived, a red Smart Fortwo hatchback, and two young women stepped out. Cole didn't recognize them. They quickly followed the reporter and camera operator as they trailed the mayor toward Cole.

His assistant swooped in, a bottle of water and...was that her makeup compact?

"I'm so sorry. If I'd known this was going to happen, I would've helped you prepare." She shoved the bottle of water into his hand. "Give me two seconds and I'll have you powdered and—"

"Did you just say *powdered*?" Cole accepted the water but took a giant step back. Unfortunately, she had him pinned against the curb.

"Yes, this is powder." She gestured to the plastic circle in her hand. "We can't have you looking shiny and flustered on the five o'clock news."

Shiny and flustered?

"Oh, just hold still."

"That won't be necessary." He held up his palm. "I'm not planning to be on the news."

"Well, you aren't going to be able to avoid it. The mayor called a last-minute press conference."

"I see that." Cole glanced toward the scene unfolding on the street behind Millie Kay. It reminded him of a similar one that played out on an episode of Avery's show. Yes. He'd watched. More episodes than he cared to admit. She had stepped out of an SUV in front of a building that she had helped renovate, her glowing ring of curls and astounding features undoubtedly captivating the viewing audience. His thoughts hopped on the Avery carousel and spun in a delightful orbit. Too bad she wasn't here to see this. Imagine the reactions if she'd emerged from that vehicle instead of Mayor Caldwell. Avery's presence would make the evening news for sure. If he and the mayor had to shovel a ceremonial scoop of dirt for the media, it would be ten times more enjoyable with her around.

*Dude, get a grip.* He couldn't keep thinking about her. Not like that. Thankfully, the mayor called his name. Cole took a quick sip of water then strode toward the entourage coming at him.

"Cole, it's a pleasure to see you out here. Is this the official groundbreaking I'm hearing so much about?" Mayor Caldwell greeted him with a broad smile and a firm handshake.

"Yes, sir," Cole said. "Thank you for stopping by."

"Wouldn't miss it, and you don't have to call me sir." He tucked his white button-down into his olive slacks. "This is a wonderful thing you're doing."

"I didn't know you wanted to be here, or I would've extended a more formal invitation."

Mayor Caldwell took the hard hat his assistant offered and lowered it over his ebony close-clipped hair. "No worries. The Camellia word of mouth brigade keeps me informed. Let's do this, shall we?"

Cole shot his assistant a confused glance. Do what?

Someone had convinced the heavy equipment operator to power down for a minute. Probably Dale, who'd arrived in the midst of the controlled chaos, a cardboard tray of iced coffees in one hand and his phone to his ear.

The press pool, if they could even be called that, closed in. The steady hum of conversation grew louder. Cole turned to face them and his breath caught in his chest. Where had all these people come from? Not that he minded Imari's Place getting the attention. And human trafficking was on more and more people's radar lately as a pressing humanitarian issue. Still, this level of coverage for a modest groundbreaking seemed excessive. He inched toward the mayor, who'd already grabbed a shovel and started chatting with a journalist like he did this all the time.

"Cole? Perhaps you'd like to share a few words?"

His face heated. Couldn't they just start throwing dirt around without saying anything? There had to be at least twenty people hugging the curb, their cameras and phones poised expectantly.

"I'll get us started and you can finish up." Mayor Caldwell grinned again then angled toward the waiting audience. "Imari's Place is one of Alabama's most important assets. We're extremely proud of this organization, which has become a haven for young women worldwide who are breaking free from the scourge of modern-day slavery."

There. The tension in Cole's shoulders lessened a fraction, his worries soothed by the mayor's speech. He was going to nail this. After a few more pithy, inspirational thoughts that kept the audience engaged, Cole hoped he'd have access to the video footage for future marketing opportunities.

The mayor caught his eye. "I think we have time for a few questions."

*We do?* Cole rocked back on his heels. He hadn't planned for any interaction with the media today, much less a Q and A. He located Millie Kay standing at the edge of the crowd, her phone trained on him. Well, at least she'd have the video he wanted.

"Folks, I'm sure you're familiar with the director of the foundation, Cole Whitaker." The mayor gestured toward the press pool with an exaggerated flourish and another wide smile, his dark eyes gleaming. "Please direct your questions his way."

They didn't waste any time.

"Mr. Whitaker, can you confirm that Avery Lansing Crawford is partnering on this project?"

The plastic water bottle crinkled in his grip. He shifted awkwardly from one foot to the other. His hesitation elicited a murmur that rippled through the crowd. When he didn't answer the leading question, everyone moved in closer, firing questions faster than he could process. *Tell us more about Miss Crawford's role. Did you ask her or did she volunteer? Will her ex-husband be involved as well?* Cole forced a smile and held up his hand in a desperate attempt to regain control of the narrative.

"Thank you, everyone, for coming today. On behalf of Imari's Place, the board of directors, our staff and our phenomenal volunteers, I'm thrilled to officially share that due to the generous contributions of Friends of the Foundation, we can move forward with our vision to provide housing and education for even more young women seeking refuge from human trafficking."

"Are the Lansings or the Crawfords the Friends of the Foundation you mentioned?"

So much for distracting them. He glanced down at the pavement, as if imaginary notes would somehow appear. A proverbial map to guide him out of this sticky briar patch.

"Have you specifically invited Avery or Pax Crawford or his partner, Trey, to help you?"

Cole hesitated. They obviously weren't going to stop asking. It couldn't hurt to mention Avery by name, could it?

"Yes, we have reached out to Avery Lansing Crawford and asked for her input."

"And did she say yes?"

"I guess you'll have to wait and see." Cole turned toward the mayor. "What do you say we move some dirt?"

Mayor Caldwell nodded and grabbed a shovel. Cole heaved a sigh, thankful he didn't have to answer any more questions. It probably wasn't a wise move to bail so quickly, especially with a cliffhanger of an answer. But if the local press had already heard about Avery's role in the project, what else did they know? Avery couldn't find out about Nana's contribution. Not now, not like this.

Of all the ways Avery had envisioned Pax resurfacing in her life, a random text message on an ordinary Tuesday morning wasn't one she'd considered.

Hello, Avery. I'm going to be in Camellia, June 17th through the 23rd, promoting the book and reconnecting with family. I'd appreciate the opportunity to see the kids, especially since I'll be around for Father's Day.

The crayon slipped from her trembling fingers, landed on the table and rolled off the edge.

"Uh-oh." Addison's eyes widened. "I'll get it."

She slid off the chair, climbed under the table and found the crayon wedged in a groove in the porch's floorboards. Blood roared in Avery's ears as she watched Addison retrieve the crayon, but she couldn't speak. Couldn't think. She could barely breathe.

Rubbing her fingertips along her collarbone, she read the message again. His imminent return to Camellia wasn't a surprise, but his request to spend the weekend with the kids had flattened her. It wasn't that she didn't want him to see his children. He certainly had the right to maintain a relationship with them. But it had been so long since they'd heard from him. He had never even held his son. How could he just re-enter their lives so casually?

"Here you go, Mama!" Addison plunked the crayon down on the coloring book. "I like your picture."

"Thank you, baby," Avery whispered. She smoothed her palm over Addison's hair.

"Are you crying?" Addison studied her, leaning in extra close.

Avery bit her lip and shook her head. She wouldn't let Addison see or hear anything about this. Not until she came up with a plan.

"Can we keep coloring?"

"Absolutely."

Through the screen panels, the fragrance of flowers blooming in Mama's garden floated on the breeze. Dark clouds crowded the horizon, blotting out the sunshine they had enjoyed during their short walk less than an hour ago.

"Mama." Addison tapped her adorable little finger on the edge of Avery's page, a half-finished picture of princesses attending a ball. "Color more, please. You haven't finished their dresses yet. Here, use pink."

"All right." Avery accepted the crayon and complied with her daughter's instructions, although she wasn't a fan of the bossy tone. That was the least of her worries right now. First, she had to deal with Pax's request. Thunder rumbled in the distance and her phone hummed with another incoming text.

*No. I'm staying focused on being present with my daughter.*

"You gots a message." Addison paused, her purple crayon hovering over her own picture of a tea party.

"That's okay. I'll check it later. Thank you for letting me know." Avery kept her voice calm, although her insides buzzed with a nervous energy that made her restless. Surely that wasn't Pax again. Wouldn't he give her more than seven minutes to respond when he had basically abandoned his family more than a year ago?

Please don't call, she silently pleaded. Her phone was face-down on the wood table. It wouldn't be easy to keep the caller ID concealed from Addison for long, though. The girl was quick. She couldn't read, but she was smart enough to recognize *P-a-x* on the screen.

The wind picked up, rippling the surface of the lake. Tree branches danced in the yard and Addison swiveled in her chair to look outside. "What's happening?"

"Storm's coming." Avery used the distraction to her advantage and plucked her phone off the table. She tucked it into her dress pocket as Addison turned back around in her chair. "Let's go in." Addison flipped her coloring book closed then clutched it to her chest and scampered off the chair.

"Wait," Avery said. "I need your help. Pick up the crayons, please."

Thunder rumbled, closer this time, followed by a bolt of lightning that cut a jagged line across the angry sky. Addison squealed as she raced toward the door and disappeared inside the house. From the portable monitor on the table, Addison saw Hayes stirring in his crib. She sighed. The weight of Pax's unanswered text bogged her down. Another clap of thunder provoked more squealing from Addison.

"Mama, hurry." Addison hovered inside the sliding glass door, bouncing up and down on her toes.

"I'll be right there." Avery quickly gathered the rest of the coloring supplies and the monitor. Lightning flashed again and Addison burst into tears. Hayes started to cry, his unhappiness from being woken up evident by the tone of his wailing through the monitor's speaker. Avery's skin prickled. Her mother, Greer and her sisters were all out for a few hours. She hadn't been home alone with her children hardly at all since they moved back. She'd quickly grown accustomed to having an extra person or two around for times like this when both kids needed attention.

"Come on, pumpkin, you can help me get Hayes up from his nap." Avery stepped inside the house and slid the door closed. She deposited the crayons and coloring book on the kitchen counter then ushered Addison down the hall to the bedroom.

"I can do the diaper." Addison squeezed past Avery's legs and pushed the door open. "Baby Hayes, I'm here."

Avery couldn't help but smile at Addison's sweet tone and her determination to help care for her little brother. Oh, how she hoped Addison would hold on to that fierce loyalty to her sibling. That was the very thing that had carried her through her own childhood trauma—her love and devotion to Julene and Harper.

Addison kept up a steady stream of chatter as Avery lifted Hayes from the crib and set him on the changing table. He fussed and rubbed his tiny knuckles against his mouth. She'd need to feed him soon. Her pocket hummed with more incoming text messages, which only heightened the anxious thoughts swirling in her mind. She had sole custody of the kids. Some petty selfish part of her wanted to tell Pax no. But that wasn't right. He hadn't committed a crime. There wasn't a viable reason why he couldn't see his children.

He'd simply chosen not to.

His departure had been his own doing. Or perhaps his choices had been subtly influenced by Trey. She didn't want to think about that right now. He'd taken up way too much of her emotional energy already.

"Addison, wait, please." Avery intervened before Addison plucked another five disposable wipes from the container. "We don't need that many."

"But I want to help," Addison whined from her perch on a short stool beside the changing table. "Hayes needs me."

Avery tried not to snap at Addison when she tickled Hayes under the chin and he cried louder. She quickly changed his diaper, scooped him up and settled him against her shoulder.

"Come on, Addison. You can watch a show and eat a snack while I feed Hayes."

"Yay!" Addison hurried out of the room and skipped down the hall to the kitchen. Avery helped her get water and a package of crackers then settled her on the sofa with a new episode of *Ask the StoryBots*, her current favorite.

Avery sat in the recliner. While she fed Hayes, she checked her text messages, starting with her most recent message from Harper.

Have you seen this morning's paper yet?

On second thought, don't look. Stay off the socials too.

Who possessed the stamina to avoid that kind of temptation? She wasn't interested in obeying her sister's directive, anyway. Not when she'd been left alone with the latest edition of the *Iron City Gazette* taunting her from the coffee table. Hayes had fallen back to sleep in her arms. Addison was occupied with her snack and her show. The morning newspaper sat directly in her line of sight. What could anyone have written that was worse than the pain she'd already endured?

Growing up in Camellia, she'd tried to remain an impartial bystander when gossip spread through the community. Some folks wore their nosiness like a badge of honor, proclaiming their duty to get to the bottom of a so-called scandal for the good of the order. After her father had left, she'd weathered the painful barbs and thoughtless speculation.

Given her past experience in Camellia, she shouldn't have been surprised that she'd made the local paper. A more self-disciplined woman would've heeded Harper's advice.

But her desperate need to find out exactly what people were saying so she could somehow find a way to control it, or manage it or repackage it into something more palatable, drove her from her chair. She set Hayes gently in his swing, turned on the motor and the peaceful lullaby then plucked the paper from the table and snapped it open.

Sadly, as soon as she scanned the headline below the fold, she longed to unsee what greeted her.

"Local reality television star's absence provokes questions."

Absence from *what*? She studied the photo of Cole and a gentleman she presumed to be the mayor wearing hard hats, smiling and holding shovels.

"Avery Lansing Crawford didn't make an appearance at yesterday's unofficial groundbreaking ceremony for the expansion of Imari's Place, although Whitaker confirmed she's on board as a consultant. She hasn't made any scheduled public appearances yet, which has provoked much curiosity and speculation throughout the community. Her ex-husband, Pax Crawford, will be in Camellia later this month as part of the promotional tour for his bestselling memoir. Sources say this will be the first time Pax and Avery have crossed paths in quite some time. Perhaps Mr. Crawford will weigh in on the Imari's Place project as well."

"Oh, no he won't." Avery closed the paper without reading the rest, folded it in half then folded it again and marched into the kitchen. "And who determines whether or not a book is a bestseller, anyway," she grumbled, stuffing the offending paper deep into the recycle bin under Mama's sink.

Hurt and confusion snaked through her like a kudzu vine overtaking a garden wall. Was she supposed to be at the groundbreaking? No one had invited her. Cole hadn't mentioned a word about it. And who were these sources the paper had quoted? She retrieved her phone from the cushion of the recliner and scrolled to Cole's number. If he'd intentionally withheld the information about the event as a means of protecting her, she'd have to let him know his plan had backfired. Besides, she didn't need him looking out for her.

Did she?

"Mama, will you watch this with me?" Addison's sweet request interrupted her internal debate.

Avery set her phone on the coffee table and joined Addison on the sofa. "Sure."

Thunder rumbled in the distance and rain pelted the windows. Addison snuggled close to Avery, the faint aroma of the apple-scented kids' shampoo enveloping her. As the animated characters in the show embarked on a grand adventure, Avery worked to untangle her snarled thoughts. She'd have to respond to Pax, even though she couldn't fathom spending a weekend away from her children. Hayes would have to start taking a bottle if they were going to be apart for more than a few hours. Cole wasn't responsible for what the newspaper printed. It wasn't fair to blame him. But she wasn't going to sit back and let people gossip about her. And experience had taught her they weren't going to stop. It was time to take control. If only she knew how.

Maribelle hadn't heard from Avery since they'd had supper together. Too much silence could really make an old lady sweat. Six days was far too long to go without any updates. She'd moved the money, now she needed Avery to do her part. Between the flyer announcing Pax's book signing, the article in the magazine then that newspaper headline, Maribelle had worked herself into a tizzy. What good were her efforts to grease the skids for Avery to get in with Cole and his project if those harebrained reporters made a mess of things with their scandalous lies?

"Front page news," Maribelle grumbled.

"Maribelle, are you all right?" Lucille barged into her thoughts. "You're talking to yourself again."

"Slow down, Lucille. I can't see where we're supposed to turn." Maribelle braced her hand on the dashboard of Lucille's Cadillac and peered out the window. "All these swanky mansions looked the same."

Her son was lower than a snake's belly in a wagon rut, but thankfully her former daughter-in-law had graciously overlooked Maribelle's genetic link to him. Maribelle had always been included in family events through the years, which is why she had no qualms about showing up at the lake house uninvited.

"Do you have the address?" Lucille slowed to a crawl then stopped on the side of the road and reached for her phone in the center console. "I can plug it into the app."

Oh, leave it to Lucille to start showing off. Trying to impress with all that newfangled technology. Maribelle didn't need an app. Or a map. She'd recognize the house when she saw it with her own two eyes. She frowned and stared at a wrought iron gate blocking a long driveway, flanked by trees. Was that the one?

A little variety in the landscaping would improve the property value, plus if they had something unique up by the road, it would help folks find the right place.

"The trouble with this neighborhood is that we can't see the houses." She craned her neck to catch a glimpse of a white brick mansion through a gap in the trees. No, that wasn't it.

Lucille chuckled. "I think that's the whole point. These families value their privacy. When were you here last?"

She wasn't about to admit it had been less than a week. "Not that long ago, but I was distracted. Greer about talked my ear off the whole way here."

"You haven't been to your daughter-in-law's house often enough to know where to turn?"

"Lucille, I could really do without your judgmental attitude." Maribelle shot her a withering glance.

"And I could do without your lack of preparation." Lucille dropped her phone in the console, checked her mirrors then mashed the accelerator. They shot forward and Maribelle flopped back against the seat cushion.

Oh, bless. Maribelle pinched her mouth closed. Lucille didn't need to talk to her that way, but now was not the time to get into a snit. Besides, once Lucille tasted Harper's chicken salad, she'd be grateful Maribelle had invited her along. Her granddaughter might be busier than a one-legged cat in the sandbox, but she made a chicken salad sandwich that was to die for.

"Turn here."

Lucille swerved quickly and Maribelle lurched forward in the seat. Glory be. Good thing the neighbors couldn't see through all those manicured hedges. They'd call the authorities right away.

*"Two old biddies in a beige Cadillac driving recklessly..."* Oh, she could just imagine the reports. Their family didn't need any additional news coverage this week.

"Advance notice would be quite helpful, Maribelle," Lucille said, angling her car up the driveway and easing to a stop in front of the gates. "I don't suppose they're expecting us."

"Not exactly." Maribelle eyed the gates and the box with a keypad mounted on a post outside Lucille's window.

"Do you know the access code?"

Well, no, she didn't. And even if she did, she wouldn't tell. Lucille was a decent person and all, but they hadn't known each other for long. She wasn't about to reveal all her business. What if Lucille got mad and sold the info to the paparazzi? Then Avery and her great-grandchildren would find strangers on their doorstep, taking ridiculous pictures and snooping around. No, ma'am. Maribelle shook her head. Too risky.

"How exactly are you planning to get through this gate?"

"Well, now don't you worry." Maribelle fumbled in her handbag for her phone.

After that comment about lack of preparation, she wasn't about to let on that she didn't have a concrete plan, but she did know how to send a text message. "I'll send Avery a message and she'll open the gates."

"Well, I hope she's home. I haven't got all day, you know." Her face puckered like she'd licked a lemon. "Bingo starts at four o'clock."

"It's best to remain calm, Lucille." Maribelle sent Avery and Harper a text announcing their arrival. "I'll have you back at your apartment in time to freshen up. I know you want to go to bingo so you can sit by Hank again."

Lucille's pale cheeks turned pink. Uh-huh. Now, that was

a bingo right there. So she *did* have a thing for Hank. They sat in silence until the gates swung open.

"See?" Maribelle patted Lucille's arm. "Ask and you shall receive."

Lucille didn't say a word. She drove the car up to the house and parked in the shade. Hopefully, Harper had made her chocolate chess pie too. Lucille needed some sweetness in her life.

Greer stepped off the porch looking quite handsome with his silver hair perfectly combed. His stone-colored shorts revealed long suntanned legs, and he wore a pale blue polo shirt and Top-Siders without socks.

"And who might this be?" Lucille quickly pulled her compact from her purse and powdered her nose.

Maribelle didn't miss the admiration in her voice. Couldn't argue with her, though. Greer was quite nice to look at. "Back off. You only have eyes for Hank, remember?"

"We might be old but we're not dead." Lucille lowered her window and waved with her fingers. "Heyyyy."

Oh, my. Maribelle shook her head in dismay. "Lucille, I can't take you anywhere."

"Good afternoon, ladies." Greer stopped a respectable distance from Lucille's side of the car and greeted them with a polite smile. "How can I help you?"

Maribelle leaned across the console and offered her sweetest smile in return. "Hello, Greer. This is my good friend, Lucille."

"It's a pleasure to meet you, Lucille. I'm Greer Huntington."

"We thought we'd drop by for a quick visit. I wanted to give Avery plenty of time to get settled before I brought Lucille by to see my great-grandbabies."

"Is that right?" Greer gave her a long look then angled his head toward the house. "Are they expecting you?"

Maribelle chuckled then unbuckled her seat belt. It took all her concentration to step out of the car on her first attempt. She tried to smile over the Cadillac's expansive hood at Greer, but feared it looked more like a grimace. "They opened the gate, didn't they?"

"And they also sent me out here to investigate."

Smart girls. Maribelle smoothed her blue-and-white-patterned tunic over her white slacks. She was going for an effortless chic summer vibe, but this outing was proving to take more energy and careful thought than she'd anticipated. Determined to talk her way past Greer, she clasped her handbag tighter to hide the trembling in her fingers. "Please let them know that Nana comes in peace."

His veneer cracked and a smile hitched up one side of his mouth. "Now, Maribelle, you and I both know that's not true. Come on inside."

Well, that was uncalled for. She motioned for Lucille to come along. Holding her head high, she followed him toward the house. He wasn't about to discourage her with his misguided opinions. She only had her family's best interests at heart. She was here to make sure Avery could see the way forward and give her a little nudge in the right direction.

"Well, that was *fun*." Julene came inside the house, her face flushed and hands balled into fists at her sides. "Before they drove away, Nana told me that I'm too old to wear a miniskirt and cropped top. Because boys don't like girls who dress like floozies."

"Oh, my." Avery grimaced and sank onto the sofa in the living room. "Mama, has she always been so—"

"Insufferable?" Harper chimed in as she scraped the remnants of their lunch with Nana and Lucille into the garbage disposal.

Avery smothered a laugh and then checked on Hayes, strapped

into his infant bouncer seat nearby. The motor hummed along, slowly lulling him to sleep. Addison had taken to her bed for a nap without argument. Maybe all the commotion of Nana and Lucille's visit had worn her out too.

Mama carried empty glasses from the table to the counter beside the sink. If Nana aggravated her, she rarely vented. Mama had always been classy that way.

"I've never been so thankful for a bingo game in my life," Julene said, crossing to the fridge. The tiered fabric on her black cotton skirt flounced as she walked. "I don't know who the activities coordinator is at Westwood Manor, but remind me to take them some treats. Their bingo game must be quite the event."

"I think it's Hank who's the main attraction." Harper loaded plates into the dishwasher. "I heard them talking about getting back in time to sit with him."

"Who's Hank?" Julene pulled two cans of flavored sparkling water from the refrigerator. "Does Nana have a man friend?"

"I hope he knows what he's getting into," Avery said. Lucille was nice and all, but Nana had been a real handful today. Going on and on about Cole and his work at the foundation.

"Why does she care so much, Mama?" Avery tucked her legs up underneath her. "I can't figure out why she's adamant that I help Cole. I've already said yes, but obviously I'm not moving quickly enough to suit her."

Mama ripped a sheet of aluminum foil from the dispenser and covered the leftover chess pie. "Maribelle has always cared more than she should about what people in this town think."

Ouch. Avery could hardly criticize her for that. Hello pot, meet kettle.

"Ever since your daddy left I think she's felt ashamed, so she's done her best to make sure that things go well for our family. Not just for me but for each of you girls too."

"But she's not all up in Harper's business."

"Not yet," Harper said. "Give her time."

The comment sent a ripple of quiet laughter through the room.

Julene handed Avery one of the cans of sparkling water. Blackberry lemonade. Her new favorite flavor.

"Thank you."

"No problem." Julene sank down beside her on the opposite end of the sofa. "You good?"

Avery hesitated then popped the top open. "Not really."

Julene's forehead creased. "Are you mad about the story in the paper?"

"It's not just the story in the paper. I'm appalled that Pax and Trey have managed to spin their side of the story into something that garners positive media attention." Her voice grew louder as anger blazed a fiery trail through her abdomen. "I was pregnant when I discovered their affair. They left me with a three-year-old and a baby on the way. Trey wiped out our savings betting on horses. *Horses.* Meanwhile, Pax somehow gets free publicity for his book tour in a front-page news story that's supposed to be all about Imari's Place and the good work Cole's doing there. It's not right."

Mama and Harper turned around, concern etched in their expressions. Julene stared down at the aluminum can. The whir of Hayes's bouncer seat was the only sound in the room.

"Wow," Julene said softly. "That's a lot. I had no idea about the gambling."

Avery pressed the cold can to her flushed cheeks.

Mama started the dishwasher then she and Harper joined them in the living room. Harper sat on the floor beside Hayes's chair. Mama stood, arms crossed over her chest. "You're right, nothing about this is fair," Mama said. "Pax and Trey made a series of poor decisions and no one faults you for being angry.

Especially when it doesn't seem like there's a whole lot of accountability."

"Um, try zero. There's been zero accountability." Avery took a quick sip of sparkling water. "Other than child support, their choices have cost them nothing."

"So why don't you say something?" Julene shifted to face her. "The press would be more than happy to hear your side of the story."

"No way." Avery shook her head. "I'll have to deal with the backlash for speaking out and he'll just sell more books."

Harper's frown deepened. "So you're going to suffer in silence?"

"What choice do I have? I'm trapped between taking the high road and pretending none of this bothers me or publicly sharing my side of the story."

"Isn't there another option?" Mama asked. "I don't want you or your children to be splashed all over the morning talk show circuit or anything, but I also don't like to see you hurting."

Mama's loyalty softened the jagged edges of her pain. "I—I don't know. The news about his book tour and the way he's being presented as Camellia's darling child is really starting to get on my nerves."

"Maybe you need to be Camellia's darling child then." Julene picked at a loose thread on the hem of her skirt. "What you've agreed to do for Imari's Place has amazing potential. That project will be far more meaningful than a forgettable memoir."

"I've already told you how I feel about your partnership with Cole and his foundation," Mama said. "But if you're feeling unsettled about your decision, don't let Maribelle or anyone else pressure you into doing something you aren't comfortable with. You have the right to change your mind."

"But if I back out then Cole has to find somebody else last-minute, and that only fuels more speculation. Doesn't feel like the right decision, either."

"Then you'll have to identify your true passion and let that be your guide. You said you want to help women find redemption and second chances," Harper said. "If that's your passion, then it's likely going to cost you something."

"That's what I'm worried about." Avery squeezed her fist against her forehead. "The Imari's Place project will help young women start over. That's meaningful work. But I'm still afraid and angry and I don't want to give the public a front row seat to my family's drama."

"Then don't." Julene reached over and squeezed Avery's knee. "I've spent some time studying your socials. Your audience adored you. So go back to what works. Reconnect with your people online, give them uplifting inspirational content, and prove that you're an expert in your profession. Because you are."

"Hardly." Avery scoffed. "There are so many people doing a phenomenal job in the home design and nonprofit spaces."

"But there's no one who sees the world or has the exact same creative flare as you. Cole offered you the opportunity because he knows you'll transform the new place into something beautiful and functional." Mama's eyes shone with pride. "We believe in you, sweetheart. You can do this."

"Thank you for cheering me on." Avery offered Mama and her sisters a grateful smile. "I'll set up a design meeting with Cole so we can get started."

Where would she be without her family to lean on? Moving home had been such a difficult decision. But their encouragement and advice helped her navigate the choppy seas of stepping back into the world professionally. If only she could figure out how to prepare for Pax and Trey's return to Camellia.

## Chapter Six

This wasn't going at all like he'd hoped. Cole sat across the kitchen table from Avery in the Huntingtons' lake house, his knee bouncing impatiently. He'd been thrilled when he got her invite for their first design consult. Beyond thrilled, actually. Insisted that Millie Kay reschedule today's meetings so he could be here.

But something wasn't right. Avery barely made eye contact with him and she'd hardly smiled since he got here. In the last thirty minutes, she'd spent more time dealing with Hayes than sharing any coherent thoughts. Magazines, fabric swatches, two samples of tile and a roll of something he couldn't identify—wallpaper maybe—were spread out around her open laptop.

"Mr. Cole, play with me." Addison's huge blue eyes carried a hint of mischief as she wrapped her little fingers around his arm and tugged.

She was such a cute kid. He smiled. "Maybe later, kiddo. Right now, your mom and I are trying to have a meeting."

Avery massaged her forehead with her fingertips. "I should've hired a babysitter."

Hayes chose that exact moment to burst into tears.

Addison released her hold on his arm and pressed her hands over her ears. "Baby Hayes, that is enough."

Cole clamped his fingers over his mouth to stifle his laughter. The scowl, tone of voice, even the tiny furrow in Addison's brow mimicked her mother.

Avery took a deep breath and sighed it out.

He banished his amusement and sat up straighter. "Is there something I can do to help?"

*Please, please don't ask me to hold him.* He had no idea what to do with a crying baby.

Avery reached for the bottle sitting between two stacks of magazines and tried to get Hayes to take it. He cried louder. This time his face turned an impressive shade of beet red.

"I'm trying to get him to take a bottle because…" Her gaze shifted toward Addison then back to Hayes. "Because it's time for him to learn."

"Not a fan, huh?"

Okay, that was a pointless question. Cole winced as Hayes grabbed a tiny fistful of Avery's shirt and turned his head away. Poor little dude. He was angry.

"Mr. Cole, come outside. We won't hear the crying out there." Addison tugged on his arm again. Cole glanced at Avery for permission.

"Would you mind? I'm sorry. I know we're trying to get this project going, but I just need a minute."

"Not a problem. Take your time."

"This way." Addison pulled him from his chair. "You gots to see the flowers."

"All right. Let's see the flowers." She led him across the

kitchen, a blur of pink and yellow as her striped cotton dress billowed around her bare legs. Temporarily detained at the sliding glass door, she slowed down long enough to yank on the handle, grunting when it didn't give way.

"Here." He reached around her and flipped the latch. Addison tugged on the handle again and this time the door slid open.

"Thanks." Addison stepped out and hurried across the porch. She pushed through the screen door, letting it slap closed. Wow, she was quick. He closed the slider, trading Hayes's crying for the whine of lawnmowers and boat engines rumbling in the distance.

He caught up with Addison out in the backyard. She stood at the edge of the raised flowerbeds, squinting up at him in the morning sunshine. The humidity wasn't quite stifling yet, but it wouldn't be comfortable for long. Hopefully the flowerbed tour would be brief, Avery could get Hayes settled down and they'd get some work done before lunch.

"These flowers will be for the butterflies," she declared, pointing to the purple coneflowers. "Butterflies loves purple."

"Is that right?" Cole shoved his hands into the front pockets of his coral-colored chinos. "Tell me everything."

Addison inched along the flowerbeds, pointing out the different varieties of flowers and keeping up a steady stream of chatter.

He couldn't say for sure if she had her facts straight. Not that it mattered. He liked hanging out with her. "Wait. I have a question."

"What?"

"How did you get so smart?"

She giggled. "My mommy."

He grinned down at her. "Your mom is very smart. So is

your grandmother. Did you know your grandmother was my teacher?"

Addison's mouth formed a perfect O. "No, she's too old to be your teacher."

He tipped his head back and laughed. "I'm a grown-up, obviously. But once upon a time, I was a kid right here in Camellia and your grandmother was my fifth-grade teacher. You can ask her. She'll tell you all about it."

Addison scrutinized him, her disbelief still obvious. He turned and gestured toward the rest of the yard. "What else do you love out here?"

"I like the water and the trees. And I like to go on boat rides because it's super fun." Addison spread her arms wide and twirled in a clumsy circle. "You can go with us next time."

"I'd like that." Cole took in the stunning landscaped yard sloping gently down toward the water's edge and the boat bobbing against the dock. Avery's family had a lovely place here. He might've owned a lakefront house nearby if he'd stayed in his first career as an attorney. But that firm would've turned him into a miserable shell of a human. And he couldn't stomach the thought of all the lives that wouldn't have been changed for the better if he'd never joined forces with Imari's Place.

Addison screamed, jolting him from his thoughts.

"My arm, my arm!"

"What happened?" He dropped to his knees in the grass beside her. Panic tore the breath from his lungs. Tears dribbled down her flushed cheeks and she cradled her arm against her chest.

"A bee stinged me," she wailed.

Oh, no. He'd been daydreaming, oblivious to the fact that Addison might be in danger. "It's okay. The bee's gone now."

He scooped her up and awkwardly carried her back to the house. Her pathetic crying grew louder, making him feel even worse. He crossed the porch in long strides, flung open the slider and stepped inside. "We've got a problem here."

Julene, Harper and Avery stood at the kitchen table, hovering around Avery's laptop. They turned toward him, their mouths agape. Then they all pelted him with questions.

"What's going on?"

"What happened?"

"Why is she crying?"

Flustered, Cole turned in a circle. Mrs. Huntington stood beside the sofa in the living room, with Hayes nestled in her arms.

Heart pounding against his ribs, Cole eased Addison onto the kitchen counter. "We were looking at the flowers together. She says a bee stung her arm."

"Mama," she cried, stretching her arms toward Avery.

"Oh, sweet baby," Avery swooped in, pulling Addison against her.

Cole stepped out of the way, pushing his fingers through his hair. How did he let this happen?

"There's meat tenderizer in the cabinet by the stove," Mrs. Huntington said. "That usually helps."

"Is she allergic?" Harper crossed the kitchen to the cabinet. "I have students who carry EpiPens for stings and bites. Is she having trouble breathing?"

Cole's stomach heaved. Allergic? Trouble breathing? He was going to be sick.

Avery leaned back, both hands clutching Addison's shoulders. "Pumpkin, look at me. Breathe. I need you to breathe."

Addison pulled in a shuddery breath then kept crying.

"Are her lips swelling?" Harper plucked the meat tenderizer from the shelf and brought it to Avery. "That's always the first sign."

"Harper, relax," Julene scolded. "If she's crying, she's breathing."

What had he done? Sweat trickled down his spine. This was his fault. He glanced toward his messenger bag and papers stacked on the kitchen table. His phone was somewhere in there, wasn't it? If they had to call for help, that should be his job. He stood still. Unable to move. His arms felt like they weighed a thousand pounds each.

"She's never been stung before." Avery ran her fingers over the angry welt on Addison's arm. "How am I supposed to know if she's allergic?"

"Do you have any allergy medication?" Julene scrolled through her phone. "This says we should give her some."

"If she has to go to the emergency room, I don't think you should give her any medicine," Harper said.

The flurry of activity made Cole dizzy. "I—I'm going to go..." He barely choked out the words. "I shouldn't be here right now."

Avery stared at him. "What?"

"I'd better... I'm going to go. I'm in the way. So sorry. I hope she'll be all right." He grabbed his bag and stuffed the papers inside then hurried toward the front door, carefully avoiding Mrs. Huntington's gaze. Wow, he was such a coward running like this. But he didn't know what else to do. Addison had been hurt on his watch. How could he possibly be a part of their lives if he couldn't even keep the kid safe for three minutes?

"Huh. That was weird." Avery glanced through the living room window toward the gate where Cole's car had long since disappeared.

"Mama, my show." Addison sat on the sofa, wrapped in a fluffy bath towel that Harper had pulled from the dryer. Evidently a warm towel, an episode of *Doc McStuffins* and a lime-flavored popsicle were all that she needed to forget her bee sting.

"Hang on, sweet girl." Avery turned from the window and focused on the remote control.

What had just happened? She scrolled through the channels looking for the correct platform to stream the show and mentally replayed the afternoon's events. Cole had seemed fine. Patiently tolerated Addison's interruptions and Hayes's crying during their meeting. If he hadn't wanted to go outside, he would've said no. Right?

"That one, Mama. That one." Addison pointed to the television screen, her popsicle dripping down her hand. She was thankful for that towel, otherwise Mama's sofa would have new lime-green accents.

"Everything okay?" Her mother came into the room carrying Hayes. He wore a clean white onesie and navy shorts. Not the outfit he'd been wearing before Addison's bee sting.

"Oh, no." Avery grimaced. "His diaper?"

Mama nodded, kissed his cheek then handed him to her. "He's all cleaned up and ready to eat. I tried the bottle again but he's not having it."

Hayes fussed and rubbed his chubby fist against his mouth as Avery scooped him into her arms. "Thank you for trying."

"No problem, sweetie. I'm happy to help."

"Grandma, watch my show with me." Addison popped up from the sofa, bouncing on her knees, the half-melted popsicle dipping dangerously close to the white fabric.

"Addison, sit down while you're eating that, please. Make

sure you keep that towel on the sofa too." Avery settled Hayes on her shoulder, trying desperately not to lose her patience.

"You feed Hayes. I'll sit with her." Mama skirted the sofa and settled beside Addison. "What are you watching?"

Avery didn't argue. She strode toward her bedroom, shifting Hayes to her other shoulder, as his cries echoed down the hallway. Through the open door, Avery caught a glimpse of Julene sitting on the floor in her room, facing a full-length mirror. She tipped her head to the side. Quirked her lips. Puckered. Her phone sat propped against the dresser, while she and the young woman on FaceTime debated the merits of Julene's lipstick.

An arrow of envy pierced her insides. Hayes's crying escalated, earning her a concerned glance from Julene.

"Sorry," Avery whispered then slipped into her bedroom and closed the door. Hot tears stung her eyes. If only her biggest problem was whether she'd bought the right shade of lipstick at the beauty counter.

As she settled in the rocking chair and fed Hayes, she let the tears flow. Wow, she was a mess. Home for less than a month and she was already jealous of both her sisters' freedom.

Or maybe these tears were more about what she'd lost? And how far she'd fallen. She didn't miss Pax. Not really. Not like she had when he'd first moved out. But she mourned the loss of being part of a traditional family unit. The sweet memories they'd built, celebrating Addison's milestones and the growth of their business.

She swiped the back of her hand across her cheeks. Life looked nothing like she'd expected. A typical day in her former life was hectic. Demanding. She managed multiple projects, handled marketing all by herself and made sure their home ran smoothly. Now she couldn't even take a simple meeting without unraveling. Worse, she relied on her mother and sisters to help care for her kids.

And how in the world would she ever help Cole with the expansion project? Especially if he flipped out every time her kids had a meltdown. She'd have to hire a babysitter. Or maybe a nanny. She couldn't take kids to a construction site and she wasn't ready to get a place of her own yet. Rent in Camellia was far more reasonable than in Raleigh, but covering first and last's month's rent plus a security deposit on an apartment felt too risky right now.

Her breathing grew shallow as her uncertainties pressed in, like a string of linebackers determined to sack the quarterback. She loved her children. And she'd find a way to provide for them. But how was she going to survive being a single working mother?

She forced herself to stare at the painting of a sailboat cutting through ocean waves hanging on the opposite wall above the queen bed. *Breathe. Just breathe. Feed your baby. He needs you.*

A soft knock sounded on the door. Avery sniffed and quickly mopped at her tears with a cloth diaper she found draped over the back of the chair.

"Come in."

Her mother stepped into the room, Avery's phone in her hand. "Sorry to interrupt but you had three calls right in a row. I thought they might be important."

Her worried expression made Avery's gut cinch tight. "Who called?"

Mama bit her lip and passed her the phone.

Avery glanced at the screen. One missed call from Whitney, and two from Pax. "I'd better call him."

"Do you want me to take Hayes?"

Hayes stopped nursing and cried out.

"There's my answer." Mama smoothed her hand over the rumpled lavender and gray floral duvet cover on the bed. Lingering. A subtle offer of solidarity.

"I'll call him while Hayes finishes nursing." Avery plastered on a brave smile. "Don't worry, I'm sure it will be a brief conversation."

Mama hesitated then slipped out and closed the door softly behind her.

Avery shifted Hayes in her arms, made sure he was content then glanced at her phone again. She could text him and insist their attorneys handle his request. Because he most definitely had a request. That meant more billable hours and more money subtracted from her meager account balance. An avoidance strategy that was too costly. Her pulse pounded like a jackhammer destroying a sidewalk as she tapped the screen to return Pax's call.

He picked up on the second ring. "Hey."

*Hey.* So casual. Like months hadn't passed since they'd spoken. Three seconds in and her fingers already itched to end the call.

"What's up?" She tried to sound bored. Exasperated.

"I'm just checking in. Had some down time in Nashville between appointments. How're the kids?"

*How are the kids?* She pulled the phone away from her ear and stared at the screen. Why was he suddenly pretending to care? She placed the call on speakerphone then silently whispered a prayer for an extra dose of patience. "The kids are fine, Pax. What do you want?"

Silence filled the line. "There's no need to be rude, Avery. I'm allowed to call and see if my children are healthy and safe."

Her scalp prickled. She resented the implication in his comment. "Have you heard otherwise?"

"Not exactly. I—"

"You have no right to question my parenting abilities, seeing as how you abandoned us and I haven't heard from you in months. Other than the measly child support payments."

"I'm doing the best I can. Life on the road is demanding."

She couldn't stop a laugh. "Oh, please. You have no idea what demanding looks like. Try parenting a preschooler and a newborn by yourself."

Hayes pulled away and stared up at her, his face wrinkling. Avery quickly tossed the cloth diaper over her shoulder and held him upright, gently encouraging a burp.

"From what I've heard, you have plenty of help."

Anger simmered in her midsection. He was *so* infuriating. "I'm not sure where you're getting your information, but I'm guessing it's your mother. Who, by the way, couldn't be bothered to speak to me for more than two minutes. And she's made zero effort to see Addison or Hayes."

"Well, I'm glad you brought that up because I'd like to do something about that."

Pax's tone was smooth. Patronizing. She wanted to scream. "Do tell."

Hayes arched back against her hand, letting her know he wasn't pleased with the interruption in his feast. He burped, making a mess on the cloth diaper. And the sleeve of her T-shirt. So gross. Hopefully he had missed the chair's upholstered cushion.

"I have two events scheduled in Camellia soon," Pax said.

"I'm well aware." Okay, that was borderline snarky. It wasn't like she could forget about his impending visit, mainly because Nana, her sisters and the local media wouldn't let her. She nestled Hayes in the crook of her opposite arm and he resumed nursing. Drawing in a deep breath, she forced herself to count to four and hold it. Then slowly exhaled. She could do this.

Pax ignored her comment and pressed on with his plan. "In case you missed my text, I'd like to spend some quality time with my children."

*No.* Fear snaked in and coiled around her insides. If Pax thought he was taking Addison and Hayes on a book tour, he was one sandwich short of a picnic.

"Both of your children? Hayes doesn't even know you."

Pax huffed out a long breath. "And that's something I'm trying to change. A boy needs his father in his life. And Addison needs to spend time with me too. I miss her. So much."

Was he for real? "This had better not be a publicity stunt. What's the matter? Are you worried about looking like a deadbeat dad in your own hometown?"

"That is not fair."

"Don't even talk to me about fair." Spots peppered her vision. A pacifier sat on the dresser and she grabbed it and popped it in Hayes's mouth. Thankfully, he accepted it and suckled away, his eyelids growing heavy.

"I'm trying to do right by you and our children. The least you could do is meet me halfway."

"The least you could do is be reasonable. I'm not letting you parade two little kids across the stage at your daddy's church. No photo ops. No public appearances. They can't ride on your bus and you may not leave the state. And Hayes doesn't take a bottle, so there's that."

Pax muttered an obscenity. "You're not making this very easy."

"Nope, I'm not." She clamped her mouth shut to keep from saying something hateful.

"I'll be in town for three days. I'd like at least one day with Addison. She doesn't need your constant supervision."

"True, but she does deserve an explanation about why you abandoned her, so make sure you have that speech memorized."

"You're the one who demanded full custody. I'll be sure to explain to Addison what that means exactly."

Heat flushed her skin. The man was impossible. "Is there anything else, Pax? I need to go."

"I want time with Hayes too."

"Fine."

"Seriously?"

"Yes, seriously. He requires two naps a day, though, so you'll need to plan around his schedule."

"I'll stay at my parents' place. There will be plenty of extra hands if I need support."

Chill bumps pebbled her skin. What did that mean? Was he traveling with an entourage? She couldn't bring herself to ask about Trey. "All right then. Father's Day weekend it is."

"Perfect."

They agreed to talk again and arrange for a hand off when Pax arrived in Camellia. Then she ended the call and tossed her phone on the bed. Her whole body trembled. What had she done? If Pax and Trey found out Cole had hired her, they'd surely tell anyone who'd listen that she wasn't qualified to design the inside of a shoebox, much less an entire house. She had to find a way to prove to Cole and everyone else that she was worthy of this opportunity.

Cole climbed out of his car and stood in the Huntingtons' driveway, the apology he'd rehearsed at least a dozen times spooling through his head. If not for the paper shopping bag of frozen custard and his desperate need to make things right, he might've climbed back in his car and hightailed it out of there. But he'd already done that once today and carried the shame and humiliation to prove it.

*Whitaker, you're a bonehead.*

Bag in hand and his stomach in knots, he trudged toward the front door. At least he was approaching under the cover of darkness, although someone inside the house had probably seen him on the security camera when he came through the gates.

*Don't overthink this. Just tell her you're sorry.*

He reached for the doorbell then hesitated. It was after eight. The kids might be sleeping already. He knocked softly instead. Shifting his weight from one foot to the other, he clutched the paper bag tighter. He half expected Greer to come to the door and block his entry with a few pointed questions, followed closely by Julene and Harper, who'd probably add their own commentary regarding his epic departure.

To his surprise, the door opened and Avery greeted him. Her brows curved in surprise. Then she spotted the bag in his hands.

"Is that frozen custard from Marlowe's?"

He could only nod. Did she know how beautiful she was? In her faded Camellia High T-shirt, denim shorts with the cuffs rolled up and her curls tamed back with a wide red fabric headband, she looked so much like the Avery he used to know that he could hardly breathe. His gaze landed on her toenails painted the color of red rose petals and all coherent thought left the building.

She didn't seem to notice that he wasn't able to speak. Grabbing his arm, she tugged him inside. "You have impeccable timing."

Ha. Not exactly. He closed the door then followed her into the kitchen.

"Greer and Mama took Nana out for supper. My sisters are gone and the kids are finally both asleep." She reached into the cabinet, pulled out two colorful enamel bowls then plucked two spoons from the drawer and set them on the counter. She glanced at him over her shoulder. "Well, what are you waiting for?"

"I—I'm sorry."

"For what?" She opened and closed drawers until she found the ice cream scoop.

"For not inviting you to the groundbreaking. And for today. I'm sorry I was such a coward, leaving you the way I did."

"Yeah, what happened to my invitation? Lost in the mail?"

"To be honest, there wasn't supposed to be a ceremony at all. Then the mayor showed up and brought the local press and things took off from there. Again, I apologize. You weren't intentionally excluded."

"It's fine." She pointed to the bag he still held. "That's going to melt if we don't hurry up."

He hesitated. "Is it really fine or are you trying to be nice? Because that story in the paper wasn't what I'd hoped it would be."

Her expression crinkled. "Yeah, that one stung a little. I'm not thrilled about the newspaper article, but I'm not holding you responsible."

"Thank you for being so gracious."

She waggled her fingers and motioned for him to hand over the custard. "I can't believe Marlowe's is still in business."

He passed her the bag. "Well, it was touch and go there for a while."

"Really? I hadn't heard."

"With you not here to keep up a steady demand for their bizarre flavors, they almost went under."

"Oh, stop."

Laughing, she swatted his arm then bumped him with her hip. He'd been there less than five minutes, and she'd already touched him three times. This apology thing was much easier than he'd anticipated.

She pulled both cartons from the bag.

"I can't believe they still have pistachio and that you remembered." She pressed up on her toes and kissed his cheek. "Thank you."

He clutched the counter's edge with both hands. Yearning unfurled, like a flag in the hands of a color guard performer at a Friday night football game. A normal person would've continued the conversation. Responded with a simple "you're welcome."

Not him.

He'd wanted her for far too long to gloss over this milestone event. His brain was obsessed with cataloging every detail of her innocent gesture. The warmth of her body fitting against his for one glorious second before she pulled away. A hint of fragrance laced with a fruity scent—melon, perhaps? He couldn't be sure. Didn't really care. The feather soft touch of her lips brushing against his skin knocked out all other sensory input.

He forced himself to step away. "I'll get us some water, if you don't mind."

"Sure." She shrugged and popped the lid off the first carton. "Is Marlowe's really in danger of going out of business?"

Pulling two tumblers from the cupboard, he filled them with ice and water from the dispenser on the refrigerator door. "They've struggled from time to time, but I think business is solid now. I don't know why pistachio is the flavor of the day. Maybe they heard you were back and whipped up a fresh batch just for you."

She didn't answer.

Oh, no. He turned around and brought their water to the counter. "What did I say?"

Dropping a generous helping of custard into the red enamel bowl, she frowned. "You didn't say anything wrong. And by the way, Addison's fine. She's not allergic to bee stings. I don't know why Harper was going on and on like that."

Relief settled over him. "I felt horrible. Again, I'm so sorry."

"Yeah, well, of everything that happened today, that was the least of my concerns, to be honest. Which kind do you want?" She gestured to the pints of frozen custard, already leaving milky trails across the countertop.

"I brought chocolate peanut butter for me. I know better than to get between you and your pistachio frozen custard."

She shook her head in mock exasperation then served him a generous portion. "Come on. Addison will hear the sound of a spoon scraping on a bowl even if she's sound asleep then she'll be out here in two seconds. And I really, really do not want to see that child until morning. Let's go outside."

"Wow. Rough day, huh?"

"You have no idea."

"Well, come on then. Let's go out on the porch and you can tell me all about it."

Gratitude brightened her eyes. "Thank you. You've always been a great listener, Cole."

"Happy to help." He forced a smile, but his insides collapsed like a punctured balloon. How could he tell her that he'd always be there for her? He'd always wanted to be there for her. And he'd like nothing more than to restore their friendship.

Nourish it. Stoke that chaste kiss on the cheek into something so much more.

*You're off your rocker. Not gonna happen.*

Her husband had betrayed her. Even though the divorce had been final for a while, he sensed that wound was still quite raw. A relationship was likely the last thing she wanted or needed right now. Especially a relationship with him. Accepting Maribelle's bribe meant vanquishing any possibility of a future romance. If Avery knew the truth, she'd never forgive him.

He followed her out onto the porch, being as quiet as he possibly could. Selfishly, he didn't really want to see Addison again today, either. The cicadas, frogs and crickets all sang their peculiar nighttime harmony. Lanterns in the yard cast a pleasant glow into the velvety darkness. Strands of vintage lights crisscrossed the screened porch. A ceiling fan whirred overhead, swirling warm air around them. Avery claimed one end of the swing and patted the cushion beside her. "Here, have a seat."

He set the tumblers on the table nearby then sat down beside her. They dug into their frozen custard. The ordinary activity of eating their favorite dessert together carried him back in time.

He couldn't begin to count how many hours they'd spent at Marlowe's back in the day. It was a perfect reward after an intense study session, and the ideal escape when they both needed to get out of their houses for an hour or two. "So what happened today after I flipped out and ran off?"

"Please don't beat yourself up. It really is okay." She pressed her hand to his pants leg above his knee, and it was all he could do not to twine his fingers through hers and hold on. "Don't give it another thought. She's fine. Kids bounce back quickly."

"I don't like...ever since..." He blew out a breath, followed by an embarrassed laugh. "Ever since Kim was abducted, I'm not great with kids getting hurt. I realize a bee sting and an abduction are on opposite ends of the spectrum, but clearly I react to an injured child by panicking. There's something about it that freaked me out."

She paused, a spoonful of custard halfway to her mouth, and searched his face. Oh, he wanted to get lost in those eyes. He hadn't said those words about his sister out loud to a woman, any woman, ever. But instead of feeling raw and exposed, he felt seen. Safe. Because he knew Avery was trustworthy. He could tell her his true feelings and didn't have to risk being ridiculed.

"Cole Whitaker, you are a remarkable human," Avery said finally. "Tell me again why you're still single?"

Oh, my word. What had she done? Her spoon clinked against the edge of her bowl as she let it go then she pressed her fingers to her lips. This was Cole, one of her dearest friends. One of the few genuine friends that she had left. And she'd gone and made fun of his vulnerability with a joke.

"I think it's my turn to apologize," she whispered. "I'm so sorry. I meant that as a compliment. You're a wonderful guy and you'll make someone very happy."

He still hadn't looked at her. Two splotches of color clinging to his cheekbones hinted that she'd probably embarrassed him. Yeah, they had made that pledge to marry each other if they turned thirty-two or whatever and they were both still single. But they'd been young and naive then. Besides, it wasn't like Cole had expressed any interest in her. Maybe he wanted to be single. Maybe he liked being devoted to an important cause.

She ducked her head and stared into the remnants of her

frozen custard. Today had been one long string of drama-filled disasters. She was in a terrible frame of mind, which meant she'd likely say and do all sorts of nonsensical things. Exhibit A—she'd already dipped her toe in the off-limits pool when she kissed his cheek. And now she was getting all worked up about a silly bargain they'd made years ago. This was a sentimental trip down memory lane on a night when she was feeling sorry for herself.

He quietly finished the last of his chocolate peanut butter custard then set aside his empty bowl and reached for his water. "Thirsty?"

"Please." He passed her the other tumbler and she drank it down in three long gulps. He raised his eyebrows, but he said nothing. Finally, his mouth curved into an effortless half smile. "Now might be a good time to talk about that napkin pledge of ours. Since, as you mentioned, I'm not married and almost thirty-two."

She groaned and pressed her palm to her face. "I'm so sorry."

"Not a problem. You aren't the first to point out my marital status."

She forced herself to look at him. "I do still have that napkin, by the way."

He slung his arm across the back of the swing and sipped his water. "Do you now?"

She angled her body toward him and crossed her legs underneath her, grateful that he'd overlooked her thoughtless comments. "I found it the other night. It's in the bottom of my jewelry box."

"Good to know."

His amused expression grew serious and she waited for a more nuanced explanation about why he hadn't married or a brief summary of who he'd dated over the years. Instead, they rocked slowly, and Avery resisted the temptation to pry.

But she couldn't stand the silence for long. "So, I've come to an important realization."

"Uh-oh." He stopped the swing with his foot. "Am I going to need more custard for this?"

"Probably not. I think you'll like what I'm about to say."

He resumed rocking. "All right. Lay it on me."

"I need to hire reliable childcare if I'm going to give our project the attention it deserves."

"You're right. I do like the sound of that."

"Pax called me today, and I've been super flustered ever since, because he wants to spend some time with the kids when he's here in a few weeks. That made me realize Hayes has never been away from me and now it's going to be super hard because he's so attached, but I'm going to have to find a way to make it happen."

Oh, boy. She was babbling.

Cole sipped his water. "Wow, you've had quite a day. How are you feeling about Pax coming back to Camellia?"

"Afraid. Irritated. Stressed." She pulled at a loose thread on the cuff of her denim shorts. "I'd kind of gotten used to doing life without him. But as much as I hate to admit it, he does have a right to see his children. I don't think Hayes is going to be thrilled, but…they should see each other."

"If anybody knows what it's like to not have a dad around, it's you." Cole's gaze found hers in the semidarkness. "I admire your willingness to foster a relationship between your children and their father."

"Well, I'm not exactly willing, but there's no legal reason why he can't. And if I say no, then I have to get my attorney involved because he'll make an issue of it, and that's just going to be expensive."

"It still sounds complicated."

"Very complicated. On the bright side, if I can hire reliable childcare and Pax and his family are willing to be involved with the kids as much as they say they are, then you and I will be free to focus on Imari's Place. Right?"

"Right." He looked down at his water and turned the tumbler in a slow circle. What was he thinking about? He'd come in here all contrite and apologetic, and not that he wasn't sincere, but there was something more behind that expression of his, something she couldn't quite pinpoint.

Was he interested in something more substantive than friendship? Heat scorched her skin for even thinking it. Of course he wasn't.

And if she flirted or teased or boldly initiated a kiss—a real kiss—she'd likely destroy this partnership they'd forged. And she wasn't willing to risk it.

"It's getting late." He pushed to his feet and gathered their cups and bowls. "I need to go."

"I'll walk you out." She followed him into the kitchen. Conflicting emotions picked teams and squared off like students in an elementary game of dodgeball. She allowed her gaze to track Cole's every move as Team You'll Be Sorry lobbed the first truth bomb.

*You'll be sorry if you ruin this friendship.*

She leaned against the doorframe and tried not to sigh appreciatively as he tucked the utensils in the dishwasher then rinsed the bowls and added them to the lower rack.

Not to be deterred, Team Romance lobbed a compelling argument. *Every healthy romantic relationship starts with a solid foundation of friendship.*

Team You'll Be Sorry came back for a second round. *But a healthy relationship requires honesty and you're not being honest.*

Ouch. Her optimistic romantic side retreated to lick its wounds.

Cole put their tumblers in the top rack, closed the dishwasher and faced her.

"Thanks again for stopping by and bringing my favorite dessert," she said. "That was really thoughtful."

His tight smile didn't carry the same warmth it had only a few minutes ago. "You're welcome. Let's talk soon. We need to schedule another meeting."

"Of course."

She followed him to the front door. Cole slowed long enough to turn the knob then step outside. "Have a great night," he called over his shoulder then strode toward his car.

"You too." She closed the door then leaned against it. What had gotten into her? She pressed her palms to her flushed cheeks. A romantic relationship with Cole wasn't something she'd ever thought about. Well, maybe once back in the day.

But not *now.*

Besides, he didn't exactly answer her question about his status. Maybe he was in a committed relationship. A burning sensation filled her chest. She pressed her hand against her sternum, as if capable of squeezing the unfortunate emotion out.

Why did she even care? A relationship with Cole was not an option. He would be a wonderful husband for someone. Just not for her.

## Chapter Seven

"The answer's no." Cole held up his palm to silence Hemby before he even got started. He'd seen that telltale look before in his best friend's eyes, and it always spelled trouble.

"C'mon, man." Hemby reached for his glass of sweet tea. "You haven't heard my proposal yet."

"I don't need another proposal." Cole squeezed ketchup into a hollow spot in his basket of fries. "I'm swamped."

Thanks to Maribelle Lansing, he didn't have to take every meeting invite that came his way, hoping it might lead to a sizable donation. Right now he had the luxury of saying no. Staying focused on the expansion instead of worrying whether he'd done enough.

"You're going to want to make space in that packed calendar of yours once you hear this."

"Doubt it."

"Someone reached out to me because they know we're

friends. They'd like to film a documentary about the great work you're doing with Imari's Place."

Cole paused then set the ketchup bottle down in front of Hemby. "No thanks."

"What do you mean?" Hemby frowned. "It's a documentary, not a TMZ exposé."

"Doesn't matter." Cole picked up his cheeseburger. "We are moving forward with the expansion. The foundation's poured. We're fully funded. I don't need to deal with a film crew."

"It's probably only three guys. Maybe four." Hemby's eyes gleamed over the rim of his glass. "You'll hardly even know they're there."

"Right." Cole scoffed. "Cameras, operators and producers are so discreet. Practically invisible."

Conversation hummed around them, punctuated by the occasional burst of laughter and the dishes clinking together as a teenage boy bused a table nearby. The lunch crowd had packed the booths and the counter at The Main Street Deli, Hemby and Cole's usual weekday meeting place.

"Your work is garnering attention. People are talking about your plans to build a larger home for trafficked women. Isn't that what you want? Positive press? This guy's an experienced documentary filmmaker. A good one. All he's asking for is a meeting."

"I can think of ten reasons why a documentary about Imari's Place is a bad idea."

Hemby reached across the worn Formica table and swiped one of Cole's fries. "And I can give you one brilliant reason why you should say yes."

"Super." He hoped his sarcastic tone emphasized his lack of enthusiasm. "Enlighten me."

"Avery." Hemby grinned like he'd just won the US Open then popped the french fry into his mouth.

"What about her?" He didn't like where this was going, even though he'd suspected this so-called friend had an ulterior motive.

"She's already had a successful TV show. People know who she is and she'll know exactly how to handle a renovation with a camera crew hovering over her shoulder."

"That's a weak argument, counselor." Cole plucked a napkin from the stainless steel dispenser. "Aren't you supposed to be a lawyer? Because you just refuted your point about how we wouldn't even know the cameras were there."

Hemby shrugged then took a bite of his chicken salad sandwich. "You can poke holes in my argument all you want. That doesn't change the fact that you know I'm right."

"I've already misled her about the funding." Cole leaned closer and dropped his voice low. "I can't ask her to be a part of a documentary."

Hemby stopped chewing long enough to roll his eyes. "You are not obligated to tell her where the money came from. She's not on your board of directors. That's between Mrs. Lansing and her family. And I'm not suggesting that you lie. Or trick her into participating. It's just a documentary."

"But she'll think I'm using her."

Hemby's brows sailed upward. "A little late to worry about that, isn't it?"

Cole dropped his sandwich back in the basket, his appetite waning. He wasn't using her. Was he?

After she'd graciously accepted his apologies last night and planted that kiss on his cheek, he'd thought the vibe between them was tilting out of the friend zone. Until she'd quashed the mood by pointing out that he was still single. Even followed up with the zinger about how he'd make someone very happy.

There was no way he'd confess he wanted that someone to be her.

But he wasn't about to tell Hemby any of that. It would only encourage him.

"You're starting to come around. I can see the wheels turning." Hemby raised his glass toward their server, hinting he'd like a refill. "Stop trying to analyze all the possible outcomes. Just ask her. The worst she can say is no."

"It's not just about her."

"Then what's the hang-up?"

"Privacy concerns, mostly." Cole picked up another french fry. "Women who live at the house currently aren't going to want a crew snooping around."

"I'm not asking you to endanger anyone or put a woman on camera who isn't ready to tell her story. But put aside your fear for three seconds and think about what this can do for the future of your organization."

Cole chewed slowly, envisioning Avery's bright smile and optimistic spirit shining like a beacon into the dark and sometimes hopeless void that comprised his work. Was it wrong that he wanted more time with her? More of her light in his life?

"If privacy is your main concern, I can have a waiver drawn up by the end of the day," Hemby added.

Cole shook his head. The privacy argument was weak. A cover for his real fear. He didn't trust himself to not fall completely in love with Avery. Because no matter how Hemby tried to spin this, she'd end up being involved in the process somehow. That meant even more time they'd be spending together.

"Don't do this."

"Don't do what?"

Hemby lobbed him a look of dismay. "Don't shoot down a great idea because you're afraid."

He hated when Hemby was right. A documentary raised the kind of awareness this crisis so desperately needed. Billboards, social media and fundraisers only went so far. He needed more artists across a variety of platforms to speak out against the social injustice of modern-day slavery if they had any hope of putting an end to it. A well-made documentary on a reputable streaming service had a greater reach. Which meant more people paying attention. Possibly more contributions. And maybe freedom for the many still caught in trafficking's suffocating snare.

Cole pushed his plate aside. "I can't give a definitive yes. Not yet. I need to think about this."

"Shocker. When was the last time you made an impulsive decision?"

"Accepting Maribelle's check was impulsive."

"I suppose one impulsive decision per decade isn't too bad."

Cole crumpled his napkin and jammed it under the edge of his plate. He didn't want to talk about how much trouble that one decision had caused already. He'd gone from vowing to keep his distance to having supper with Avery and her family and sharing frozen custard on the porch swing. Every minute spent with her chipped away at his best intentions to guard his heart. Hemby didn't mind playing fast and loose, but Cole was a man who liked order and careful analysis. Besides, he'd already said yes to Maribelle's bribe. If he said yes to a documentary, what would he risk losing next?

"I have a suggestion." Avery picked at the seam of the cardboard sleeve on her disposable coffee cup and avoided Cole's gaze. Her skin prickled, bracing for rejection. It had been ages since she'd pitched a creative idea. Especially one of this magnitude. Trey had often shot down her suggestions, or offered false praise then quietly eliminated her contribution from the final design plans.

"Do tell." Cole leaned his elbows on the table, granting her his undivided attention. Conversation hummed around their small table tucked in a corner of Camellia's popular new coffee shop.

"What would you think if the women at Imari's Place had jobs making a line of products?" The words tumbled out. She forced herself to make eye contact, quietly assessing his reaction.

"We've discussed it a few times, but nothing ever panned out." Cole slid his own coffee cup closer then shifted in his chair. "It can be challenging to raise enough funds to cover all the residents' needs. We've made housing and vocational training outside the facility our main focus."

Was that a no? She couldn't quite interpret his neutral expression. He hadn't shut her down, so she kept going. Flipping open her new notebook that housed all the thoughts and musings, she turned to the last page she'd filled with her research. "I've done some fact-finding. There are a few programs similar to Imari's Place that make products available at a retail location. It's a way for the women to recover and transition back to life in the world. Handbags, jewelry and other accessories."

Cole craned his neck to get a better look at her notes. "Wow, I'm impressed. You've done your homework."

"I found this organization in Nashville. They've had success with a variety of products."

"Yeah, the founder's a friend of mine." Cole sipped his coffee.

She splayed her hand over the page and ducked her head, blood rushing to her cheeks. She was so presumptuous, trying to tell Cole about a cause he'd devoted his whole life to.

"Hey." His voice was warm. Gentle. He dipped his chin

and found her gaze again. "I wasn't criticizing you. Simply acknowledging that other organizations have done this well and we can certainly look at emulating them. Tell me more about your idea."

She straightened. How refreshing. Instead of discrediting her like Trey had done countless times, Cole wanted to hear more. The fact that he hadn't dismissed her idea injected her with confidence. "Well, you know me. I want to do something unique, something no one else is doing, but the overhead might be too high and we don't really have access to a warehouse or a manufacturing space."

"All excellent points. We can get to those details later. Talk to me about the products."

"Candles, bath bombs and soap are top of mind. Perhaps essential oils and lotion too if we had the bandwidth. Women helping women, and women building each other up is so important. I know a lot of people who would love to buy products made by people rescued from trafficking."

Cole's fingers moved along his jaw. "I have some contacts on the ground in other countries where women make jewelry and sell it in their community. That can be sort of a feast-or-famine kind of thing. The slightest amount of political instability or the unpredictable nature of consumers, and the whole operation is off the rails. To your point, a facility here in Camellia or close by would be huge."

"I've spent a lot of time thinking about the women who will stay at Imari's Place."

He nodded. "Me too."

"I've done some reading about trafficking, nothing compared to what you've researched and observed, I'm sure, but I'd love to create more opportunities for women who need a fresh start here in Camellia. Vocational training that sets them up for long-term success in roles other than food service and the hospitality industry."

"Agreed."

She stared at him. His skin was smooth and slightly flushed from the heat. She'd looked at Cole hundreds maybe even thousands of times. He was incredibly handsome. She'd never noticed the smattering of freckles on his cheekbones or that tiny divot above his eyebrow. Had he told her the story about that scar?

"Avery?"

Her name on his lips was gentle. Patient. Tugging her back to the conversation.

"Did you have something more you wanted to say?"

"I was doing some research about how women in developing nations try and contribute to their families. Harvesting coffee beans, making handbags and jewelry are all common. Those seem like labor-intensive options. I mean, it takes a long time to make a beaded necklace and not everyone has the patience. Or the skills necessary. And Camellia isn't a developing nation."

"Despite the stereotypes that linger about Alabama, no." Cole's smile was effortless. Confident. "This isn't a developing nation."

Avery's heart took a Texas-sized leap in response. What was *wrong* with her?

"Some of the women we bring to Imari's Place are originally from a poverty-stricken community in another country," Cole said. "They once worked in agriculture and only came to the US because someone coerced them. Preyed on their vulnerabilities and convinced them they'd have a better life here. Often all they really want is the freedom to earn a decent living and send some money back home to their children."

"So, this is way beyond the scope of this project, but what

if we opened a factory here and manufactured a product or several products? Wouldn't we be teaching them a skill set they can use here in Camellia? Or are we focused on equipping them to return home to their families and communities and make positive contributions?"

His jaw drifted open.

"What?" Her fingers fluttered self-consciously to her neck. "That was a dumb question, wasn't it?"

"No, it was a brilliant question." Cole's hand extended and his fingers brushed affectionately up and down her bare arm. It was a gesture so unexpected, so intimate that he pulled back immediately. Avery didn't know what to say, but she was acutely aware of the trail of heat his fingers left and the way her body wanted to lean into his touch.

Even though it lasted only a millisecond.

Cole leaned back and linked his arms across his chest. "Your suggestion about a manufacturing facility and a product line is fantastic. This is an ongoing conversation in board meetings and among other people who direct similar nonprofits devoted to fighting human trafficking."

"It is?"

He nodded. "Rescuing someone from trafficking isn't as simple as you'd hope it might be. Separating the person—most often for us it's a woman—from the source of her security and the person who has convinced her she is nothing without him is a huge battle."

His words pricked at a wound. Avery swallowed hard against the unexpected emotion tightening her throat. "I've just been thinking about how hard it is to start over. Reinventing yourself feels overwhelming, especially if you have children." She ducked her head. "Sorry. I made this about me."

"Avery."

There it was again, her name on Cole's lips. So kind. So reverent. Making her feel like she could become or do anything.

"You can always tell me what's on your mind. And I always want to hear your recommendations."

Cole's kindness made her want to weep.

"You don't need to worry about reinventing yourself, by the way. You're going to be just fine."

"That's sweet of you to say. I feel like Pax and Trey left and took the blueprints for our future with them."

"Make your own way forward," Cole said. "You don't need them."

"But I feel adrift creatively right now," she confessed, staring past him. "I know it's weird to be admitting that when you hired me as your consultant, but it's true. All I know for sure is that I want women to feel proud of what they've accomplished at the end of the day."

"Me too." Cole frowned. "It's getting more and more difficult to convince trafficking victims to choose freedom over bondage."

His words pierced her. Bondage. She wasn't trafficked but she'd certainly found herself in bondage to ideas, opinions and even the choices made by her former spouse and business partner. Not to mention her own expectations and people's judgments about her life circumstances.

Had she really sacrificed her own happiness and the security of her children to please her adoring fans? The same fans who turned on her? Was her whole life a facade? Shame slithered in. How long had she lived this false narrative, convinced it was what she had to display for the world to see? It was all a lie. A perfectly curated, filtered lie of a life. She'd actually thought the social media version of her family was the one worth saving.

Panic flooded her limbs with the urge to run. She flipped

her notebook shut. "I have to go. Harper's babysitting for me and I promised I'd be home by—"

"Wait." Cole's hand shot out and covered hers. "There's something I have to tell you."

*Give her an opportunity to shine…make her believe she can't live without you.*

Oy. Hemby. His advice had climbed inside Cole's head and taken up residence. Now he couldn't shake his best friend's so-called wisdom.

"This won't take long, but it's important." He pulled back and reached for his coffee again. As if the dregs of his mocha could fuel enough confidence to get the words out. Really he just needed someplace to put his hands, instead of letting his thoughts wander to the way her skin had felt when he'd touched her a few minutes ago. How her skin was smooth and warm and she looked incredible in a pale pink blouse and…

"I can stay for about ten more minutes." She remained seated across from him in the coffee shop. "What's up?"

He finished his coffee and gathered his courage. Their impromptu brainstorming session had pulled them into an intimate conversation and Avery had revealed more of her struggles. That had always been their way. She had always been so honest. So real with him. And he hated that she'd felt so trapped in her relationship with Pax. That her partnership with Trey had been so costly. He longed to help her find freedom from all the things that weighed her down. Why couldn't she see about herself what he and the rest of the world saw?

"Cole? Is everything all right?"

"Yeah, we've just had some new developments." He picked up his pen and thumped the end against his yellow notepad. Outside the coffee shop window, he caught a glimpse of Pastor and Mrs. Crawford walking toward the door. His stomach clenched. *Please keep walking, please keep walking.*

Maybe he should tell Avery everything, starting with Nana's arrival in his office. The giant chunk of cash she'd donated and his foolish promise to hire Avery. He met her cautious gaze. But if he told her everything, she'd never speak to him again. And the thought of moving forward on this project, especially when she shared his vision for the potential of Imari's Place, well, he just couldn't bring himself to jeopardize that.

"So Hemby told me he got a phone call from someone who films documentaries. They've heard about the work we're doing here for human trafficking, and they'd like to feature… They'd like to feature us."

Her eyebrows tented. "Us? Like you and me, us." She wagged her finger back and forth between them.

Warmth heated his skin. One simple word conjured so many daydreams.

"We're hardly doing anything that's worthy of a documentary," she said, opening and closing the cover on her notebook. Her gaze skittered toward the coffee shop's front door and her expression hardened. The Crawfords must've arrived.

"Well, that's debatable." He shifted in his seat, wishing with everything in him that he could somehow shield her from another painful interaction with her former in-laws. "You're clearly invested in this project. Based on the meetings we've already had, you've agreed to consult on the expansion. Before I tell them yes or no, I wanted to have a conversation with you."

"Are you asking for my permission?"

He nodded.

"I don't know. The last time I was on camera, it did not go well for me."

"That is so not true." The words were out before he could stop them. "You were stunning."

*Like always.* At least he had the good sense to keep that last part to himself.

Voices hummed behind him, punctuated by boisterous laughter. Cole winced. Pastor Crawford's arrival had provoked a reaction inside the shop. He was good at that. Avery gnawed on her lower lip.

Cole scrambled to hold her attention. "I have absolutely zero experience, but I would imagine a reality TV show for a major network has a slightly different objective than a documentary."

"True." Her gaze floated away, and he could see her fiddling with the clasp on her handbag. She'd always fidgeted when she was nervous.

"I don't have to give them an answer right now, but they're going to want to hear from me soon. It wouldn't be fair for me to move forward without your blessing."

"But you don't want to tell them no." Her beautiful eyes pierced his. "I'm trying to understand your perspective."

He pushed his fingers through his hair. "I've worked so long and so hard to bring awareness to what these women are going through. So many times I felt like I was just shouting into the void."

"Don't say that." She frowned. "Countless lives have been changed by the work you've done."

"But think about how many more could be impacted if people paid attention. The more we talk about human trafficking, the more people might be moved to get involved. To want to make a difference. It's the hope that I cling to. That's what keeps me going."

She tucked her notebook into her handbag. "And you're confident that a documentary will reach the target audience and educate people in a way that motivates them to donate money or shop more intentionally?"

"Yes."

She got quiet then cast another furtive glance behind him. "I've got to go. Let me think about it and I'll let you know. Are we still meeting next Friday?"

"Absolutely. Let's meet at the job site. I'll have the project manager stop by and we can chat. Make sure we're all on the same page about next steps."

"Perfect. I'll be there." Her smile didn't quite reach her eyes. "Thanks for your time."

"Of course. Want me to walk out with you? I've got to get back to my office."

Her nervous glance toward the shop's counter confirmed he was wise to offer.

"Please do."

They stood and pushed their chairs in. He collected their cups and tossed them in the trash nearby. Pastor Crawford stepped into his path as he pivoted toward the door. "Cole Whitaker? Is that you?"

Cole forced his mouth into a smile. "Pastor Crawford."

For a man whose arrival created quite a stir, he was rather small. Cole towered over him. Pastor Crawford rubbed his hand over his bald head. His leathery tan skin crinkled as he offered an artificial smile. "I'd forgotten you and Avery were so close."

"Pardon?"

Pastor Crawford brushed past him without responding. Cole turned to see Avery's reaction. "Hello, Dalton."

Cole sensed the weight of customers' curious stares. Poor Avery. Irritation burned in his chest. It was unfortunate that she had to run into the Crawfords in a busy coffee shop.

"Whitney mentioned you were back in town." Pastor

Crawford folded Avery into a hug. Her polite smile quickly faded, replaced by a pinched expression. She looked like she'd rather encounter a snake than hug this man. Cole jammed his hands in his pockets, powerless to intervene.

"Yes, the kids and I are visiting my family." Avery pulled back and swung her purse strap over her shoulder. "I need to run. My sister is watching them and Hayes will need to be fed soon."

"Oh, I'm looking forward to seeing those rascals. Bring them on by sometime." Pastor Crawford's voice echoed off the walls. Undoubtedly he wanted the whole place to know what a doting grandfather he was.

Cole glanced at Whitney, still speaking with a woman near the end of the coffee bar.

Avery hesitated. "I'll have to check my calendar then touch base with Whitney. Let's talk soon."

"You know where to find us." Pastor Crawford's gray eyes swiveled to Cole. Something undecipherable flickered across his features.

Cole gave a brief nod. "Have a good day, sir."

Avery strode toward the door like the place was on fire. Thankfully, Whitney continued her conversation and didn't glance in their direction. Cole recognized a couple of friends he played tennis with sitting by the door and offered a quick wave.

Avery strode outside, her chin held high. The midday sun greeted them like they'd stepped into a furnace.

"That was dicey," he said, once the door swung shut behind them.

"Sure was. Thanks for sticking with me. That's the first time I've seen him since, well, since I was still married to Pax." She offered a quick wave before she turned toward her vehicle parked down the street. "See you Friday."

"Yeah, see you Friday." He walked back to his office, guilt weighing him down. Had he handled that well? Was he supposed to run interference between Avery and the Crawfords? To an outsider, that was probably a harmless interaction. But the unspoken words and the tension hovering in the air had been impossible to ignore.

She hadn't said no about the documentary. She hadn't said yes, either. He was glad he hadn't mentioned anything about Maribelle's donation. He could see little hints that Avery was healing. Like a cherry tree about to blossom in the spring, she was slowly stepping forward out of the aftermath of her divorce. So maybe he was being selfish, but he could live with that if it meant partnering with Avery to achieve a common goal. Because that's all this was about. Nothing more.

If there was one thing she lived for it was Sunday lunch with her people. Maribelle settled on the sofa and heaved a contented sigh.

Harper smiled at her. "Feeling good, Nana? Are you ready for a nap?"

"By golly, I believe so." Maribelle smoothed her hand over the sofa's white linen fabric. Greer sat in the recliner, newspaper on his lap and remote in hand. He'd put a baseball game on the television. Maribelle loathed baseball. Not enough action and the games dragged on for hours. She could hardly complain, though. The man had been good to her and her family.

Addison's protests filtered down the hallway as her grandmother coerced her into getting ready for a nap with the promise of reading three stories instead of two. Julene stood by the window with Hayes nestled in her arms. She swayed gently back and forth. Maribelle made a mental note to put finding a husband for that girl on her to-do list. She was young, and she'd make an excellent mother. How had the single men of Camellia not noticed her?

Unless they had come calling and Maribelle hadn't been informed. That did not sit well. She shifted, trying desperately to stay awake. Now was the perfect time to glean important details about what these women were up to. If she fell asleep, she'd miss everything.

Harper joined Avery at the table in the dining room. Maribelle longed to be a part of that conversation. The fried chicken and potato salad had been especially delicious today. She'd even scored a slice of chocolate chess pie. This sofa probably cost a fortune, but it was quite comfortable. Her eyelids grew heavy. She let her chin dip to her chest.

"I don't know, Harper. A documentary is a big deal. That might mean doing an interview, being on camera and answering a whole lot of questions that I'm not ready to answer." Avery's soft voice broke through Maribelle's hazy thoughts. A documentary? Cole hadn't mentioned a word about that.

"Cole must value your perspective or he wouldn't have asked you to be a part of this," Julene said. "I think it's sweet that he asked for your permission before committing to anything."

Maribelle silently agreed. He was so smart, that Cole. All he'd needed was a little incentive.

"A documentary can bring a lot of positive attention to an important cause," Harper said. "Did you look up the production company to see what other films they've made?"

"I didn't get that far yet," Avery said. "I'm leaning toward saying yes, but I need to think about it some more. We meet again on Friday and I'll decide by then."

"I think you should go for it," Harper chimed in.

"Yes, indeed," Maribelle mumbled.

The ladies laughed.

Maribelle sat up with a start. She glanced around the room. The girls were all looking at her and smiling. Had she said something out loud? Greer's newspaper crinkled as he gave her the side-eye. "We thought you were asleep."

"This old bird's always listening, dear." Maribelle smiled sweetly. This conversation was just getting good. She had to stay awake. At least for a few more minutes. She pinched the tender skin between her thumb and her index finger to keep from nodding off. Maybe she could talk her body into cooperating and moving to an empty seat at the table.

"Did I tell you that Cole asked me about our napkin pledge?" Avery asked.

"What are you talking about?" Julene moved closer to Maribelle, studying her. "Nana, are you all right?"

"I'm a bit thirsty, sweetie. Could you help me sit at the table and perhaps bring me a glass of tea?"

Julene nodded. "Um, sure. Greer? Can you help, please?"

"Absolutely." Greer set his paper aside and stood. "Maribelle, let's bring you over to join the ladies."

Normally she wasn't a fan of being handled like a sack of rice but her legs just weren't interested in obeying any reasonable commands today. "Thank you, Greer."

"Oh, yes, I remember the napkin pledge," Harper said. "I can't believe you brought that up."

Maribelle concentrated on putting one foot in front of the other. Greer braced her elbow and gently guided her toward an empty upholstered chair at the dining room table. She sank into the armless chair with a sigh of relief.

"I'll get you that glass of tea." Greer patted her shoulder then strode into the kitchen.

"Now, what's all this talk about a napkin?" Maribelle scanned the girls' faces. This sounded like something she needed to be aware of.

"If Cole and I are going to be working together, we're probably going to talk about all kinds of things. We have quite a history," Avery said, flipping open her notebook.

Maribelle studied her. Was she blushing?

"He came by the other night and brought ice cream. He felt terrible about the way he handled Addison's bee sting." Avery pulled a cocktail napkin from a pocket inside the notebook's cover. "Here it is."

"Oh, can I see it?" Harper held out her hand. "This is quite the relic."

Maribelle's head was spinning. She was so tired she could hardly keep up, but this was a development she'd never anticipated.

"Aren't you glad you skipped your nap?" Julene teased. "This is breaking news."

"Well, I can't miss out on my girl time now, can I?" She leaned closer, itching to get her fingers on that wrinkled napkin. "Oh, by golly. Would you look at that? It's almost like the two of you were meant to be."

Silence blanketed the table. Avery's cheeks flushed a deeper shade of pink. "I wouldn't go that far, Nana. We'd both been disappointed by our dates. It was a rough night. We made a joke to make ourselves feel better. I don't know why I've kept this all these years."

"But here you are both single and interested in similar things." Julene sighed. "Sometimes timing is everything."

Avery angled her head toward Hayes. "I'm also a single mother of two. Cole hasn't indicated he's real interested in becoming anyone's stepfather."

Greer returned with Maribelle's glass of sweet tea. "It's nice work if you can get it."

The girls all laughed.

"Thank you, dear." Maribelle reached for her tea. Maybe a few sips and the sugar would make her more alert.

"I think that boy is married to his work," Harper said.

"I do believe you're right," Maribelle said, shaking her head in mock dismay. "It will take a special woman to help him realign his priorities."

Okay, so she was laying it on a little thick. But she couldn't let her granddaughters know what she'd been up to. They'd never forgive her for all this meddling in their affairs. Even if she had the best of intentions.

Harper whipped out her phone. "Let me take a picture of this."

"Oh, do it. Let's post it on Avery's socials." Julene grinned. "People will go bananas."

Avery snatched the napkin back and slipped it inside the notebook. "No, no pictures. I wanted to show you, but now it's going back into hiding."

"If it's not a big deal, then why do you still have it?" Harper asked.

Avery lifted one shoulder. Her mouth tipped up in a smile. "Cole's always been a good friend to me. I like to reminisce, that's all."

Oh, boloney. Maribelle took another sip of her tea to keep from saying what she was thinking. She carefully filed all the details of this discovery away. This was better than anything she could have concocted on her own. To think these two had set this plan in motion decades ago and now all she had to do was give them more nudges. They couldn't have made it any easier. My oh my, she couldn't wait to tell Lucille about this. It wouldn't be long and these two would be riding off into the proverbial sunset. Together.

# Chapter Eight

Avery sat alone at the kitchen table with her phone, laptop and a sketch pad in front of her. She had one day until her meeting with Cole at the construction site. One day. Between taking care of the kids and stressing about them spending an entire weekend with their father, she hadn't been able to focus. Hayes no longer cried and turned away when offered a bottle, but she was still conflicted about being away from him for two whole days.

But showing up unprepared for her meeting wasn't an option.

After flipping through her mother's old issues of *Southern Living* and *House Beautiful*, and spending more hours than she'd cared to admit scrolling online and watching home renovation shows, (although not her own—she avoided those episodes), a cohesive plan for the home's interior still eluded her.

Maybe the solution was to stop thinking about Cole and that silly napkin. Her conversation with Nana and her sisters on Sunday afternoon kept replaying in her head. She opened her notebook and took out the napkin again. Harper and Julene had been right. A throwback post on social media about the napkin and her bond with Cole would resonate. Even her fickle audience would go bananas for a glimpse into her personal life. But Cole had given her the courtesy of asking her opinion about the documentary. She owed him the same. Sure, they had a past. But were they willing to put it all out there for public consumption?

She opened an app on her phone and scrolled to a recent post. Since Julene had put up that picture of a view from the lake house and launched her return to social media, she'd added a few more posts on her own. It hadn't been so bad, really. A sunset view from the dock, a gorgeous bouquet of flowers on the kitchen island and an adorable image of Hayes's bare feet had all garnered plenty of likes and pleasant comments.

A notification alerted her that someone had tagged her. Uh-oh. She hesitated then tapped the screen and read the caption.

Staycation photo dump! Hubs and I have had the most amazing week off, enjoying all the incredible venues our beautiful Camellia has to offer. Wasn't gonna post EVERYTHING I saw downtown, but this was too good not to share. Look who has a new man in her life! Is it just me or are sparks flying? Be sure to swipe to the last one. The camera doesn't lie. Am I right?

An icy tingle danced along her spine.

She swiped to see all the photos. The first five featured mediocre shots of downtown Camellia, plus the pond she and Mama had walked around with the kids. She swiped again. The image of her and Cole at the coffee shop together wasn't unflattering. They leaned toward each other at the table. Her expression looked earnest. The camera had been angled to catch only part of Cole, but had included enough to clearly indicate his smile. To any casual observer—or nosy social media frenemy—they appeared to be engaged in a deeply meaningful conversation.

Which wasn't misleading. They'd both been excited about their shared vision for Imari's Place. Still, the caption implied something romantic. Okay, so she'd thought about a relationship with Cole, especially after he'd dropped by with frozen custard. But nothing had happened. They weren't dating. And she resented the online speculation implying that he was her new man.

This was once a platform where she was revered as the queen of home decor and could pop in for a virtual visit and receive dozens of comments and questions on any given day. Sadly, if one post plunged her into a tailspin, what would happen if the documentary was filmed?

Was she foolish for hoping to encounter support and affirmation?

She should've put down the phone. But that comment about sparks flying in the post wasn't something she could ignore. Or the reference to the camera not lying. Worse, the last photograph featured her speaking with Pax's father. Her features were twisted into an aggravated expression.

Her hand shook as she scrolled through the comments. Several had garnered dozens of "likes."

Gurrrrl, these photos are gold. Can't believe you didn't post sooner. So is this her new man??

I always knew something sketchy was going on with this family. Seriously, how can anyone's life truly be that perfect? It's nice to know things aren't as they seem.

"Thank you for your honesty, Liza MacGregor." Avery resisted the urge to neutralize all those "likes" with a comment of her own featuring only the angry face and barfing emojis. "You didn't seem to think I was sketchy when you hired us to redecorate your home two years ago, now did you? And I didn't hear any complaints when the project was featured on the cover of *Alabama Living*, either."

The MacGregor project had been one of the few where Trey hadn't monopolized their creative pitch or dismissed her design ideas. To her surprise, he'd seemed content to play a supporting role. Avery shook her head in disgust but still she kept reading, appalled at the venomous judgment oozing from every word. Didn't any of these women have strained relationships with their extended family? Wasn't that part of normal life?

Maybe that was where she went wrong. Assuming a normal life was even possible anymore.

Just goes to show you can't have it all. Sure, she's rich, famous and gorgeous, but she obviously can't keep her husband satisfied. #Justsaying.

Avery gasped and pressed her fingertips to her mouth. Rich and famous? And now the intimacy in her marriage was up for debate? She shouldn't be surprised. Of course it was. The crass words and flippant observations cut deep, though. What did people hope to gain from commenting publicly on her family's demise? And why was Pax's decision to step outside their marriage her fault? Her stomach twisted. She was about to abandon the app when the name of the next commenter caught her eye.

No.

It's a real shame that people refuse to admit when they've let their careers take precedence over their families. I wish I could say I'm surprised, but I've seen this coming for years.

"You have?" Avery smacked her palm against the table. "Then why didn't you say something, Genevieve? If you knew my husband was gay, it would've been super helpful if you'd mentioned it to me, because I had no idea!" she ranted at the screen.

"Avery, who are you yelling at?" Julene swept into the room, clutching her phone in one hand and an iPad in the other, her perfect brow marred with concern.

Tears slid down Avery's cheeks as she held her phone toward her sister. Genevieve ran the children's ministry program at The Oasis. They'd known each other since high school. Avery had vacationed with this woman, belonged to the same youth group and attended numerous dinners at Pax's parents' home with Genevieve and her family. Until now, Avery would've considered her a close friend.

"Is this how we treat each other now? We shame people publicly then tell them we always suspected they were failures?" Avery swiped angrily at the moisture on her cheeks.

Julene studied the screen, scrolled quickly then powered off the phone and set it on the table.

"Unbelievable." She sank to her knees beside Avery's chair and flung her arms around her. "I'm so sorry. I'm the one who posted that first picture when you moved back home and told you to get back out there, and now this happened."

Avery sniffed and leaned her head against Julene's. "This is not your fault."

"But I feel partly responsible for your suffering. People in this town love to tear each other apart. They use social media as a way to say things that they would never say to you in person." Julene pulled back. Tears glistened in her eyes. "Listen to me. You are smart, your children are amazing and you have a tremendous gift of sharing beauty with the world. Don't let the haters get you down."

The front door opened. "Mama?" Addison's voice echoed through the house, followed by her flip-flops slapping against the hardwood.

Avery's breath caught in her throat. She fumbled for a tissue in her handbag then quickly swiped at her cheeks. Addison came into the kitchen, her face flushed and a telltale ring of chocolate surrounding her mouth. "Mama, are you crying?"

Avery nodded. "Just a little."

Julene smiled then stood and turned to Addison. "Sometimes grown-ups are mean, sweet girl. But don't you worry. Your mama is strong and she's going to be fine. How was the ice cream shop?"

"Good." Addison grinned then pushed past Julene and climbed into Avery's lap. "I had chocolate with rainbrow sprinkles."

Avery smiled at her cute mispronunciation and breathed in her sweet, sugary scent. "Sounds delicious. Did you bring me any?"

"No silly. Too melty. You'll have to get your own." Addison leaned forward and studied Avery's drawings. "Whatcha making?"

"I'm helping Mr. Cole decorate a nice house for some ladies to live in."

Addison settled on Avery's lap, craning her neck to study the magazine spread open on the table. Glossy pages featured a stunning kitchen with a white subway tile backsplash and sage green cabinets. "This is pretty." She licked her finger then flipped the next page. "I'm not a big fan of those lights."

Avery pressed her lips together to contain her laughter. She and Julene exchanged smiles. Evidently Addison had been paying close attention to all the home decorating shows they'd been streaming lately.

"Me, either." Avery had never accepted design ideas from her preschooler. In this case, she had to give Addison credit. The vintage style chandelier suspended above the island in the photograph wasn't the best fit. She made a mental note to choose lighting for Imari's Place. There was still so much to do.

Addison softly hummed a song while she kept flipping through the magazine.

"You're like two peas in a pod," Julene said.

"I wouldn't have it any other way." Avery gently undid the barrette pinning Addison's hair out of her eyes and attempted a do-over.

"No, Mama. I don't like that clippy anymore." She slid from Avery's lap and out of her reach. "I want to color."

Avery sighed and set the barrette on the table. "Go find your coloring book and crayons then."

"And stickers. I need lots of stickers," Addison called over her shoulder as she hurried into the dining room.

Julene watched her go. "How do you keep up?"

"I don't."

Avery checked the time on the stove's digital clock. Hayes was taking an extralong afternoon nap. She quickly jotted some notes in her notebook then folded down a corner of the page and closed the magazine. By the time she had her computer shut down and her notebook and magazines stacked, Addison had returned with her coloring supplies. "Mama, are the ladies nice?"

"Sit here." Avery patted the chair beside her at the table. "Which ladies?"

"The ladies that you're building this house for and making it pretty. Are they nice ladies?"

"I haven't met them yet. I'm sure they're very nice."

"Good 'cause mean people stink."

Julene and Avery chuckled.

"That's true, mean people do stink." Julene pulled out a chair opposite Addison. "Was someone mean to you at the ice cream shop?"

"Nope, but Papa Greer saw someone being rude and he whispered it to me." Addison selected a crayon from the box and started coloring a fresh page.

"Huh." Avery studied her daughter. Surely no one at the ice cream shop would discuss her personal life with Greer in front of Addison. The thought sent a fresh wave of anger coursing through her. Greer hadn't come inside yet. He'd probably gone down to the dock to fiddle with the boat. Avery reached for her phone to text him and make sure everything had gone okay, but Julene snatched it first.

"Hey, I need that."

"Not right now. Why don't we all color together?" Julene produced some scratch paper then handed Avery a piece, along with a meaningful look. "I know I'm the one who told you that you need to spend some time on social media but right now you need to take a breather. I'll handle your next couple posts and keep an eye on the comments."

Avery opened her mouth to object.

"The next time you post, it needs to be a behind-the-scenes video with you on camera talking about your goals and your vision for this project. People will love that, it will draw engagement, and doesn't invite criticism."

"Ha. Everything I post invites criticism." Avery sketched an outline of the lake on her paper with a blue crayon.

"Featuring the project and sharing a brief glimpse helps you look focused instead of…"

"Floundering?" Avery said.

"Exactly."

Addison slid off her chair again. "Mama, can I have a snack?"

"Didn't you just come from the ice cream shop?"

"Yeah, but I'm still hungry."

Avery glanced at the clock again. It would be a couple of hours until they had supper on the table. "How about some carrot sticks, apple slices or yogurt?"

"I'd like a cheese stick, please."

"Here let me help you with that." Julene followed Addison toward the refrigerator.

Avery chose another crayon, a forest green this time, and sketched trees around the lake. Coloring with her daughter was supposed to be relaxing, but her thoughts returned to the online comments she'd read. Addison was right. Mean people did and said some stinky things. Avery couldn't let their words seep in and take root, though.

There wasn't any point in defending the end of her marriage, not even to the people who had been the closest to her and Pax. She was stepping forward into a new life and this was the opportunity God had given her. No, her circumstances didn't look the way she thought they would, but she couldn't let her unmet expectations keep her from growing. These women needed a home and even though she still wondered why Cole had picked her, it was time to fulfill her commitment and stop wondering if he should have chosen someone else.

On Friday morning, Cole parked his car in front of the construction site, grabbed his messenger bag from the passenger seat and climbed out. Nail guns, saws and the aroma of fresh plywood greeted him. The walls had been framed and the joists for the roof were going up.

Two guys wearing cargo shorts and T-shirts with unfamiliar logos hovered near the bumper of a well-loved gray SUV. They stared at their phones. Disposable cups from a local fast-food restaurant sat on the bumper. The men looked about his age, maybe a little younger. Hemby had offered to meet with them and make a formal introduction, but Cole declined. His friend had meddled enough.

"Cole Whitaker?" The taller of the two put his phone away and offered a friendly smile. "I'm Max Johansen."

Cole shook Max's hand. "Nice to meet you."

"This is my brother, Charlie."

The other guy glanced up from his phone and gave a polite nod. "What's up, Cole?"

They both had the same strawberry blond hair, inquisitive blue eyes and smiles that bordered on mischievous.

The knot of tension between Cole's shoulder blades loosened a fraction. He'd expected documentary filmmakers to be…well, he wasn't sure what he expected. More polished? Older dudes with fancy equipment and a luxury car? Instead, Max and Charlie looked like guys who'd lived in his dorm in college.

"Thanks for taking time to meet with us," Max said. "Hemby mentioned you might have some questions."

"He's right." Cole pinched the strap of his bag between his fingers, feeling foolish for not being more articulate. "Tell me again how you know Hemby?"

"Our sister is a paralegal at his law firm," Charlie said. "What's your connection to Hemby?"

"Friends," Cole said. "He's the closest thing I have to a brother."

"Ah." Max nodded. "It all makes sense now."

Cole narrowed his gaze. "What makes sense?"

Max and Charlie exchanged glances. Charlie took a sip of his drink as if punting the conversation to Max.

Max shoved his hands into his pockets. "Our objective here is to tell a compelling story. There aren't any secrets on our end. Whatever we can do to make this more palatable, feel free to ask. Folks usually want to know about the filming process, who we might interview, the implications of appearing in a documentary...that sort of thing."

"Max is being too nice. What Hemby actually said is we'd have to talk you through your hang-ups." Charlie smirked. "That sounds like something a brother would say, right?"

Max offered a can't-argue-with-that shrug.

"Yeah, Hemby's not afraid to say exactly what he thinks." Cole looked away. Oh, how pathetic was he for wanting Avery to be here right now? Not because he couldn't speak with Max and Charlie on his own. Ever since they'd met in the coffee shop last week and she'd shared her ideas about creating a line of products manufactured in Camellia that incorporated vocational training, he couldn't stop thinking about her. She'd been so tentative about accepting the role as a consultant on the project, yet she'd already taken the foundation's mission to heart.

He'd never been prouder of her. And he didn't want to do any of this without her by his side.

"Cole?" Max prompted. "Would you like to walk us through the site now?"

Cole shifted his gaze toward the house. Dale had a crew of six guys working today—a couple of the men were from a local home building company and a few more were volunteers from a men's group at the church on Pine Street.

"If anyone is around, we'd love to chat. Charlie has waivers for everybody to sign." Max rattled the ice in his plastic cup then took another long sip. "No one has to be on camera who doesn't want to be."

"Hold up," Cole said. "We haven't officially given the documentary a green light yet. Not everyone that will be impacted has agreed."

"I'll grab the exterior shots." Charlie left his cup on the hood of the vehicle. Before Cole could object, the guy was moving toward the house.

"Doesn't he need a camera or something?"

"Typically we start our research with a few still shots. Getting the lay of the land, so to speak. Then we'll storyboard and brainstorm, conduct interviews, finalize a shot list and then production officially begins."

"Interviews?" Cole palmed the back of his neck. "That might be a challenge. Did you not hear me? We haven't agreed this is a sure thing. The design consultant we've brought on board hasn't said yes."

"Perhaps we should start with you? Not that anything you say here will make the final cut. I want to give you an idea of my style. It's different than speaking with local media." Max tapped the screen on his phone then held the device toward Cole's chin.

Cole's limbs itched to take a giant step back. Sweat dampened his shirt. Couldn't they have this conversation in a coffee shop? Someplace with sweet tea and robust AC?

"Tell me about your foundation, what you hope to achieve with Imari's Place and why people should care enough to invest emotionally or financially in your cause."

Thoughts of Avery, sitting at the table in the coffee shop, with her notebook and her bold vision for the foundation's future filled his head. Too bad she wasn't here. She'd felt slighted when she hadn't been part of the groundbreaking ceremony. He didn't want to make that mistake twice.

Except he wasn't being entirely honest with himself. What he really wanted was to see her again.

Somehow he had to find a way to separate the documentary about his work with the foundation and his friendship with Avery. He could do that, right? People struck a healthy balance between their work life and their personal life all the time.

Except he'd never been one of those people.

"Take me back to how this all started," Max coached him. "What was that initial spark that inspired you to advocate for trafficking victims?"

Thoughts of his beautiful sister, perpetually eleven years old with her sable hair, contagious laughter and wide-set eyes, filled his head. Followed by Avery buying him frozen custard because she didn't know how else to help him. He'd been so distraught.

"My sister, Kimberly, was abducted seventeen years ago. She was later murdered. I've always felt compelled to do something to help people, but couldn't quite identify my passion. At first, I worked long hours at a law firm. One day on my commute, I heard a podcast interview about an organization in Nashville that helped women rescued specifically from human trafficking. That inspired me to leave the firm and take the role as director of Imari's Place. I'll never be able to bring my sister back, but this is meaningful and important work, and I truly believe we're making a difference."

Max nodded, his Adam's apple bobbing as he swallowed

hard. "That's cool, man. I had no idea. I'm so sorry about your sister."

"Thank you." Cole gestured toward the house. "Generous folks here in Camellia, across the country and strategic global partners made the existing facility possible. Now we're focused on a substantial expansion, so we can bring more women here. Ideally we help them get an education, either with additional vocational training or through a college or university. There's counseling, medical care and each is responsible for caring for a certain aspect of the home."

Cole paused then dug in his bag for a bottle of water. He could go on and on.

Max stopped recording and pocketed his phone. "Nicely done."

"Thanks." Cole drew a long sip of water, swallowed then twisted the cap back into place.

"One thing I failed to mention. The consultant I mentioned earlier has a much bigger vision. She'd like to see a separate facility constructed here in Camellia that would allow the women to produce a particular product line. Perhaps household goods or toiletries, something of that nature. The sales of which would go back into operations, community outreach, etcetera."

Max studied him. "Sounds ambitious."

"Indeed."

Max clapped Cole on the shoulder. "Great start. My brother and I are on a fact-finding mission today. We want to chat with you, get to know you and your team. If you don't mind, I'd like to connect with the consultant you mentioned. We're going to want to hear more about that additional facility."

"I'll see what I can do," Cole said. "She left the reality

television world and would prefer to stay off camera for now. Maybe she'll change her mind later."

"Maybe so." There was that mischievous smile again. "After all, it didn't take much to get Hemby to change your mind. Can you ask him to speak to this consultant?"

No way. "Where's Charlie? Let me take a look at those waivers."

After spending most of the night with an inconsolable baby, the last place Avery wanted to be in her sleep-deprived, irritable condition was Dalton and Whitney Crawfords' driveway. But the invitation had arrived via text at the last minute yesterday. She couldn't keep putting this off. Addison deserved to know her grandparents better.

"Whoa. Is this where I'm swimming today?" Addison asked, unbuckling herself and scrambling out of her car seat.

"This is the place. Pretty nice, right?" Avery infused her voice with as much optimism as she could muster. Mama and Greer's house was equally impressive in comparison to the Crawfords' sprawling white brick home nestled on a hillside in Camellia's most sought-after neighborhood. Much like her own family, Dalton and Whitney had embraced a more lavish lifestyle. Mama had mentioned that The Oasis had several thousand members now. Quite a change from when they launched in a modest apartment complex clubhouse almost fifteen years ago. Avery shook her head. So pointless, sitting here overanalyzing why her former in-laws had purchased this ostentatious home. Frankly, it was none of her business.

"Come on, Mama. Let's go inside."

"I'm right behind you, baby." Avery turned off the ignition and unlocked the car doors so Addison could get out. When Whitney had first mentioned she wanted to have the kids over to swim, Avery hadn't expected to hear from her. Maybe Pax and Trey's arrival next week had something to do with it. Whitney must've realized she'd be helping with the kids and decided a short visit today would make future visits more palatable.

"I want to swim, Mama." Addison scampered around the back of the car, dancing and twirling.

"I know you do. Let me get Hayes." He'd been fussing off and on most of the night and tugging at his ear. Avery had called the local pediatrician's office and begged them to work him in. Thankfully a friend of the family managed the practice and had agreed. Avery had meant to schedule his first well visit as soon as she moved back to town, but the task had slipped to the bottom of her to-do list.

Avery opened the passenger door and unbuckled Hayes from his car seat. The pitiful tears on his pudgy cheeks and flushed skin made her wince. Poor thing. He looked miserable. "Come on, sweet pea. This will just take a minute."

With Hayes tucked gently against her shoulder, she helped Addison get the tote bag with dry clothes, a towel, goggles, floaties and a few toys from the back of the car.

"That's not the pool, is it?" Addison pointed toward the impressive water feature in the center of the well-manicured lawn. Three ornate tiers spilled water into a large round basin.

Avery chuckled. "No, that's a fountain to make the yard look and sound nice. There's probably a bigger pool around back."

The water was soothing. Far more enjoyable to listen to than the grouchy baby she carried in her arms.

"I'm so excited." Addison squealed and skipped along the flagstone path.

*Glad somebody is happy to be here.* Avery's stomach clenched.

Hayes wailed louder. She patted his backside and followed Addison up the steps to the front door. Addison pressed the smart doorbell button.

"Hello there, my little cutie patootie," Whitney's voice greeted them. "I'll be right out."

Eyes wide, Addison glanced up at Avery. "She can see me?"

"Yes, her doorbell is very smart. A camera talks to an app on her phone."

The front door opened and Whitney appeared, wearing a leopard print knee-length dress over her swimsuit. Her smile seemed surprisingly genuine. Bangles and a charm bracelet jangled on her lean tan arms as she sank to her knees. "Hi, sweet girl. Don't you look adorable. I'm so glad you're here. Give me a hug."

Addison hesitated then stepped into Whitney's outstretched arms. "Hi, Grand— I mean, Mimi."

Avery swayed back and forth, desperate to soothe Hayes.

Addison pulled away and reached for the tote bag. "I'm ready to swim."

"Me too." Whitney straightened. "Hello, Avery. It's nice to see you again."

"Likewise, Whitney. Thank you for the invite."

Whitney formed her ruby red lips into a pout. "What's wrong with the little mister? Is he hungry?"

Hayes twisted in Avery's arm, shoving his fist in his mouth.

"I'm taking him to the pediatrician. Pretty sure he has an ear infection." Avery carefully shifted him to her other arm.

"Oh, dear. I was so hoping he'd get to stay."

"I'm afraid not." Avery angled her head toward the bag Addison clutched with both hands. "Addison brought plenty of toys, her goggles and floaties. She'll need to wear those when she's in the water."

"I'd really like for you to come inside and meet Olivia Claire. She's studying elementary education at Auburn and grew up at The Oasis. Her family is lovely and I'm certain you'll approve."

"Approve of what?"

"I've hired her to help look after your children." Whitney stepped back and motioned for them to come inside.

"I trust your judgment. We really need to get going." Avery forced the words out, determined to keep her tone neutral.

Whitney didn't even try to mask her disappointment. "That's unfortunate. We need to spend some time reconnecting."

"We've crossed paths twice now, Whitney. You were either in a hurry to get to lunch or occupied with another conversation."

The silence between them was thicker than the Alabama air after a thunderstorm.

A muscle in Whitney's contoured cheek twitched. "Addison, why don't you scoot on in to the kitchen. Olivia Claire's waiting. The two of you can play for a few minutes and then we'll go out to the pool."

"Bye, Mama." Addison dashed into the next room without looking back.

Avery drew a deep breath and forced herself to meet Whitney's fiery gaze. "I'll be back at 1:30 to pick her up. She doesn't have any food allergies, but she needs constant supervision in the pool."

Whitney heaved a sigh. "I know how to supervise children in my own pool, Avery. As I mentioned, we've hired Olivia Claire so Addison will have more than enough attention."

"I am not questioning your abilities. Only making my expectations clear." Avery offered a thin smile, even though she wanted to scream right along with Hayes. Oh, this was not going well.

"If we're going to have a discussion about expectations, then I have a few of my own to share."

Unbelievable. Avery huffed out a laugh. "Now is not the best time."

"Don't worry, I'll keep it short." Whitney linked her arms across her chest and raised her voice to be heard above Hayes's meltdown. "I'd like for you to be mindful about how you conduct yourself in public."

"I—I don't understand."

"You seem to think I'm not paying attention, but I'm fully aware of who you're spending time with. So clever, aligning yourself with someone who's well respected in Camellia."

Her stomach churned. "Are you referring to Cole? We've been friends for years."

Whitney smirked. "So I've heard. I can see that you've attached yourself to an important cause. I hope you're not spreading yourself too thin and that your intentions are genuine."

"I have no intention of saying or doing anything that would reflect poorly on you, your husband or your son." Anger seeped into her voice, but she refused to be disrespectful. "I'll be back at 1:30. Please take good care of Addison."

She turned and strode back to the car. Hayes was crying so loud the whole neighborhood could probably hear him. He screamed and arched his back as she tucked him into his car seat. Fumbling in the diaper bag, she found a pacifier attached to a string and a clip. Usually he refused, but this time when she offered it, he gladly started sucking. Mercifully, his eyelids grew heavy then fluttered closed.

*Thank You, Lord.* Avery quietly shut the car door then slid behind the wheel and started the car. Her pulse sped as she pulled out of the driveway then worked her way down the hill toward downtown Camellia. Whitney's comments made an unwelcome visit, spooling through her head and provoking several snarky comments that she sort of wished she'd come up with before she'd walked away.

Did people really think she'd agreed to help Cole to make herself look good? And was that true? She cringed then gripped the steering wheel tighter. She'd always struggled with craving other people's approval.

Admitting that, even to herself, stung. As she drove, she silently offered a prayer. Something she hadn't done on a consistent basis for quite some time.

*Lord, I need Your help. I can't navigate these family dynamics on my own. This all feels so convoluted. I want Addison and Hayes to spend time with their grandparents and to have healthy relationships with Pax and Trey. But I'm still so wounded and, if I'm honest, a little angry. My life does not look the way it used to, and I know I'm supposed to be thankful and use this as an opportunity for growth. I'm fumbling in the dark here. Please, please don't let me cause irreparable harm to these precious children. I have so many issues because my dad left and I want to protect them from feeling that pain.*

Tears burned hot against her eyes. She pressed her hand to her mouth and swallowed back the sob cresting in her throat. She would not show up at the doctor's office looking like an emotional wreck.

*Please make a way forward for our family, despite the hurt. Teach me to forgive, Lord. Even though I really, really, don't want to.*

The late afternoon sun baked Camellia with its unforgiving heat, like a pizza in a wood-fired oven. Cole nudged the AC in his car up another notch then sighed and glanced at his phone.

Avery was late. Twenty-two minutes, by his calculations. He glanced in the rear-view mirror. Waves undulated across the pavement. The only vehicle in sight was the white van with its dented bumper and extra ladders mounted on the top. Roberto and his crew didn't let humidity or temperatures in the nineties set them back. They'd been hard at work framing the walls for the expansion project all day, only stopping for lunch and brief water breaks.

Cole stared through the windshield, imagining the day when the whole project was finished and the women had moved in. His brain veered off track, delivering a mental picture of a familiar woman with long brown hair and a wide smile bringing gift baskets by the house. What a cruel trick his mind played on him sometimes, like a twisted puppet master, fabricating a grown-up version of his sister, Kim, and what she might be like as a young adult.

"Of course you'd be here, serving others, trying to make this house a home," he whispered. "You had a heart as wide as the Mississippi."

He slumped against his car's headrest and squeezed his eyes shut. If he hadn't shirked his brotherly responsibilities that horrific day and Kim was still here, would his personal and professional life look any different? Would he have kept practicing law? Married Evangeline and started a family by now?

Groaning, he opened his eyes and cut the engine. That miserable train of thought took him into a dark and ominous tunnel of what-ifs every single time.

Not today. He plucked his phone from the console and exited his vehicle. The humidity enveloped him like a wet bedsheet suspended from his grandmother's clothesline. Avery had exactly five minutes to text him her ETA or he was calling. Max and Charlie wanted to start filming early next week, so he needed to know whether she was on board with the documentary. Or not.

He shoved his phone in his pocket and resisted the urge to pace the sidewalk. Since his conversation with Max this morning, he'd grown increasingly attached to the idea of a documentary. But he wouldn't go back on his word to let Avery weigh in.

He checked his phone for a text from her. Still nothing. He kicked at a pebble on the sidewalk.

The breeze kicked up, rustling the leaves of the giant magnolia tree in the yard behind him. A discarded plastic bottle skittered across the pavement, landing in the well-manicured lawn of a local resident. Cole chased after the litter and snatched it, along with an empty potato chip bag. He quickly disposed of both in the trash bag he kept tied to the back of his passenger seat in his car. All the permits had been approved for the home's expansion, but he knew the residents in this established neighborhood didn't appreciate the construction equipment and crew descending on their turf. The last thing he wanted was to field complaints about trash blowing through their yards.

A vehicle turned the corner. He glanced at the black luxury sedan. Not Avery. Cole waved to the gentleman behind the wheel as he did a slow roll past the construction site. Where was she? Another vehicle rumbled toward him. The pungent aroma of a diesel engine confirmed that this one wasn't Avery, either. Unless she'd borrowed a dual-axle silver pickup with an extended cab.

Dale, the project manager, waved through the windshield as he eased to a stop and claimed the shaded parking spot behind Cole's car.

Dale silenced the engine then shoved the door open. "Hey, buddy."

"Hey." Sweat tunneled down Cole's spine and he wished he'd worn shorts and a T-shirt instead of khaki pants and a collared polo.

"Somebody steal your lunch money?" Dale's eyes crinkled at the corners as he climbed out of the truck then slammed the door.

"Excuse me?"

Dale grinned and hiked up the waist of his jeans. They promptly met the fortress that was his prodigious belly and retreated to hanging low on his hips. "You look a little miffed is all. What's going on?"

"I'm waiting on the designer to show up. She's…" He checked his phone. "Almost thirty minutes late."

"Ah." Dale brushed some crumbs from the front of his green polo shirt. "Waiting on a woman. I get it."

Cole opened his mouth to say something polite about how he normally didn't mind when folks ran late, but that wasn't true. He did mind. A lot, actually. A vehicle turned the corner and drove toward them. Cole studied the front of the SUV and caught a glimpse of Avery's blond hair through the windshield.

Dale followed his gaze. Avery applied the brakes and parked behind Dale's truck. When she opened the door and stepped out, Cole noted Dale admiring Avery's shapely legs and yellow slip-on shoes. He fisted his hands at his sides, but hardly could he admonish Dale, because he was staring too.

Avery stepped onto the sidewalk, closed the door then offered a tight smile. She'd tamed her hair in glossy platinum ringlets. Aviator sunglasses shielded her eyes. A gray-and-yellow-striped dress skimmed her knees. Her arrival sparked something inside, brightened his glum mood, like he'd captured a whole jar of fireflies before bed.

"Ah." Dale's gaze swung back to Cole. "Now it all makes sense."

Cole narrowed his eyes at him, hoping he'd telegraphed his irritation. Gah! Did he have to be so transparent all the time?

Dale ignored him and ambled closer to Avery, pairing a handshake with a welcoming smile. "Hi, I'm Dale."

"Avery Crawford." She shook his hand. "It's nice to meet you."

"I'm the project manager. It's a pleasure to meet you, Miss Crawford. Let me know if I can be of any assistance." Dale turned and winked at Cole. "Looks like your day just got a whole lot better."

Cole angled his head toward the construction site. "Roberto said he needed to see you. Something about a plywood delivery."

Dale's belly jiggled as he laughed. "Sure, I'll go find Roberto."

Avery stood quietly beside Cole, hands clasped in front of her until Dale walked away.

"Sorry I'm late," she said.

"No problem." He studied her. She hadn't removed her sunglasses. The downward turn of her mouth and the pink splotches of color clinging to her cheekbones hinted that she might've cried during the drive over.

"Are you okay?"

She hesitated, trapping her lower lip behind her teeth.

His gaze landed there and suddenly he didn't mind that she'd kept him waiting.

"Pax and Trey are going to be in town soon." She looked away, the breeze lifting some of her curls. "We agreed that he'll see the kids while he's here, so Addison spent some time at Dalton and Whitney's this morning and it didn't go quite like I expected."

Uh-oh. The hair on the back of his neck stood on end. He'd heard Millie Kay bragging about the tickets she'd scored to Pax's book signing. Something about limited seating at an exclusive event at The Oasis.

"How are you feeling about this arrangement?"

"I want to throw up."

"Well, by all means." He gestured with an exaggerated flourish toward the lawn behind them. "I'm sure the neighbors won't mind."

Her lips twitched. "Very funny."

"The guys who want to make the documentary came by earlier. They're ready to start conducting interviews and filming. Are you on board or…"

She nodded. "Let's do it."

He wanted to pump the air with his fist. Instead he kept his hands in his pockets. "Do you have any questions?"

"Just one." She removed her sunglasses. "Do you think I'm using you?"

His heart squeezed in his chest. "Excuse me?"

"Whitney implied that I was helping you with this project to make myself look good." She wrinkled her nose in disgust. "Is that what people are saying?"

"It doesn't matter what people are saying." He stepped toward her, his arms lifting of their own accord. He gently cupped his palms against her bare upper arms. "I asked you to do this because you're smart and talented and more than capable of designing a beautiful functional space."

*And because your grandmother bribed me.*

Her doubtful gaze nearly flattened him. He was being so

selfish. So feckless with her fragile emotions. This was his out. His opportunity to tell her everything. "Avery, I—"

She stepped out of his reach and slung her bag over her shoulder. "I'm okay with the documentary, by the way. I'm sorry I doubted you. It sounds fantastic."

Her weak smile brought little relief.

He shoved aside the guilt niggling at him, harassing him to tell the truth. At least he'd been honest about one thing. She'd asked if he felt she was using him. The answer was no. Regardless of Maribelle's philanthropy, he would've asked for Avery's input anyway. At least that's what he kept telling himself.

## Chapter Nine

"There has to be a way I can convince those two they can't live without each other." Maribelle sprinkled a healthy dose of brown sugar on top of her oatmeal. Oh, how she hated oatmeal. It was worse than an egg white omelet, which was the other less than desirable breakfast option today. But her cholesterol levels had become her nemesis. Her doctor was going to order blood work next week and give her a lecture if her numbers weren't good. So now it was oatmeal for breakfast every single day. A guy who lived down the hall told her that was the secret to throwing the numbers. Probably the brown sugar wasn't in her best interest, but they just needed to let her live her life. She'd made it nearly ninety years. Clearly she had a few things figured out. Since she was still kicking and all. Why weren't folks more receptive to her advice?

"Avery and Cole are being particularly resistant. They've been given ample opportunity to go on a proper date and nothing's happening. I'm not giving up, though. What if I arrange for them to be—"

"Now, listen." Lucille set her spoon delicately on the saucer under her teacup and pressed her lips into a line. "You've done more than your fair share of meddling. It's time to give it a rest."

*Well, I'll be.* Maribelle stared at her, blinked then stared some more. Usually firing a meaningful look Lucille's way made her wilt. Then she'd comply and go along with whatever scheme Maribelle had cooked up. This time was different. Lucille stared right back, her expression unusually frigid and her spine ramrod straight.

"Lucille, I do believe you're having a stroke because that is complete and utter nonsense."

"Maribelle, you are testing my patience. I suggest you proceed with caution before your family turns their backs on you. Then you'll be miserable and alone." She leaned across the table, her fingers trembling against her cloth napkin. "Is that what you want?"

"Gracious me, of course not." Maribelle shifted in her chair. "My family is everything to me. I'm only doing this for them."

"That's preposterous." Lucille slid the pitcher of cream closer. "You're doing this for you. It's always all about you."

Maribelle pressed her palm to the front of her floral print blouse. "I have no idea what you're talking about."

Lucille calmly poured cream into her tea. "Again, with the lies. You won't rest until you've orchestrated every detail of your grandchildren's lives. When will you learn that's a fool's errand?"

"Such harsh language."

Lucille arched one very thin brow. "I'm just getting started. When Avery finds out what you've done and disowns you, you are going to be a bitter, stubborn old woman."

Maribelle's stomach churned and it wasn't because of the oatmeal. "Who said I was bitter?"

"How else do you explain your behavior?"

Her body flashed hot then cold and the breath she sucked in was wobbly. Maybe she was having a stroke or heart attack. Did her jaw feel tight? Was her arm sore? She circled both arms quickly, windmill style.

Lucille's eyes widened. "What are you doing?"

"Making sure I'm not having a stroke. I feel funny."

"That's called guilt, Maribelle." Lucille took a tiny bite of her buttered toast. "It's consuming you."

Well, didn't she look all smug. And why was she eating butter on her toast? Her cholesterol was probably fine. Lucille rarely did anything dangerous. Come to think of it she rarely did anything even remotely questionable. So boring.

"I know what you're thinking by the way." Lucille primly dabbed at the corners of her mouth with her napkin. "I haven't taken a lot of risks in my life, but in case you hadn't noticed my family isn't drowning in a heap of drama."

"I am not responsible for the drama that Avery is dealing with. She has her ex-husband to thank for all of that mess."

Lucille hesitated then took another bite of her omelet.

Maribelle leaned forward. "You think I'm responsible?"

"You certainly haven't improved the situation. If you hadn't interfered—"

"Lucille, being philanthropic is not a crime. I'd hardly call being generous an interference." Maribelle raised her voice enough to draw stares from the neighbors dining at the next table. She dialed it back a notch and tried to convince her galloping pulse to slow down. "My generous contribution to Cole's foundation will make it possible for lots of women to start over. You are not going to make me feel guilty about that. And did you know they are going to make a movie about what Cole is doing over there at that residential facility?"

"Your generosity is to be commended," Lucille said dryly. "And who would watch a movie about girls who've survived trafficking?"

"Plenty of people, especially if Avery's in it. Don't forget, she had that TV show everyone loved."

Lucille reached for her glass of orange juice. "Until it was canceled."

It wasn't canceled. Was it? Maribelle opened her mouth to protest then clamped it shut. Lucille only had one oar in the water if she thought they were going to sit here and argue about this.

"Mark my words, it's the bribery that's going to cause a problem," Lucille said quietly.

Maribelle pushed her oatmeal away, accompanied by a dramatic eye roll. Everyone was making such a big deal about how Avery was going to feel when she found out about Maribelle's agreement with Cole. Now, that was preposterous. How in the world would she ever find out? Even if she did, she'd probably be grateful. Not angry. Thanks to her quick thinking, Avery had an opportunity to make a fresh start. This was her time to shine. When all was said and done, she'd have herself a new man and a project that she could be proud of. Still, Maribelle couldn't shake the nagging sensation that maybe Lucille was right. If her family got so upset that they refused to speak to her she'd be crushed. Lights out. Game over. She couldn't live with herself if she didn't have her family. Apart from them she was nothing.

She couldn't wait to get to Imari's Place. Avery mashed on the accelerator a little harder than necessary and sped toward the gate. She had to leave before Harper, Mama and Greer changed their minds. Laughter bubbled from her lips as she envisioned Harper swinging a grappling hook superhero style down the driveway and snagging her bumper. Addison was in a mood tonight. It would likely take all three adults and the patience of Job to keep her occupied until bedtime. Hayes thankfully had cheered up since yesterday. The liquid antibiotics the pediatrician prescribed must be working.

Visiting Imari's Place wasn't how she'd initially planned to spend her Saturday evening. But Cole had sent her a text that he'd arranged for her to chat with Wendy and Shayla, two women who had lived at the home for more than a year. After visiting the site, she had several questions. Cole's suggestion that Wendy and Shayla could share their insights had infused her with a creative energy she hadn't experienced in months. Meeting women whose lives would be directly impacted by her design choices gave her a sense of purpose.

Long rays of sunlight filled her car with a golden glow. Freedom beckoned. Still, she paused and waited for the gate to slide open. Hayes had finally taken a bottle yesterday when she'd been at her meeting with Cole. The pediatrician had even suggested she offer baby cereal this morning, which she'd done. He'd eaten a few bites. But what if he refused to take the bottle tonight and cried until she got home? What if Greer and Mama placated Addison's tantrum with too much sugar and processed junk?

They wouldn't. Pax and Trey would be in Camellia in less than six days, regardless of how things went tonight for her children. There was no denying she'd be handing them off in less than a week, and she had to get used to letting go.

She drove through the open gate and onto the road, drawing deep, calming breaths to soothe her anxious thoughts. Pax had turned out to be a not-so-great husband, but she had to keep reminding herself that initially he'd been a wonderful dad. Patient and attentive to Addison's needs. Even during her colicky phase, he'd spent many an evening driving her around Raleigh to give Avery some relief from the constant crying. There wasn't a reasonable explanation for why he'd abandoned his kids. Part of her wanted to blame Trey for wooing Pax away from his responsibilities as a husband and father. Okay, most of her wanted to keep blaming Trey. But Pax had to take responsibility for his own actions. If he wanted a relationship with Addison and Hayes, then she'd have to dredge up the courage to graciously offer him the opportunity.

Even though the thought of a shared custody arrangement still made her stomach lurch like she was riding the Tennessee Tornado rollercoaster at Dollywood.

Tonight, she had to stop obsessing over her children and focus on the gargantuan task at hand. Dale, the project manager, had mapped out an aggressive timeline. He recommended they choose flooring, countertops, plumbing fixtures and lighting as soon as possible. The sooner the expansion was finished, the sooner more women could move in, ideally by Christmas. She gnawed on her thumbnail while she drove, the other hand white-knuckling the wheel.

Did she have the knowledge or ability to take this on? Not like she could tuck tail and run. Instead, she'd show up with sustenance and get Shayla and Wendy to tell her more about what they needed to thrive in their home environment.

Less than thirty minutes later, she pulled into the cul-de-sac in front of Imari's Place with fried chicken sandwiches, four large orders of fries, diet and regular soda, sweet tea and lemonade. All picked up from the drive-through of a favorite local fast-food restaurant. She reached into the paper bag, snagged a french fry and popped it in her mouth, wincing as the heat singed her tongue. Lights glowed from the front windows of the house next door, although the construction site was completely dark.

Greer had offered her two camping lanterns, battery powered, which she'd tucked on the floorboards behind her seat. After she chatted with Wendy and Shayla, and they ate their meal, she wanted to spend some time in the unfinished building. The absence of the crew and somewhat cooler evening temperatures might make it possible for her to think and plan and dream.

When she climbed out of the car, another vehicle pulled in behind her. The driver parked, cut the engine and climbed out. Cole. Delight swelled in her chest. She rubbed her palm against the cotton fabric of her V-neck T-shirt. What was that about?

"Hey." He strode toward her, his tall athletic frame clad in gray cotton shorts and a vintage Auburn T-shirt. Her gaze fell on his muscular biceps then slipped to his broad chest.

"Thanks for meeting me here." She jangled her keys, forcing her eyes to inch upward.

"No problem." His amused glance sent heat to her face. Had he noticed her checking him out?

"Although I'm sorry to tell you, Wendy and Shayla aren't going to make it."

"Oh, no." She tipped her head toward her car. "I have enough supper in here for at least four people."

"You didn't have to go to all that trouble."

"It's fast food. No trouble at all. Besides, I didn't want to show up empty-handed."

"I'm sorry. They are normally quite reliable. Shayla picked up an extra shift at work, and when Wendy found out, she bailed. Since she had the night off, she probably wants to hang out with some friends."

"I understand." She bit her lip, trying to mask her disappointment.

"I don't want to go into the house if we're not meeting

Wendy and Shayla," Cole said. "That's intrusive. Do you want to eat in the construction site?"

She glanced toward the unfinished building. The exterior walls and the roof were up. A temporary set of steps were in place, assembled from cinder blocks and extra plywood. "Sure. Can you grab the drinks?"

"Of course." She circled around the front of her car to the passenger side. Cole took the cardboard drink carrier and she grabbed the bags of food. After nudging the car door shut with her hip, she picked her way across the yard, grateful she'd worn white canvas slip-on shoes instead of flip-flops. No telling what was lurking in the red clay.

The smell of sawdust and new plywood greeted her when she passed through the open doorway, mingling with the aroma of the fried food wafting from the bags in her hands. Cole set the drink carrier down and quickly made a table from two sawhorses and two-by-fours stacked nearby. The sun wouldn't set for another hour or two, but without any electricity inside, shadows crept in.

"Greer gave me some battery-powered lanterns." She put the food on the makeshift table. "They're still in the car behind the driver's seat."

"I'll get them." His sneakers thumped against the floor as he went back outside. A few minutes later, he returned with a lantern bobbing in each hand. He set them on the table beside the bags of food. The silvery blue light flooded the room.

"Probably not the ambiance you envisioned, but it'll do. Were you really planning to work tonight?" Cole reached inside the bag and lifted out a carton of french fries and a sandwich wrapped in a foil-lined paper bag.

"After I talked to Wendy and Shayla, I was hoping I'd have a chance to think and dream without so many people around." It was true. Mostly. Yeah, she'd wanted to hear about Imari's

Place from a resident's point of view. But she also needed extra time to come up with a beautiful functional space. Frankly, Whitney's comments about her motivations had stuck with her. She still hadn't been able to shake the implication that this was somehow all about her.

Cole handed her a packet of her favorite dipping sauce. She took it and smiled. "Thank you. I can't believe you remembered. First the frozen custard and now my favorite sauce."

"How could I forget? You're the only person I've ever met who doesn't like ketchup with their fries."

Avery pulled a face. "Then you haven't met very many interesting people."

He chuckled and unwrapped his chicken sandwich. "I've met you. That's what matters."

His words gave her pulse an excuse to frolic. She quickly batted away the compliment. "There are plenty of people who could help you make this building a true home. I just happened to be your conveniently unemployed friend."

He gave her a narrow-eyed look while he finished chewing. "That is so not true." The air between them crackled. "We've been over this already. You matter, Avery. Your happiness matters too. I've known you for most of my life, and I believe you can do this."

Again with the kind words she didn't deserve. Eyes downcast, she focused on dipping her fry in the sweet sauce.

"I can tell you don't believe me." His voice carried a gentle tone. "Where's the confident, self-assured girl I knew in high school?"

"Ha." She punctuated the air with another fry. "I was socially awkward, dealing poorly with my abandonment issues and this hair was wild and untamed."

"I disagree," Cole said. "Girls would've killed for those curls. Most guys were too scared to ask you out, by the way."

"Are you sure we went to the same school?"

His expression grew serious. "Stop selling yourself short."

"Thank you for being so kind and believing in me." She gestured toward the tube of rolled-up paper beside him. "Are those the blueprints?"

He wiped his hands on a napkin then spread out the plans between them.

She moved closer and stood beside him. Her shoulder brushed against his, and a familiar yearning rippled through her. One that might quickly morph into something danger-ous if she wasn't careful.

*Pull yourself together.*

"Tell me the biggest need for Imari's Place right now. In a perfect world, what would make this expansion useful for years to come?"

Cole palmed the back of his neck. "That question is beyond the scope of this project. And our budget."

"Why?" She studied him. "In my experience, that means you have something spectacular in mind. For now, give that budget a mental shove and tell me your vision."

His hazel eyes tangled with hers. "That's another thing I've always admired about you."

She faced him. "What's that?"

"Your ability to see beyond the surface. Deeper than what's on the exterior. You see the potential and that's a gift."

Oh, how his tender words were like rain on the desert wasteland of her heart. He reached up and gently tugged on one of her curls. She leaned into his touch, letting his warm palm caress her cheek. Cole's eyes dropped to her lips.

Over his shoulder, she caught a glimpse of a hooded figure lurking outside and she screamed.

★ ★ ★

The unmistakable flash of a camera jolted him back to reality. She gasped and clutched his arm. "Who is that?"

He turned and hurried toward the entrance. Outside, a person wearing shorts and a hooded sweatshirt cut across the yard. "Hey! What do you think you're doing?"

The guy broke into a jog. His hood slipped back, revealing a mop of unruly dark curls. His skin was pale between the hem of his shorts and black socks and sneakers. He ran toward a gray older model compact car idling in the street.

Cole contemplated going after him, but tackling some dude in the street and smashing his camera wasn't a wise move. Instead, he turned back to Avery. She stood beside the blueprints spread across the table, her arms wrapped around her torso.

"He ran off," Cole said. "Maybe it was one of your loyal fans? Or a nosy neighbor trying to see what we're building?"

"That wasn't an amateur. Nobody's neighbor has a camera with a lens like that." Her gaze ricocheted around the framed-in space as if she was looking for a place to hide.

"Avery." He moved toward her, his arms aching to pull her close. "Relax. We're not doing anything wrong."

"We're here alone. It doesn't look good."

Really? He stopped short. Anger flashed hot in his gut. After all she'd been through, keeping up appearances was still a priority. "You're divorced. We're looking at plans and eating chicken sandwiches and french fries. Hardly a scintillating Saturday night."

The shallow dip of her frown made him wince.

Drat. He'd messed that up. Clearly his words had landed all wrong. So much for being logical and pragmatic.

He didn't care who was taking pictures of them. As far as

he was concerned, they weren't doing anything wrong. No contracts were being violated. But her pain was still very raw and maybe he'd been too bold. There wasn't any way he could stop the following and the speculating and the covert picture taking. So why get worked up about it? But he could tell from the panicked expression on her face and the slump of her slender shoulders that she was mortified.

Or maybe the fact that he'd almost kissed her had sent her into panic mode. When he'd tugged on that curl and she leaned into his touch everything in him wanted to claim her. To kiss her and finally taste those plump full lips for the first time. Want and desire simmered in a dangerous internal cocktail, and he fought for control. If only that guy outside had been thirty seconds slower.

He worked his jaw in a tight circle. At least the intrusion had kept him from doing something he'd never be able to undo. Because deep down inside he knew there would be no turning back. He'd dreamed of kissing her for years. To be honest, he was still longing to kiss her now. Instead he had to find a way to be what she needed him to be. Self-controlled. Her problem solver.

"I should go." Her hands trembled as she packed up her uneaten food. "I think it would be best if I went home now," she repeated herself, as if trying to convince them both.

*No!* He wanted to shout. *That's not what's best.* He swallowed back a frustrated sigh.

"All right, if that's what you want."

"I'm sorry. I should've left when Wendy and Shayla canceled. I don't know what I was thinking."

"You were thinking you wanted to be free. You were thinking you feel most alive when you're creative."

A spark of disbelief ignited in her eyes. He stepped closer.

"It's true, isn't it?"

Her mouth drifted open and her fingertips fluttered at the V in her T-shirt. He shelved his hands on his hips and stared at her. "All the stuff in the periphery, it just fades away when you're being creative. I've known you a long time, Avery, and you are your happiest, your most fulfilled when you are creating something."

She trapped that plump lower lip behind her teeth and it was all he could do not to close the last of the distance between them and kiss her senseless.

She nodded slowly. "You're right."

"Then why are you letting the things you can't control hold you back?"

Hurt flashed in her eyes for the second time in five minutes. Oh, he was really messing things up tonight.

Her smooth brow furrowed. "You have no idea what it's like to be in this position."

"You're right, I don't. But I do know that you're letting all these negative voices get inside your head. You're allowing people's opinions to hold you captive. Avery, you can't change what's happened. You can't stop the speculating, the social media posts or hurtful things. You'll never get people to stop talking about you down at Harry's when they've had one too many. Watching somebody else come undone is a spectator sport here in Camellia. It stinks but that's the way it's always been."

She skewered him with an angry look. "I'm sick and tired of being in the center of the arena." Her tone was frigid as she quickly packed up her things. The walls were closing in. She was refurbishing her protective shell and bracing to go back out into the world. "Will you please walk me to my car?"

He stared at her and let the silence grow uncomfortable. There was so much more he wanted to say. Since he felt at least partially responsible for her current emotional state, he acquiesced with a nod.

He rolled up the blueprints and tucked them under his arm. With a lantern in each hand, he followed her outside into the warm muggy air. A subtle breeze whispered through the magnolias. The gray car with its mysterious intruder was long gone.

Avery strode toward her vehicle, keys jangling. She opened the door and shoved the food and the drinks inside. Cole added the lanterns. She slammed the door then circled around to the driver's side without looking at him.

"Avery, I—"

She held up her hand. "Don't worry about it."

He grabbed the edge of the door and clung to it while she climbed behind the wheel. "I am worried. I don't want to fight with you."

Her blue eyes still glittered with irritation as they met his. The last light of the day bathed her skin in a cotton candy pink. "We're not fighting, Cole." Her stiff smile said otherwise.

She tugged the door from his grasp. "See you around."

"Yeah, see you around," he said softly as she started her car then circled the cul-de-sac and drove away. He stood there for a long time, replaying their interaction. Memorizing the sensation of her silky hair twined through his fingertips. For one fantastic instant, he'd believed that she could be his. He'd been so close.

And that was a dilemma that wouldn't vanish like an unwanted visitor. Because he'd never be able to forget the way his heart hammered against his ribs, or the way her chin tipped up, with her eyelashes fluttering against her creamy skin. Almost like she wanted him to kiss her.

No, he wouldn't be able to forget any of that. Now he only wanted her more.

## Chapter Ten

He'd almost kissed her.

And she would've kissed him right back.

Oh, she'd love to pretend that she would've had the self-control to step away, but in her heart of hearts, she was certain that wasn't true. When Cole's eyes had dipped to her lips and he'd leaned in, she'd responded by tipping her chin up and fluttering her lashes like a modern-day Scarlett O'Hara.

Avery sat on the screened porch with Hayes nestled in the crook of her arm. He'd fallen back to sleep after she'd fed him. Her chair squeaked as she rocked and savored her morning coffee. Addison still hadn't climbed out of bed yet, which provided Avery with ample opportunity to ponder last night's encounter with Cole. The intruder peeping in with his camera and snapping her picture had rattled her. But it was her exchange with Cole that had far greater impact.

Did she want to be single forever? Of course not. She had come home to rebuild her life and lean on her family for support. Starting a romantic relationship with one of her most cherished friends had never been on her radar.

The door slid open and Harper poked her head out. "Sorry to interrupt your peaceful morning. You'd better come in here."

Goose bumps pebbled her skin. Oh, no. She stood slowly, her mind already spooling through worst-case scenarios. Had Addison sneaked out of bed and tried to make her own pancakes? Did someone get through the gate and come to the front door unnoticed? Were they demanding an interview?

*That's a bit of a stretch, isn't it?* The more logical side of her brain stepped in and tried to take charge, like a principal in a classroom full of unruly students.

The pungent aroma of coffee filled her nostrils as she stepped into the kitchen. Harper must've started another pot because a steaming mug sat on the counter.

Harper twisted her hair in a messy bun and secured it with an elastic band. She wore a cotton floral robe over her matching pink pajama set. She grabbed her coffee then gestured toward the flat-screen television mounted on the wall in the living room. "It's a commercial break right now, but when they come back on the air they said they're going to feature you in their pop culture corner."

Avery swayed back and forth, Hayes still asleep in her arms. Her sister might as well have been speaking another language. "Who's featuring me? Harper, what's going on?"

Harper's sleepy eyes filled with confusion. "Don't you watch morning television?"

"Not anymore." She glanced down at the child asleep in her arms then met Harper's puzzled gaze. "If we have the TV on in the mornings Addison usually picks what we watch."

It was true. She hadn't been in charge of the remote since, well, probably since she and Pax binged *Breaking Bad*.

"You need to see what they're talking about so you'll know how to respond." Harper sat down on the sofa and blew on the coffee in her mug.

Respond to *who?*

Avery skirted the end of the sofa, her legs quaking, and perched on the cushions beside her sister. Hayes stirred in her arms and she patted his back, making soft shushing sounds. His perfect little lips hung open and he stretched one arm over his head then clenched a tiny fist.

Adrenaline pulsed through her veins as the commercial on TV ended. Although she hadn't watched morning television in ages, the weekend anchors sitting behind their sleek desk hadn't changed. An orange and blue icon filled the screen, teasing their pop culture corner. And there above the splashy graphic was a picture of her and Cole. Last night. Her mouth went dry.

The photographer had captured a compelling profile shot. Probably that gazillion-dollar lens he'd angled through the cutout for the future living room window. She and Cole stood face-to-face next to that makeshift table. His palm hovered next to her cheek, and she looked at him like he was the greatest thing since sliced bread. Her skin tingled at the memory of his touch.

A savvy intern had done their homework. Thankfully the broadcaster stuck to the facts. Still she leaned forward, forcing herself to breathe against the tightness constricting her chest.

Blood roared in her ears as he mentioned Cole, the name of the foundation and referred to Camellia as their hometown.

Harper leaned over and pressed her cool fingers to Avery's arm.

The host straightened his stack of notecards with an efficient tap and offered a cheeky smile. "This photo begs the question, is Avery Lansing Crawford discreetly returning to the world of interior design and can we expect another reality TV show—perhaps with her new beau as her sidekick?"

"Okay, that's enough." Avery plucked the remote from the cushion between them and silenced the television.

Harper gave a weak smile over the rim of her mug. "Look on the bright side. Imari's Place gets their fifteen minutes of fame."

"That's exactly why I'm worried." Avery stood and paced the room, her hand automatically patting Hayes's back again. More to soothe herself than anything else. "I knew I shouldn't have stayed."

"What do you mean?"

"Last night. We were supposed to be at Imari's Place for an interview, except the women we were going to speak with stood us up. I'd brought food to share, and Cole had rolled out the architectural plans and we were just talking."

"Then someone came out of nowhere and took your picture? Who was it?"

"I—I don't know. Cole went to the doorway and looked, but the guy had a car waiting and he took off."

"He must've acted quickly." Harper set her mug down on the coffee table and pulled her phone from the pocket of her robe. Her eyes grew wider the more she scrolled.

Avery's stomach churned. "What is it?"

"I have an alert set up so I can keep track of when your name is mentioned on social media. A little trick Julene taught me."

Splendid. "W-what are people saying?"

"Well, the picture has already been posted online. Let's focus on how you're going to respond, now that this is out there. That's really the only thing we can control."

"I'm not going to do anything because nothing happened."

"Nothing happened yet, you mean." Harper frowned and glanced at her phone as it continued to ping with notifications.

"Cole and I have been friends for ages. Our relationship isn't like…that. Why won't you believe me?"

Harper heaved an exasperated sigh and looked heavenward. "Dear Lord, please don't let today be the day I strangle my sister."

"What? Why?"

"Because for someone who is so successful, you can be ridiculously myopic."

"What does that mean?"

Harper lowered her voice and leaned close. "Cole is in love with you, Avery. He has been for years. I don't know why you can't see that."

A heady mix of excitement washed through her, chased immediately by a fresh wave of fear. Something had shifted between them last night. She couldn't deny that. But now they'd be the subject of endless speculation. All she wanted was an opportunity to live a quiet life, raise her kids and figure out how to co-parent effectively with Pax and Trey. It wasn't fair dragging Cole and his foundation into this. His work was too important to be sullied by melodramatic gossip. Yes, maybe once a long time ago they'd teetered on the edge of dating, but they hadn't. Then she'd been married for ten years and had never given her friendship with Cole much thought.

She sat back down beside Harper.

"Can I see the picture again?"

Harper hesitated then scrolled and swiped, before turning the device toward Avery.

She scanned the image. Warmth unfurled in her chest. If someone was going to take her picture without her permission then blast it all over the world, at least she was with Cole. He was kind and good and his expression looked so tender.

"Is it that obvious?" She barely choked out the whispered words.

Harper nodded.

"To who?" She shook her head at her own inane question. "I mean, who else knows? Or can tell? Or whatever?"

"Well, anyone who has access to this picture now or spends five minutes with the two of you." Harper dropped her phone in her lap. "The question is, what are you going to do about it?"

Hayes's eyes opened and he blinked against the morning sunlight then started to fuss. "I'm going to take things one step at a time. First, I'm going to get the kids dressed, then I'm going to get ready and then we're going to church. You're welcome to join us."

Harper gave her the side-eye. "Seriously?"

"Seriously." Avery lifted Hayes to her shoulder and pressed a gentle kiss to his smooth cheek. She wouldn't be so foolish as to step foot inside The Oasis. That was only asking for a drama-filled encounter she didn't possess the strength to navigate. No, she'd find a more traditional service, something with a nursery and a preschool class, and a pew in the balcony where she could worship without dozens of prying eyes tracking her every move.

"Go big or go home, right?" Hemby grinned and clapped him on the shoulder. "I never thought I'd see the day when you'd go public with your relationship on a national news broadcast."

"I didn't go public with anything and we're not in a relationship." Cole glared at Hemby then tugged at the tie knotted at his throat. It wasn't really all that hot or humid out yet, but his body felt like it was over a hundred degrees already. He'd been a fool to put on this suit and an even bigger fool for stopping to speak to his friend after church. Maybe he should've stayed home altogether.

Folks were being polite, but they weren't shy about staring. Not a single person had offered any empathy or compassion, either. Least of all his best friend.

Hemby jammed his hands in the pockets of his linen trousers. "What did Avery have to say about the morning news?"

Cole lifted one shoulder. "Don't know. We haven't spoken."

Hemby tipped his head toward the church entrance behind them. "Well, now's your opportunity."

Irritation prowled through his insides like a hungry mountain lion. "C'mon, man. Don't do me that way."

"I'm serious." Hemby tipped his chin up. "Turn around."

Cole hesitated. His irritation morphed into nervousness. This feeling arcing and twisting in his gut was worse than waiting for his bar exam results. He wasn't ready to speak to Avery. Not yet.

A rivulet of sweat trickled down his spine. He forced himself to turn around. All coherent thought evaporated as she walked toward him. She wore a simple blue dress with a square neckline and a knee-length skirt. A diaper bag dangled from one shoulder and she carried Hayes, wedged on her opposite hip. Greer hovered at her side, his eyes crinkling as he glanced down at her and smiled. She laughed and his gut clenched.

Man, he wanted so badly to be the person escorting her and her children out of church. Making plans. Trading inside jokes. Looking forward to a leisurely Sunday afternoon together.

Sure, he'd had that same thought countless times. But today he needed to know for certain that she was okay. And he needed her to know he wasn't responsible for what was broad-casted on television and shared on the internet this morning.

Harper had her phone pressed to her ear and she gestured with one hand as she spoke, trailing behind her family. Mrs. Huntington walked beside Avery, holding Addison's hand. Addison's curls were tamed into two pigtails and her sleeveless pink dress flared out at the waist. She saw him first.

"Mr. Cole!" Addison tugged her hand free from her grand-mother's and ran toward him.

"Now's your time to be the hero, buddy." Hemby clapped him on the shoulder. "I'll catch up with you later."

Before Cole could ask him to clarify what he meant by hero, Hemby was cutting long strides across the parking lot toward the lawn where his wife and kids chatted with friends in front of the church.

"Mr. Cole, what are you doing here?" Addison demanded, staring up at him, one hand propped on her hip while the other waved a piece of paper in the air.

"Hey, Addison." Cole sank to the ground to meet her at eye level, grateful for her enthusiasm to distract him from his own thoughts. "My family goes to church here too."

"Oh." She quirked her little mouth to one side then thrust her artwork toward him. "Look what I made."

He took the paper and eyed the mosaic cross she'd pieced together from small squares of brightly colored paper. "Wow, that's beautiful. Did you make this all by yourself?"

She took it from his hands. "I had some help with the glue part."

Cole chuckled then met Avery's gaze. "Good morning."

Oy. Why did he have to sound so awkward?

"Hey." Avery's smile didn't quite reach her eyes. "How are you?"

*Better now that you're here.*

Maybe this wasn't the time to be quite so honest. That probably didn't meet Hemby's definition of heroic. "I'm hanging in there. This is a nice surprise. Do you usually attend the second service?"

"First time visitors." Avery set the diaper bag on the ground then shifted Hayes to her other arm. "I heard there's a strong children's program and lots of families with little kids."

"We've worked hard to make this a place that families want to attend." He smiled and rocked back on his heels, like he could claim responsibility. He couldn't. He had nothing to do with the programming. But now that she'd visited, he wanted her to come back. Hoped it would become a regular occurrence. If she sat beside him next time, he'd be thrilled.

"Cole, how about a boat ride?" Greer asked. "It's a beautiful day."

"I don't want to impose on your family time."

"You're not imposing," Greer said. "I just invited you. Come on, you bring the sandwiches. We've got plenty of chips back at the house, and I'll ice down some sodas. Avery, it's about time we take that boy on his first boat ride."

Avery's brow furrowed. "What about Nana? She'll be miffed if no one picks her up for Sunday lunch."

Cole palmed the back of his neck. He'd never get tired of spending time with Avery or her family, but he'd defer to her preferences.

Harper ended her call. "That was Julene. She's going to pick up Nana and bring her out to the house. They'll have lunch together."

"See? Nana's all taken care of. The weather is perfect and the water's like glass. We ought to get out there before a thunderstorm rolls in." Greer reached for Addison's hand. "C'mon, pumpkin. Let's get in the car."

Evidently Greer wasn't backing down. He and Mrs. Huntington were already steering Addison toward a vehicle parked nearby. Harper gave him a polite smile and followed her mother, Greer and Addison.

"If you'd rather not, feel free to decline his invitation," Avery said.

"Do you not want me to come?"

"Of course I do. I'm also aware of how much getting involved with my family will cost you."

"Involved?" He frowned. "I thought we were friends."

"We are. And I don't want my *friends* to be tomorrow's headline news."

Oh. "Too late for that." He shrugged. "Greer had me at the weather is perfect."

"All right. We'll head home and get ready. It's going to take us a while."

Doubt that. With her curls exploding everywhere and her eyes the exact color of her dress, she looked incredible. Cole tamped down the compliment. Probably best if he kept comments like that to himself. She didn't need anything complicated in her life right now. Besides, she'd clearly established his place with her friends comment.

An hour later, Cole stood on the dock, passing Greer plastic bags of ice for the boat's cooler. Per his instructions, Cole had arrived with bags full of chicken salad sandwiches from the deli, a six-pack of bottled water and a dozen chocolate chip cookies. Blue-green water lapped against the fiberglass hull of the twenty-six-foot boat. Greer's prediction had been mostly right. Except for white billowy clouds gathering on the horizon, the weather was almost perfect.

A warm breeze swirled around him. After he carried the groceries on board, he claimed a spot on the buttery soft bench seat facing the house. The rumble of a boat's engine sliced through the silence. Greer straightened and waved to a neighbor cruising by on their ski boat.

"I'm glad you're coming with us." Greer dumped the last bag of ice in the cooler underneath the boat's bench seat then added the bottled water and cans of soda.

"Thanks for the invitation."

Greer shoved the empty plastic bag in the trash can stowed in a compartment. "You're good for her."

"Pardon?"

"You heard me, son." Greer's smile creased his weathered skin. "Pax is all about Pax. But you—you are a man who sees the bigger picture."

Cole winced then slid his sunglasses in place. He saw the bigger picture all right. But was he any better than Pax? He'd accepted a bribe from Nana to further his cause. And buy him time with Avery.

"I've known Avery since we were children." Cole accepted the water Greer offered. "I'm pretty sure she sees me as the brother she never had."

Greer shot him a long look. "She needs you."

*Not as much as I need her*, Cole thought.

A baby's squeals interrupted their conversation. Avery walked down the dock with Hayes in her arms. Cole's breath caught. He was grateful for his sunglasses to conceal his eyes. She wore a red sundress with a loose skirt that skimmed her knees, revealing bare legs and brown leather flip-flops. Her blond curls were loose and free and he caught a glimpse of a swimsuit strap tied halter style around her neck. She carried a canvas tote bag on her shoulder and Hayes in her arms, his head mostly covered with a brimmed sun hat. Addison skipped down the dock, singing an unfamiliar song.

Avery's mother followed behind carrying her own tote bag and wearing a wide-brimmed straw hat and a green cover-up over a bathing suit. Harper wore a navy blue bucket hat and a red cover-up over her bathing suit. She'd draped a red-and-white- striped beach towel over one arm and carried a tall water bottle in her hand. Addison climbed on board without any help. Greer reached for her and effortlessly maneuvered her into the boat.

"I have a brand-new life jacket. It's just your size," Greer said.

Addison pushed out her lower lip. "No life jacket."

"No life jacket, no boat ride. It is as simple as that." He held open the life jacket for her. Pale pink with purple and teal stripes. "Are you ready, little girl?"

She hesitated, her lip pushed out even further. Cole sat back and watched the whole situation unfold.

"Addison." Avery's voice carried a warning.

Addison finally complied with a dramatic sigh and let Greer snap the buckles shut.

"Why don't you come up here and help me drive?"

Addison tucked her hand in Greer's and let him lead her to the captain's chair.

Cole stood and moved toward Avery. "Can I help you with anything?"

"Sure, how about you take my bag?" Her smile was a radiant light that only made an already exquisite day even better. He took her bag then offered a hand to help her on board. After she had both flip-flops on the deck, he held on a second longer than necessary. Then squeezed her hand gently before letting go.

*You're pathetic.* The critical voice in his head gave him pause. Maybe so. But it was too late. He couldn't stop these feelings from escalating even if he wanted to.

The warmth of Cole's competent hand holding hers rocketed a pleasant feeling of attraction straight through her. She widened her stance, mentally blaming the boat bobbing in the water for her flustered state. Except the boat wasn't moving that much and Hayes seemed surprisingly calm. Cole let go but didn't sit down. The woodsy scent of his aftershave was so appealing she wanted to make sure she sat right next to him. This only magnified her internal turmoil and her skin flushed. Now her comment in the church parking lot about them just being friends seemed silly.

"Would you like me to hold him while you get settled?" Cole asked.

"Please." She thrust her son into his arms without a second thought. Hayes's little face crumpled and he started to fuss.

"Hey, little buddy." Cole's soothing voice latched onto something dormant in her heart and brought it to life. Made her want to pluck a soda from the cooler, pop the top and stare at him for the rest of the afternoon.

*Stop.* The rational voice barged in, squelching her romantic notions. She sat down on the bench seat opposite Cole and pretended to rearrange the contents of her tote bag. He'd acted like he didn't have much experience with children but wow he looked good holding her baby. She averted her gaze to check on Addison but snuck another glance at Cole and Hayes. Thankfully she'd worn her biggest, darkest pair of sunglasses.

Hayes grabbed for Cole's sunglasses, giggling as Cole leaned out of reach. Hayes tried again and Cole turned him outward, so Hayes faced Avery. "There. That's a much better view, don't you think?"

Even through his polarized lenses, she felt the heat of his gaze. A telltale swirl of attraction danced behind her knees. Oh, she was in a heap of trouble.

Cole had traded his Sunday best, slacks and a button-down shirt with a bow tie, for orange board shorts that showed off his tan legs and a graphic T-shirt. She allowed her gaze to linger on the corded muscles in his arms as he carefully supported Hayes with both hands.

"All right, everyone ready?" Greer's question intruded on her delightful observations. She managed a nod and quickly checked to make sure Addison hadn't ditched her life jacket already. She sat on the bench in the bow of the boat, kicking her legs against the seat's base and singing a song.

"Cole, if you'll grab that stern line, we'll be on our way," Greer said.

"I'm happy to hold him again." Cole stood and passed Hayes to her. "Give me a second to help Greer."

"No problem." She squeezed the words from her decidedly parched throat. Did he sense the chemistry arcing between them? Or had she crushed him with her pretentious speech about the cost of her friendship?

*Why* had she said that? She'd probably regret that comment for the rest of her life.

"Come here, pumpkin." She welcomed Hayes into her arms. He cried and reached for Cole.

Cole paused on his way to untie the line from the cleat on the dock. The corner of his mouth tipped up in a half smile. "I'll be back in a flash, little buddy. Don't cry."

She watched Cole as he untied the line, gently nudged them

away from the dock then hopped back into the boat like he'd done it a thousand times.

Hello, hotness.

Her cheeks flamed again. He casually slid onto the cream-colored vinyl cushion beside her and stretched his arms toward Hayes. "May I?"

"Of course." She passed Hayes back, letting her fingers brush against Cole's then settled in her seat and let the warm sunshine sink into her skin. Greer motored out into the lake, obeying the no wake zone. Harper and Mama sat on the bench seats at the bow of the boat. Addison stood next to Greer, her little hand beside his on the wheel.

"Do you have anything he can chew on?" Cole asked. "Or is he hungry?"

Avery studied Hayes. He'd been fed and changed already. He had one finger jammed in the side of his mouth and he looked quite comfortable tucked in the crook of Cole's arm.

"I brought a couple of toys." She fished a set of baby's keys from her bag. Cole took them and playfully jiggled the rainbow-colored plastic together. Hayes gave a slobbery grin then batted at the keys.

She forced herself to look away before that warm fluttery feeling washed over her again. They were supposed to be working on designing and decorating a new house, not falling in love. She'd not made much progress on her assigned tasks yet. Part of her expected Dale to get aggravated with her indecisiveness and tell Cole she'd never come up with a feasible plan. She could whip up a couture ball gown faster and with more confidence than she could figure out what to put inside a residence for women.

He was going to be so disappointed with her when he found out he'd chosen the wrong person for the job. Not to mention that photo was just going to get everybody talking all over again.

In an effort to channel her frustration into something posi-tive, she'd accepted an offer to collaborate with a local business that sold Alabama-made housewares. Product placement on her social media and short-form video promoting a summer-themed flat lay on an outdoor table was right up her alley. People couldn't be cruel about table settings and centerpieces, could they? Focusing on being an influencer carried so much less risk than having her personal life overanalyzed by people she'd once considered her allies.

Oh, she never should have let Cole convince her she could do this.

"Hey, are you all right?" The warmth of Cole's shoulder brushing against hers muddled her thoughts all over again.

She tried for a smile. "I have a lot on my mind."

There. That was true.

"Same."

The tension knotted between her shoulder blades eased a bit at his admission. Had he seen their photo on television or online yet? He hadn't seemed nearly as upset by that guy tak-ing their picture as she had been. Maybe he considered any publicity for the foundation a good thing. Greer increased their speed and they glided across the lake. Hayes let go of the keys and his eyes grew heavy.

Cole gently readjusted the brim of the baby hat.

"Where did you learn to hold a baby?"

"I've been learning as I go. Hemby has kids. Most of my friends have at least one child. I mean, I'd never volunteer in the church nursery or anything but sometimes people trust me enough to let me hold their offspring."

She laughed. "If you can get that boy to sleep on a boat I'm going to call you the baby whisperer."

He grinned and the skin at the corners of his eyes crinkled. "Challenge accepted."

Addison glanced back over her shoulder. "Mama, take my picture with Papa Greer."

"I left my phone on the kitchen counter," Avery said. "I'm sorry."

"Here, I brought mine." Mama pulled her phone from her bag and handed it to Harper. "Why don't you take the picture?"

"Sure." Harper took the phone and held it up toward Addison and Greer. "Say *cheeseburgers*."

"Cheeseburgers!" Addison propped her fist on her hip and looped her other arm around Greer's. Harper took a few photos. Addison immediately scampered over to review them. "Here. I knowed the filters I want."

Chuckling, Avery shook her head. "She's something else."

Cole gently nudged her knee with his own. "You've got to admire a girl who knows what she wants. Another trait she gets from you, I'm sure."

Her amusement evaporated. She turned her lips inward to keep from snarling at him.

"Oh, no." Cole's voice dropped low. Instantly contrite. "What did I say?"

"Nothing. I'm just—it's fine."

"Please. I can tell you're irritated. What's wrong?"

Was she overreacting? Maybe. He'd meant it as a compliment. But his words stung like lime juice in a paper cut.

A ski boat zipped across the lake, towing a skier and churning up a sizable wake.

"Hang on," Greer called out.

She clutched the railing behind Cole. Greer slowed down, but their boat rose and fell abruptly as they crossed the choppy water.

Cole cocooned Hayes in his arms, carefully protecting him.

After Greer guided them to a quieter part of the lake, Avery let go of the railing and shifted in her seat to face Cole. The breeze lifted his hair, tousling those honey-gold strands. She had the weirdest urge to reach out and smooth her fingers through the strands that were amiss.

"Avery?" Her name on his lips was gentle. Patient. Drawing her back to him. "Are you going to tell me what's going on or do I have to guess?"

"I never wanted to come back here. Did you know that?"

A muscle ticked under his eye. "I assumed that was the case."

"Moving back in with Mama and Greer, as a divorced single mom who faked her way through one season of a reality TV show was humiliating. I'm still so ashamed. When you describe me as someone who's confident and capable, I bristle because I'm not that person. You keep saying how much you believe in me and I don't get it."

Her voice broke. Fresh tears threatened to fall. She should stop talking before she came completely undone. Greer had pulled back on the throttle. They were barely moving. He and Mama, Harper and Addison could hear every word. But she didn't care. She had to get this out.

"I'm sorry. I—"

She held up her hand. "Let me finish. I'm still not sure what I want to do with my life. Help people find redemption? That's a lofty goal. But I know what I don't want. To be mocked online. And I don't want to be a woman who embarrasses you and your foundation because she can't choose the right paint colors or the best luxury vinyl tile. Or worse, a woman that people see as nothing but a washed-up beauty queen trying to feed her kids by posting pictures of pretty things online."

Cole's crestfallen expression swam in her blurry vision.

"No one who truly matters believes any of that is true," he said softly.

"That doesn't mean my feelings aren't valid."

He tilted his head to one side. Probably choosing his words carefully so she didn't come completely unglued.

"Is this about that photograph or is there something more significant bothering you?"

"I can't pretend that photo never happened, Cole. People aren't going to ignore it." She fidgeted with the clasp on her bracelet. "And if you've changed your mind about hiring me as a consultant, I'd understand."

His brow crimped. "Why would you say that?"

"Because I'm creating too much drama. People are obsessing over us." Shame made her insides froth. "I—I don't want to be the reason Imari's Place gets lost in the—"

"You are not responsible for that photograph or the way it's being shared." He draped his arm across the back of the seat behind her and it was all she could do not to lean into him. Find comfort in his strength.

But acting on her sudden attraction to her dearest friend was foolish. Her heart wasn't ready for a relationship. Obviously. Look at her. Blubbering in the middle of an afternoon boat ride. She refused to jeopardize their project any more than she already had. If she didn't want people gossiping about her, then she needed to keep Cole at arm's length.

Since when was a boat ride more important than Sunday lunch?

"Oh, no." Julene peeked inside the paper bag containing their food. "They left out half of our order."

"That's okay, darlin'. We can share."

Julene pinned her with a look. "You don't mean that. I'll

run back over to the deli right quick and get the rest. It will only take a few minutes."

Maribelle pasted on her most gracious smile. "Maybe get them to throw in some fried chicken to make things right."

Julene hesitated. "Will you be all right here by yourself?"

"Absolutely."

"Help yourself to something to drink. There are snacks in the pantry too." Julene grabbed her keys and sailed out the door.

Julene was sweet and all, picking her up and bringing her out to the house. They'd had a lovely chat in the car. Hopefully the deli would right their wrongs. She had her mouth set for some fried chicken. They always fixed it just the way her mama used to.

She shuffled in a slow circle, one hand braced on the counter. She'd taken to watching church on television these days. All the bother of getting dressed, fixing her hair then getting a ride to church—by the time she got herself in the pew she was too exhausted to pay attention. And forget all that standing up and sitting down for the singing part.

Not to mention that band. Oh, the band. Far too loud for a proper worship service. Who decided to bring a band to church, anyway? Whatever happened to a good old-fashioned piano? Or a regal pipe organ. As much as it pained her to admit, church had become a young people's game. She was more than happy to stay in her own place and watch that cute fella from Atlanta tell her how to improve her life.

Except this morning her decision to attend church virtually had backfired. She'd been irritable since breakfast and couldn't concentrate on the sermon. The next thing she knew, her neighbor at Westwood Manor had knocked on the door to alert her that Avery's photo had been on a television show.

Maribelle had been too proud to admit that she'd been resting her eyes in the recliner and didn't see a stinking thing.

Now she had so many questions.

She'd have to be extra accommodating during lunch if she wanted to get any crucial information out of her granddaughter. Sometimes the girl kept the facts locked down tighter than the gates of Fort Knox.

An ugly familiar sensation roiled inside. She pressed her palm to her abdomen. Probably hunger pangs or maybe all that oatmeal she'd been eating wasn't agreeing with her. Surely that wasn't envy slithering in like a copperhead snake and making itself comfortable.

Nonsense.

Her family evidently had big news to share but hadn't bothered to tell her yet. So what?

A phone hummed nearby. She grew still. The temptation to look at the illuminated screen inches away wrestled with the tiny modicum of good sense she had left. Other people's text messages weren't meant for her eyes.

But she was hurt that her family had left her out. Why didn't Avery tell her that she was going to be on that morning show everybody watched? No, this wouldn't be her proudest moment, but she was feeling a bit vindictive. So she fumbled for her reading glasses wedged on top of her head, slid them onto her nose then leaned closer and read the text.

Hey, Avery. Hope you're having a great weekend. This is a friendly reminder that we need to start filming tomorrow at 10:00 a.m. Does that still work for you? Let us know.

*Filming?* As in the movie? Maribelle gripped the counter with both hands and let out a whoop of delight. If she were a younger woman, she'd do a little victory dance. A slow grin pulled at the corners of her mouth as the recent conversation with her granddaughters replayed in her head.

The napkin. It would make the movie so much better if the producers knew about Cole and Avery's teenage pledge to marry one another. Who didn't love a story about two people destined to be together? Now, where was that thing?

A delightful hum of anticipation swept through her as she closed her eyes and tried to recall the details. Maybe being in a mostly empty house was a serendipitous opportunity. She peeked through the window above the sink and made sure Julene was gone. Then she crossed to the screened porch and peeked out toward the lake. The boat wasn't at the dock. Good. That meant it would take a while for anyone to get back to the house. She had plenty of time to find what she needed.

With her hand trailing along the wall, she walked deliberately down the hall to the room where Avery slept. Now, where would Avery keep her most treasured possessions?

Maribelle paused to study a photograph of Avery with her children in a silver frame on the dresser. So precious. But she wasn't here to admire scrapbooks or reminisce. No sir. She was a woman on a mission. She opened and closed the top drawer then the second, rummaged through some clothing. Nothing. Her fingers trembled as she fumbled with the lid on the jewelry box. The hinges squeaked. Only a few pairs of earrings, a broach that had once been Maribelle's and a strand of pearls sat on top of the crushed velvet lining. Not big enough for a napkin. She closed the lid then shuffled toward the nightstand. A stack of folded laundry sat in the middle of the cedar chest at the end of the queen-sized bed. Maribelle eyed the chest. A tried-and-true container for sentimental items, but she'd try the nightstand next.

She eased the nightstand drawer open. A Bible, small notepad and a pacifier sat inside. Maribelle paused, shifting her weight from one foot to the other. Any Southern woman worth her monogram hid crucial things between the pages of the Bible. Doubt niggled. Lucille's warning about provoking family because she'd overstepped echoed in her head. She dismissed that thought faster than a sneeze through a screen door.

"Lucille thinks she's so wise, spouting her advice," she whispered.

Cole might get a little irritated if he found out she'd meddled in his personal affairs, but he'd get over it. Avery would be overjoyed when this was all said and done. Those two were precious. But painfully slow.

She rifled through the pages of the Bible and checked inside the front and back covers. Nothing. Pushing the drawer closed, she sighed then turned and surveyed the room. The edge of a notebook sticking out of a tote bag on the floor beside the armoire caught her attention.

That's right. Avery had that notebook where she kept her important project details. How had she forgotten?

Maribelle didn't have time for people to be so reluctant and indecisive. Before she left this world she needed to know that Cole and Avery were on their way down the aisle. She could tolerate a little momentary irritation from them if she knew that in the long run they'd be together. Stepping into their happily-ever-after.

Her heart pattered in her chest as she crossed the room and carefully retrieved the notebook. She quickly flipped through the pages of notes, sketches and a few pieces of magazine articles folded and tucked inside. At last she found the napkin sandwiched between the final page and the cover. It slipped out and landed near her freshly pedicured toenails, which she'd had painted in a delightful shade of lavender.

"Bingo." Maribelle held on to the edge of the dresser and bent down, praying she didn't keel over. She retrieved the napkin and turned to leave. Wait. What was she thinking? Stealing it was way too obvious. If Avery paid close attention, she might discover its absence before Maribelle had time to put her plan into action. A picture. That's what she needed.

Sometimes she was so brilliant she could hardly stand herself. Wearing a proud smile, she ambled back out toward the front door where she'd left her pocketbook. Photographic evidence was all she needed to plant some seeds. Give the movie people some ideas of where they could go with this. Oh, they were going to eat this up. Everybody loved a story about love, right?

Maybe they'd even put her name in the credits. Wouldn't that be something?

Of course she had no idea how she'd get them the photo. She'd likely exhausted all her favors with Lucille. And she wasn't about to ask Olive.

A woman named Genevieve had started volunteering at Westwood Manor. Maribelle sensed a connection. Genevieve had offered to do anything to help. She'd even left her number on a card. Maribelle had tucked the card in her Bible for safekeeping. She'd call and ask Genevieve to help her as soon as she got back to her apartment.

She arranged the napkin on the dining room table, retrieved her phone and snapped several photos. Her eyes weren't what they used to be and she had to be certain she got this right. No do-overs. Satisfied, she slipped her phone back in her pocketbook then returned to Avery's room as quickly as her tired old legs allowed. Her hands trembled, but that was probably just from excitement. Or nerves. To be honest, she had been more nervous than a cat in a room full of rockers when she'd put the napkin on the table.

Her family had chosen a boat ride over eating lunch together, but she'd turned a disappointment into a victory. Too bad she'd have to keep her plan under wraps for now. She was so focused on putting the napkin back and rearranging the notebook in the bag the way she remembered that she didn't hear footsteps in the hall.

"Nana?"

Maribelle gasped and whirled around.

Julene stood in the doorway, clutching two bags from the deli. The aroma of fried chicken floated on the air.

"Darling, you scared me to death." Maribelle pressed her hand to her chest and willed her pulse to quit racing.

Julene's eyes toggled between the bag on the floor and Maribelle. Her brows tented. "Nana, what are you doing in here?"

## Chapter Eleven

"I'm in way over my head." Cole dragged his palm over his face. "I should have told her the truth long before now."

He sat with Hemby in a back booth at The Flowering Vine, drowning his regret with a tall glass of soda and loaded nachos. Sunday evening's thunderstorm had turned into a dreary Monday. Rain still spattered the window beside them. Their weekly tennis match was a washout so they'd convened for an early dinner. Hemby's wife and kids had left for vacation in Gulf Shores. Hemby wasn't joining them until Thursday, making him a captive audience for Cole's pity party.

Except Hemby wasn't having it. "We've been over this already. You don't owe her an explanation."

"You weren't on that boat with us yesterday. She's upset. People's comments are hurting her, and that's my fault." Cole jabbed at the ice in his soda with his straw then reached for another chip from the platter between them. He didn't want to keep having this conversation but he couldn't shake the ominous feeling that stalked him. Some desperately optimistic part of him hoped that tonight might be the one time Hemby finally said something that assuaged his guilt. So far this was not that time.

"Listen, she never has to know her grandmother made a significant contribution to your foundation. I'm assuming a portion of that is covering Avery's consulting fee?"

"Yes, we're paying her."

"Good. Then all I have to add is I'm disappointed you haven't kissed her yet." Mischief gleamed in Hemby's eyes as he pulled a chip from the pile of nachos. Cheese stretched in a trail from the plate. He plucked the strand free and draped it over the black olive and tomatoes already heaped on top of the chip. "You're getting all torn up over nothing."

Cole snorted. "I'd hardly call this nothing. Someone took our picture and leaked it to the press. She's told me from the get-go that she's the wrong person for this project, but I didn't listen. When she finds out her grandmother's been meddling she is going to be irate."

Avery had always wanted to be known and appreciated. He'd be lying if he argued that she didn't enjoy the limelight at least a little bit. He sighed. "Here's the thing. I'm starting to worry that if the two of us are all anyone really wants to hear more about, then our relationship will overshadow the foundation."

"You've got to hop off this train of thought. It's taking you in a pointless circle." Hemby pulled his soda closer. "This might not be playing out exactly like you'd planned, but you absolutely did the right thing for the foundation. Human trafficking is now part of the daily conversation in this country because of you. You and Avery together. That photo shoved

Imari's Place into the national spotlight. So how about you flip the script, my man? What's better than that?"

"And ignore the collateral damage?"

Hemby rolled his eyes. "Are you hearing anything I'm saying? The house will be spectacular when it's finished, so keep focusing on everything that's going right and who will benefit."

Yeah, he'd tried that angle. It only made him feel better for a few minutes then he imagined the devastation when Avery found out he'd duped her. She'd been so honest. So vulnerable. He'd dismissed her concerns at every turn. What if this all came back around and caused more heartache than he'd ever anticipated?

"The way I see it, you gave Avery a legitimate opportunity to do some damage control. She tried retreating and hiding out at her folks' place or whatever but this project has brought her right back into the public eye."

"That's the problem." Cole shot him a look. "They're making a spectacle out of our…relationship and the focus should be on the larger cause."

"No, what she's doing is on brand for her wholesome image. Trust me. This is all going to work in your favor."

"Are you moonlighting as a marketing expert now?"

Hemby finished chewing then took a sip of his drink. "Mock me if you want but you know I'm right. People are curious about her. And about you. They admire people who are doing something that truly matters. Remember, there's no such thing as bad publicity."

Ha. Unless it crushed Avery's spirit and made her not want to have anything to do with him. "Pax and Trey are coming to town this weekend. She hasn't said much, but I know they're promoting the book and spending time with the kids."

Hemby's expression turned serious. "That could be tough to navigate. Like I said, flip the script. Use the circumstances to your advantage. Post more pictures."

"I haven't posted any pictures. Besides, is that really our objective here? To be some kind of wholesome brand ambassador?"

"My goal is to get you to stop obsessing over a nonissue. She's divorced. That means you both have the freedom to pursue a relationship. So what's holding you back?"

Heat crawled up his neck. "A kiss isn't going to bring any clarity to the situation."

Hemby laughed. "You clearly haven't kissed anyone in a while."

Ouch. "Not helping." He glared then popped a chip in his mouth.

"Somebody has to give you some tough love."

Cole crunched on a nacho and pondered Hemby's perspective. He didn't want to cause Avery any more pain. She'd endured too much already. But how could he pursue a meaningful relationship with her? How could they build a life together on top of the rubble that remained of her heart?

"What do you think about her kids?" Hemby asked. "Have you ever dated a woman who's also a single mom?"

Cole shook his head. "Addison's a handful but she's also a lot of fun."

"And what about the baby?"

Their server stopped by with refills of their sodas. Hemby tipped his chin in acknowledgment. "Thanks."

"Hayes is mellowing some. He fell asleep in my arms on the boat." Cole smiled. He wasn't about to confess how much he'd enjoyed holding Hayes, or the way the space between him and Avery crackled and fizzed when they'd first boarded the boat. Hemby would only take that information and run with it. Cole popped his straw into the fresh glass. "I never thought about what it meant to be a stepdad. I guess because I never had one. My mom stayed single all these years and I don't keep up with my dad and his wife. That's quite a leap from where we are now, so I'm trying not to think about it, to be honest."

Hemby studied him then grinned. "There's still hope."

"What's that mean?" Man, being this vulnerable was exhausting. As soon as he finished eating, he was out of here. Torrential rainfall or not. He'd take getting soaked on his way to the car over spilling any more of his feelings tonight.

"You're easy to read, my friend. I can tell that you're not giving up on the possibility of a relationship." Hemby rubbed his palms together triumphantly. "Things are about to heat up. I can feel it."

No, he wasn't giving up. The faint embers of hope still burned inside. No matter how messy and convoluted this whole thing had become, he'd never be able to snuff out the feelings he carried for Avery. But could he step forward and be the man she needed him to be?

His phone chimed on the table and he leaned over to read the text message.

Hey Cole. Quick question. What's this about a napkin and a pledge?

Oh, no. Cole's stomach plummeted. He read the rest of Charlie's text message. You've been holding out on me, man. We had no idea. Let's talk soon about how to incorporate this into the documentary.

"Oh, no. Not again." Julene's words clamped like icy fingers around Avery's heart. Squeezing. Clenching.

"What's wrong?" Avery glanced up from the tablescape she'd put together featuring products from a local shop. Vibrant pinks and splashy turquoise fabrics with hints of paisley here and there acted as a backdrop for the pewter serving dishes. At the last minute, Avery had reached out to a local florist who'd happily contributed a stunning floral centerpiece. In exchange for a mention in the social media post, of course.

She ran her fingertip over a pewter ring encircling a cloth napkin.

Not bad. Not bad at all. She couldn't stop a smile as she admired the flat lay. Her first styled tablescape since she'd left Raleigh. The collaboration had given her a boost of confidence and a place to channel her nervous energy in the four days leading up to Pax and Trey's arrival.

The morning sunlight filtering through Mama's kitchen windows had been perfect. Julene had shared a few tips she'd learned from styling a photo shoot at the magazine and together they'd captured the essence of the product line. She had less than an hour to edit and post the image before she had to pick Addison up.

The leader of the children's program at Mama and Greer's church had casually mentioned an opening in their vacation Bible school. Avery had claimed the spot before anyone else snatched it. She wasn't the only one wound up about Pax and Trey's arrival. Addison had her on pins and needles ever since Avery had told her that her daddy and Uncle Trey were coming. The news had sent Addison into a spiral of never-ending questions and understandable excitement. Every hour that Avery could keep her occupied was better for everyone.

Julene's face was pale as she stared at her phone.

"Jules, what's wrong? You're white as a sheet."

"I—it's—I think you'd better sit down."

Avery checked the images one last time then pocketed her phone. She bumped her hip against the corner of Mama's table, knocking a tumbler over as she moved closer to her sister. She winced as water spilled across the nearest place setting. Bummer. She righted the tumbler then slid the damp place mat to a dry spot. "I'm cutting it close. As soon as this is posted, I've got to go. Just tell me. Better yet, show me."

"Okay." Julene's hand shook as she slowly held out her phone. Avery leaned in for a closer look. Was that—no. Couldn't be.

"That's a picture of my napkin. Who…who did this?"

Dark spots peppered her vision. She stared at the username on the social media account. *Genevieve*. How did she get a photo?

Julene shrugged then pulled her phone back and started to scroll. "I'm guessing you didn't give it to her?"

"Of course not. I have the napkin so no need to take a picture of it. Other than Cole, I've never discussed it with anyone outside the family." Oh, what a disaster. She wiped her clammy palms on her dress then pulled her phone from her pocket.

"Maybe you should talk to Cole first before you do anything else? He's been tagged in the photo too."

Right. She checked her notifications. People had already tagged her. White-hot anxiety zipped through her veins. Her phone pinged, alerting her to more activity. She swiped all the notifications out of the way and quickly sent a text to Cole.

We need to talk. When can you meet? I'm free in an hour.

"Oh, my word, these comments." Julene slid her fingers over the screen. "People are brutal."

Avery's stomach turned inside out. She wanted to clamp her hands over her ears and sing one of Addison's favorite songs at the top of her lungs. Or maybe she should dive into bed, hide under her covers and sleep for the rest of the week.

"Whatever you do, don't look at those." Julene shoved her phone into the back pocket of her shorts.

Avery let out a bark of laughter. "Sure, I've always been supergood at ignoring what people say about me. I'll avoid looking at social media for the next week? Month? A century?"

Julene chewed her lower lip, studying her. "Why don't you let me get Addison? Mom is here. She can take care of Hayes when he wakes up from his nap. You need to meet with Cole ASAP."

"I promised Addison we'd get a treat on our way home today."

"No problem. I'm on it." Julene plucked her keys off the counter. "What do I need to pick her up? Photo ID or some kind of special permission slip?"

Avery massaged her forehead with her fingertips. Shock and anger clouded her mind, blotting out the practical thoughts. "Photo ID. You are already on the approved list of people to pick her up."

"Good. Don't worry, I've got this. Take as much time as you need to sort this out."

"Thanks." Avery hugged Julene. "I couldn't do this without you."

"We're here for you." Julene patted her arm then strode toward the door. "Keep me posted. I'll meet you back here later."

Her phone pinged with a text from Cole.

Let's meet at Imari's Place. How soon can you get here? Max and Charlie have already got wind of this, by the way.

Oh, dear. Her heart climbed up into her throat. Charlie and Max. What would they want with this information? It had nothing to do with human trafficking or building a residential facility. She quickly texted back and confirmed her arrival. She'd filmed one segment for the documentary yesterday but the heavy rain had kept them from doing any of their exterior shots. She'd promised to meet with them again this week and hopefully she could talk to Wendy and Shayla soon. They'd been reluctant to reschedule so she'd made her final selections for the home's interior without talking to them. Her deadline with Dale had come far too soon. She still wasn't confident she'd made the best choices, but she ran out of time over-thinking every flooring option, backsplash tile and paint chip.

Another text message arrived. This time from Harper, who was away on her beach trip with Mary Catherine.

**What is going on? How did that photo even happen?**

Great. So news was spreading. As predicted. Avery started to reply then deleted the text.

There was nothing she could say to her sister that would make the situation any better.

A quick check of the video monitor on the counter revealed Hayes was still asleep. Mama was reading on the screened porch. She had enough time to post the shots she'd just styled with Julene, grab some drinks at the coffee shop then get to her impromptu meeting at Imari's Place.

She refused to let this take her down.

Cole wasn't a DIY kind of guy. At all. He lived in a condo with an HOA and a maintenance team who handled all the minor issues that cropped up. His mom had to call somebody when things went wrong in her house because he wasn't qualified to fix much other than a light bulb.

But right now he desperately wanted a project. Something he could do with his hands. More anger surged through his system than a driver with road rage on a jam-packed interstate. If only today was demo day like those other famous home renovation shows on television. He could really go for a sledgehammer to put through some drywall. Instead he drew a calming breath then flexed and straightened his fingers.

The abhorrent words spray-painted in red and blue graffiti at the construction site spanned three sheets of plywood. The vandals had propped their artwork against the unfinished house.

"So disgusting." Cole shoved his fingers through his hair. Vandalism was one thing but vandalism that denigrated women, especially the women who lived here, was a special brand of horrific.

Dale stood a few yards away, surveying the damage, with his phone pressed to his ear. He gestured wildly with his other hand. Hopefully he was getting Roberto and his crew out here to clean up the mess. If Roberto was busy, Cole would take care of it with his own two hands. He had to get the awful words covered up before any of the residents saw them. Imari's Place was supposed to rescue women who'd been trafficked. They'd encountered more than enough shame in their journey toward healing. No one needed to pile on more, least of all bored, thoughtless locals on a spray paint rampage. This expansion was never supposed to be about gaining approval or social proof on Instagram. He'd certainly never meant for this house to be a platform or a battle ground. But he couldn't help but wonder if that's what was happening anyway.

Was this the work of restless kids, or a more calculated attempt by someone in the community who didn't want to see his foundation succeed?

Anger scorched through his extremities again. He had to do something. He couldn't stand here, waiting for Dale or Roberto or anyone else to take action. Pulling his phone from his pocket, he forced himself to catalog the evidence with pictures. Then he scrolled through his contacts until he landed on the name and number of Camellia's police chief. His fingers jabbed the screen as he composed a brief text, attached the photos then requested a follow-up call.

Ugh. This all made him want to vomit.

An approaching vehicle caught his attention. He jammed his phone in his pocket then turned to see Max and Charlie's van pulling up to the curb. Charlie wasn't even out of the driver's seat before Max had his sneakers on the ground and his camera filming.

Cole strode toward him. "You are not seriously going to film this?"

Max pulled back from the camera's viewfinder, his eyes wide. "I most certainly am."

The door slammed and Max jogged over to join them. "Hey, Cole. What's up?"

Cole stepped closer, barely concealing his anger. Charlie and Max exchanged concerned glances.

"This is vandalism. It's cruel and thoughtless and I'm removing it in the next three minutes. This is not the time for you to get your next fifteen seconds of sensational footage."

Charlie fisted his hands on his hips. A muscle in his jaw knotted. Max at least had the decency to put the camera down.

"It's cute the way you stand up for people like some modern-day knight," Charlie said. "Much respect. But the graffiti on that plywood is like a gift from above. You can't ask for a more telling summary of how the community feels about your organization."

Oh, he desperately needed to smash a stationery object now. "It's *vandalism*, Charlie. Maybe if you'd try harder to preserve people's dignity rather than exploit their weaknesses, you'd actually have a decent documentary."

He was yelling now, but he didn't care.

Max muttered a curse word then walked away.

Charlie stood his ground. His eyes sparked as he angled his head to one side. "Is that right? I'm glad we had this talk, Cole."

Then he brushed past him and followed Max toward the unfinished house.

Charlie's comment landed like a lit match on the anger and frustration already kindling in his gut. He turned and stormed across the muddy rock-strewn yard. Dale had ended his call and pocketed his phone.

"Unless you've got a better idea, I'm moving that plywood before any of the women who live here or the local news crew shows up."

"No argument here," Dale said. "I'll help you."

He approached the first sheet of plywood, praying it wasn't nailed to the side of the house. Max and Charlie came back outside. The familiar hum of another car approaching sent Cole's pulse rocketing into overdrive. Max already had his camera on his shoulder and Charlie was grabbing footage with his phone.

Cole shook his head in disbelief. It was like they hadn't even had a conversation. Was it too late to back out of the documentary? He'd have to consult the foundation's attorney.

The rough edge of the plywood scraped against his hand as he tried to drag it away. In his panic, he didn't see the discarded bricks nearby until he nearly went down. This was so much easier the way he'd envisioned it in his head.

Dale came to his rescue. "That's Avery's car. If you don't want her to see this, let's flip it over right quick. We'll leave it facedown for now."

"Genius." Cole formed his lips into a smile. They made short work of flipping all three sheets over into the red clay. "Thanks, man."

Dale clapped him on the shoulder. "Sure thing. It's the best we can do. I'm running late for a meeting on another project. Y'all take care."

Cole nodded. "See you."

A car door slammed then Avery walked slowly toward him carrying takeout cartons with enough iced drinks for four people. Her smile didn't quite reach her eyes. "I know smoothies and iced coffee won't fix everything, but I thought it might help a smidge."

Her kind gesture dissipated the tightness in his chest. How did she know they'd all need a bit of cooling off before they regrouped to discuss the photo of that napkin?

"That was sweet of you. Thank you." He took one of the cartons from her hands then led the way inside. He'd mitigated one part of their disastrous day and shielded her from more unnecessary pain. But had he done enough?

Avery followed Max, Charlie and Cole inside the unfinished building. The rough framing had been completed and the roof finished. Sadly, it didn't seem like they'd made much progress since the last time she'd been here with Cole. When she'd given Dale her final selections, he had mentioned the window factory had run into a supply chain issue. The plumbing and electrical contractors hadn't started yet, either. That explained why it was about eleventy bazillion degrees inside. No sign of a breeze, either. She held the tray with plastic cups filled with cold drinks as they stood in an awkward circle in the center of the unfinished room. Already the cotton fabric on her dress was sticking to her torso.

"Thanks for coming." Cole stood beside her, his cheeks flushed and his expression firm. Unyielding. She gave him the side-eye. With the hem of his vintage T-shirt, he swiped at the perspiration on his forehead. She caught a glimpse of his toned abdomen and forced herself to look away.

"Max and Charlie, make it quick, please." Cole linked his arms across his chest. "Avery needs to get back to her kids."

The hair on the back of her neck prickled. It was hot and things were tense. Why couldn't Max and Charlie give her and Cole privacy to sort this all out?

"Cole and Avery, that napkin is a relic from your past." Max grinned then held out his phone. "What an interesting twist this adds to our production plans."

She shot him a pointed look. He had the same picture on his phone that Genevieve had already posted. "Who gave you that picture?"

"I'm less concerned about how you got the picture and far more interested in knowing why you feel it needs to be incorporated into the documentary," Cole said, his voice low and sharp.

Avery turned to Cole. "Evidently it's been shared on social media too."

Cole's eyes sparked with irritation. "Of course it has. Which underscores my point. Why include a sentimental item from our childhood in a documentary about human trafficking?"

"Between this new information plus the signs outside, we feel we could tell a much richer story," Charlie said.

Avery rattled the ice in her plastic cup. "What signs outside?"

"It's not a big deal," Cole said, without looking at her. "Let's decide what to do about this picture first."

Charlie released a sardonic laugh. "That's not what you said a few minutes ago."

"Somebody was probably bored and thought it would be funny to spray-paint something nasty." Cole's gaze slid to meet hers. "I don't believe it's directed toward you, if that's what you're thinking. I'd rather we spend the limited time we have together talking about what we can control. Do you really want our personal relationship incorporated into a documentary that viewers can access from a major streaming service?"

Honestly, why was he being so stubborn? "If you don't tell me, I'll flip that stinkin' plywood over and read it for myself."

He released a frustrated groan then chucked his half-finished drink in the industrial-sized garbage can nearby. "Why do you want to know so badly?"

"Because I already know it was something significant by the way y'all are acting." She resisted the urge to stomp her foot, Addison style. She could be an adult about this. "Don't keep things from me."

A heavy silence blanketed their semicircle. Max stared at his phone. Charlie's curious gaze pinged between her and Cole.

"Tell me what was on the sign, Cole."

"Fine." Cole gestured over his shoulder with his thumb. "Someone spray-painted the words *hooker, whore* and another word I refuse to repeat on sheets of plywood. Our friends here think it makes for a compelling story. I disagree."

Oh, he was so compassionate, trying to protect these women from more shame and humiliation. And he was so good at it too. "Frankly, I'm not sure what's worse. Vandalism with lewd words or people's comments on social media."

Cole's eyes narrowed. "What kind of comments?"

"Julene told me I shouldn't look, so I didn't. Not yet, anyway. But the picture of the napkin has evidently generated several comments. Probably not many of them are kind."

Cole faced Charlie and Max. "Can you give us a day or two? We need some time to discuss this."

Charlie hesitated. Then nodded. "Shoot us a message when you're ready. We truly believe this adds a rich layer to the overall story we're trying to convey. The two of you and your long-standing friendship speaks to your commitment to this community. That's worth sharing with the world."

"Noted." Cole dismissed them with a curt nod. "We'll be in touch."

Max and Charlie filed out.

Cole scrubbed his fingertips along his jaw then paced the room. "Avery, this has to stop."

She tapped the end of her straw against her lips. "What has to stop?"

"You getting involved with Imari's Place was never about exploiting you or your personal life."

"Ha." Her bark of laughter earned her a wince. "I'm sorry, I didn't mean to be cavalier about this. I hate that someone has vandalized the property, but it's a little late to be worried about my feelings."

He pressed the heels of his hands against his eyes. "I never should've agreed to this."

"Agreed to what?"

He dropped his hands to his hips again then shook his head. "Bringing in a high-profile consultant. We should've bid this out to a local design firm. This has turned into a monster that we can't tame."

"I told you from the beginning that there were better designers out there and you didn't listen." She tried for a smile and pointed her straw at him. "So that's on you."

So much for levity. His face maintained the same sullen, barely controlled expression. "One thousand percent. This is all on me."

"Here's the thing. I'm fed up with people digging around in our personal lives, saying horrible things and trying to throw us off our game." Avery sipped the last of her drink then tossed the cup in the garbage. "This vandalism feels like an attack on our mission, and I'm not going to sit back and take it. Let's go make an offer on that empty warehouse at Fifth and Jasmine. Are there funds available? It's an ideal location for that production line I can't stop thinking about."

He tunneled his fingers into his hair again and blew out a long breath. "I—I don't know, Avery. That's a huge undertaking."

"But we won't know unless we try, right?" She looped her arm through his. "Mama and Julene have my kids for another couple of hours. Let's at least peek in the windows of that warehouse and see what we can see."

Cole grunted in agreement then let her tug him toward their vehicles outside. She had no idea what had inspired this sudden onset of overconfidence. The Avery of a few weeks ago—even the Avery of two days ago—would've absolutely assumed those nasty spray-painted words were targeted at her. She wasn't thrilled about her and Cole's pledge to marry becoming public knowledge and later, in a weaker moment, she'd probably ignore her sister's advice and read every single comment that had been posted. But for now, the only weapon she had for battling Genevieve's shenanigans, Pax and Trey's impending arrival, and the doubt plaguing this project was her friendship with Cole.

He believed in her.

That's what mattered. So they had to stay strong. She was determined not to let anything or anyone else derail their plans. They had to keep working together. These women needed help starting over. Imari's Place could be a sanctuary and a stepping stone by providing both a house and a job that produced a line of products other women would love. If she could stay focused and remember why they'd started this project, then maybe the public commentary would be easier to ignore.

## Chapter Twelve

Cole walked toward his office the next morning, coffee and a bacon, egg and cheese biscuit in hand. Not the healthiest of breakfast choices, but after yesterday's interaction with Avery, he required sustenance in the form of comfort food. Summer-like weather in Alabama was in full swing. Record-breaking temperatures dominated the weekend forecast. All the up-coming Father's Day festivities would require plenty of cold drinks and cranked AC's. Not that he planned on paying any attention. He'd send the obligatory brief text to his dad. Then he'd probably receive a text of acknowledgment, followed by a selfie of his father on some local golf course.

He picked up his pace, the uncomfortable feelings about his almost nonexistent relationship weighing him down. There wasn't enough energy in his emotional well to draw from today. He'd have to bench that topic and revisit it on Sunday. Even at eight in the morning on a Wednesday, folks were moving about on the downtown sidewalks at a much slower pace. Or maybe it was the gaggle of people blocking the entrance to his office.

He slowed his steps then craned his neck to see what the fuss was about. A local news van idled at the curb. The same reporter who'd attended the groundbreaking ceremony stood with her camera operator on the sidewalk.

"Mr. Whitaker, how do you feel about the vandalism outside Imari's Place? Is there any connection between the vulgar language on those signs and your relationship with Avery Crawford?"

"What? No." Cole clamped his mouth shut to keep from saying anything more as he pushed through the curious onlookers. The strap of his messenger bag slid off his shoulder and he had to fumble to keep from dropping his coffee and bagged breakfast.

"Will you and Miss Crawford be making any official statements or issuing a press release before her ex-husband arrives in town today?"

His teeth bore down on the inside of his cheek as he sidestepped a particularly aggressive observer brandishing a smart phone. That's right. Pax and Trey were expected in Camellia for a week. Yet another reason why he longed to shield Avery from additional pain.

He'd been so naive, thinking the local media wouldn't find out about the vandalism. Or maybe it was good old-fashioned denial. After nearly losing his temper with Charlie and Max, then trying and failing to conceal the horrible vandalism, he'd shoved yesterday into the never-want-to-do-that-again pile then tried to move on.

Judging by the people hovering behind him, phones and cameras poised to catalog his reaction, yesterday wasn't going to be so easy to forget. Sure there had been a few curious glances and a couple of people whispering behind their hands while he waited in line for his coffee. He'd tried to pretend he was blissfully unaware as he scrolled through his email messages and mentally composed a game plan for the day.

He had meetings this morning with different contacts who had boots on the ground in the eastern US. Both advocates were working tirelessly to rescue more victims. Since recent arrests of women working in a Memphis massage clinic, victims of human trafficking seemed hesitant to come forward and seek life beyond the only one they knew. Cole gritted his teeth. His organization and many like it offered hope and a future, but it could be understandably difficult to bring the women out of the darkness and into the light.

They'd been tragically manipulated into believing that modern-day servitude and selling their bodies for empty promises was all they were worth.

Oh, what he wouldn't give to find a way to blot out those lies and convince these women and girls that they were worthy of walking in freedom.

He managed to get inside his building without saying anything he'd regret later. Sweat pooled under his arms and beaded along his forehead as he climbed the stairs to the foundation's office. Somehow between his morning meetings, he'd promised Avery he'd reach out to the Realtor representing the warehouse they'd looked at yesterday. Maribelle's donation had been more than enough to cover the expansion and this additional purchase. But he'd need the board's approval not only to make an offer but also to pursue product manufacturing.

Cole strode into the office then almost turned around and left again when he saw Millie Kay and Cassandra Nelson, the wife of one of their board members, huddled around Millie Kay's computer. When they saw him they broke apart and jump-started a casual conversation about their weekend plans. Whatever. He knew better.

"Ladies, good morning," he said. "What's going on?"

Millie Kay hesitated, her dark eyes darting toward her co-conspirator. "It's complicated."

"We're just worried about you, sugar." Cassandra rounded Millie Kay's desk with her arms outstretched. Wait, was she going to hug him?

"That's a lot of media attention for our sweet Cole to handle. We're here to help."

Wow, okay. What was he, seven? And since when had Cassandra Nelson appointed herself as his protector? Warning bells clanged in his head. Her sweet perfume and pouty pink lipstick both needed to be avoided at all costs. She rubbed his bicep before he took a giant step toward his office. Heat climbed up his neck. He didn't know whether to break into a run or play dumb, so he went with the latter option and forced a smile. "Appreciate the concern, but I'm doing fine. Millie Kay, please don't disturb me unless it's an emergency. I have back-to-back meetings this morning."

She regarded him with flat-lipped silence. He raised his coffee cup and walked backward toward his office. "Thanks again for your concern. Couldn't do this without you."

Taking a fortifying sip of his coffee, he headed into his office and kicked the door shut with his foot. Word was spreading. Splendid. So much for believing that he'd somehow be the exception and when it came to him the nosy people of Camellia would graciously mind their business.

He sat down at his desk, turned on his laptop then unwrapped his breakfast. He took a bite of the lukewarm sandwich, savoring the salty combo of eggs, cheese and bacon on a buttermilk biscuit while he waited for his computer to boot up.

*It's a little late to be worried about my feelings… I told you from the beginning that there were better designers out there and you didn't listen.*

Avery's declaration had tunneled inside his head and built a fort. That was the problem. She'd been brutally honest, and he'd kept things from her. Plenty of things. And it was getting harder and harder to cling to his own false narrative that he'd made the right choice. Oh, he could keep lying to himself. Keep pretending that all he needed to do was bide his time until the expansion was finished. Deny that he felt anything more than platonic friendship for her. Maribelle's donation was already in the foundation's account. If he held on a little bit longer, they'd wrap this thing up and no one would ever be the wiser.

Except the guilt was slowly eating him alive.

He took another sip of coffee then slumped back in his desk chair.

How could he possibly endure being so close to Avery and not tell her the truth? Not just the truth about Nana's donation but the truth about how he felt? Or was now the time that he finally looked her in the eye and told her that he fell in love with her a long time ago? And that he never stopped loving her. That she had had his heart since he was sixteen years old?

Against his better judgment, he scrolled through social media until he found a post featuring their napkin pledge.

Evidently they were trending. Hashtag *complicated*. Ah, so Millie Kay had been mocking him.

"Awesome," he grumbled under his breath.

He scrolled a little further, his blood pressure rising. The cheesy GIFs were everywhere. Along with rampant speculation about what Pax and Trey thought of his and Avery's marriage plans.

He closed out the app then finished his breakfast, quietly

mulling his options. What a three-ring circus. Or maybe he was the fool who'd been swept into the most bizarre turn of events ever. If he stepped away now who would Avery have on her side? Sure, she had her family. Harper and Julene had been fantastic, and their mother and Greer completely supportive. Which was ironic given that Cole had taken a bribe from her grandmother and that's what got him in this mess to begin with. He groaned and tipped his head back then closed his eyes. *Lord, I'm officially terrible at being the hero of this story. Please send help before I cause irreparable harm.*

She was an absolute hot mess.

"Is my daddy coming yet? Does he have any new toys for me? Why does Hayes get to come?"

Oh, my. Avery gulped past an exasperated groan. "Your daddy will be here any minute, Addison."

Friday had arrived much too soon. The constant stream of questions made her want to sprint outside and cannonball off the end of the dock. Shed her worries like a cicada molted from its shell. Even though she'd made the arrangements for Pax to take the children for the weekend, she'd underestimated her anxiety over handing them off. She still wasn't at peace with letting Hayes out of her sight for more than a few hours.

But Pax had been persistent in his requests to spend quality time with both of his kids. He'd sent texts and emails, including a letter of reference from the family Olivia Claire had babysat for last summer. It was the most they'd communicated since they'd separated. Avery had finally agreed to let both kids stay with Pax from noon on Friday until Monday morning.

Hayes swung contentedly in the baby swing she'd set up by Mama's living room window. He smiled and cooed at the mobile dangling above his head, a happy trio of sea life in shades of blue and turquoise and orange.

Avery folded another bib and tucked it in the side pocket of his diaper bag. He'd finally drunk a whole bottle of formula last night with Julene holding him. Avery had had to go outside because she couldn't handle the uncertainty of knowing whether he'd eat. What if he went on strike while he was with Pax? What if Addison decided she was miserable and begged to come back to the house?

Addison twirled in circles around the living room, humming a song from an animated movie soundtrack. Avery checked and rechecked the diaper bag. She'd loaded it with plenty of diapers. Pax remembered how to change a diaper, didn't he? Memories of those early days at home together with Addison crept in. She mentally shook them off. He'd have to figure it out. Diaper cream? Check. Extra pacifier and a teething ring? Yes and yes. She glanced at Hayes again and studied him with a critical eye. Was he teething? He shoved a tiny finger in the side of his mouth and grinned at her.

"Hey, sweetheart." She kept moving, because if she stopped and thought too much about what was going to happen in a few minutes, she feared she'd melt into a puddle beside the sofa. She lifted the lid on the plastic bin and recounted the diapers. She'd thrown in more wipes, extra clothes, a blanket and a handful of toys.

"Darling, are you all right?" Mama came into the room, sipping water from a tall plastic tumbler. She hovered behind the sofa, the weight of her concerned stare heating Avery's skin.

She refused to look at her mother. "Making sure I have everything is all." She checked the time on her phone. "He said he'd be here at four."

"Anything I can do to help?"

"Pray that I don't come unglued. I'm having second thoughts. Scratch that. I want to back out. This is a horrible idea."

"I understand why you're concerned," Mama said. "It's only forty-eight hours, right?"

"Closer to seventy-two. But who's counting." Avery tunneled her hands through her hair and pressed her palms against her scalp, willing her brain not to conjure up every possible worst-case scenario.

"He's probably going to drive the kids straight to his parents' house, anyway."

"That's what I'm afraid of." Avery groaned. "Addison hasn't seen Dalton and Whitney very much and Hayes doesn't even know them."

Addison stopped turning in circles and looked up. "Who do I not knowed?"

Drat. Why did kids always hear the juiciest parts of adults' conversations?

Avery exchanged worried glances with her mother then reached over and smoothed Addison's hair back. "Your dad's probably going to have some people with him that you haven't seen in a while."

"Like strangers?" Addison's eyes saucered. "I'm not supposed to talk to those."

"That's right you're not." Avery's heart squeezed. "Don't worry, your daddy is going to take good care of you. Your grandmother Whitney, Papa Dalton and Uncle Trey will be with you too. Maybe your new friend Olivia Claire will come over to play."

She silently prayed that she hadn't offered her precious child an empty promise. She had zero control over what happened with Addison and Hayes once they left here. Past experience had proven Pax to be an involved, attentive father. Trey had always been great with kids. If this was their new normal, she'd have to be brave and embrace it.

"Someone's at the gate." Greer ambled into the room, staring at his phone. "Cadillac Escalade. Black with Alabama plates. Do you want me to talk to him?"

Oh, dear. Not a good idea. Avery shook her head. "Let him in." She could do this. She was a grown woman, capable of handling this exchange like a mature adult. She forced herself to suck in a deep calming breath.

"Is it my daddy? Is it him?" Addison scampered after Greer as he strode toward the door.

"Addison, wait." Avery called her back. "Why don't you go get your suitcase and your pillow?"

"Oh, yeah." Addison reversed course then raced down the hallway toward her bedroom.

"Well, if this cloud has a silver lining, I think it's safe to say you don't have to worry about her." Mama's weak smile didn't fully mask her concern. Greer stepped out on the front porch and quietly closed the door.

Avery rubbed her palm across her chest, as if to smooth down the jagged pain this interaction provoked. She didn't want to see Pax. She didn't want him to take their kids, not even for an hour. How could she possibly spend a whole weekend away from Addison and Hayes?

"Want me to get Hayes in his car seat?" Mama asked.

Avery hesitated. Mama would handle this for her if she stepped aside. But if she was ever going to reach a place where she'd forgiven Pax and Trey, then she had to take small steps forward. And keeping the kids from seeing him wasn't right. Yet even though months had passed since she'd breathed the same air or even lived in the same zip code, she still felt ill-equipped to speak to him again.

A few minutes later Addison barreled into the room, pillow tucked under her arm and her tiny wheeled suitcase in tow. "I'm ready, Mama." She grinned, as if destined for a week-long visit to a deluxe villa at a theme park.

"Good girl. One second while I get your brother buckled in his car seat."

"No, no more seconds. I don't want to wait," Addison whined. She dropped her pillow on the floor and popped a fist on her hip then shot Avery her most exasperated glare.

Avery's mother snorted then smothered her laughter behind her palm.

"Addison," Avery scolded. Except she didn't really have any clout. Her father was about two minutes from swooping in like a hero in a fairy tale and whisking Addison away from all the boring demands of her life, like structured bedtime and no sassy talk.

"Here, let me help you carry your things to the car." Mama set her tumbler down.

"Oh, thank you." Addison heaved a dramatic sigh then ran toward the front door, her suitcase tipping on two wheels as if it could hardly keep up.

"See you later," Avery whispered, hot tears burning her eyes. Once Addison saw Pax, she probably wouldn't even bother with a hug and a kiss. "Come here, sweet boy." She freed Hayes from the baby swing, settled him in her arms then nuzzled his neck. She drank in the delightful baby fragrance and he rewarded her with a happy screech as he grabbed a fistful of her curls.

She didn't want to let him go.

"A boy needs his father, Avery," she grumbled, parroting Pax's comments from their previous conversation. She intentionally exaggerated his Southern drawl for her own amusement. And also to keep from crying. Hayes gnawed on his finger, his eyes studying her as she buckled him into his car seat. His brow puckered then he arched back, resisting her efforts.

"I know exactly how you feel." She forced herself to click the buckles into place.

A car door slammed outside then Addison's shrill greeting punctured the air. "Daddy!"

Hayes burst into tears. Avery blinked back the moisture forming in her eyes, forced herself to stand then carted him toward the door.

Iron bands tightened across her chest. Hot sticky air enveloped her as she stepped outside. Pax stood at the bottom of the steps chatting with Greer. Their conversation stopped as soon as Avery joined them. Pax's smile faltered. Was he nervous too?

"Hello, Pax." She clutched the rubbery handle of Hayes's car seat. Pax wore a pale blue T-shirt from a popular seafood restaurant on the Gulf Coast. Huh. That was odd. He detested seafood and never wanted to visit that part of Alabama when they were married. His skin wasn't the golden tan she remembered and his hair was longer than she'd ever seen it. Not that her opinion on his clothing or his hairstyle mattered anymore.

"Avery." He tipped his chin in a casual greeting, moved closer then stopped and tucked his hands in the pockets of his navy blue shorts. "You're looking well. How are things?"

"We're doing fine, thank you." She let her gaze slide toward the Cadillac Escalade, bracing for Trey to hop out of the vehicle and waltz back into her life. Through the windshield she recognized Whitney riding in the passenger seat up front. Once again, she had a phone pressed to her ear. Hopefully much like their encounter in the coffee shop she'd refrain from joining them. Addison had already dragged her suitcase over to the vehicle and struggled to put it inside. Mama had gone after her and stood beside the back door, undoubtedly offering last-minute words of encouragement.

Hayes ramped up the crying, drowning out all possibility of a lengthy conversation.

Pax's brow furrowed. "Is he all right?"

"A little out of sorts." Avery fought to keep the emotion from creeping into her voice. She lowered the car seat to the top step and set the diaper bag beside it. "I sent you an email with detailed instructions."

Pax chuckled. "Of course you did."

"Don't." Avery glared at him. "Please don't make fun of me. This is extremely difficult for everyone."

Greer cleared his throat and shifted his weight from one leg to the other.

Pax sobered. "I understand. I'm sorry. I didn't mean to make light of a challenging situation."

Avery acknowledged his kind words with a nod. That was progress, right?

"If I have any questions, I'll be sure to let you know." Pax leaned forward and braced his hands on his hips. "Hey, buddy. It's good to see you. We're going to have a good time together, aren't we?"

Avery stepped back, clenching her hands into fists at her sides. If she focused on the pain of her nails digging into her palms, maybe that would prevent her from saying something she'd regret. It wasn't a golf outing or football game. He was an infant.

"Addison, come give me a hug, please."

Addison broke free from her grandmother's embrace and sprinted toward the porch. "Bye, Mama. I'll be good, I promise."

That nearly did Avery in. She scooped Addison into her

arms. "I know you will, baby girl." She hugged her until Addison squirmed to get down. Avery set her daughter on her feet then forced herself to meet Pax's gaze again. "Please take care of them. I mean it. They are my everything."

Oh, she hadn't meant to say that.

Pax's brows sailed upward. Then he took Addison's hand in his and pulled her close. "I'll bring them back on Monday like we discussed."

Avery nodded, blew Addison one more kiss then turned and went inside. Her steps quickened to a jog, propelling her down the hall and into her room. She dove onto her bed, buried her face in her pillow and sobbed.

"Olive, can't you move any faster?" Maribelle snapped like a branch on the ancient live oak tree in her granddaddy's yard. The crowd in the sweltering parking lot outside The Oasis had swallowed the last of her patience. Men and women of all ages streamed toward the church's entrance, parting like the Red Sea around their sad little gaggle. Oh, she hated being so slow.

"She had her hip replaced six weeks ago, Maribelle. Have a little grace." Lucille's frigid gaze did little to dial back Maribelle's impatience.

"If it weren't for Olive, we wouldn't have these tickets," Nell added.

"At this rate, we're going to get stuck in the back row of the auditorium," Maribelle argued. "Or worse, they'll give our seats away because we didn't get there in time." Oh, she was so angry she could spit nails. Why didn't Olive give her ticket to someone who could move faster than a snail?

Olive's walker thump-thump-thumped across the asphalt as she methodically made her way from the church's parking lot to the front entrance. Her mouth tightened, but she didn't make any effort to increase her speed. She'd probably slowed down on purpose. Just to spite her.

"I'm surprised they're even going to let you in, Maribelle." Olive's voice sailed toward her, a velvet harpoon of sweetness covering a dagger of contempt. "Given your granddaughter used to be married to that Pax fella. You must be so pleased to see her picture splashed all over the news."

Oh, my. Maribelle opened her mouth to launch a barbed comment back, but nothing came out. Lucille clamped her bony fingers around her arm and propelled them forward into the crowd.

"We'll save you seats," Lucille called over her shoulder.

Maribelle stumbled along. "Did she just say—"

"Yes, yes she did. Now, keep quiet and let's go find our seats."

Distracted by the indignant rage boiling inside, she was forced to comply with Lucille's instructions. Olive's insult had stunned her into submission. Not a single coherent thought rattled around in her addled brain.

"Here." Lucille let go of her arm long enough to reach inside her pocketbook and pull out a pair of white sunglasses. "Put these on."

So tacky. Maribelle grimaced. "No, thank you."

Lucille shook her head. "You are so obstinate. Did you think you were going to get inside this event without anyone saying anything to you about your family?"

"I don't expect anyone will be nearly as uncouth as Olive."

"What are you planning to do when we get inside?" Lucille still held the sunglasses. As if Maribelle might somehow be convinced to change her mind.

"I'm going to get the book that I've already paid good money for and wait in line until it's my turn to speak to Pax."

"That's what I was afraid of." Lucille shook her head. "I don't think that's wise."

"Why not?"

"Because I know you and you're going to try to give him a lecture. First you'll list all the things he's done wrong to hurt your granddaughter's feelings then you'll probably go on and on about how he's abandoned his children—"

"Well, yes. I was maybe going to mention some of that." Maribelle sniffed then tugged on the hem of her royal blue tunic. She'd worn it because it was her favorite and frankly, it looked stunning paired with her bright white slacks. Besides, she'd heard somewhere that blue projected power. Boy, she needed all the power she could muster. She needed people to listen and get out of her way, not hold her back and boss her around.

"Let's keep moving, Lucille. This crowd is fierce." Maribelle started toward the entrance again.

"Maribelle, for once in your life, listen to my advice. You cannot go in there and make a scene." Lucille's kitten-heeled pumps clacked along on the pavement. "Do you understand?" Maribelle huffed out a breath and walked faster. Except somebody bumped into her and she stumbled. Her heart hammered in her chest.

Lucille clasped her elbow again, holding them both upright in the throng. They had less than ten minutes until the event was scheduled to begin.

"See? I wasn't wrong. There are so many people here we're never going to get inside before they start." Panic laced her voice and Maribelle tried in vain to increase her speed again.

"I'm not going one step farther with you until you promise me that you are going to keep your mouth quiet." Lucille emphasized each word like Maribelle was a first grader. Honestly, Addison got more respect than she did.

"I will promise you no such thing, Lucille. I have every right to be here and speak my mind."

"No, you don't. Not if you're going to embarrass me, your friends and more importantly your family. Do they know you're here?"

She avoided answering and kept her eyes locked on the ground.

"Answer me. Did you tell them you had a ticket and that you bought a book?"

"What difference does it make?"

"I'm trying to get you to think of someone or something other than your own emotional state. If I were Avery, I would not want you in here, especially after the week she's had. Let sleeping dogs lie and all that."

Lucille might have a point, but Maribelle was not going to give her the satisfaction of admitting it. Lucille didn't know what it was like to have your only son walk out and never come back. She and Lucille were both widows, but Maribelle's loss still seemed far greater. When her husband died, she'd lost her only ally, the one person who shared her heartache.

Not that he ever wanted to talk about it.

He'd been a good husband. A good man who possessed a gift that she did not. The mind-boggling ability to let things go.

Maribelle glanced from Lucille to the front door of The Oasis then back to Lucille. "All right, you win. I'll behave."

"Outstanding." Lucille smiled. "Now, let's go have a good time."

Inside, the thick fragrance of floral perfume and spicy cologne swirled around them. They let the crowd carry them into the atrium of The Oasis with its high ceilings and vast corridor dividing the building. Four young women with long hair styled in loose waves, flawless makeup and stylish outfits flanked both sets of double doors leading into the auditorium. Maribelle battled back an unexpected wave of nausea.

What was wrong with her? She fumbled in her pocketbook for something to fan herself with.

Lucille shot her a concerned look. "Everything all right?"

"Just a little warm." Maribelle found her paper ticket that she'd folded in half. As they waited for the line of people to file further inside, she flipped the paper back and forth in front of her face. Her mouth had grown dry and she could feel annoying little beads of perspiration forming at her hairline.

"It will be cooler once we sit down." Lucille tightened her grip on Maribelle's elbow and guided her toward the young ladies waiting to greet them. Maribelle managed to twist her mouth into a smile. The rumble of conversation grew louder, punctuated with bursts of laughter and the animated sounds of friends greeting one another.

Her legs turned to melted butter. She rarely wanted anyone's help but she was secretly grateful for Lucille's attentiveness. "I—I need to sit."

"There's a bench right here."

The tightness in her chest and light-headed sensation making her brain feel foggy kept her from arguing. She sank onto a rustic wooden bench right beside a life-size cardboard cutout of Pax. Oh, dear. Not at all who she wanted to stare at while she tried to pull herself together. Even the fake version of him was too much to take. Maribelle intentionally angled her body away. At least she made it without passing out.

Lucille sat down beside her. Concern pressed her lips into

a thin line. "We can wait here as long as you need to. Olive and them will be along in a few minutes, I'm sure."

Hot tears pressed against the backs of her eyes. What in the world?

"Forgive me for saying this, Maribelle, but you do not look well. Are you ill?"

"I—I don't know. Maybe that lettuce in my salad was bad." She fanned the paper faster. The fog in her brain grew soupier. Her breaths came in little pathetic gasps.

"Maribelle?" Lucille's fingers were blessedly cool as they gripped her fiery-hot arm.

Maribelle couldn't make the words flow from her brain to her lips. Something about coming here. Not this building specifically, more like the symbolism of the event, how it represented her family's betrayal paraded onstage for all of Camellia and beyond to ogle. Naming the problem sent her heart dropping to her toes. It all ripped the scab off an old wound. Yes, she'd known that wound had never healed. But the way the pain returned with a vengeance floored her.

"Maribelle, I'm getting you some help." Lucille's voice sounded so far away. Like she shouted from the opposite end of a tunnel. Yes, help sounded nice. Preferably a good-looking man in uniform. Maybe a whole platoon would swoop in here and whisk her away to safety. Upstaging Pax and Trey in the most socially acceptable way possible. She chuckled.

Except no one else laughed. Then her eyes fluttered closed, she slumped forward and Lucille screamed.

Cole baited the hook on his fishing line then cast out into the lake. The rod released with that refreshing, familiar zing. Then the bobber landed with a ploop in the blue-green water. He sat on the grassy bank at the edge of a pond only a short walk from the cul-de-sac where he'd grown up. The neighborhood hadn't changed much and he'd easily found his way along the worn footpath.

Tension had coiled his muscles into hard knots. Every breath of thick, evening air tinged with the scent of jasmine and wisteria sent him careening back in time. He'd spent countless hours fishing here. If he closed his eyes and concentrated, he could almost hear Kim's laugh as she learned to skip a flat stone across the glassy surface of the water. Dad had sat with him too, not far from this very spot, teaching him to fish. Instilling the value of patience. He'd caught a good bit of fish here over the years. Tonight he didn't care if he caught anything at all. His T-shirt clung to his back and he swabbed at the sweat on his brow with his sleeve. The crickets and the bullfrogs chattered, while a family of ducks swam by. He adjusted the tension on his rod. Sunlight filtered through the dense green trees on the opposite side of the pond. Wisps of orange-and-pink-tinged clouds dotted the sky overhead.

It had seemed as though all of Camellia was at The Oasis. He'd avoided the heavy traffic and taken the back way to his old neighborhood. He craved a quiet and understated retreat. His mom had tickets to tonight's big event and had offered him one, but he declined. Not his scene. Besides, he couldn't be trusted not to approach Pax and confront the guy for all the pain his actions had provoked. The only person he really wanted to be with tonight was Avery. He'd debated driving out to the lake and checking on her, maybe even offer to take her to the movies or out to dinner.

Anything to distract her.

The night wasn't over yet. He'd still held out hope of mustering his courage. Instead he'd steered his car the opposite direction, returning to his old neighborhood. Now, here he sat fishing his cares away. He had no idea if there were still fish in this pond. He'd seen zero evidence of any jumping or biting. He just wanted a quiet space to think and be. Mom had sold the house a long time ago and moved to a condo downtown.

Dad had remarried and moved to Georgia, back to his new wife's hometown. Even though he had zero ties legitimately to this neighborhood anymore, fishing in this pond would always feel like home. A merciful breeze kicked up, stirring the thick evening air. The rumble of a car engine caught his attention. He glanced over his shoulder and recognized Avery's SUV. He couldn't stop a smile as she parked, climbed out of the car and picked her way down the dirt path.

"Mind if I join you?"

She looked incredible, as always, in a pair of khaki shorts and a white blouse with short fluttery sleeves. Her curls bounced against her shoulders as she sank down beside him.

"You're always welcome here. Did you bring a fishing pole?"

"I didn't come here to fish."

The pleasant fragrance of her shampoo or lotion wafted toward him. After their almost kiss at the construction site last week, he hadn't been able to stop thinking about his next opportunity. What he wouldn't give to reel in his line, set the pole aside then pull her into his arms. He banished those thoughts. "What brings you by?"

"I wanted to see you. I don't know why this was my first stop. I suspected I'd find you here."

Her words sent a flush of warmth to his face. "What's on your mind?"

*Please say us, please say us, please say us.*

"Pax and Trey are in town."

"Really? I hadn't heard." He reeled his line in.

Her winsome laughter filtered into the air. "Evidently The Oasis is the place to be. I didn't want to be there tonight."

Cole secured the empty hook on his fishing pole then leaned it against his tackle box. "That makes two of us."

She glanced at him. "Thanks. I appreciate that."

"Mainly because I didn't trust myself not to do or say something regrettable."

"Same."

He met her gaze and offered his full attention. "I'm sure this is tough to navigate, co-parenting with your whole town watching."

She looked away then tugged her knees up to her chest and wrapped her arms around her legs. "Pax and Trey are grown men. They have the freedom to make their own decisions. I'm still worried they will bring the kids onstage. After everything that's happened recently, the thought breaks my heart."

"Did you ask Pax not to do that?"

She was silent then nodded slowly. Moisture hovered on the edge of her lashes. His heart squeezed in his chest. He slid his arm across her shoulders and pulled her close. Her eyes fluttered closed and she leaned into his touch. There was no one around. It would be so easy to kiss her.

No. He couldn't. Not right now.

She straightened, putting space between them.

He tried to mask his disappointment.

"I trust Pax and Trey and whomever Whitney hired to help tonight to keep the kids safe. I want to believe they won't use Hayes and Addison for a publicity stunt, but Pax insisted that the children be a part of the event tonight, and now I'm nervous."

"That's understandable. Addison and Hayes are quite young to be at such a large event."

"I won't rest until we're back under the same roof."

"It's a new normal. You have to find your rhythm," he said, leaning back on his hands to keep from touching her again.

"How did you keep moving forward after Kim was gone?"

The question had been asked at least a dozen times. Still, it gutted him. "We didn't know how to live without her. Our family was never quite the same. We got up every day and did what we needed to do, but my parents were always fighting and my dad blamed me."

"No, he didn't."

"Yes. He did." Cole picked up a pebble from the ground and tossed it into the water. "We always stayed at that same place in Destin. Dad told me every morning at breakfast that I was supposed to keep an eye out for her. But I got distracted…" he trailed off, dipping his chin to his chest to get control of his emotions.

"Cole Whitaker, look at me."

He didn't.

"Look at me," she insisted.

Slowly he lifted his chin. Empathy tinted her gaze, somehow soothing the ache of Kim's absence.

"You are not responsible for your sister's abduction. Or her death. It was an evil, twisted crime."

"For as long as I live I'll never forget the look on my parents' faces when I had to tell them that Kim was gone. I've spent hours in therapy trying to work through the things my father screamed at me. The way my parents fought until their marriage imploded. Avery, if I hadn't lost my sister that night my whole life would have been different."

"But look at all the good that has come from a senseless crime," she reminded him. Her hand encircled his bicep then squeezed.

He forced himself to listen carefully to her words and not think about how those slender hands of hers might feel tunneled in his hair.

"You've changed so many lives. Sacrificed a lucrative career. I know none of that can bring your sister back or fill the hole her absence left in your family, but you have got to let go of the weight of that burden."

"You first."

An air of disbelief cloaked them. "What did you say?"

"I said, 'you first.' When you let go of the burden you're carrying, maybe I'll drop mine too."

"I have to go." She stood and dusted off the seat of her shorts. "I'll see you around."

Anguish lodged in his throat. He stood and chased after her. "Avery, wait."

He caught up with her on the path.

She whirled and faced him, eyes glittering.

"Please, don't run away. Not again."

"I'm not running."

"Oh, but you are." He inched closer. Blood roaring behind his ears. He forced himself to move slowly, like he was approaching a skittish, wounded animal. "I'm not the enemy. Don't you see? You're beautiful and smart and you've been hurt deeply. I get that. But all I want to do is see you thrive."

So, that wasn't exactly true. Maribelle had preyed on his weakness. Convinced him to make an offer they all suspected Avery wouldn't refuse. As he stood in front of her, his eyes roaming her gorgeous face, the desire to kiss her overwhelmed him.

"Why do you care so much about me, Cole?" Her voice was barely above a whisper.

*Because I love you.*

He couldn't go there. Not yet. Even if it was the absolute truth and his reason for chasing after her. The reason he'd never stop pursuing her. Gently, he lifted his hands and cupped her cheeks with his palms. She grew still. His heart climbed into his throat. But she didn't pull away.

"You are one of the most incredible women I've ever known. Please, please stop letting the world tell you that you're not enough. Let go of the burden of other people's opinions and walk in freedom."

She tipped her chin up. He braced for rejection, fully expecting her to push him away. He'd planned to respect her reaction, whatever it was, and calmly walk her to her car.

Again, she stayed. Those fathomless blue eyes searched his face. Her hands found their way to his shoulders. He couldn't last two more minutes with those lips full and pink and plump and oh so kissable in front of him. Those long curls that his fingers ached to tunnel through tickled the backs of his hands. He was a good man, but he wasn't perfect. She was too tempting to resist. Her eyes fluttered closed and her lips parted. Her breath hitched, drop-kicking the last of his self-control into the lake like a punter in an Alabama-Auburn football game.

"I'm going to kiss you now, Avery Lansing Crawford, like I've wanted to for a couple of decades now." He meant to say all kinds of things, but she angled her head to one side and leaned into him. Then his hand slid into her hair and his mouth claimed hers. She tasted sweet and she was warm and she molded her body to his. The silky feeling of her hair twined through his fingers and her palms gliding from his shoulders to the nape of his neck as he deepened the kiss confirmed that holding Avery in his arms was the best thing he'd ever done.

# Chapter Thirteen

Cole's lips on her skin made her feel alive again. His kisses sent delicious shivers down her spine as he found the delicate skin behind her ear then left a scorching trail back to her mouth. Oh, she wanted to be closer. This moment needed to last forever.

But it couldn't. This was Cole. They were supposed to be in a professional relationship, not careening down a danger-ous path like two reckless teenagers.

Not that she didn't want to be a tiny bit reckless. He'd awakened something in her. A passion she hadn't believed could be rekindled.

Reluctantly, she pulled back, her chest heaving.

His grin stretched wide, confirming he felt the same.

"Wow," she whispered, tracing her fingertip along the out-line of his swollen lip.

Cole groaned then captured her hand in his and delicately kissed each fingertip. He'd kissed her. What had he said? For a couple of decades he'd wanted to do that?

Why had he waited?

She surveyed his features, memorizing the curve of his mouth and the planes of his cheeks. The tone of his skin had transformed to a tawny shade in the gathering twilight. She'd known him for years, but tonight she saw him through a different lens. They'd launched out of the friend zone and catapulted straight into something more with that epic kiss.

Desire glittered in his eyes and she let her gaze drop to his mouth. They should talk. Map out a plan. Except she didn't want to spoil the moment by labeling whatever this was sparking between them. She leaned in, brushing her lips against his. Going back for more. He splayed his hands on the small of her back and deepened the kiss. She let him, sliding her hand slowly up the curve of his bicep then squeezing. All her worries about co-parenting and expenses and finishing an intimidating project slipped away. Warmth exploded in her chest. He tasted faintly of chocolate with a tinge of salt. His affection for her breathed life into the wounded places of her heart. The parts of her that, if she was honest, still stung from Pax's rejection.

Wait. Was she ready for this? Dating and romance and wow, she had her children to think about. Sure, this rollercoaster ride of emotions was fun and boy, could he kiss. But this was Cole. They'd joked about a relationship before, but should they really take this leap? Panic flooded in. She inched away, set her palms on his muscular chest then pressed gently, putting some much-needed space between them.

Cole frowned and he palmed the top of his head. "What's wrong?"

"I just—I mean—" She crossed her arms over her chest and looked away. Oh, brother. Listen to her. She couldn't even form a coherent sentence. Cotton candy clouds and the golden glow of the sun setting gave her pause. A perfect night for a romantic kiss in a place that had been a huge part of their childhoods.

"This changes everything," she whispered, forcing herself to meet his troubled gaze. "You're my dearest friend, Cole, and now we've crossed over into a place that's so tender and fragile. What have we done?"

"We kissed." His knowing smile made her pulse hum. "It was incredible at least from my perspective."

"It was and that's why this is so hard."

His smile faded. "What are you trying to say, Avery?"

"I'm afraid that when people find out we're romantically involved, when they realize that photograph shared a few weeks ago was an accurate picture of our feelings, I'm so worried that everything you worked for is going to be diminished. Cheapened." She gulped in a breath then carved the toe of her sandal through the dirt at their feet. "People are going to forget about what Imari's Place means and instead they're going to focus on you and me."

Cole lifted one shoulder. "Spoiler alert, they're already plenty focused on you and me. I used to worry about that, but like you said, tonight changes everything."

"I thought our mission was to bring awareness to human trafficking and raise money for an important cause."

He stepped closer. "The mission hasn't changed. We'll always be intentional about helping more women escape bondage."

She stepped back and bumped against the hood of her vehicle. "The social media crowd is going to have a field day with us."

"Who cares?"

"I care."

"Why?"

"Because it just about kills me that Pax and Trey get nothing but accolades and a book tour, while my every social media post and coffee date and professional decision is scrutinized."

A muscle in his cheek twitched as he closed the distance between them. The woodsy scent of his cologne enveloped her as he leaned closer, bracing his hands on either side of her. "I meant what I said before I kissed you."

His eyes dipped to her lips. The need to feel his mouth on hers filled her with a desperate ache.

"Those words have never been more true. I care about you, Avery." His eyes roamed her face. "I care about what happens to you. The things that hurt you hurt me as well. I want so much for you to not care anymore what people think of you."

"I want that too."

His eyebrows sailed upward. "Do you though?"

"Yes, of course."

She shivered, already missing the warmth of his touch. They'd connected. Genuinely connected. Their kiss had been next level as Julene would say.

Her phone rang and she hesitated, hating to interrupt this conversation.

"Ignore it." His voice was husky. His mouth only inches from hers. "Please."

Oh, she wanted to. How she wanted to. Thoughts of Hayes crying and resisting the bottle flashed in her mind, and she plucked her phone from her pocket. "I can't. I'm sorry."

Cole groaned and dropped his chin to his chest.

Pax's number filled the screen. "It's Pax. I have to take this."

Cole nodded and stepped away, bracing his hands on his hips.

She swiped her trembling finger across the screen then pressed the phone to her ear. "Hello?"

"Hey, it's me."

*Me.* That one intimate word in his familiar southern drawl used to make her heart turn somersaults. This time Pax's voice didn't make her do anything other than flip out. "What's wrong? What's going on? Are the kids all right?"

"The kids are fine. They're back at the house with that amazing nanny my mother hired. I've checked on her twice. She says they're doing great and Hayes is already asleep."

His reassurances did nothing to settle the anxiety buzzing in her veins like a swarm of angry honeybees. "Then why are you calling?"

"It's your grandmother. Someone just told me that she went down in the lobby waiting in line to get into the auditorium."

"Wait, where are you?"

"The Oasis. I'm supposed to be speaking right now, but the event's been delayed a few minutes because the ambulance had to come for Nana."

"My nana?" She squeaked out the words.

"Yes. I wish I had more information. Do you know if she came with anyone?"

"I—I don't know." She paced the ground in front of her SUV. Nana had tickets to Pax and Trey's event. Who knew? She glanced at Cole, who tracked her with that still-smoldering gaze. Willing her to end the call.

"Thank you for letting me know."

"Hang on a sec." He spoke in a muffled voice to someone nearby. "My mother said to tell you they took her to Camellia Community Hospital."

"I'm on my way there now. Thank you, Pax."

"You're welcome. Avery?"

She paused. "Yes?"

"You'll text me later and let me know that she's all right?

It's been a while since I've seen her, but your nana is a special lady. I'd hate for anything to happen to her."

"Yes, of course. I'll let you know as soon as I hear something." She ended the call then pocketed her phone. "It's my grandmother. She fell down waiting inside The Oasis. Pax was calling to let me know. His book signing or whatever has been delayed because of her medical emergency."

Cole's forehead crimped. "That's awful. Do you know where she is now?"

"Yes. Whitney says they took her to Camellia Community."

"Do you want to go?"

She nodded.

"Are you okay to drive?"

"Yes, I think so."

"Then I'll follow you there."

"Thank you." She turned and got into her car. Worry threaded its fingers around her heart. Nana was exasperating sometimes, but they couldn't lose her.

Cole fed both the dollar bills he'd found in his wallet, plus a handful of quarters scrounged from the tray in his vehicle, into the hospital's vending machine. Then he chose peanut butter M&Ms and a Twix bar. The candy dropped to the bottom of the machine with a satisfying thunk. He grabbed the water and the candy and strode back down the hall to the waiting room.

Avery sat in a beige plastic chair in the corner, one leg crossed over the other, and her sandaled foot tapping the air. A nervous posture reminiscent of how she'd often sat in high school when they'd waited for their teachers to return their graded exams.

"Hey." He sat down beside her. "Options are limited around here."

She eyed the chocolate in his hand.

"I have fresh water bottled at the source, as well as your choice of gourmet chocolate."

"Thank you." She accepted the water and took the peanut butter M&Ms. Selfishly, he'd hoped she'd go for the Twix bar instead.

She leaned over and brushed his cheek with a kiss. He froze. It took everything in him not to turn his head ever so slightly and capture her lips with his.

"You're welcome." He sat back then tore the wrapper off the candy bar. Avery removed the cap from her water and took a long sip. He couldn't help but let his gaze slide to her slender neck. The muscles working as she swallowed. Not long ago, he'd taken his time exploring the space between her mouth and her ear. Savoring the way she smelled. How her body felt pressed against his.

*Stop.* He quickly twisted off the top on his own bottle of water and took a long gulp. *This isn't about you, remember?* "Any news?"

"A physician assistant came out a few minutes ago. They wheeled Nana down for a CT scan. She's breathing on her own but not opening her eyes yet. They're concerned about head trauma. They want to rule out a brain bleed." She grimaced. "I've called Mama and Greer. They're on their way."

"I'm sorry this has happened." Cole reached out and squeezed her knee with his hand. "Your grandmother strikes me as a fighter. I'm sure she'll pull through."

She had to. He didn't want to deal with the fallout of telling Avery the truth without Maribelle around. Not that she'd offer much moral support. Still, she was partly responsible for this mess.

He shoved those thoughts right back where they came from. This wasn't the time or the place.

"I didn't even know she was going to Pax's event," Avery said, sorting the candies by color in her palm. "I hope she didn't go there alone."

"I've seen her out and about in town with a group of ladies. They're quite active. I doubt she went by herself. She doesn't drive anymore." He took a bite of the candy bar and thought about that night at the restaurant when Maribelle sat down at his table and made sure he knew that Avery had come back. He'd been so distracted, waiting to meet a woman for a first date who'd never showed.

"I hope she wakes up soon and that there's nothing wrong. We're not ready to be a family without Nana."

Oh, man. The lament in her voice pierced him. What if Nana didn't recover and he had to tell Avery the whole convoluted tale on his own? The chocolate and caramel gummed together in his mouth. He grabbed his water and took a long pull. He kept waiting for the ideal circumstances, but what did that even look like? She'd given him yet another opportunity to come clean. But he couldn't. Not here. Not when she didn't have her family to be with her if she got upset.

And he was confident she'd get upset.

"Are you planning to stay until she's discharged?"

"I'm planning to stay until Mama and Greer get here, and we find out the results of her CT scan."

He checked the time on his phone. Ten fifteen. "I'm sure at this point they'll keep her overnight."

The automatic doors parted and he looked up expecting to see Avery's family. Instead, Pax stepped inside wearing bright blue slacks, a pale blue shirt and a silver-and-blue-striped tie. His honey-brown lace-up oxfords tapped out a determined rhythm on the grungy tile as he strode toward them.

His brown hair was coiffed sky-high and an orange-brown layer of makeup covered his face. Probably to accommodate the bright lights of The Oasis stage. Avery's packet of M&Ms slipped from her hands, scattering candy all over the waiting area.

"Pax, what are you doing here?"

"Hey." He flashed a brilliant white smile their direction, side-stepped the candy and took a seat across from them.

Cole offered a curt nod then dropped to his knees and scooped the candy into his hand.

"The kids are asleep. My parents are there with Trey. I wanted to stop by and check on your grandmother," Pax said.

Super. Cole's stomach clenched as he stood and carried the trash to the can positioned by the elevator. He didn't belong here, but he wasn't confident he should leave Avery alone with Pax. Then again, they used to be married. He turned back toward Avery, willing her to look his way. To reassure him that she needed him by her side.

She met his gaze. Her fingers rubbed the back of her opposite hand, but she didn't say anything.

He pulled his keys from his pocket. "I'm going to go. You'll let me know if anything changes, right?"

"Of course." She tucked an errant curl behind her ear but stayed in her chair.

Disappointment fisted in his chest. Couldn't she at least give him a hug or a chaste kiss? Offer to walk out with him so he could kiss her properly? He felt the weight of Pax's curious gaze sizing him up.

"Thanks for everything."

Her slow smile sent a frisson of warmth curling through him.

"No problem." He turned and strode out into the sticky night, his frustration building with every step. *No problem?* Maybe he was being childish. Maybe his guilt clouded his thinking. Maybe he shouldn't have kissed her at all. Then he wouldn't be in this rock-and-a-hard-place predicament, clinging desperately to this new phase of their relationship yet fearing he'd already wrecked everything.

She should go after him.

Avery bit her lip, watching as Cole strode into the darkness of the parking lot. He'd been so kind and attentive. She should at least give him a hug and kiss. Tell him thank you. After their encounter near the pond, she felt the tiniest bit guilty for not walking him out.

She glanced at Pax.

He studied her. "Is that—"

"Cole Whitaker, director of a local nonprofit, Imari's Place."

"Is that all he is to you?"

"Does it matter?"

He smirked.

Her stomach curdled. Maybe eating that candy was a bad idea. "Why are you here, Pax?"

His expression sobered. "I told you I was concerned when I heard that your grandmother fell inside my parents' church at an event where I was speaking. I wanted to be doubly sure that she's okay. Since you didn't text me or answer my calls, I thought I should see for myself."

She plucked her phone from her purse and glanced at the screen. He had texted her twice and called twice. "I'm sorry. I don't think the reception is all that great in here. It's nice of you to stop by. We're waiting for Nana to get a CT scan."

"Oh, wow." Pax tugged at the knot on his tie then pushed his hand into his hair. Tried to anyway. It was gelled and sculpted within an inch of its life. "Since we're alone, I think now would be a good time for a candid conversation. Don't you?"

She picked at the label on her water bottle. "Conversation about what?"

"Life. Hayes and Addison. Your plans for the rest of the summer. We're divorced, but that doesn't mean I don't care about the kids or what's going on in your life."

Where was all this coming from? She opened her mouth then closed it. She couldn't move. Couldn't speak. Overhead, a woman's voice came through the loudspeaker, paging a doctor. The doors slid open and closed. Footsteps came and went. She stared at him.

His brows scrunched together. "Avery, are you all right?"

Oh, how she wished Cole hadn't left. "I'm…confused, Pax. What are you up to? Why are you saying all this? Why now?"

"All valid questions." He huffed out a breath then leaned forward, elbows on his knees. "Look, I didn't go about this in the right way at all."

She dug her nails into her palms. Her whole body flashed hot then cold. "You don't say."

"I realize now that my decision to leave you when you were expecting was irresponsible, to say the least, and not to mention incredibly selfish. I own that."

"Don't forget you left your daughter *and* your son. Also, our business caved, I had to move back in with my parents, and we haven't heard from you in a year." Her voice trembled. Okay, that probably wasn't what she should've started with. But if he wanted to have a candid conversation, she wasn't about to pretend he hadn't hurt them.

"A year? That's a bit of a stretch. I've checked in from time to time."

"Pax. Checking in——" she quoted the air with her fingers "——that's what former college roommates or childhood friends do. You are their father. Trey is your partner and one of the most important grown-ups Addison had in her life. And you both vanished. Hayes never even met you before this week. How can——"

"I know, I know." He pulled his tie off completely then dropped it in the chair beside him. "You're right. Look, I'm not here to fight with you. I came by to make sure your grandmother was all right."

"So why are you asking about my summer plans and suddenly pretending to care?"

Misery dragged his mouth into a frown. He hesitated, rubbing his palms on his pants. "When I walked in and saw you sitting here, I thought I should take the opportunity to apologize."

Oh. She leaned back, crossed her arms over her chest and fixed him with her most pointed stare. "Let's hear it then."

"I'm sorry." He clasped his hands in front of him. "There's no excuse for leaving you the way that we did. Trey and I deeply regret how we've handled our relationships with you, with the kids, and I——we——want to do better."

"Define better, please."

"To be honest, we've been ridiculously self-absorbed. The thrill of creating a successful show, building a thriving business so quickly and having a beautiful family all went to my head. Yet I felt so trapped. So hopeless. I had everything a man could possibly want. But I struggled with my attraction toward Trey and felt strongly I should be committed to our marriage."

"So you decided to cheat and then leave me with a house and two kids to manage all by myself?"

Okay, that wasn't kind. Or probably even necessary. But the weeks and months of Pax and Trey roaming free with barely any responsibilities, while she slogged through single motherhood and fielded criticism at every turn, had drained her emotionally and physically.

His chin slumped with his shoulders. "That's a fair question. Again, you're right. There's no excuse for cheating, especially when you had Addison and you were pregnant with Hayes. We took the easy way out instead of giving you the honest explanation and support you deserved." He dragged his gaze to meet hers. "There's nothing else I can say other than I'm truly sorry, Avery. I hope someday you can forgive me."

His words shocked her. She could only stare at him, her jaw lax.

"Please. Say something."

She shifted in the uncomfortable chair. "I accept your apology. Really, I do. But if I'm being honest, I've still got miles to go when it comes to forgiving you and Trey."

"I understand." Pax pinched the back of his neck with his fingers. "Going forward, I'd like to establish a home base here."

"Wait. What?" Blood roared behind her ears. Their fragile truce was already fraying around the edges. "You're moving back to Camellia?"

"You're here. My folks are here. It's a great place to raise kids. I'd like to be in their lives."

"What does that mean exactly?"

"Well, we're starting with one weekend. What if it was two weekends a month? Eventually I'd like to work up to co-parenting. An equal fifty-fifty arrangement."

"Are you serious?" She sprang to her feet and paced the cramped walkway between their rows of chairs. Fifty-fifty?

"I want to make up for being gone for a year. Legally, there's no reason why I can't parent them. I'm their father and Trey's my partner."

She whirled to face him.

He'd kept his voice calm. When she'd popped out of her chair like a firecracker, he'd stayed sitting down, his expression so earnest.

"They can't travel with you. I mean, vacations and outings, things like that are fine, but you can't just scoop them up and haul them off to Kentucky for a long weekend because Trey wants to see a horse race."

"I understand your concern."

"It's a legitimate concern, Pax. They're too little to be dragged around the country."

He worked his jaw in a tight circle. "I can promise you, we won't be doing that."

She massaged her forehead with her fingertips. "Do you have jobs? Something a smidge more ordinary than a book tour?"

"Trey's going to sell real estate, and he's agreed to seek professional help for his gambling addiction. I'm taking a job in pharmaceutical sales. We'll have a steady income. Will Addison start school in the fall?"

"She's starting with transitional kindergarten at a local preschool. If that's okay with you." She tacked on that last part. Frankly, it felt weird, asking his opinion, even his permission when it came to decisions regarding their daughter. She smoothed her sweaty palms on the legs of her shorts. The doors parted again and a bald man wearing green scrubs under a long white coat stepped into the room. "Family of Maribelle Lansing?"

"Here." She lifted her hand and waggled her fingers. "I'm her granddaughter, Avery."

"Dr. Knight." His tired brown eyes turned toward Pax. "Are you family as well?"

Pax shook his head. "I'll leave you to it. Hope everything's okay. I'll give you a call tomorrow." He stood, gently squeezed her elbow then gave the doctor a brief nod before he left the building.

Avery shifted her attention toward the doctor. "How is she?"

"Stable and resting quietly. There's no sign of head trauma. When they brought her in, they said her companion reported she'd been sitting on a bench, basically slumped over."

"Did she have a stroke or a heart attack?"

Dr. Knight shook his head. "Everything looks normal. Blood pressure's a little high and she's severely dehydrated. We're going to keep her overnight for observation. If all is well tomorrow, then she can go home, although I don't believe I would leave her alone. Where does she live?"

"She lives at Westwood Manor, but she can stay with my parents until she's feeling well. Can I see her for a few minutes?"

"If you'd like."

"Please." She scooped her purse and water bottle from the floor. Hopefully if Mama and Greer showed up they'd ask at the registration desk for instructions.

Dr. Knight turned and strode toward an area clearly designated for hospital employees. He swiped his badge, the doors parted and he stepped through. She followed him into a wide-open area that felt more like the control center at NASA she'd seen on television than a hospital. Computers sat on workstations; medical people moved about with startling efficiency. Phones rang, patients were rolled in and out on gurneys. Avery wanted to make herself very small and stay out of the way. Somewhere a machine beeped, and a siren grew louder as an ambulance approached the building.

"This way." Dr. Knight slid a curtain back on a small private alcove. "You may sit with her for a few minutes, but then you'll need to go. We don't have formal visiting hours down here. We're going to move her upstairs as soon as there's a room available."

"I won't be here long. Thank you, Dr. Knight."

He nodded then turned away, zinging the curtain closed behind him.

Avery swallowed hard then approached the bed, clutching her purse with both hands. "You really gave us quite a scare, Nana."

Oh, she looked so frail. Her makeup was smudged and her hair matted. A cannula pumped oxygen into her nostrils. Nana's bony hands rested at her sides. Clear liquid flowed from a bag on a stand into her arm.

Avery lowered her bag to a chair pushed against the wall then moved beside the bed and clasped Nana's hand in hers. She delicately traced a purple vein visible beneath Nana's papery, wrinkled skin. "I know you hate to be bossed around, but you really need to get some rest. Then we'll bring you home and feed you all your favorite foods."

Emotion thickened her throat. "Get better, Nana. Please. I don't know what we'd do without you. I love you."

# Chapter Fourteen

So, this just happened. Super exciting!

Cole tapped the video Avery had included with her text message. A man rolled open his box truck's back door and revealed brand-new cabinets for Imari's Place. The second video she'd sent featured a crew carrying them inside.

Avery could handle taking delivery, but he still sort of felt like a coward for leaving.

Okay, a lot like a coward. Because he'd done his best to avoid her for the past three days. Ever since Pax showed up in the hospital waiting room, he'd been rattled. That kiss had rocked his world. Finally, Avery Lansing Crawford was his.

And now he was going to go and mess it all up by telling her he'd caved to her grandmother's schemes and accepted a bribe. She was going to be crushed. Especially after what he'd said to her at the pond.

*I care about what happens to you. The things that hurt you hurt
me as well.*

He'd meant all of that. He really had. But, caught up in
the moment, he didn't think about how they'd sound later.
Once she knew the truth. She'd been so honest. So vulnerable. Every time she pulled back the proverbial curtain and
shared her fears about not being good enough, she'd offered
him another opportunity to confess that he'd allowed her
grandmother to manipulate him.

Avery had leaned on his belief in her to push through the
doubt, and he didn't even have the decency to honor her brav-
ery by coming clean.

"Hon, are you all right?" his mother asked. They were on
their way to Tupelo, Mississippi. She stared straight ahead, her
hands positioned on the steering wheel at a responsible ten and
two. Her cruise control was set at a steady 65 mph. Always a
rule follower, his mother.

"I've messed up big-time, Mom."

The classical satellite radio station played a familiar concerto
through the sedan's speakers. She fiddled with the volume then
cast a quick glance his way. He could almost hear her brain
formulating an optimistic, nonjudgmental response. That had
always been her go-to coping strategy. What he wouldn't give
to see her just one time emote something that resembled rage.
To rail at the unfairness of all she'd lost.

"I'm glad you can get away for a few days. I know this isn't
exactly a vacation what with your speaking engagement in
Oxford and all but maybe putting some miles between you
and Camellia will help you gain a fresh perspective."

A fresh perspective about his lie of omission and hasty exit
from the hospital? Yeah, well, he'd tried to spin that in a more
positive light a dozen times already.

The truth was impossible to ignore.

He ripped open the bag of cheese-flavored chips then plucked one out and shoved it in his mouth. His phone chimed again. He dusted the cheesy powder residue from his fingers then looked at the screen. She'd sent a selfie, featuring that megawatt smile he'd loved since forever.

**Have a safe trip. Counting the minutes until you're home.**

He doused the groan climbing up his throat with a swig of diet soda.

Add total dirtbag onto his list of undesirable qualities. Usually, he'd nod in agreement. Feign acceptance of his mother's sound advice. Because pushing back with anything other than optimism was akin to poking a bunny with a sharp stick. He couldn't bring himself to be thoughtless and short-tempered with a woman who approached all of life on such an even keel.

Until Avery sent him a text like that. Her message filled him with longing to hold her in his arms again. And for a hot minute, he considered begging his mother to take the next exit, whip around and drive straight to the Huntingtons' lake house.

But worry quickly squelched the desire to get back home. Back to Avery. He had zero excuses for not telling her the truth before now. Nana's health scare had bought him some time. He'd used her hospital stay and his commitment to take this quick trip as valid reasons to keep his distance. But now that Maribelle was out of the hospital and expected to make a full recovery, he couldn't rely on her mishap as a reason to keep avoiding Avery.

"Do you have your speech prepared?" Mom asked.

"It's a fundraising event at Uncle Art and Aunt Linda's

country club," he said. "Between you and me, I have a standard speech that I recycle for certain audiences."

Her laughter filled the car and lifted his spirits. She had the best laugh.

"What I hear you saying is, you don't need to hole up in their guest room. You'll be free to visit with your aunt and uncle and your cousins this evening."

"Absolutely." He plucked another chip from the bag and popped it in his mouth. The salty, crunchy snack wasn't nearly as satisfying as he'd hoped. They had stopped at their favorite interstate convenience store a few miles back and bought some snacks to carry them through until they arrived at their relatives' house in a couple of hours.

"Do you want to talk about what's bothering you?"

No. Yes.

"It's a mess, to be honest. I guess you heard Avery Lansing Crawford has been helping out with our big project, the expansion of Imari's Place. We're struggling with the media coverage. Folks in the community have not been real encouraging."

"Yes, I saw a rather disturbing conversation online last night. What is with people these days? The comments were quite—"

"Crass?" he finished her sentence for her.

"Yes. Crass. That's a good way to put it."

"There's been quite the focus lately on Avery and me, which is something we hadn't expected or really even encouraged."

A patrol car with flashing lights had pulled onto the shoulder of the road, right behind a bright red sports car. His mother tapped her turn signal, cautiously checked her mirrors then glanced quickly over her shoulder before merging into the next lane.

"Are you and Avery an item?"

He bit back a smile at her choice of words then unscrewed the cap on his soft drink and took a long sip. The sweet carbonated liquid didn't do much to quench his thirst. Or maybe his frazzled nerves had turned his mouth cotton ball dry.

How to answer that? Since the night beside the pond had been interrupted by Maribelle's fainting spell at The Oasis, he and Avery hadn't had more than five minutes to themselves. Their face-to-face communication had consisted of interviews with Max and Charlie so they could finish filming their footage for the documentary. Then they'd exchanged whirlwind text messages with Dale to keep on top of the schedule as the project moved forward more quickly than they'd anticipated. Now they were on track to have new residents move in by late October. Max and Charlie wanted to finish the documentary this fall as well. And ever since Pax and Trey returned to Camellia, the whole stinkin' town had been caught up in their business.

He was officially over it.

"I've cared deeply for Avery for years, Mom. Working with her on this project hasn't changed my feelings."

Her concerned gaze warmed his skin. He stared straight ahead, afraid that if he made eye contact, he'd tell her everything. And he was too ashamed to be that honest.

"I'm sorry to hear that not everyone in Camellia is thrilled with your work. I, for one, am extremely proud, and if Kim were here, you know she'd be cheering you on."

Her tender words wound around his heart. An unexpected tightness in his throat had him reaching for his soda again. "I'm sorry that I couldn't save her."

He barely choked out the words before taking another sip of his soda.

Mom's gasp startled him. In a very un-Mom gesture, she slammed on the brakes then steered the car onto the side of the interstate. Twisting in her seat, she pinned him with a hard look. "Cole Whitaker, what did you just say?"

He studied her as he slowly twisted the cap back onto the bottle. "I—I said I'm sorry that I couldn't save her. Dad told me to watch her and I did, for a minute, but then I got distracted. When I looked back, she was gone."

"Oh, honey." Mom's expression crumpled and her green eyes filled with tears. "She was abducted. I've never blamed you."

"But Dad did."

She pressed her mouth into a thin line then angled her head to one side.

"You don't have to take up for him. He yelled at me and said it was my fault."

Mom heaved a sigh then glanced down at her wrist. The classical piece filtering through the speakers carried a somber tone. She fidgeted with her charm bracelet. "Your father was so angry. He said a lot of horrible things to you and to me."

"Is that why you didn't stay together?"

"One of the reasons." She sniffled and raised her head then offered a sad smile. "I love you, Cole. You're my son and there's nothing you can do or not do to change how I feel about you. Please don't feel guilty for Kimberly's abduction or her death."

Oh, man. He did not want to fall apart right now. Not here. Maybe later, alone in his aunt and uncle's guest room, he'd replay this conversation and let the weight of her words wash over him. "I love you too, Mom. Thank you for saying that."

"You're welcome." She reached inside her purse and pulled out a travel-sized packet of tissues. "Would you like one?"

He smiled. "Nope, I'm good."

She dabbed at her tears then cleaned her hands with the sanitizer that lived in her console. A few minutes later, they were back on the road and cruising toward Oxford.

Cole stared out the window. He should feel relieved, right? That his mother had released him of this thousand-pound burden he'd dragged around for decades.

But he couldn't shake the guilt. It had spread like a kudzu vine, choking out his happiness. Hiding the facts about the funding for Imari's Place was going to destroy him. Not even that incredible kiss he and Avery had shared could overpower the sickening sensation lodged in his gut. He had to tell her what he'd done.

Avery held up her phone and filmed a quick video of the installers carefully lifting the front window into place. She couldn't wait to show Cole. She snapped several pictures then checked to make sure there was no traffic coming before she stepped out into the cul-de-sac for a better angle.

The camellias along the property line were in full bloom. Their gorgeous pink blossoms and vibrant green leaves added brilliant pops of color to the unfinished construction site. She angled her phone to capture the new window, the camellias and feathery wisps of white clouds dotting the summer sky.

Windows. They finally had windows. She let out a little whoop of joy, which earned her a curious glance from two of the installers, but she didn't care. Less than two weeks ago, the manufacturer had warned them of a ridiculous delay. Somehow, the crisis had been avoided and they'd taken a giant leap toward the finish line.

She was about to put her phone away when a message from Cole appeared on her screen.

I'll be back home in about an hour. I've made arrangements for your mama and Greer to watch Addison and Hayes. Can you meet me on the dock at 4:15?

Blinking, she read the message again. Well, wasn't he the sweetest thing? She quickly responded. I would love to meet you on the dock at 4:15. Can I bring anything?

Nope just your gorgeous self.

A smile creased her cheeks. Can't wait. She resisted the urge to attach a cheesy kissy face emoji. Oh, I almost forgot. Family dinner at 6. I need to be back for that. You are welcome to join us.

Three little dots bounced then stopped then bounced again. Next door Wendy and Shayla stepped out onto the porch followed by Max, Charlie and their sound technician.

She quickly glanced down at her screen. Cole's message arrived in a telltale whoosh she'd grown to anticipate with the giddiness of a lovestruck teenager.

I'd love to stay for dinner, but only if Nana's there.

She chuckled. It wouldn't be a family dinner without Nana. We're celebrating her release from the hospital.

This time she sent an adorable pink heart. He'd only been in Oxford for a day and a half, and less than a week had passed since he'd walked out of the hospital waiting room. But so much had happened since that last evening they'd been together. Their intense conversation, the kisses they'd shared then Pax's unexpected interruption and his heartfelt apology—the dizzying pace of her own life left her feeling off-kilter and slightly overwhelmed.

Selfishly, she longed to slow everything down and reconnect with Cole. There was so much they needed to work through. The expansion project's accelerated timeline wasn't allowing for much downtime, either. It would be a huge blessing if they finished ahead of schedule, but she could hardly keep up. On top of all that, she'd accumulated an impressive list of influencer campaigns for her social media platforms through the end of the year.

Wendy and Shayla were posing for still photos near the blooming camellia bush. Thankfully, they'd agreed to be a part of the documentary. It took tremendous courage for them to speak up and be willing to appear on camera. As the women embraced and grinned for another photo, Avery blinked back tears. The more time and energy she invested in this project, the more she realized what an impact the foundation had made. Goose bumps shot down her arms as she envisioned the house full of more young women, with jobs and opportunities to further their education. She'd struggled to find her place here, but now that she'd dipped her toe in the pool, she didn't want to stop being involved. Her plans to get the production line up and running still felt a little too pie-in-the-sky, but she wasn't giving up.

Her phone chimed with an incoming text message.

She glanced at the screen. Trey.

Hey, Avery. I'm sure you're quite busy, but I'd like to speak with you. I need to apologize in person. Wondered when we might schedule a time to chat?

Oh, dear.

Avery glanced back toward Wendy and Shayla. She didn't have time to speak with Trey. At least not right now.

Before she could respond to his request, her phone buzzed

again, this time with a notification that someone had tagged her in another post. Since she'd been back in Camellia, every time she'd stumbled across people in the community gossiping about her, their thoughtless words had sent her into an emotional free fall. She didn't have the emotional energy to get upset right now, especially not before she spoke to Wendy and Shayla. They'd both achieved big milestones recently—a promotion at work and successful completion of an associate's degree at the local technical college. Not that they needed her praise, but she was so excited for them and didn't want to miss the opportunity to offer her congratulations.

Avery silently offered a prayer for help. Part of her felt foolish asking for wisdom about online encounters when she stood a few yards from a residence for women who'd endured the unimaginable. But when she'd tried to handle harsh criticism on her own, she'd bungled it every time.

Maybe it wouldn't hurt to see who'd tagged her. Why not give people the benefit of the doubt? Not every post or comment was malicious. Sometimes people offered gracious encouragement.

*Stop. Don't do this.*

Again, the voice of reason whispered for her to steer clear.

Avery jammed her phone into her handbag without responding to Trey. She'd give careful thought and pray a few times before she made any meeting arrangements with him. Even though he said he wanted to apologize, that wasn't a conversation she felt equipped to handle yet.

Whoever had tagged her on social media would be just fine without her acknowledgment. Spending this summer in Camellia had taught her a few things. She'd learned to set boundaries. To trust the Lord had good plans for her, although that was often still a daily struggle. And she'd embraced the importance of being mindful of encounters that caused her pain. She wouldn't let the negativity get to her today or dampen her enthusiasm for Wendy's and Shayla's success. The women at Imari's Place had inspired her to grow. To believe in the possibility of second chances. She was still a work in progress, but she'd definitely learned that she didn't need likes, comments or shares to determine her worth.

He had less than two hours to confess the whole sordid truth, apologize and plead for forgiveness.

The dock wobbled under Cole's Top-Siders as he paced alongside Greer's boat. This was a horrible idea. Overhead, birds soared in an indigo sky. Late afternoon sunshine warmed his skin through his linen shirt. Greer had helped him secure the canvas Bimini cover over the boat's cockpit so they'd have plenty of shade during their ride. Maybe he should've opted for a quiet dinner at a secluded booth at the Italian restaurant downtown. Then if Avery got upset—*when* she got upset—all she had to do was walk out and get in her car.

Because he knew for certain his betrayal would deeply hurt her.

He should've told her about Maribelle's donation that day they met in the coffee shop and she'd proposed developing an entire production line. Instead, he'd let his unrequited romantic interests drive his decisions. They'd blown past all professional boundaries with that kiss beside the pond.

And he had no one to blame but himself.

Cole climbed aboard then lifted the cushions on the boat's bench seat up and double-checked the cooler. Cans of Avery's favorite sparkling water greeted him. He made sure the plastic lid on the fruit and cheese plate he'd picked up from the deli hadn't come undone. Satisfied, he hopped out of the boat and back on the dock. This was the only place he could think of that no one would be able to interrupt them. Sure, it might be a tense ride back after he confessed, but at least she'd have her family waiting inside, preparing for supper.

Avery emerged from the house. Every word he'd planned to speak vanished as he drank in her appearance. Her short-sleeved light pink dress complimented her curves, and the long flowy skirt swirled around her legs as she walked across the grass. Her wide smile captivated him. He stood rooted in place, spinning the boat's key ring on his finger and grinning like he didn't have a care in the world.

She paused in the grass, toed off her sandals then hurried toward him. His heart banged against his ribs. Avery picked up her pace then broke into a jog.

*This. This right here is what you've dreamed of. And now she's yours. So why mess it up?*

He shunned that tempting thought then stretched his arms wide.

A peal of her infectious laughter filled the air as he swept her into his embrace then buried his face in her hair. "I missed you," he murmured, drinking in her now-familiar vanilla fragrance.

"I missed you too." She looped her arms around his neck, molding her body to his. The fabric of her dress was smooth beneath his hands as he held her close. She pulled back slightly, and her blue eyes surveyed his face before she pressed up on her toes and kissed him.

She tasted sweet and the tenderness in her touch was perfection. He mined deep for his last ounce of self-control and reluctantly pulled away. "I'd like nothing more than to stand here on this dock until supper and kiss you senseless," he murmured, cupping her cheeks with his hands.

"Who's stopping you?" she whispered, her voice breathy as she claimed his mouth again.

He groaned then brushed her lips with one more chaste kiss before he stepped back and clasped her hands in his. "Greer was kind enough to loan me his boat and babysit your kids—"

"So let's go before they change their minds?"

"Exactly."

Boy, this was not going to be easy.

"Thank you so much for doing this." She held on to his hand as he helped her onboard. "I couldn't wait for you to get home because I have so much to tell you."

"Is that right?" He forced a smile. "That makes two of us, I suppose. You first."

She smiled again and his heart rate rocketed into orbit. He released his grip on her hand and gestured toward the bench seat. "Would you like something to drink? Your mama and Greer were kind enough to stock the cooler for us."

The sunlight streaming through the trees cast a glow around Avery's platinum curls. She had never looked more beautiful. The realization nearly flattened him. Did he really have the nerve to tell her everything?

"Wow, you've thought of everything tonight, haven't you?"

"I don't know about everything." He squeezed the words past his parched throat, grabbed a can of soda from the cooler and turned away.

"Want me to undo the cleat line?"

"Please." He popped the tab on the can, took a long sip then set the soda in the cupholder. He wiped his clammy palms on his shorts then sat down in the captain's chair. Avery untied the line and returned to the seat beside him, can of sparkling water in hand. He turned the key in the ignition and the motor rumbled to life.

"So where are we headed?"

"Have you ever anchored in the cove at the western end of the lake?"

"No, I don't believe I have. Good plan."

They rode in comfortable silence with the warm breeze washing over them. Avery turned her chair toward the windshield and slipped her sunglasses on. His gaze lingered on her slender neck and warmth flooded through him as he thought about trailing hot kisses from her collarbone to her ear.

*Easy, there. That's not what tonight is about.*

He took another sip of his drink then put it back and concentrated on steering the boat safely across the lake.

A few minutes later they arrived in the cove. Cole slowed down, the boat rocking gently from the wake of another passing vessel. He turned off the engine then dropped the anchor. A handful of other boats had anchored out, facing the western edge of the lake. They still had several hours until sunset, but plenty of people were taking advantage of the gorgeous weather and spending the evening on the lake.

Cole opened the cooler and brought out the fruit and cheese tray.

Maybe he should skip the small talk and romantic hors d'oeuvres. Stalling only delayed the inevitable.

He sat down across from her on the bench seat, deliberately putting space between them. His hands trembled so he tucked them beneath his thighs on the buttery-yellow seat cushion.

"There's something I need to tell you."

Her flirtatious smile and spark in her eyes muddled his thoughts. "Oh?"

A tiny ribbon of doubt slithered in.

Two tiny divots formed in her smooth brow as her smile faded. "Wait. Is this bad news?"

"Um, well—"

"Because if it is, I'd rather hold off. You can tell me another time. We have too many wonderful things to celebrate tonight. Let's deal with the negative stuff tomorrow."

Oh, no. He palmed the back of his neck. Avery took a dainty sip of her drink. He finished his off then stood and dropped the empty can in the container under the sink.

"W-would you like some cheese and crackers or fruit?"

"No, thank you. I'm not hungry."

"Avery." Her name left his lips in a pathetic groan. He sank down on the seat farthest away from hers and tunneled his fingers through his hair.

"Cole, are you all right?" She set her drink in the cupholder then moved closer. "You're not quite yourself tonight."

Before he could respond, she sat beside him and pressed her hand against his arm.

"Wait. Is this about the photo?"

Panic welled. He couldn't move. Couldn't think. Not with her sitting so close and her blue eyes locked on him. "What photo?"

"Someone took a photo of Pax and me sitting in the waiting room at the hospital. They shared it in an online group and evidently people are...commenting."

He clenched his jaw. "What kind of comments?"

"Does it matter? I didn't look. Harper mentioned it to me. People are probably being nosy and thoughtless. If you had seen it, I just wanted you to know there was no reason to worry." She slid her palm up his arm and started massaging the knots at the base of his spine. "Wow, you're all worked up. I'm sorry if I've added to your stress. Did something happen while you were away?"

"It's not—it wasn't—my trip was fine." He blew out a long

breath then faced her, resting his hand on her knee. "More than fine. Mom and I had a great conversation and the fundraising was successful."

Her expression softened. "Good, I'm so glad."

"Avery, I—"

She silenced him with a finger pressed against his lips. "Can we just enjoy being us? Please? Whatever's on your mind, I promise we'll get through it together."

Oh, if only that were possible. He swallowed hard. Then hesitated. Her eyes searched his face.

"Us. I like the sound of that."

"Me too." Her lashes fluttered against her skin. "Now, let's get to the part where you kiss me senseless."

Then she leaned in and silenced his worries with a searching kiss.

"The expansion of Imari's Place will provide additional housing and vocational training for thirty-six women, more than double the number of people initially assisted when the project launched eight years ago." Smiling, Julene glanced up from the story she was reading in the latest issue of *Alabama Living* magazine. "Way to go, y'all."

Avery met Cole's gaze across Mama and Greer's dining room table. He gave her a knowing grin and formed a heart with his fingertips. With his hair still tousled from their ride on the lake and his skin flushed from the late afternoon sun, he looked more handsome than ever.

What a gift he was. She'd never imagined when she'd packed up and moved back home that he'd walk back into her life.

Addison had already left the table and gone out onto the porch to host a tea party for her dolls. Hayes babbled in his high chair beside her then blew raspberries before picking up a piece of avocado and stuffing it in his mouth. Avery chuckled. He wasn't willing to surrender the spotlight for long, not even for a worthy cause.

"Wait, there's more." Julene held up her finger. "Well-known documentary filmmakers Max and Charlie Johansen have been in town for several weeks. They anticipate release of their next documentary featuring Imari's Place early next year."

"Here, here." Greer lifted his glass of lemonade. "Congratulations, Cole and Avery. We're so proud of you."

"The house really is beautiful." Mama's eyes glistened with tears. "Harper showed me the photos online. The women who live at Imari's Place will feel so blessed."

"Thank you, Mama." Avery smiled. That was the part that made her feel the most fulfilled. Wendy and Shayla had shared parts of their story with her already. She couldn't wait to see the finished film. "Hopefully our plans for the production facility will become reality. Think of the jobs that will add to help more women get back on their feet."

"That's the best part of the whole story," Cole said.

"I don't know about that." Avery held his gaze. "There's other parts that aren't mentioned that are pretty good too."

"For once they kept your personal life out of the story," Harper said. "How ironic is that?"

"Well, I guess the old nana's still got it, right?" Nana clasped her hands and beamed proudly as if she'd just been elected to political office.

An awkward silence blanketed the table. Avery shifted in her seat and faced her grandmother. That was like Nana to try and take credit for something she had nothing to do with. A small voice in her head counseled her to overlook the offense. After all, they'd gathered around the table tonight to celebrate Nana's quick recovery. But there was something about her words and facial expression that caught Avery's attention. And this time she couldn't let it go.

"What are you talking about, Nana?" Avery handed Hayes his new sippy cup. He banged it against the tray of his high chair. The plastic against plastic was the only sound in the room. Avery let her gaze ping around the table. Why wasn't Cole looking at her? Greer shifted uncomfortably in his chair.

"Oh, I meant that my helping Cole see how much he needed your expertise on the project really paid off." Nana's smile wobbled as she reached for the cloth napkin and its holder. "Darling, you simply must update these napkins and holders. They really aren't fit for company and—"

"Nana, don't change the subject." Avery plucked the napkin and its holder from Nana's hands and set them out of reach on the table. "What are you not telling me? How did you help Cole?"

"Avery…" Harper's tone carried a pleading note. As if begging her not to look behind the closed door for fear of what she might find. Her days of letting people sweep things under the rug were over. She couldn't not pursue this.

"And are you complicit in this too?" Avery's voice shook as she glared at her sister and then at her new boyfriend. "Cole? What did you do?"

"There are a few things you should probably know." Cole cleared his throat. "About Imari's Place."

"All she needs to know is that the house looks beautiful and those women are all going to be so happy," Nana said.

"Maribelle."

"Mrs. Lansing."

Mama and Cole spoke in unison, both scolding Nana.

Anger and impatience burned a trail to her heart. "One of you had better start talking. Now."

Nana heaved a dramatic sigh. "Okay, fine. I'll go first. I offered Cole and his board of directors an incentive to include you in the expansion project."

Blood pounded in her ears. "What kind of an incentive?"

"Just a small donation. It really wasn't much. I—"

"Two hundred and fifty thousand dollars," Cole said. He looked like he wanted to vomit.

Avery gasped. "What? Where did you get that kind of money? And why did you bribe him?" She glared at Cole. "And why did you accept it?"

Her voice got louder with every question. Hayes burst into tears.

"I'll take him." Harper stood and extracted Hayes from the chair, swept him into her arms then gently settled him on her lap with a pacifier she retrieved from the table. He leaned against Harper's shoulder and drew a deep withering breath as the pacifier wiggled in his mouth.

"Now, honey, this was all for your own good." Nana shot Cole a nervous glance. "Tell her."

"Oh, please. That's what people say when they've done something thoughtless and cruel." Avery tipped her chin up and narrowed her gaze at him. "How could you?"

"I have no excuse," he said quietly. "It was wrong and I never should've agreed to the deal."

"Turncoat," Nana growled.

Avery's chest compressed. She couldn't breathe. Her legs itched to run, but she had to stay and hear the truth. Every last ugly bitter detail.

"And the napkin?" Avery shifted her attention to Harper.

"Whose brilliant idea was it to tell the production team about that?"

Again, no one spoke. And all eyes dropped to the table. "You people are a bunch of cowards."

"Greer told me about the napkin." Mama slowly raised her hand and met Avery's gaze. "I took it to a friend who works for the local news station. She was planning to do a story, but someone beat me to it."

Mama pinned Nana with a meaningful look.

"Mama." Avery didn't have any other words. Her own mother was in on this twisted scheme?

"Look at your life, Avery. You've gone from the pit of despair to having everything you've ever wanted in less than six months. Nobody's life turns around that fast." Mama's eyes glistened with unshed tears. "This is the happiest I've seen you in years, so I absolutely will not apologize for trying to do what was in your best interests. Especially when you weren't going to do it for yourself."

"Since we're having our come-to-Jesus talk, I asked a woman who volunteers at Westwood Manor to drive me to the house y'all are building. I had sneaked a picture of that napkin and showed it to the nice boys with the movie cameras."

Cole cut Nana a glare, but he didn't say anything.

The only sound was Hayes sucking on his pacifier and Addison singing off-key through the screen door to the porch.

"Hold up." Avery shook her head, determined to track that rabbit trail as well. "Who helped you?"

Nana grimaced. "That's not important."

"Tell me."

Nana avoided eye contact and smoothed a nonexistent wrinkle from her coral-colored slacks. "Genevieve."

Avery barked out a laugh. "Why am I not surprised? Is that

what you all think? That I'm not capable of making good choices, so you made what you thought were the best ones for me? That is wrong on so many levels."

"Or it's exactly true and you don't want to admit that we were right," Nana quipped.

Honestly, that woman didn't know when to keep her mouth shut.

"This is unbelievable." She stood, knocking her chair to the floor. "My own family conspired against me."

"I don't blame you for being upset. Please know that we had only the best intentions," Cole said.

"Oh, is that right?" Avery didn't even bother to keep the snark from her voice. "Well pardon me for not being more grateful."

He winced and looked away.

She wanted to scream. Those same lips that had kissed her passionately this afternoon had kept a scandalous secret from her. Was she doomed to betrayal by the men in her life forever? The sins of the fathers visited on the sons and all that?

"Avery, please. Don't do us that way," Greer said.

"If you want to be angry at somebody, be angry at me," Nana said.

"I can be angry at all of you," Avery fired back. "Cole, you need to leave."

Cole's mouth tightened. "All right, if that's what you think is best."

"You know what, maybe it's better if I go." She spun around, spots peppering her vision. "Addison, time to go home."

Her heels clicked on the hardwood as she started shoving Hayes's blanket, toys and sippy cup in her diaper bag lying on the floor beside Mama's couch.

"Avery, honey, you're upset." Mama's voice was soft as she

moved toward her. "Where are you going to go with two little kids?"

"Mama, don't talk to me. I cannot stay here another second with a house full of people who betrayed me."

"Avery, don't go." Julene's eyes welled with tears. "We can help you work this out."

"There's nothing to work out. Harper, please put Hayes in his car seat. I'll get Addison and meet you in the driveway."

Harper nodded then slowly stood. The overhead light highlighted the tears glistening on her cheeks. At least one person that she loved was expressing remorse. Avery grabbed her purse and strode out onto the porch to collect Addison and her dolls.

"C'mon, baby." A chill raked her spine. "We're sleeping at a hotel tonight."

Addison's eyes grew wide. "Oh, fun. Can I sleep in your bed with you, Mama? I don't want you to be lonely there all by yourself."

Avery bit back a sob. "Sure, baby girl. Thank you."

## Chapter Fifteen

That boat ride had gone all wrong.

Cole stood on the screened porch facing the lake, rehearsing the words he should've said the last time he'd been here. If he'd been honest then, or at any point in the last several weeks, they wouldn't be in this mess. Avery sat alone at the end of the dock, her back toward the house.

Three days had passed since Maribelle confessed everything at the supper table. Somehow Julene and Harper had persuaded Avery to check out of the hotel and move back to the house. He'd also heard from Millie Kay who'd heard from her Realtor friend that Avery had already looked at a townhouse in the same neighborhood as Pax and Trey.

He jammed his hands in the pockets of his chinos. Not that her future plans were any of his business. She'd probably shove him into the water as soon as he approached. But he had to talk to her. Ask for forgiveness. Explain. Even though anything he said would probably just sound flimsy and self-serving.

He had to fight for her.

He left the refuge of the porch and strode down the grassy slope. Dark clouds had gathered on the horizon and the wind picked up, lifting her curls from her shoulders. She hugged her legs to her chest. When he moved onto the dock, his footfalls on the wooden slats gave him away. As he moved closer, he saw her swiping at her cheeks with the backs of her hands. Her pain knifed at him.

"Hey," he said, his voice rough. "Mind if I join you?"

So lame. Of course she'd mind. Shame carved a desolate cave in his abdomen.

She tipped her chin up and stared out across the lake. "Go away."

Well, that was slightly better than being shoved into the water. Cole rocked back on his heels and stared at the sky because he didn't know what else to do. "I'm afraid I can't go until I've said what I need to say."

She hesitated then lifted one shoulder. "Fine."

He lowered to the dock and sat down, keeping a safe distance from her, and let his legs dangle over the edge. The air carried the pungent scent of rain, although none had fallen yet. The wind blew harder, whispering through the leafy trees nearby. His arms ached to hold her. To pull her close and tell her—show her—how sorry he was. Instead, he tucked his fingers under his legs to keep from touching her.

"I'm waiting." She gave him the side-eye.

He cleared his throat. "I'm sorry. I need to ask your forgiveness. I wish I could go back in time and tell you about my... arrangement with Nana. I—"

"Your arrangement? Is that what you're calling it?" Her words carried a bite. That same snarky tone she'd used at supper when she'd found out the truth. He really hated that. "She bribed you, Cole. And you let her."

He bristled. "I didn't let her."

"You used me for your own selfish gain." Her lower lip trembled, driving another stake of pain straight through him.

"It wasn't completely selfish. Imari's Place benefited. The women are going to be thrilled when they move in. You are so talented, Avery. Something good and beautiful has come out of a terrible situation."

"Don't try to make this sound better than it is. I'm so tired of men using me to get what they want."

"That's not what I did." Anger and shame burned together and the words bubbled out before he could stop them.

She met his gaze then, glittery and fiery, and simply arched one eyebrow at him. That lone gesture spoke volumes. She was challenging him. Worse, she'd parked him in the same camp as Pax and Trey. He'd been wrong to mislead her, but he didn't deserve that. "Don't compare me to your ex-husband and Trey. Breaking news—you're not the only one who knows what it's like to be used and then pushed aside when something better comes along."

Her mouth slackened and her complexion paled. "What's that supposed to mean?"

His laugh carried a brittle edge. "Oh, please. That napkin pledge? What was that to you, anyway? Some sort of drunken promise made in desperation? Sure, I'll marry you, Cole, when I've exhausted all my other options."

Her spine stiffened. "I was *not* desperate."

"But you didn't act like that night meant anything to you. Then you went off to college and chased after the first man who wooed you." He was walking a tightrope now. One verbal misstep and he'd incinerate their relationship. These words were a long time coming, though. If she'd planned on never speaking to him again, he had to get it all out. "Don't you see? I love you, Avery. What we wrote on that napkin wasn't a silly vow. Not to me. I accept full responsibility for not telling you about Nana's donation and her request that I invite you to help us with our project. I confess that it was an opportunity for me to get close to you again. If that's selfish and despicable, then I guess I deserve your disdain."

She fixed him with another flinty stare. "Is that your idea of an apology? Because if it is, I'm afraid it's woefully inadequate."

He clamped his lips together and challenged her gaze. "Then I don't have anything else to say."

Her gaze slid away in a slow, painful dismissal. All right then. Boldly, he leaned over one last time and pressed a kiss to her temple. Her sharp intake of breath nearly undid him. Pushing to his feet, he hesitated. Lingering. She remained motionless. Her jaw set.

"Goodbye, Avery." Two simple words but he could barely force them out. Fighting to contain his emotions, he turned and walked away, his legs trembling with every step. Her rejection had just about flattened him. He'd expected her to be fired up. No one got over being lied to quickly. But nothing could've prepared him for this frigid, closed-off version of Avery. How could she sit there, stubbornly clinging to her hurt, so completely—

"Cole, wait."

He loved her?

Those were the words that propelled her to her feet and sent her running after him.

"How long?" She stopped in front of him, the wind blowing her hair across her face. Pinning her errant curls back with one hand, she found his gaze.

"How long what?"

"How long have you…loved me?"

Confusion resided in his eyes. He shoved his hands in his pockets then glanced down at the dock, scraping the toe of his shoe across the weathered plank. "Does it matter? What sort of answer would be enough for you?"

She winced. His questions were barbs, digging into her tender wounded places. His words had brought them to this uncharted space in their relationship, but now he was going to back off and pretend his feelings were irrelevant? Worse, why wasn't he willing to acknowledge that a relationship couldn't be built on a lie?

Her memory offered up a highlight reel of the time they'd spent together, stretching all the way back to middle school. Study sessions, afternoons near the pond in his neighborhood, reading novels from their required summer reading list in neighboring hammocks. That dance with the infamous cock-tail napkin pledge that had now gone viral.

Their recent intimate kisses.

Her cheeks heated and she glanced past him toward the house. Despite her hurt and her anger, she couldn't forget the way he'd shown up here in her darkest hour, swooping in when she needed him most and rescuing her. Addison couldn't get enough of him, and he'd playfully interacted with Hayes whenever he could. There probably wasn't any man in the world her family thought more highly of than Cole.

After all, they'd practically defended him at supper when Nana bragged about her underhanded schemes.

"Why didn't you tell me?"

He scoffed. "If I'd showed up outside your sorority house in Raleigh and told you how I felt, would you have listened?"

The breeze rippled across the water and she shivered.

*No.*

She'd been too distracted. Too self-absorbed. Too busy worshipping Pax. Shame slithered in, churning her stomach. Cole had wanted so much more than friendship, but he'd never said anything. And now she couldn't trust him because he'd turned out to be a selfish liar.

"Do you know how hard it was to watch you marry Pax and become übersuccessful?" Cole's voice held a texture she hadn't heard before. Gravelly. Emotional. She forced herself to look at him.

His features were etched with pain and his eyes had darkened to a mossy green. "The two of you were splashed across the magazine covers, and the billboards. I can't think of one place I traveled that I didn't have to see an image of the two of you advertising your TV show."

"Cole—"

He silenced her with his outstretched palm. "Avery, it nearly killed me to watch you be happy with someone else, knowing I'd lost my opportunity."

Her confusion morphed into anger. "But if you love me then why did you lie? We've spent a lot of time together, Cole. You had numerous opportunities to mention my grandmother was the reason Imari's Place had the resources to expand. I was so brutally honest about my insecurities. That I couldn't do what you asked me to do. But you kept telling me I could. That you believed in me. Was all of that a lie too?"

"No! I do believe in you, Avery. You're incredibly talented. And by the way, I came very close to spilling the whole story. I wanted to so many times but couldn't find the words." He gestured toward the boat tied off behind her. "We were right here just a few nights ago. What do you think that boat ride was for?"

She flung her hands in the air. "I thought we were reconnecting. You made it seem romantic. We'd kissed and then Nana's episode interrupted everything. Then you went out of town, I was juggling the kids and multiple projects. How was I supposed to know a boat ride was going to be your big tell-all?"

"And when you kissed me and told me you wanted to enjoy spending time together, that whatever was bothering me could wait, did you mean that?"

"Please don't put this back on me."

"But what happened to getting through whatever life throws at us together?"

"Now you're using my words against me." She glared at him. "Don't do that. I'm so hurt right now, Cole."

Agony filled his eyes. "I accept full responsibility for not telling you the truth. I hate that you found out the way that you did. To be perfectly honest, I was afraid."

"Afraid?" She scoffed. "Of what?"

"I felt guilty for not telling you about Nana's donation, but I was also afraid that you'd be crushed. That you would accuse me of being maliciously deceitful and you wouldn't want anything to do with me."

He clamped his mouth tight and looked away.

She rubbed her palm against the painful ache behind her sternum. In the distance, thunder rumbled.

Cole cleared his throat.

Was he trying not to cry?

"As it turns out, I was right. Because this conversation—"

he paused and waved his hand back and forth between them. "This is why I didn't tell you."

"Were you *ever* going to tell me?"

"Yes."

"When?"

He blew out a long breath, pushed his fingers through his hair then dropped his hands to his sides. When his eyes found hers the sadness in his gaze made her throat tighten with unshed tears.

"Here's the thing. I am so very sorry. There's nothing I can do to change what has happened. I understand that you trusted me when it wasn't easy for you to trust. And I realize you see a lie of omission as a betrayal. You'll never know how much I regret not speaking up. But please know this. I've loved you since forever, Avery. And that hasn't changed."

He turned and cut long strides back down the dock. The wind blew harder. Fat raindrops fell and thunder rolled through the darkening sky overhead. Avery turned away. Gulping back a sob, she clapped her hand over her mouth. She refused to watch him as he walked out of her life. This time for good. Because she couldn't be in a relationship with a man who kept secrets.

## Chapter Sixteen

Had he been too honest? Too vulnerable?

This was the question Cole had wrestled with since he'd left Avery standing on the dock almost a week ago.

Moping on the beach hadn't provided any answers. Or eased his distress over losing her.

Brown pelicans soared over the Gulf Coast waves then dived into the surf. Cole sat alone under the canvas beach umbrella Hemby had planted in the sand early this morning. Families with young children basked in the summer sun, running in and out of the tide pools. A little girl about Addison's age plopped down in the sand nearby. Another child joined her and their exuberant chatter filtered toward him as they ran back and forth, water sloshing from their buckets.

His heart fisted with regret and he looked away. Was this how it would always be? He'd slog through life forever reminded of what he'd had for a hot minute before he went and messed it all up.

*That's a bit melodramatic, don't you think?*

Hemby wasn't even out here, and Cole still couldn't escape his best friend's snarky insights.

He pulled another can of soda from the cooler stationed beside his chair then popped the top and took a long satisfying sip. Burrowing his feet deeper into the warm sand, he stared out at the horizon. The tide had slowly crept in since he'd parked in his chair shortly after breakfast. Now the sea-foam lapped closer to his toes. A toddler screeched as it touched his bare feet then ran into the arms of the grown-up standing watch nearby.

Was Hayes going to be crawling soon? Did Avery plan to bring her kids to the beach this summer?

He took another sip of his soda and tried not to think about Hayes and Addison. After his colossal failure of an apology and Avery's prompt rejection, Hemby had hauled his pathetic tail down to their condo in Gulf Shores. Cole mentally waded through the muddled wasteland that was his brain and made a note to get Hemby and his wife a gift certificate for a nice dinner out. They'd been more than gracious to him as he tried to piece his shattered heart back together. A week had passed and he'd made almost zero progress. Their time away from reality was ending. Hemby had to get back to Camellia and Cole had a grueling schedule to keep. After his conversation with Avery, he'd requested that Millie Kay pack the next three months with as many fundraising and speaking opportunities as possible.

Turned out that wasn't all that difficult when one's photo had gone viral.

When Millie Kay sent him his itinerary, he'd initially regretted leaving town when the expansion project was about to wrap. But Dale had been stellar to work with and Cole had no doubts about Avery's ability to oversee the final phase of the project. Max and Charlie had both texted to let him know the documentary was moving into production phase. They had already closed the deal with a major streaming platform.

In a serendipitous turn of events the board of directors at the foundation had hired someone to manage converting the old factory into a usable facility. Avery's vision for a product line of women's lotions and candles made by women was quickly becoming a reality. Not that he'd bother telling her. She clearly wanted nothing to do with him. Since he'd been at the condo with Hemby, he only slept in fits and starts, often waking from a terrifying nightmare. It always involved trying to save Avery from a burning building or rescue her from a vehicle dangling over the edge of a cliff. Every time, he woke gasping for air, his T-shirt soaked with sweat and the sheet tangled around his legs.

This couldn't be his new normal. Could it?

He blew out a breath and tipped his head back against the edge of the chair. The familiar scent of coconut and cocoa butter wafted toward him. He'd tried to protect her. Instead, he'd ruined everything.

When would he learn that the people he loved always got hurt?

"Hey." Hemby plunked a chair next to his and held out a sub sandwich wrapped in paper. "Are you hungry? This is turkey and Swiss, no tomato and extra mayo."

Cole stared at the food, taken aback by Hemby's thoughtfulness. "Thanks, man. I'm starving."

"Thought so." Hemby sat down then put a plastic grocery bag on top of the cooler. "I brought chips, cookies and more water."

Cole unwrapped the sandwich and took a generous bite.

The fresh bread combined with the salty deli meat, his favorite cheese and the tangy mayo hit the spot.

Hemby tossed him a small bag of his chips. Cole caught it before it slid off his lap and into the sand.

"What have you been doing out here?" Hemby asked around a mouthful of food. "Reading?"

Cole's gaze swung to the unopened paperback—a thriller written by one of his favorite authors—sitting on top of his flip-flops. He reached for his soda. "Thinking."

Hemby paused, his sandwich halfway to his mouth. "Yeah? How's that working for you?"

"Not great." An attractive young couple walked between their chairs and the encroaching waves. The guy pulled the girl closer, and she smiled up at him. Then they stopped and shared a kiss. Cole scowled. Was everyone on this entire beach in love except for him?

Seagulls swooped in, hovering over the sand nearby. Hemby shooed them away.

"Do you want to talk about it?" Hemby asked.

Cole set his sandwich down on the wrapper he held in his lap. "Why am I such a disaster when it comes to relationships?"

Hemby squinted at him, his mouth hanging open.

"Huh." Cole ripped open the bag of chips. "I can't recall the last time you were speechless."

Lifting his visor, Hemby scratched his head then jammed the worn brim down low on his brow. "It's, uh, tough to put a positive spin on this one, buddy."

"So I am a disaster."

"That's not what I said." Hemby took a bite, chewing slowly.

Cole's chair creaked as he shifted his weight.

"I know you have strong feelings for Avery and I respect

that," Hemby said. "And I owe you an apology because I said quite a few things that contributed to your current situation."

"That's nice of you to say, man, but this is all on me." Cole forced a smile. "Even if you did egg me on."

Hemby frowned. "Yeah, I feel terrible about that."

Cole studied him. This kinder, gentler version of his best friend might take some getting used to.

"I'm not sure what I can say that hasn't already been said or that you probably haven't figured out on your own." Hemby glanced out over the water. "Avery's a wonderful woman and you're a great guy. But you both have some junk to work through."

"Some junk?" Cole tipped his head to one side. "Such as?"

"Avery's going to have to forgive her ex-husband for leaving her, and you're going to have to forgive yourself."

Ouch. Cole's lunch turned to cement in his gut. "Yeah, that's asking a lot."

"Do you believe that you deserve another chance with Avery?"

"No."

"Listen, I'm the last guy who should be telling you to see a counselor or to take your concerns to the Lord. We both know I've got a few hang-ups of my own." Hemby's usually quick smile didn't materialize. "I try to avoid those cliché Sunday school tidbits, but in this case, I think the only way you and Avery have a shot at making this relationship work is through radical forgiveness."

Cole shook his head. "She's never going to forgive me."

Hemby pinned him with a long look. "I'm talking about you, bro. You have to forgive her for blowing you off after high school, and you have to forgive yourself for hurting her."

Cole rewrapped the rest of his sandwich, tucked it in the

cooler then eased out from under the umbrella. "I'm going for a walk. See you back at the house in a few."

He strode down the beach, saltwater splashing around his bare feet and Hemby's words repeating in his head. Radical forgiveness. That was a tough assignment. Especially the part about forgiving himself. People had shared all sorts of opinions about how they thought he should deal with the trauma of losing his sister. Even now, all these years later. But they weren't the ones who had to live with the guilt. They weren't the ones who'd been distracted by a dumb arcade game. He'd only wanted to play *Daytona USA* one more time. Kim had promised she'd stay beside the machine with the claw and the stuffed animals like he told her to.

He had scored a personal best in the game, but when he'd turned around to tell her, she'd disappeared. They never saw her again.

The midday sun scorched his bare shoulders. He shouldn't be out here without any sunscreen on. But he wasn't ready to turn back and face Hemby. Not yet.

Even if there had been plenty of truth and wisdom to glean from his best friend's words.

Cole stopped and planted his hands on his hips. Chest heaving, he faced the ocean, letting the incoming wave break across his shins. He had grown weary of hauling the guilt around like an overstuffed suitcase with a broken handle. And he wanted to believe that forgiveness was possible. Just like he wanted the women he helped rescue to step out in faith and seize their fresh starts.

If they had the courage to walk in freedom, why couldn't he?

"Where would you like the side table?" Greer mopped the sweat from his brow then gestured to the last piece of oak furniture he'd helped carry in from the moving truck.

"Between the armchairs, please." Avery carried the groceries into the kitchen. She had found a beautiful townhouse for rent in the same neighborhood where Pax and Trey had moved last month. A charming community park separated their front doors. Mama had warned her that might be a bit too close, but Avery was determined to try. For the sake of their children. Hayes and Addison couldn't go back and forth independently, obviously, but she hoped this was the first of many steps toward forging a more peaceful co-parenting arrangement.

Before she'd signed the lease and put down any money, she'd met with Trey and Pax over coffee. Trey had offered a heartfelt, genuine apology. It hadn't been an easy conversation. He and Pax had been united in their earnest quest to seek her forgiveness. She'd wrestled with lingering bitterness. Maybe some part of her always would. But by the end of their time together, she'd been able to forgive them.

"We have more groceries." Mama, Julene and Harper followed her inside then set the bags down on the hardwood floor beside the island.

"This is so cute." Julene straightened then ran her hand over the cabinets, which were painted a soothing shade of sage green. A basic subway tile backsplash in classic white, stainless steel appliances and modern brass lighting made for a bright, appealing space. The large window over the sink that faced the park was the kitchen's best feature, in her opinion.

"I'll make up your beds if you show me which box has the sheets," Mama offered.

"Oh, you don't have to do that." Avery unpacked the groceries that needed to be refrigerated first. "Y'all already helped us move."

"But the kids are going to be here soon," Mama said. "Don't you want to feel settled?"

Avery checked the time on the stove's clock. Mama was right. They were supposed to pick Addison and Hayes up from Pax and Trey's place in less than thirty minutes.

"I'll help make the beds if Julene will go over and get the kids." Harper unloaded crackers, peanut butter and a container of almonds into the pantry.

"Sure." Julene quickly unpacked a small box with dish soap, a package of sponges and a hand towel. "Is your stroller still in the back of your car?"

"Yes." Avery found her keys and handed them over. "Please make sure you get the diaper bag from Pax. It has Hayes's current favorite pacifier."

"Got it." Julene pocketed the keys. "I'll help Greer arrange the living room furniture then I'll go."

"Wait." Avery folded her mama and sisters into a spontaneous group hug. "Thank you for everything. I couldn't have done this without you."

"We're going to miss living with y'all, but we understand you need your own space," Harper said, blinking back tears.

Avery's throat tightened with emotion. "I'm going to miss living with you too. At first it was so hard to move in with y'all. I really didn't want to be back in Camellia. But now that I've had the opportunity to make a fresh start and see other people get their shot at redemption, I'm glad we all get to be here together."

"That makes me so happy." Mama's eyes glistened. "It's good to see you getting your sparkle back. And I'm so sorry about everything that's happened. We shouldn't have meddled in your business."

"It's all right." Avery gently rubbed her mother's back. "I know you all acted with my best interests in mind."

"What about Cole?" Harper swiped at the moisture on her

cheeks with her fingertips. "Did he have your best interests in mind?"

Avery pulled the plastic lid off a container of chocolate chip cookies. "I don't know. I'm not quite ready to go there yet."

"I was hoping you'd be his date for the gala this weekend."

Avery wrinkled her nose. "We haven't spoken to each other in a while."

Three months to be exact.

Mama leaned against the counter and reached for a cookie. "He loves you, sweetie. Has for years."

Avery sighed and grabbed two cookies. "Evidently that was obvious to everyone except for me."

"I'd better go help Greer." Julene squeezed Avery's arm then left the room.

"And we'd better get the beds made." Harper tugged on Mama's arm. "C'mon, she doesn't want to rehash all this right now. Today is supposed to represent a fresh start."

"Thank you." Avery slanted a grateful look toward her sister. "Well said."

Harper and Mama climbed the stairs to the second floor. Avery polished off both cookies, took a long sip of water from the bottle she'd carried in her tote bag then went into the living room to check on Greer.

"This looks great." She ran her hand along the back of the faux velvet sofa she'd found in a consignment shop.

"You like it?" Greer stood in the middle of the room, hands on his hips, surveying the cozy space. He'd arranged the side table between the high-back armchairs she'd found at a local thrift shop. They'd been recovered in a stunning blue paisley print.

The coffee table sat in front of the sofa and would serve as Hayes's temporary play area. He'd started cruising around furniture lately. She'd intentionally bought a benign, inexpensive table because he'd undoubtedly slam anything he could get his hands on against the flat surface.

"Your mama and I are very proud of you," Greer said quietly. "I hope you know that."

Avery grew still, gripping the corner of the sofa with her fingers. She'd always had a great relationship with Greer. He wasn't big on words of affirmation, though.

"Thank you, Greer. I appreciate everything you all have done for the kids and me. I'm sure it wasn't easy having us invade." She tried for a smile but Greer's expression remained serious.

His gray eyes found hers. "Cole never meant to hurt you. Maribelle didn't execute her plans in the most conventional manner, but her heart was in the right place. We all just wanted to help you succeed."

"I made Addison's bed. Where are your—" Mama came into the room then stopped abruptly. "Uh-oh. What kind of serious conversation am I interrupting?"

"Greer was telling me how much Cole cares for me. But I can't be with a man who betrayed me. Not again."

Mama's expression grew serious. "Honey, I know you don't want to hear this, but just because your husband left you doesn't mean every man will leave you."

"I wish I could believe that, Mama."

Mama and Greer exchanged glances.

"You are loved, Avery. Your beauty is genuine and runs deep on the inside, although you are beautiful on the outside too." Greer's smile creased the lines beside his eyes. "Remember, Cole fell in love with you long before you were a world-famous home decor expert."

His kind words provoked a fresh wave of tears. "I am not world-famous."

"Instagram famous then." Mama chuckled. "Julene showed me your latest posts."

Avery lifted one shoulder in a helpless shrug. Some of her influencer campaigns had taken off like bottle rockets over the lake on the Fourth of July. She wasn't thrilled about the so-called fame, but she did enjoy the work and the income made this move possible.

"Cole wants to be with you and your children," Greer said. "We haven't spoken since he was over at the house for supper, but my guess is he feels horrible about what happened."

"I'm not real proud of the way I behaved, either," Avery said, turning away from Greer. She opened a plastic bin and unboxed some board books and a few basic puzzles. She crossed the room and tucked them inside the chest Mama had let her bring from the guest room at the house.

"What are you talking about?" Harper stacked the empty containers that held the linens by the front door. "You didn't do anything wrong."

"I was not very gracious when he apologized." Avery closed the lid on the chest then sat on it. "He took a big risk employing me, even if Nana had way too much to do with his offer. I didn't have the skill set to pull off that design project, but he believed in me, and that made all the difference."

"The new residence is gorgeous," Harper said. "When the women move in, they're going to love everything about it. Y'all have done an incredible job."

"Thank you. It was a real team effort. Taking on that role with Imari's Place taught me a lot. The gossip and criticism were over-the-top, and I let it get to me." Avery rubbed her fingertips across her forehead. "If I'm ever going to date anyone or even think about getting married again, I have to learn to be okay with being myself, instead of what other people want me to be."

Greer smiled then reached inside a box and pulled out a framed photograph. "That's a lifelong process, darlin'. You'll get there."

She studied the photo of her and Addison sitting on a bench at their favorite park near the house in Raleigh. Addison's gingham dress with the hand smocking on the bodice complemented Avery's pale blue sundress. They both had their curls tamed back with headbands. Avery held newborn Hayes swaddled in her arms. She didn't want to go back to the agony of those weeks and months.

But was she ready to move forward and embrace love again?

"Cole and I both hurt each other deeply, and I don't know if we'll ever get past that."

"You won't know until you try," Greer said.

The door burst open and Addison rushed in, her cheeks flushed and bits of hay stuck in her hair. "Mama, guess what? Uncle Trey and Daddy took me to a pumpkin patch and it was amazing!"

Avery stood and swooped Addison into her arms. "That sounds super fun. Let's go wash your hands and then we'll have a snack and you can tell me all about it."

Julene came inside with Hayes in her arms. Greer, Mama and Harper encircled them, cheering as he immediately squirmed out of his aunt's arms and crawled across the floor.

Avery half listened as Addison chattered about her adventures. Greer's wise words had climbed inside her head. She helped Addison find some soap and a towel then adjusted the water temperature in the bathroom sink. Her feelings for Cole hadn't changed. Had she allowed anger to cloud her judgment? Yeah, probably.

Her family sure hadn't surrendered their positions as his number one fans. They had patiently supported her and tried to empathize with her circumstances, but they didn't hold back when it came to reminding her that Cole loved her.

*I've loved you since forever, Avery, and that hasn't changed.*

She revisited his declaration, turning the words over and over in her mind, like a rare piece of sea glass discovered in the sand. Maybe she needed to forgive him. Maybe it was time to let go of the hurt and embrace a second chance. Every part of her wanted to believe that was possible. But she'd wielded her pain and fear of rejection like a shield for so long, what if it was too late for her and Cole?

## Chapter Seventeen

Cole hovered in one corner of the ballroom at the Altamont hotel, his stomach a tangled mess of nerves. The live band opened their set list with a cover of Pharrell Williams's "Happy," filling the dimly lit room with a festive vibe. A spinning mirrored ball sprinkled the dance floor with rainbow-colored dots of light. He was not the least bit interested in dancing tonight. Camellia's most generous citizens mingled around him, dressed in their finest attire. Cole tugged at the punishingly tight collar on his tux, wishing he'd gone with a business casual vibe for tonight's function. He was supposed to give a speech in a few minutes but the right words eluded him.

A waiter stopped in front of him and offered a glass of sparkling cider. Cole accepted with a curt nod. Pinching the cool stem between his fingers, he allowed himself a slow perusal of the room.

They'd gathered to celebrate the expansion of Imari's Place. He hated spending money on stuff like this. Hated thinking about how much they could do with the funds instead of paying for live music and appetizers. And he hated that Avery wasn't by his side.

No, he hadn't personally invited her, but he'd made sure Millie Kay sent her an invitation to the gala on behalf of the foundation. They hadn't received a response. Hemby and his wife stood nearby, chatting with a couple who served on the board of directors. A woman in a black formal gown and blond hair twisted into an updo came into the ballroom. His breath caught. When the woman smiled and waved to one of her friends, Cole realized his mistake.

She wasn't Avery.

He'd suspected she wouldn't attend, not after the harsh words they'd exchanged. Months had passed, the project had finished, and still she'd only communicated through Dale. Harper had picked up an order from the deli when he'd been there for lunch last week. They'd exchanged awkward small talk, both carefully sidestepping any mention of Avery.

He missed her so much that it physically hurt.

The air in the ballroom shifted as someone made an entrance. Murmurs of approval rippled over the people seated at round tables covered in white tablecloths. Heads swiveled toward the double doors, and Cole's heart took flight. Maybe she'd changed her mind. He glanced toward the door as two coaches from Auburn University's athletics program strode in with their wives on their arms.

Cole blew out a deflated breath.

"Why are you here alone? More importantly, where is my granddaughter?"

Cole turned at the sound of Maribelle Lansing's familiar voice. "Hello, Mrs. Lansing. You're looking lovely this evening."

She stared up at him, clutching a designer handbag that co-ordinated perfectly with her pale blue pantsuit. "Thank you, darling. Now, answer my questions."

He couldn't help but smile. "I don't know where Avery is. Perhaps spending time with her kids?"

Maribelle's ruby red lips pursed. "Yes, perhaps. I had hoped you'd bring her as your date this evening."

"Yeah, I don't think so." Cole palmed the back of his neck. "She and I aren't on good terms right now."

"Oh?" Maribelle's thin brows arched toward her white curls. "What did you do?"

"I hardly acted alone, Mrs. Lansing. Correct me if I'm wrong, but you played a role in this too."

"Is she still upset about the napkin and the money?" Maribelle fluffed her curls with her manicured fingertips. "I was just trying to give your relationship a little jump start."

"It's more than just the money." Cole tried to keep his tone even. He certainly didn't want to offend one of his donors. But she was complicit in this convoluted scheme and frankly, he was irritated that she didn't claim responsibility. He might've lost Avery for good this time. Maribelle's dismissive tone grated on his last nerve.

"Perhaps my methods were questionable." Maribelle surveyed the ballroom.

*You think?*

"My intentions, however, have always been pure."

Cole stifled a snort. She was a master at spinning the evidence in a positive light.

Her blue eyes were fierce when she leveled him with her gaze. "Avery is a beautiful woman with exceptional talent. She's angry right now, but that will blow over. And when she is ready, you need to be on her doorstep, young man."

"You bribed me, Mrs. Lansing. Avery isn't going to get over that anytime soon."

"No, I made a sizable contribution in support of a cause we both believe in." She rose up to her full height of barely five feet tall. "You gave Avery an opportunity to do what she does best, make something beautiful out of nothing. While she might resent the circumstances that got her involved, the outcome is amazing. So many wonderful young women have an opportunity to turn their lives around because of you and Avery and everyone who is involved with Imari's Place."

Wow. Cole wanted to applaud. Maybe Maribelle should give his speech tonight.

"Don't let her walk out of your life again, Cole Whitaker."

Before he had a chance to respond, she was on the move, headed toward an older couple seated at a round table nearby.

He wanted to ask if she had a plan for how he might win Avery's heart once and for all. Because he'd professed his love and she'd shredded him. He hadn't forgotten the moment on the beach when he'd sensed the Lord prodding him toward deep emotional work. Several appointments with his counselor later and he felt like he'd made a smidge of progress when it came to releasing his guilt and shame over Kim's death.

But this newfound peace hadn't resolved his feelings for Avery. He'd meant it when he told her he'd loved her since forever. But maybe she'd been so deeply wounded that those words meant nothing to her now. It wasn't going to be easy, but he'd have to find a way to move on.

Ah, sweet relief.

Avery slumped against the wall in the short hallway between the kids' bedrooms and whispered a prayer of thanks. Hayes and Addison synchronized their bedtimes. They'd fallen asleep quickly and so far Addison hadn't climbed out of bed asking for another story or a sip of water. That meant at least an hour or maybe even two of uninterrupted time to herself.

Eager not to waste a second, she padded barefoot down the stairs and into the cozy family room. Board books about construction equipment mingled with a family of unicorns on one end of the sofa. Avery smiled as she stacked the books neatly on the coffee table. Hayes and Addison had settled into their new house without complaint. Sometimes Avery missed having Mama, Greer and her sisters close by, but unpacking in their own space had felt liberating. A new season. The fresh start she'd craved ever since they'd left Raleigh.

The hollow ache still lingered, though. She frowned and lined up the three unicorns in the middle of the coffee table next to the simple collection of unscented candles she'd arranged on a white square platter. As she picked up one of the blankets Hayes insisted on dragging around behind him as he cruised along the furniture, a smart phone thumped against the sofa cushions.

"Uh-oh." Avery recognized Harper's lock screen. She must've left the phone when she'd stopped by to visit before supper. Avery knew she'd secretly been on a mission to check on her and the kids. Ever since they'd moved out, her family had been extra attentive. Avery was grateful for the spontaneous visit. Other than Pax and Trey stopping by to hand off the kids or pick them up, she hadn't had any guests yet.

She took Harper's phone into the kitchen and set it on the counter then retrieved the remote control from a high shelf in the pantry. Hayes destroyed almost anything he could get his hands on, so she'd learned the hard way to stow electronics out of his reach. She went back into the living room and flopped on the sofa. Her thoughts returned to Cole as they often did when she was exhausted and alone. He certainly hadn't been by to see her new place. Hadn't helped her move in. Hadn't called or sent any texts. If she needed to communicate about Imari's Place, she spoke with Dale or Millie Kay.

"I miss him," she whispered. "Lord, have I made a terrible mistake?"

Her conversations with God had not flowed freely until recently. Until Cole was absent from her life. Their parting words on the dock that night almost four months ago had left their mark. She'd had the opportunity to see him but at the last minute, she'd ignored the invitation to the gala and stayed home.

A soft knock sounded at her front door, pulling her from her thoughts. Harper must've realized she'd forgotten her phone. Avery hurried to the kitchen and grabbed it then strode toward the door. She turned the deadbolt then twisted the knob without checking the peephole.

"Forget some—"

Her words died on her lips. A man stood on her front porch, wearing dark gray cargo pants, a vintage T-shirt featuring a classic rock band and black sneakers. Avery's heart hammered in her chest as she slowly noted his appearance. Taking in every detail. He wore his silvery blond hair short, as though he'd served in the military, but his posture looked anything but confident. She met his gaze with her own. That particular shade of blue was familiar. She saw it every time she looked at Addison.

"Hello, Avery." Moisture glistened in his eyes. He clenched and unclenched his fists at his sides.

"Dad?" she whispered, Harper's phone slipping from her fingers and clattering on the hardwood. That voice. Those eyes. The divot in his chin. This couldn't be happening. Her knees quaked. "W-what are you doing here?"

He cleared his throat. "I need to speak with you. Please, Avery. It's important."

"Eighteen years." She splayed her hand across her chest, fighting to keep her voice even. "I haven't seen you in eighteen years and *now* you say you need to speak with me?"

His brow furrowed. "I'm not here for money, if that's what you're worried about. I'm here to make things right. To apologize. To tell you the whole truth."

Did she want the whole truth? Lately the truth had done nothing but hurt. She hesitated. The earnestness in his gaze and the almost desperate tone in his voice won her over. She stepped back and opened the door. "Come in. Please speak softly, my kids just went to bed."

He stepped inside then reached down and picked up the phone she'd dropped. The scent of his aftershave awakened a dormant memory. She'd sat on the commode in their bathroom, watching him shave. A ritual that brought her comfort. He patiently answered her questions and made her laugh while he finished his morning routine. It was just the two of them, before anyone else woke up.

"Can I get you anything? Coffee? Tea? Water?" She gestured for him to sit down.

"Water, please." He handed her the phone then slowly rounded the sofa, pausing to study the framed photo of her and the kids hanging on the wall. Did he even know he had grandchildren? His gaze swept the room then he sat down and leaned forward, resting his elbows on his knees. Awe swept over his face as he took in the toys, books and Hayes's discarded blanket beside him.

"I'll be right back." She pocketed Harper's phone and strode into the kitchen. Her own phone sat on the counter. Should she text Mama or Julene? Did anyone else know her father was here? Her mind raced, the questions stacking up like the precarious foam block towers Julene built for Hayes and Addison.

If he wasn't here for money, then why had he resurfaced? Was he battling a terminal illness? Her stomach pitted at the thought. She scooped ice cubes from the bin inside the freezer and gently placed them in the glass so she didn't wake the kids. How had he found her? Was she his first stop? She filled the glass with water from the dispenser in the refrigerator door.

Instead of texting anyone, she turned away from her phone and returned to the family room. Her father hadn't moved.

"Here you go." She set the glass on a wooden coaster in the middle of the coffee table to avoid touching his hand. He hadn't tried to hug her yet, thankfully. She wasn't ready. He'd left so long ago that she'd stopped daydreaming of a happy reunion.

"Thank you." He reached for the glass and took a sip. "I'm sure you have questions."

"A few." Avery settled in the closest armchair and tucked her feet under her.

He smiled at her attempt at humor. The curve of his mouth reminded her of Julene. She had to tell her sisters he was here. They deserved to know. But selfishly, she wanted a few minutes alone with him. Just like the old days in the bathroom.

"You can ask me anything." He met her gaze. "What do you want to know?"

"Why did you leave?"

He hesitated, the glass halfway between the coaster and his face. "You want to get right down to brass tacks, don't you?"

"It's my most pressing question."

He sat back against the tufted cushions. "What did your mother tell you?"

"We haven't talked about you very often."

"That's fair." The ice cubes rattled in his glass as he took another sip.

She smoothed her hands over her plaid pajama bottoms. Her pulse fluttered in her throat. What if she wasn't prepared for his answer?

"I'm an addict."

Her breath hitched in her chest. Of all the scenarios she'd conjured, addiction had never been on her list of reasons why he'd leave.

He leaned forward and set his glass on the coaster. "Been sober for sixteen months."

"Wow, that's great." She twisted the hem of her T-shirt around her fingers. "I had no idea."

"I was a coward. Started using occasionally when I was out with my buddies on the weekends. We played in a garage band, and thought we were hot stuff. We weren't." He gave a nervous laugh. "Your mom was home a lot by herself with you girls. She told me I needed to clean up my act. I didn't listen. She was patient and gave me more chances than I deserved, but at the end of the day I made my choice. It was the wrong one. I left and never looked back."

"Where have you been all this time?"

"I've held down a job as a roadie with a professional touring musician. Addiction is part of the lifestyle. That's no excuse, I'm just saying that's the way it is. I've lost a lot of friends over the years to a variety of health conditions. So I finally decided it was time to make some changes."

She offered a gentle smile. "That's good."

"Part of addiction recovery is making amends to the people

we've hurt. So I promised myself that before the end of the year, I would reach out to you, your sisters and your mama." He drew a long breath. "And Nana."

"Oh, my." Avery grimaced. "That's going to be a tough conversation."

"Yeah I'm feeling pretty anxious about that." His mouth tightened. "I'm thankful she's still alive. One of my biggest regrets is that—"

He paused, fighting for control of his emotions.

Her heart ached for him. What a brave decision, coming back home to face his family.

"It's too late for me and my dad to reconnect. I regret that I left Camellia and we never spoke to one another again."

"Granddaddy was a good man," Avery said. "He loved you very much."

Dad nodded then scrubbed his hand over his face.

She blinked back tears. "I'm glad you're here, Dad. I just hate that it took you so long."

He raised his head and met her gaze. Tears slid down his gaunt cheeks. "I know."

She stood and crossed the room.

Slowly, he pushed to his feet. "I'm so sorry, sweetie. Can you forgive me?"

"Absolutely." She stepped into his embrace. Tears flowed freely.

"I love you, Avery."

She wept into the cotton fabric of his T-shirt. "I love you too, Daddy."

Well, her cheese must've finally slid off its cracker.

That was the only logical explanation for the hallucinations.

Maribelle squinted. Avery and a middle-aged man who bore

a striking resemblance to her son stood near her recliner. He had less hair, and his face looked sort of skinny, but she'd know those blue eyes anywhere. The prominent shape of the chin too. Even now after all these years, he still favored his daddy.

"Mrs. Lansing." The woman who checked on her in the afternoons leaned closer. Her pleasant smile and warm eyes made Maribelle want to comply. Or maybe it was the fresh chocolate chip cookies she snuck in every now and again. "Wake up. You have visitors."

"I'll wait outside," Avery whispered then squeezed his arm and left the room.

"Hey, Mama." He sank to his knees beside her recliner. "Sorry to wake you."

She blinked. This couldn't be happening. She blinked once more, slower this time. Maybe she wasn't hallucinating. Maybe she was dead.

But surely her estranged son wouldn't be the first one to greet her at the Pearly Gates? No sir. Because if that were the case, then she and the Big Guy were going to have a chat first thing. If Heaven was indeed perfect, He'd missed the mark there. She'd recommend He upgrade His welcoming committee.

Keith's face paled and he shot a frantic glance toward the nursing assistant. "Ma'am? She isn't speaking. Is that...normal?"

"Um, no, she usually has plenty to say. She might be annoyed that I didn't bring her any cookies today." The woman returned to Maribelle's side. "Mrs. Lansing, do you recognize this young man? He says he's your son."

"Oh, for crying out loud, Keith Albert Lansing, you've been gone for eighteen years." Maribelle glared at him. "I'm old, son. Nearly ninety. I'm allowed to be surprised by your sudden reappearance."

The woman chuckled then patted Keith's shoulder. "She's fine, sir. I'll leave you to get reacquainted."

Her rubber shoes squeaked and her scrubs whisked together as she strode toward the door then quietly slipped out, pulling the door shut behind her. Smart girl, that one. Lucille would be over here in a hot minute to see who'd dropped by. Maribelle wasn't quite ready for the whole place to know her business. Especially if he was just here to borrow money.

"What are you doing here?" She surveyed his face then drew in a deep breath. His eyes looked bright and alert. He didn't smell like whiskey. Not that she'd know what that smelled like, mind you.

"Not exactly the warm welcome I was hoping for, Mama." His eyes gleamed with amusement. "I suppose it's only reasonable that you'd question my intentions."

"Where have you been, Keith?"

He pushed to his feet then crossed to the chair opposite hers and sat on the edge. She shifted to face him, struggling for a glimpse of the little boy who'd resided in her memories. Oh, that belly laugh. Sure, he'd kept her on her toes with all those trees he'd climbed and his bizarre need to drive things at high speed. The only time he stayed still was when he fished for hours or followed his daddy everywhere.

Tears pricked her eyelids, but she stubbornly willed them away. Her only son had come home. It was a blessing she didn't deserve. But there was no way she was going to let him see her cry.

Not yet.

"I've been to all fifty states, Canada, Australia, New Zealand and the UK." His gaze fell to the floor and he rubbed his palms together slowly. "If there's a stage, an arena or an amphitheater, I've probably been inside it."

She slanted a look toward him. "Are you trying to tell me that you're famous?"

He chuckled. "No, ma'am. I work for someone who is. We've toured the world together."

"Do you play an instrument?"

"I move the instruments. I'm a roadie."

"Are you telling me a story?"

Keith's smile faded. "I'm here to tell you the truth, Mama."

"You'd best get started then. I take a lot of naps these days and I don't want to miss any of the important details."

"I won't keep you. The first thing I need to say is that I'm an addict who's in recovery. That's the main reason I'm here and I just wanted—"

He paused then rubbed his fingers along his jaw. "I've lost so much time, being away all these years. I just wanted to come home and see my family."

His expression crumpled. He dropped his chin to his chest. The sound of his quiet sobs undid her.

Maybe it was the sight of him crying, or maybe it was guilt over him leaving. She'd always secretly feared that she'd done or said something to drive him away. Or maybe she'd flat had enough of trying to make everything all right all the time.

There was no fighting back the tears. She didn't have the strength. The emotion welled like a king tide under a full moon. Tears fell unfettered, sliding down her cheeks and into the valleys and crevasses of her neck.

Keith stood then crossed to her dresser and picked up the box of tissues. When he brought them to her, the torment swimming in his eyes made her heart nearly split wide open.

"I'm so sorry, Mama, for all the hurt and pain I've caused.

There's nothing I can do to change the past, but if you'll let me, I'd like to be part of your life again."

She blubbered like a baby. They could probably hear her downstairs in the commons, but for once she didn't care. Plucking a tissue from the box, she swabbed at her tears. "I never thought I'd hear you say those words to me."

"I'm just glad I was able to say them to you out loud."

"I forgive you, son," she whispered, her mouth trembling.

He sank to his knees beside her chair again and she wrapped him in her arms. They wept together.

Her boy. He was back. She held him tighter and turned her eyes heavenward. Oh, how she'd longed for this moment. To see Keith and hear his voice and savor that mischievous smile. Despite all of her missteps and her meddling, God had graciously brought them full circle. *Thank You, Lord, for Your tender mercies.*

The door opened and Avery stepped inside.

"Oh, my darling girl, come here." Nana motioned for Avery to join them. "Did you find my son and bring him to me?"

Avery crossed the room, her chin wobbling. Tears clung to her lashes as she sank down beside her father at Nana's elbow. "I drove him here, Nana. That's all. Visiting you was his idea."

"Oh, look at you. Deflecting the credit. You've always been so humble." Nana reached for her hand and clasped it between her own. "Sweetheart, I am so very sorry. You were so upset with me and I didn't take your feelings seriously. Please forgive me. But more importantly please forgive that sweet Cole Whitaker. He's brokenhearted without you."

Avery leaned closer and gently kissed Nana's forehead. "That's sweet of you to say, Nana, and I forgive you. I'm so glad that you and Daddy can be together again."

Nana swiped at her tears again with her crumpled tissue.

Oh, Mylanta, would she ever stop crying? Avery hadn't mentioned forgiving Cole, but that was a problem to be solved another day. She had her boy back and Avery had forgiven her. Those were two precious gifts from above so she'd have to try her best to be grateful.

## Chapter Eighteen

The icy wind kicked up, sending brittle leaves skittering across the asphalt. An unexpected December storm loomed in the forecast. Rumors of an epic snowfall had spread through Camellia. Avery was skeptical, but the granite-gray skies overhead and tangy bite in the air made her wonder if perhaps the forecast was right.

Thankfully, she'd had worn something sensible. Skinny jeans tucked into her knee-high brown boots and a beige cable-knit sweater layered underneath her green double-breasted jacket. At the last minute, she'd found gloves in the hall closet and brought them along.

She opened her handbag to double-check that she hadn't forgotten her notebook with her brief prepared speech. The edge of the infamous napkin peeked out from between the last page and the back cover. Her heart pinched. She slipped the napkin from the notebook and held it carefully with both hands so the wind didn't snatch it.

How could a note scrawled on an old napkin cause so much drama?

Man, she missed Cole. Hopefully they'd have a few minutes to talk after the ceremony ended. They'd both turn thirty-two in the spring and although they wouldn't be married like they'd pledged on the napkin, she couldn't deny that her friendship with Cole had changed her life for the better. She'd always be thankful for the way he believed in her when she couldn't believe in herself. She tucked the napkin back inside the notebook and closed her handbag.

Her curls bobbed against her shoulders as she stomped her feet to keep warm. Mayor Caldwell had invited her to do the honors at the ribbon cutting for the new manufacturing site, but the event was not about her. This might've been her vision initially, but the board of directors had taken the concept for a product line of home goods and toiletries and knocked it out of the park. Moving forward the products would be created on-site by the women who lived at the residence.

"Hey, Mama. Hey!" Addison's little voice rang out and Avery smiled then waved. Addison stood with Mama and Greer. Julene held Hayes. He kept trying to pull his red knit hat off. Harper joined the small crowd gathering on the street, along with Pax and Trey. Hayes spotted them and squealed. Pax smiled and reached for him. Hayes was moving at top speed these days. It would take every single one of her people to keep her kids entertained until the ceremony was over.

Her family might be unconventional, and her kids might make a scene, but she wouldn't want to do this without them. Today was a celebration of a vision she'd tentatively shared, never imagining it could become a reality. Much less a reality in less than six months. The facility represented a new chapter for so many women. Including her. After all she'd been through, she was learning to see the blessing that had come from her deepest wound. If she hadn't endured a divorce, she might never have come back to Camellia and become involved with the foundation.

She let her gaze wander, hoping Cole was among the fifty or so people fanned out in front of her. The mayor stood nearby, speaking to someone on his staff. She kept waiting for Cole to come forward. But there was no sign of him. His absence planted a hollow ache in her midsection. They never would've pulled this off if it weren't for his passion and commitment.

"Keith, slow down. In case you hadn't noticed, I'm using a walker these days."

Oh, dear. Avery bit her lip. Leave it to Nana to make an entrance.

Several people turned to see what was happening.

A feeling of warmth spread through Avery's chest when her father came into view, slowly walking beside Nana. Olive, Nell and Lucille made up the rest of Nana's entourage. She had broken her hip shortly after Thanksgiving. Evidently her recovery hadn't kept her at home. Avery smiled, waved and blew her nana a kiss. She supposed today wouldn't be possible without Nana, either. For all her foibles and her mistakes, Nana loved her family. And if not for her generous donations—and yes, her meddling—the product line wouldn't have been possible.

"Are you about ready, Miss Avery?" Mayor Caldwell handed her the biggest pair of silver scissors she'd ever seen.

"Yes, sir." She carefully took the scissors from his hands. A wide lavender ribbon had been strung across the front doors of the new manufacturing place anchored on either side by silver stanchions.

"Ladies and gentlemen, if I may have your attention please," the mayor said. "We are delighted to have Miss Avery Lansing

Crawford here to celebrate the opening of Camellia's newest achievement, which will directly benefit the women who live at Imari's Place."

A shiver of anticipation raced down Avery's spine.

"Miss Crawford, if you wouldn't mind saying a few words." The mayor stepped back with a flourish, officially giving her the opportunity to speak. The crowd wasn't all that grand. She didn't need a microphone or her prepared notes after all. Her words mattered not nearly as much as what was going to happen behind the closed doors and four walls of this incredible facility.

"Thank you all for coming. It means so much to us to see you here," she said. "As you may have heard, I returned to Camellia because my life took an unexpected turn."

The crowd shifted nervously. "What I've learned through all of this is that love is a powerful force and can drive us to do amazing things in this world."

"That's right, child." An older woman wearing a purple knit cap and vivid pink parka, standing on the sidewalk, jabbed the air with her finger.

Avery smiled then continued. "When I met the women who lived at Imari's Place, I was heartbroken to hear of the suffering they'd endured. In partnership with the foundation, I was moved to act. The expanded residence along with this new facility is proof that when we stand together, we can make our community better. Hopefully, we'll see the end of human trafficking in our lifetimes. For now, our immediate goal is to create jobs and opportunities for the women who live at Imari's Place. So I am thrilled to not only cut this ribbon today but also proclaim that at 7:00 a.m. tomorrow morning, production will begin. The first batch of candles, soaps and lotions will go on sale online, in local stores here in Camellia and at select retailers across the Eastern United States. Thank you to my family for supporting me, for the generous donors whose financial contributions made this happen and especially Cole Whitaker, who helped me see that a project like this was possible with hard work, dedication and a little faith."

Applause echoed off the buildings and cheers punctuated the crisp air as Avery posed with the mayor for photographs then sliced through the ribbon.

Mayor Caldwell faced the journalists and camera operators. "Any questions?"

"I have one."

Avery's pulse sped at the rich sound of Cole's voice.

"Excuse me, please. Pardon me."

People standing closest to her moved aside, forming two groups, like the parting of the Red Sea. Cole halted his steps at a respectful distance from her and the mayor. Phones slid out of coat pockets and the camera operator accompanying the local newscaster angled his lens their way.

Avery's whole body trembled, both from the chill in the air and the sheer relief that he'd shown up.

"Miss Crawford, what would you say if I told you the foundation had secured funding for an additional residential facility and operating expenses for the next fiscal year?"

Her heart swelled. "I'd say that's fantastic news, Mr. Whitaker."

"I have another question to ask, if I may." Cole's expression remained unreadable. He wore a long black peacoat over gray slacks and black dress shoes. Stubble clung to his jaw and dark circles rimmed his lower lashes. She didn't care. His arrival held her captive.

"Please." She gestured with her gloved hand. "The floor is yours."

"Excellent. Thank you. Miss Crawford, what would you say if I told you the foundation would like to offer you a full-time position as the executive director for special projects?"

Her mouth ran dry. A smattering of applause broke out.

"I—I don't even know what that means," she said, half tempted to steal a glance at her sisters to confirm they'd heard his words. To be honest, she couldn't look away. Cole's kind eyes held hers.

"Sorry to hog the Q and A, folks, but I just have one more thing I need to ask."

Avery literally leaned forward, gripping the microphone with both hands. Her heart fluttered in her throat and she was certain the whole town could see it.

"Perhaps we could meet after and discuss the details of the offer?"

She couldn't stop a smile. "Yes, I'd like that very much."

Avery stepped away from the microphone and moved toward her family. Applause swelled as Mama embraced her.

"We're so proud of you, sweetheart. Well done."

"Thank you," Avery murmured into Mama's shoulder, her head still spinning with Cole's unexpected job offer. She'd need more information, but directing special projects for the foundation sounded like a role created with her strengths and passions in mind. How ironic that moving back to Camellia had once felt like defeat. Today had proven that she couldn't have been more wrong.

Cole had never been so thrilled about a snowstorm in his life.

The Huntingtons had invited him and a few other folks back to their house to celebrate after the ribbon-cutting ceremony. Snow had started falling in thick white flakes a few minutes ago. Greer had rolled out a propane heater, and

Avery had asked him to join her on the porch. The informal party continued inside. Hayes had fallen asleep in his swing and Addison was occupied decorating a sugar cookie with Harper. This was the first time they'd been alone since their miserable interaction on the dock four months ago.

Avery shivered then reached for a plaid blanket and spread it across her lap. Was she nervous too? He couldn't tell.

He swiped his clammy palms across his pant legs. It might be twenty-eight degrees outside, but his anxious feelings over seeing Avery again had him in a cold sweat. "Your family sure knows how to throw a party."

"Want to go in and say hello to anyone?"

"Nope." If she was going to give him her undivided attention, then he wasn't about to squander it.

The platter of sugar cookies and hot cocoa on the kitchen counter could wait. A miniature tree decorated for the holidays stood on the side table, its lights twinkling in the gray afternoon.

"Nana is really in her element, isn't she?" Avery craned her neck to assess the crowd gathering inside.

Cole looked for Maribelle through the porch door. She stood just inside, leaning on her walker. Keith hovered at her elbow, chatting with Avery's mama.

"There's a sight to behold," Cole said quietly. "Did you ever think you'd see your parents in the same room again?"

She shook her head. "I'm still amazed that my dad is here and we're all mature enough to attend the same party."

"How are your sisters doing since he's come back?"

"They're working through some things. Julene especially. She was only two when my dad left. Greer has been more of a dad to her. I'm praying that they can establish a good relationship."

"Are you happy he's back?"

"Of course." She gave him her full attention. "You know what else I'm happy about?"

Her playful tone made hope take flight. "Tell me."

"That you're here and we can finally have a conversation." She tugged at a loose thread on the blanket's edge. "Your job offer sounds intriguing."

"I'm glad you think so. I was scared to death."

*Still am, actually.*

Avery studied him. "You were? I couldn't tell. You seemed so confident. That delivery was quite smooth."

"I was worried sick wondering whether you'd even take my questions."

Her expression sobered. "Before we talk more about the offer, I need to apologize. I'm so sorry that it's taken me this long to speak to you."

"Avery, you have nothing to be sorry for."

"That's very gracious and so not true." She uncrossed then crossed her legs again, one boot tapping against the other. "I regret many things about how I've reacted since I found out Nana meddled in my life. There's something I should've said when you came to see me on the dock that day."

Oh. "Say more."

She dragged her gaze to meet his. "You apologized and poured your heart out. I should've offered forgiveness right then."

Relief flooded in. "You were hurt and upset and needed time. Betrayals aren't easy to bounce back from. I get that."

"I shouldn't have punished you because Pax and Trey had hurt me. That wasn't right. Or fair. I am so sorry."

In a bold move, he stood from his seat in the rocker and knelt beside her. He pressed his finger to her chin and tipped it up.

"Look at me. All of that is behind us now. We did what we set out to do. The ladies are all moved in, the factory is open and people are watching the documentary. By the way, the instant you proposed your vision I knew you were going to nail this thing."

She tenderly brushed her lips against his then pulled back. "Thank you for believing in me."

"I love you, Avery. I'll always believe in you."

"I love you too." She shifted slightly, angling her body toward him. "Because of you and your invitation to help expand Imari's Place, because of your love for me..." Her voice wavered. "I can finally let go of my obsession over other people's opinions."

He caressed her cheek with the pad of his thumb. "Mission accomplished."

She leaned into his touch. All he wanted to do was kiss her.

"You are the most beautiful, most creative and most intelligent woman I have ever known. I don't want you to worry anymore about what other people think. You outshine their criticism with your creativity and your compassion every single time. I'm so proud of you."

"Thank you." She closed the distance between them, her breath warm on his skin. "You are a gift from above, Cole Whitaker. I will thank God for you every day."

"Same." His eyes dipped to her lips. "I've loved you since forever, Avery Lansing Crawford. That will never change."

"I love you too." She hovered, her mouth only inches away. "Shout out to that napkin pledge for making this relationship possible."

He laughed then kissed her again.

# Epilogue

The morning breeze swirled across the yard and the camellia blossoms bobbed and danced. On the lake, Greer's boat zipped by, towing Addison and Hayes on a chair-shaped inflatable. Avery smiled and waved, although the kids were just two bright spots of color in the middle of the water.

Cole spread a waterproof striped blanket on the lawn then patted the space beside him. "Why don't you rest for a few minutes?"

She rubbed her aching back then complied, carefully sinking down beside him. She rested her head on his lap. He leaned back on both hands, staring out at the water, giving her the perfect view of his jawline silhouetted against the bright May sky. The weight of this full circle moment wasn't lost on her. She released a contented sigh, which drew his attention back to her.

A slow, easy grin lifted the corners of his mouth, sending

her heart cartwheeling all over again. Oh, she loved that smile. And that mouth. A delicious warmth spiraled through her.

"What's on your mind, Mrs. Whitaker?"

"I think you know what's on my mind."

His grin widened and she caught a mischievous gleam in his eye. "The kids are with your mama and Greer for another hour or so."

"Well played. I do believe that's how you got me in this current predicament, isn't it?"

His eyes smoldered as he splayed a palm across the curve of her very pregnant abdomen. "I happen to love your current predicament."

Cole's voice was husky and rich. Oh, how she adored this man. "You're going to be an excellent father."

"Thank you. I hope so." His thumb caressed the cotton fabric of her maternity shirt. "Do you still want to name him Walter Walden Whitaker?"

"Absolutely not. That is hideous."

He chuckled. "How about Laura Lansing Whitaker?"

"That's slightly better than your first suggestion." They'd agreed—mostly—on waiting until the baby's arrival to find out the gender. Choosing potential names for a boy had been a challenge.

Addison was seven now and Hayes was almost three. They'd campaigned heavily for their favorite names, although Hayes changed his mind on a regular basis. With a few weeks left until her due date, Avery was more than ready to deliver.

"You know if we have a girl I'm insisting we name her Kimberly," she said, trailing her fingertips along his forearm.

"If you keep rubbing my arm like that, you can name our kid anything you want," he said, his eyes lingering on her lips.

"I'm grateful for another pregnancy and hopeful that we'll

have a beautiful, healthy child." She sat up slowly, overcome by a sudden wave of emotion. As usual, her hormones fluctuated by the minute.

Cole's brows furrowed. "What's wrong?"

"Nothing." She sniffed, trying not to ugly cry. "I'm just happy is all."

"Aw, sweetheart, don't cry." He held her face with his hands. Those gorgeous hazel eyes locked on hers. Then he gently grazed her lips with his.

She pressed her palm to his chest, feeling the warmth of his skin through the soft cotton of his T-shirt. He was such a gift. She silently offered another prayer of thanks. God had given her the most wonderful man. These moments of gratitude still surprised her. The freedom they'd found in their relationship with one another still floored her in the best possible way.

Reluctantly, she pulled away and tucked her head into the crook of his neck.

The last two years had been a whirlwind. After a brief engagement that generated plenty of speculation, they had a small spring wedding at Greer and Mama's church in Camellia. They'd come home from their honeymoon in time to attend the premier of the documentary, which was now one of the most watched on a major streaming platform. She'd juggled working as the executive director for special projects for the foundation, and Cole had maintained a busy schedule. His speaking engagements had taken him coast to coast. When the kids were with Pax and Trey, she'd traveled with Cole. Their trips had established a sweet foundation for their newlywed life.

Imari's Place now had residential space for fifty women, and the Camellia factory was going strong. Together they'd bought a house in the neighborhood where Cole had grown up. A true fixer-upper. They'd hired a crew who'd renovated it in time for them to move in last week.

This season hadn't been all romance and weekend getaways. Navigating their complex family dynamics had been difficult. Hayes and Addison spent half their time with Pax and Trey. She'd lost more than a little sleep over behavior issues, worrying that she'd expected too much of her kids. They'd had to adapt to some major life changes in a short amount of time. Their family didn't look like everyone else's. She seemed to be the one most concerned about all of that.

Forgiveness had come easier than she'd anticipated. Another reason to thank the Lord for His work in her life and in her heart. Nana had slowed down considerably. She didn't maintain quite the social calendar that she once had, but there was a peace about her now that her son was back in Camellia.

"Do you think your dad will be able to come and see the baby when he or she is born?"

"I hope so." Avery braced her hand on her forehead and tried to find Greer's boat. She'd promised Addison she'd pay attention. The girl had no fear and begged Greer to intentionally fling her off and into the water.

Her father had gone back on tour as a roadie. The months between his return to Camellia and his recent departure with the band had granted her and her sisters some sweet times with him. It was a big, beautiful life they were living. She'd come a long way since she drove into town a single mom with a broken heart.

"Thank you for loving me." She kissed Cole tenderly. "I wouldn't be who I am today if it weren't for you."

A smile played at the corners of his mouth. "Nonsense."

Every now and then someone posted a picture of her on social media when she was out with her kids. Or tried to take a picture without her permission if she crossed paths with Pax and Trey around town. She didn't say yes to nearly as many social media campaigns as she used to, but occasionally the comments turned ugly on one of her more engaging posts. She'd hired an assistant specifically to manage that aspect of her online community. It was so refreshing to devote her time and attention to what truly mattered, rather than getting hung up on petty conversations that nobody won. Camellia had its foibles, but that's why she loved living here. This place was part of her story. *Their* story.

Cole twined his fingers through hers and gently kissed her knuckles. They had each other, their home and their family. Forever.

★ ★ ★ ★ ★

# Acknowledgments

*One Southern Summer* is about navigating life's plot twists, who we run to when we encounter the unimaginable, and the sweet blessings we experience after we've endured heartache. I think it's safe to say that this novel has taken the scenic route to publication. There have been countless plot twists in my life and multiple revisions of this manuscript since the day Avery arrived in my imagination, insisting that I write her story next. Getting this novel into your hands, dear readers, would not have been possible without the help of many generous and talented people.

To my original critique group, Angela Couch, Laura Hodges Poole, Janet W. Ferguson and the late Marion Ueckermann, thank you for being such wonderful writing friends. I was so nervous to share the earliest iterations of this manuscript because I'd never crafted a character quite like Maribelle before. Your kind words and insightful feedback helped so much. I'm grateful for each of you.

To my former literary agent, Jessica Kirkland, thank you for believing in me as I took those first tentative steps into the world of traditional publishing.

Steve Laube, you're a delightful human and a fantastic literary agent. I'm grateful for your integrity, kindness and wisdom. It's an honor to be a part of your agency.

Susan May Warren, Rachel Hauck, Lisa Jordan and everyone at My Book Therapy, thank you for teaching me how to write well, giving great pep talks and celebrating wins along the way.

I'm extremely grateful for the whole team at Love Inspired. Thank you for all you do. I appreciate the opportunity to branch out into southern women's fiction. Thanks especially to my editor, Shana Asaro, for helping me shape and polish another book. This one will always be extra special.

Lee Tobin McClain, RaeAnne Thayne, Kristy Woodson Harvey, Kathryn Springer and Julie Cantrell, your endorsements are a gift. Thank you.

A huge thank you to the booksellers, early readers, bookstagrammers, podcasters and the publicity team at UpLit Reads for helping this book find its readers. I'm super grateful for each one of you.

Books are written in solitude, but there's often a whole network of people who generously offer a helping hand. Carla Biesinger, Amy Porterfield, Thomas Umstattd Jr. and my Author Media mastermind group, thank you for sharing your wisdom and equipping me with the proper marketing tools to learn and grow as an author and entrepreneur.

To my local church community as well as my incredible friends and family scattered near and far, thank you for cheering me on and telling everyone you know about my books.

Finally, to my husband, Steve, and our kids, Luke, Andy and

Eli, I'm certain that it's a challenge to do life with someone who spends so much time interacting with fictional characters. Thank you for supporting my dream with your encouraging words, graciously overlooking unfinished tasks that I've abandoned or forgotten about and tackling chores you'd probably rather not do. I love you to the moon and back.

## IF YOU ENJOYED THIS BOOK
## WE THINK YOU WILL ALSO LOVE

# LOVE INSPIRED
## INSPIRATIONAL ROMANCE

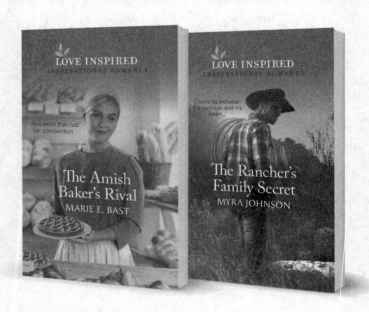

*Uplifting stories of faith, forgiveness and hope.*

Fall in love with stories where faith helps
guide you through life's challenges, and discover
the promise of a new beginning.

**6 NEW BOOKS AVAILABLE EVERY MONTH!**